FUELED BY OBSESSION

A Romance and Suspense Novel by
Sara K. James

www.ten16press.com - Waukesha, WI

For information, please contact:

www.ten16press.com
Waukesha, WI

Cover design by Therese Joanis

Acknowledgments and Author's Note

I'd like to first thank my partner in fiction crime. Whenever my characters find themselves in trouble (and I find myself struck with writer's block), you're the one I turn to for help in bailing them out. To my early draft readers – Jan, Jackie, Lucy and Mary Ann – your encouragement and insight into the world of romantic suspense convinced me that the characters in this book had a story to tell and that I was gifted enough to be the one to tell it. Also, special thanks to my team at TEN16 Press: Lauren Blue, editor; Therese Joanis, graphic designer; and Shannon Ishizaki, owner.

Footnote: I hope that my readers will excuse any liberties I have taken with fictional references and location descriptions in order to enhance the continuity of the storyline.

For all the enthusiastic readers of my first novel who were kind enough to hound me for another one . . .
This one's for you!

PROLOGUE

An explosion of lightning cut across the room followed by a bone jarring crash of thunder. The man hunched over the corner desk reading by the light of a small florescent lamp didn't even flinch. He barely heard the rain as it drummed steadily against the single-pane glass window, his full attention glued to the eyes of the woman appearing on page fifteen of *Brushwork* magazine.

His fingers slowly trailed across the sable-colored hair and down the sleek, finely-toned body of the woman pictured. He momentarily wondered if she kept that shapely figure from one of those trendy California gyms, or if it was inherited genes. Either way, it didn't matter. It wasn't her body that he was interested in.

He knew her name. It was Katie Nolan, only daughter of Robert and Marian Nolan of Long Beach, California. An up-and-coming painter and photographer who, at the age of twenty-seven, was headed toward unquestionable success in the art community. *"Ms. Nolan has a rare talent for breathing life into every piece of artwork she creates,"* the article quoted. *"In this writer's opinion, she's as good as they come."*

The man happened to disagree. In his opinion, she deserved absolutely nothing and shouldn't be allowed to breathe the same air he breathed.

It was a fact that while the younger Katie Nolan had been attending the best schools money could buy, he had gone to a run-down, graffiti-ridden public school in a neighborhood that had been labeled "blighted" by the city council way before he'd even been born. And while Marian Nolan had been hosting the garden club in her fancy suburban home, his mother had been working three jobs to put food on the table and pay the rent on a microscopic one bedroom basement apartment.

Yet it was Judge Robert Nolan that the man held the most contempt for. While the judge had been brokering deals on the ninth hole with corrupt attorneys and state prosecutors, his own father had been forced to spend years in a dirty, cramped prison cell. One day even that had been brutally taken from him.

For twenty years now, the man had been living with the injustice of his father's death and the pain it had buried deep inside his mother's heart—an unrelenting pain that had finally broken her spirit. For the past three years, nothing seemed to matter to her anymore. He took care of her, much like she'd taken care of him when he'd been a child, yet half the time she didn't even comprehend that it was her son who was providing for her. It troubled him to think that most days she didn't even care if she lived or died.

He re-read the article that accompanied the photo and felt that all-too-familiar fury begin to bubble inside. Rationalizing that now was not the time to surrender to his anger, he was content to imagine how he would end Katie Nolan's life if only he had the chance. As he visualized how she would struggle while he plunged his steel knife deep into her flesh, he could almost feel the pleasure he'd get when he bathed himself in her screams. Her muscles would twitch and her arms would flay uselessly under the weight of his body. She would plead for him to stop, but he wouldn't. Instead he would use her words to fuel his need for revenge until at last, she drew her final breath.

Movement from the back bedroom momentarily distracted him. Glancing briefly toward the partially closed door, he heard his mother's low-pitched voice call out for him. Slowly rising from his chair, he tore the page out of the magazine, then walked over to the kitchen sink.

It was too late to make Judge Nolan—who was the person truly responsible for his parents' misery—regret the decisions he'd made. But shouldn't someone be held responsible for the death of his father and for the suffering his mother endured? Holding his father's cigarette lighter against the corner of the page, he swore that Katie Nolan was the most logical choice. She needed to be the one to accept responsibility for the sins of her father. Only then would justice be served.

CHAPTER ONE

Katie Nolan found herself racing around her stylishly modern kitchen trying to make up for the time she'd lost after hitting the snooze button on her alarm clock. Twice.

She popped a sliced bagel in the toaster, poured coffee into her bright red travel mug, then dragged a bag of dog food over to Winston's bowl. She glanced over to where the Alaskan malamute was lying, watching her through thoughtful eyes. After the bowl was filled, he slowly rose to all fours and ambled over to begin breakfast.

Next, it was Tabitha's turn, and as soon as Katie reached for the can opener, the calico cat leaped off the windowsill and raced across the room, stopping only long enough to swat the dog's nose. Winston, who was accustomed to the behavior, didn't even seem to notice.

"Good grief, Tabitha," Katie scoffed as the cat started to whine and rub against her ankle. "At least wait until I can get the can open before you pounce. You don't see Winston carrying on, do you?"

At the sound of his name, Winston lifted his head, glancing in her direction with anticipation showing in his eyes. "Sorry buddy, you're not going with me today," she said, snatching the now toasted bagel and slapping on some raspberry jam. "I'm flying up to Oregon so you'll be staying with Grandma Nolan." With a sigh, the dog lowered his head and went back to cleaning out his food dish.

Katie picked up her carry-on bag and checked to make sure her camera equipment was all there and securely packed. Although photography wasn't her first choice of professions, it basically helped pay the bills and kept her living in the style to which she'd become accustomed. Even more than that, it provided her with the income necessary to support her true love—painting. It wasn't that she minded getting behind the camera and producing what she knew were artistic and fashionable photographs. It just didn't bring her the pure joy that a brush and palette could.

She grabbed her car keys off the counter and took a final glance around the kitchen. She saw Tabitha hadn't moved away from her tuna breakfast and Winston, who had lived with Katie for the past four years, had already returned to his rug in the corner to nap. Hopefully both would continue to ignore each other until her mother came by to pick up the dog. Tabitha was a recent addition to the household, and while everyone was trying to get used to her domineering ways, Katie's mother had insisted that a welfare check once a day was all the rescue cat needed during the short time her daughter would be away.

As Katie reached her car, the familiar sound of bluegrass came floating out of her purse. She dug for her cell phone and smiled, tucking the phone between her shoulder and ear so she could take the call while wrestling the carry-on bag into the car without dropping the travel mug or bagel.

"Hello, handsome," she said as she opened the back door.

"Good morning, gorgeous. Miss me yet?"

Her smile expanded as she listened to the deep southern drawl of her fiancé, Evan Hogan, a computer software consultant who spent a great deal of time traveling to and from clients. For the past two days, he had been in Nebraska conducting a seminar on a new software application his company had recently developed.

"I missed you the minute you walked out the door," she said. "How's the conference going?"

"Better than I expected it would. What about you? You're photographing the Freeman's condo today, aren't you?"

It never failed to please Katie that Evan remembered her specific assignments. He cared about what she did and took pride in her work. He often joked about how he was just riding her coattails until she made that defining sale which would skyrocket her to the top. Then he'd be able to retire and live off her wealth.

"I'm leaving the house now to head for the airport," she said, sliding behind the wheel of the car. "It'll be my first time on a private plane, and needless to say, it'll be a real sacrifice not to take commercial. Photographing the home of the CEO of one of the top private jet brokerage firms has its demands."

"I truly feel for you, Katherine Gayle," Evan said dryly as Katie chuckled on the other end of the phone.

"You know, my company has done consulting with Andrew Freeman," he continued, watching a group of participants from his seminar trickle into the conference room, slowly making their way to their tables. "When he began Freeman Air Jet Services, I helped him with their computer security. He's got an internal tech team now, but they still use us from time to time. I've seen their condo by the way, and the place certainly has class. Not my style though. There wasn't a dirty towel on the floor anywhere."

"Or sweat pants or underwear or smelly tennis shoes?" Katie asserted.

"For the record, the tennis shoes are yours. And you can leave that sexy black underwear of yours lying around the house any time you want. You'll hear no complaints from me."

"So noted," Katie said, turning the key in the car ignition. "When do you think you'll be home?"

"My return flight is the day after tomorrow and we should be touching down by noon."

"I'm not sure if I'll be back by then to pick you up."

"No problem," Evan replied. "The company is going to have a rental available for me."

"Sounds good," Katie said as she pulled out of the driveway.

"Well, looks like the room is beginning to fill up so I better get going. I love you, sweetheart."

"I love you too, Evan. Have a safe trip home."

"I'll pass your request along to the pilot, and you do the same. See you soon, babe."

And he was gone. She disconnected and tossed the phone on the passenger seat. "Yeah, see you soon."

CHAPTER TWO

Katie sat on a comfortable vintage wing chair sipping iced tea from a crystal glass and nibbling on what was surely the most magnificent chocolate chip cookie in the universe. Not what she had expected to be doing halfway through her photo shoot of the Freeman condominium. Especially not while the wife of one of the most highly respected air transportation executives sat calmly on a curved antique sofa doing the same.

Katie had no doubt that most men would describe Christina Freeman as an exceptionally beautiful woman. From the bio Katie had received, she knew Christina had recently celebrated her thirtieth birthday. Although younger than her husband by a good fifteen years, she inherently possessed the sophistication often seen in a CEO's wife. Her honey-colored hair was pulled back into a simple French braid and her soft brown eyes sparkled behind trendy small-framed glasses. Dressed in a white, over-sized silk blouse and black wide-leg trousers, she sat barefoot across from Katie, casually talking about her home.

"Most of what you see is based on sketches I did myself," she was saying. "I knew what I wanted, how I wanted our home to look, and then hired the CK Carlyle Agency to help take my vision from paper to this." She ran a slow, satisfied look across the spacious room. "As a teenager, I had dreams of going into fashion. Then I audited a class in interior design at college and fell in love with it.

I even worked briefly for a small exclusive firm in Pasadena before Andrew and I met. After we married, I joined him at Freeman Air, running the front office."

Smoothing her hand along the edge of her pant leg, she continued. "When the company had grown enough to where Andrew could afford a full staff of experts, I went back to design on a part-time basis and now do strictly consulting. Having the final say on which clients I work with allows me to manage the time I spend with my daughter."

As Katie was about to ask about Christina's little girl, a blond curly-haired head poked up from behind the sofa. "Hi. My name is Melanie," the spirited seven-year old said. "I have the same name my grandmother had but she died before I was born." Melanie turned her head toward her mother and asked, "What does that make me, Mom? I forgot the word."

Christina ran her fingers through the little girl's hair and laughed. "You're her namesake, sweetie."

"That's right. I'm her namesake," she repeated, turning back to Katie. "What's your name?"

"My name is Katherine, but everyone calls me Katie."

"It's nice to meet you, Katie."

"It's nice to meet you also, Melanie."

"As long as you've managed to sneak past the sitter, why don't you come on around here and have a snack," Christina said.

Katie laughed at how swiftly Melanie made it around the sofa and to the tray of cookies. Taking the one on top, she sat primly on the edge of the cushion, close to her mother's knees. As she enjoyed the generous mouthful of chocolate, Katie shifted her attention back to Christina and was touched by the look of pure love that was now sparkling in those brown eyes.

As Melanie took another bite, the sitter came hurrying into the room with her apologies for letting her charge escape. Christina casually waved the girl away as Melanie spoke. "I go to school but

I have the day off. My teacher is going to school instead," she said, grinning. "I guess she needs to learn stuff, too."

"There isn't a person alive who knows everything," Christina said. Looking back at Katie, she added, "It's a mandatory training day for the special education teachers. Melanie wanted to stay here instead of going to her friend Tawny's house, and I finally relented. Although I never suspected that she'd break away from Karen."

"Mommy told me you were taking pictures of our house," Melanie mumbled as she finished off the cookie.

"Yes, I am. The pictures are going in a magazine called *Tailored Elegance.*"

"I know. We have a cription."

"Subscription," Christina gently corrected. "Melanie loves to page through it every month and uses it to gather ideas whenever she wants to redecorate her bedroom."

Looking craftily at her mother, Melanie asked, "Are you going to be in any of the pictures?"

"Yes, I am. And no, you're not."

"But, why?" she asked with some passion. "Don't you think I'm pretty?"

"I'm not even going to dignify that with a response, young lady. You know perfectly well how pretty you are."

Katie was impressed. Christina had managed to subtly reprimand her daughter while in the same breath reassure her that she was a beautiful child.

"Daddy says I get my looks from you," Melanie pointed out, still trying to sway her mother's decision.

"Your father is absolutely correct," Christina said.

"I understand the magazine has only contracted with me for photographs of you and your home," Katie said to Christina, "but if you don't have any objections, I'd like to take some extra photographs of you and Melanie that you can keep for yourselves."

Melanie didn't say anything, but the pleading look she sent her mother could have melted rock. Christina sighed softly and said, "I would like that very much, Katie. We've snapped several photos over the years, but haven't had anything taken professionally, although I'm not sure why. We'll pay you of course."

"Maybe Dad could be in the picture, too."

"Maybe he could. Why don't you go on back to Karen now? Katie and I have to finish up here."

"It was very nice meeting you, Katie."

"Same here, Melanie."

As soon as the girl was out of hearing range, Katie said, "I hope I didn't overstep with my offer. It was out of my mouth before I completely thought it through. I shouldn't have made the offer in front of Melanie without first running it past you."

Christina laughed and picked up her tea. "Actually, I'd been thinking about asking you to take a family photo. Because of Melanie's Down syndrome, we sometimes find ourselves sheltering her, having experienced how cruel people can be. She's still so young and . . . I guess the correct word is vulnerable. Unfortunately, my decisions sometimes take away her freedom to enjoy being a little girl."

"I'm guessing that raising a child with a disability would be difficult at times."

"It is. But she's getting older, and I'm afraid that I need to let her test her wings. I'll talk to my husband. If he agrees, you can submit one of the photos you'll be taking with Melanie. No promises, though."

When the door chime sounded, Katie observed the subtle change in Christina's posture as she transformed from the relaxed, doting mother back to the conservative executive's wife. "I've been expecting a delivery from Andrew's office, and I'm guessing that's the courier service," Christina said as she rose from the couch. "If memory serves me correctly, you have the dining room slated in next. Why don't you go on ahead. This shouldn't take long."

Katie had been home from her assignment in Oregon for just over a week and now found herself running behind schedule. Evan had already left for work, thankfully having fed Winston and Tabitha. But even with one less chore to do, she was still moving at warp speed in order to make it out the door by nine.

When the kitchen phone began to ring she debated whether or not to answer it, mentally clicking through the names of possible callers. Her mother rarely called on a workday morning, so she could cross her off the list. Of course, it could be the magazine's editor or office assistant. Or maybe it was one of Bryna Grant's handlers, calling to say that the high-profile actress broke a nail and couldn't possibly go through with the publicity shoot today. With a sigh, Katie reached for the phone.

"This is Katie Nolan," she said as she scooped some sliced fruit into a round plastic cup.

"Hey, Katie. It's Bethany. Hope I'm not catching you at a bad time. Like maybe in the middle of making mad passionate love with that sexy fiancé of yours."

"If I was in the middle of mad passionate lovemaking," Katie asserted, "I certainly wouldn't be taking the time to answer the phone. Which leads me to wonder how your lovemaking is going these days if you honestly think it's acceptable to break away for a phone call?"

Katie's childhood friend offered up a ladylike snort. "Never you mind about how I'm doing in the bedroom. I will say, however, things get better once you tie the knot. That old Catholic guilt attached to pre-marital sex finally disappears."

"Thanks for the heads-up. Now what's so important at this time of the morning?"

"Matt and I are having a dinner party on Saturday and wanted you and Evan to come. One of Matt's old college roommates is flying in from out east for a couple of days, and it seemed like the perfect opportunity to get everyone together. It'll be informal, maybe fifteen of our nearest and dearest friends. Matt said your computer geek will probably know a few of the attendees."

"Evan hates it when you call him that, you know," Katie said as she packed the fruit cup into her insulated bag next to a container of cottage cheese and an apple juice box. "And I must regretfully decline your invitation. The geek and I are heading out to spend four blissful days in the wilderness."

"Not camping?" Bethany moaned. "How can you two go out there and play pioneers when there's so much you can be enjoying right here in Long Beach? It's not natural, Katie."

"Actually, it's all natural. I'm even trying to convince Evan to leave his cell phone at home."

"Good lord, what's come over you?" Bethany exclaimed with a laugh. "I bet there won't be one good shoe store within miles of where you're pitching that tent."

"I hope not. Thanks again for the invite, but Evan and I haven't had a lot of alone time in the past few months, and we both agreed not to change our plans. Why don't the four of us get together for dinner next week? Maybe you and Matt can come over here."

"We accept. Call me when the two of you make it back to the civilized world."

Katie disconnected the call. Stealing a final glance at the clock, she realized it would take a miracle for her to reach the Los Angeles studio ahead of the infamous actress. The best she could hope for now was that Bryna's reputation of never being on time was accurate.

CHAPTER THREE

It wasn't quite three a.m. when Katie turned, reaching for Evan. But he was gone.

Groggy from a long day of hiking and rock climbing in a remote section of the Shasta National Forest, she didn't give it much thought other than to conclude that he'd needed to relieve himself in some nearby bush. She curled her legs up until she was resting in a fetal position, pulled the sleeping bag tighter around her shoulders, and fell back to sleep.

Two hours later, a small cluster of birds started to sing their ritual awakening which stirred Katie for a second time. Again, she reached for Evan but the realization that she was still alone had her sitting up and taking inventory of the small, restricted space.

She lowered the zipper on the sleeping bag, threw back the flap on the tent entrance, and stepped out into the chill of the morning. She noted that the fire they had built the previous night was still cold, and the rented SUV was still parked at the far end of the campsite, their cooler resting undisturbed on the ground near the rear tire. Maybe he'd had trouble sleeping, she thought, and had decided to spend the night in the car rather than disturb her with his tossing and turning. Katie strolled toward the vehicle only to discover it was empty.

With panic on the rise, she slowly turned in all directions, hoping to spot him. He could have decided to take an early morning hike without her, although she found it hard to believe that he would have left her alone for so long. She called out his name, but received no response.

Fearing now that he had wandered off and could be lying somewhere hurt and in pain, Katie sprang into action. She went back to the tent and quickly pulled on her jeans and a hooded sweatshirt, then located a flashlight and walking stick before heading down a path that led to an area where she knew two other campsites were set up. One was occupied by a single camper she and Evan had yet to meet; the other belonged to Jeremy and Nathan Hunter, brothers they had encountered on their hike yesterday. Deciding the two brothers were the better choice to help with her search, she made a sharp left at the bottom of the path.

Evan would no doubt chide her for overreacting if she found him safe and sound, but she was willing to take that chance. And because that little voice in her head was telling her she was quickly running out of time, she picked up her pace until she was sprinting toward the brothers' campsite.

Katie spotted the scuffed hiking boot first and took off on a run down the unmarked trail. Jeremy caught up to her by the time she reached the edge of the bluff, and they both leaned over and saw Evan.

He was lying on his back with his arms sprawled out to either side and his left leg bent at an impossible angle. Katie saw the blood under his head and the empty look in his eyes which seemed to stare right through her. She gasped and then screamed his name. Jeremy's brother, Nathan, was already climbing down the side, scraping over rocks and gravel.

"Stay where you are, Katie," he shouted up at her, keeping his gaze on Evan. "Keep her up there, Jeremy. It's tricky here."

Jeremy was already pulling out his cell phone and dialing 911 when Katie pushed past him trying to descend the side of the steep embankment. He grabbed her around the waist as he gave the dispatcher their location, pulling her back up as he spoke. Although she struggled to get free, she was no match for Jeremy's strength and determination to keep her in place.

Disconnecting the call, he tried his best to calm her. "Let Nathan get to him, Katie. He's a doctor and he'll know what to do. He'll take care of Evan. You can't do anything right now, so let's both stay here."

She dropped to the ground, shaking uncontrollably. Jeremy draped his arm around her shoulders and spoke quietly to her while they waited. He knew that Evan was either dead or as close to it as any man could get, having seen his share of death during his tour in Afghanistan. But he would let her hold on to the hope that her fiancé would survive. The impact of what had happened would come crashing down on her with no mercy soon enough.

Twenty minutes later, the area was filled with medical personnel and park rangers. Two of the paramedics tended to Katie who had become almost comatose with shock. Jeremy stayed close by, all the time speaking in a low soft voice, telling her that Evan was in good hands. It was only after the medical team finally got her in the ambulance and pulled out of the campground that he went to stand with his brother.

"He's dead, isn't he?" Jeremy asked, even though he was sure he knew the answer.

"Yes," Nathan replied. "Probably a couple of hours. It appears that he broke his neck in the fall." Brushing the dirt off his jeans, he asked, "Where's Katie?"

"They took her to the hospital. She was pretty shaken up."

"Yeah, I bet she was. Why don't you go on to the hospital and stay with her. I'll go pack up their stuff and meet you there. See if you can get a hold of a family member or friend, and we'll stay with her until they get here."

As Nathan led the way back up the trail to the campsites, his brother took a final look at where Evan's body had been found. "What was he doing out here in the middle of the night?"

"Your guess is as good as mine. Come on, let's get moving."

CHAPTER
FOUR
Fourteen Months Later

Katie stepped out of the closet with a handful of sweaters and blouses. She walked over to the bed where she had two suitcases laying open—one still empty and the other halfway full.

"I don't understand why you have to go so far away, Katie," her mother said quietly. "There are plenty of opportunities right here in Long Beach. It hasn't been that long since you lost Evan, and I think it's too soon for you to be completely on your own. You should be around your family and friends."

"It's been over a year," Katie said, glancing over at her mother. "And moving on doesn't mean I've forgotten Evan or that I ever will."

For a long time, Evan's death—which had officially been ruled an accident—had left everyone in shock. His reasons for going out alone that morning had remained a mystery until Katie had found his cell phone inside the knapsack he'd taken with him. The stored photos had provided the most logical explanation. There were five of them, taken approximately five minutes apart. Photos documenting a rising sun, its beauty magnificent in its simplicity.

She could still remember his now haunting words, spoken on the first day of their trip. *"If only we could bottle that,"* he'd said, pointing to the burst of color splashed across the skyline. *"We could pull it out at the start of every day and bask in the beauty."* And as sure as Katie had ever been about anything, she'd known that Evan had gone out that morning, wanting to immortalize that view. For her. Except he'd been unfamiliar with the area, and that unfamiliarity had led to his death.

Glancing at the wall where she had the framed photos hanging in a sequentially ordered display, she felt the jolt of regret that always came with the knowledge that Evan had never gotten the chance to bask.

"His death wasn't your fault," her mother said. "And you have to stop thinking it was."

"That's hard to do sometimes." Turning away from the photos, Katie added, "I know this must be hard for you, my leaving. I hope you don't see it as some sort of desertion."

"Of course not, sweetie. It's just that lately I've been thinking about all the loss you and I have endured over the years. First your brothers and then your father. And of course, Evan."

"And even though it's different, it feels as if you're losing me, too," Katie said sympathetically as she crossed the room to sit next to her mother on the edge of the bed. "I'll be a phone call away whenever you need me. We'll probably talk more now than we ever have. You're not losing me. I promise."

Marian wiped a stray tear from beneath her eye. "You always were a sweet-talker, even though you have a smart mouth. I can't figure out which I'll miss the most."

Katie grabbed her mother up in a bear hug and gave her a noisy kiss on the cheek. "It's not forever. Eight months, a year at the most. And I'm holding you to your promise to come visit me. Or, I'll make the trip back here to spend time with you. It's all going to work out, Mom."

"If you say so," Marian said as she began folding a stack of sweatshirts. "And, even though we've been over this before, it still makes me nervous that you know so little about the man you'll be working for. I'm concerned that you're making a rash decision flying off to Oregon. Who asks a virtually unknown artist—no offense intended," Marian added quickly when Katie raised her eyebrows, "to simply pack up and leave her home? A man in his position could have hired anyone. He certainly has the money, but he commissions you, a woman who's recently lost her fiancé, making her particularly vulnerable."

Katie was a little surprised by the judgment she heard in her mother's voice, suspecting that her concerns went deeper than just her little girl leaving. When Katie had attended the San Francisco Art Institute and then went to Paris for several months to study, her father had still been alive. But now, her mother would have no family nearby and the reality of that was taking its toll.

She'd adjust, Katie thought for the millionth time since she'd made the decision to leave. Re-creating three family photographs on canvas for one of the most connected men on the west coast was an opportunity she couldn't pass up. Not to mention the freedom she'd have to work on her own paintings—a selling point that had pleased her agent. He'd been pressuring her for both photographs and artwork to exhibit in the upscale gallery he owned, and had even hinted that if Katie could pull enough work together, a one-woman show wouldn't be out of the realm of possibility.

"I need to do this, Mom," Katie said as she rummaged through her dresser drawers. "It's a mother's right to worry about her kids, but this job could give me a real opportunity to open some doors in the art community."

When Marian didn't say anything, Katie decided it was useless to try and change her mother's mind, so she chose instead to lighten the mood. "If you think about it, I'm not the only one who benefits here. With me out of the picture for a while, you'll be able to concentrate on you. Don't you think it's time you re-enter the dating pool, maybe go find me a new daddy?"

Observing the horrified look spread across her mother's face, Katie let loose a sidesplitting laugh. "I'm sorry, Mom, but that look on your face is too precious. Where's my camera?"

Marian was not amused. "I fail to see the humor in that remark, young lady, and I'm perfectly fine on my own. Robert Nolan was your father, and although he's no longer with us, he cannot be replaced." She stood up and strolled toward the door. "Now get moving. You have all that packing to do and, as usual, you're running late."

CHAPTER
FIVE

Thankful that she had put the top down on the newly leased convertible before leaving the Eastern Oregon Regional Airport, Katie found herself smiling like an idiot as the wind carelessly ruffled her long, sable hair. She drove through the countryside feeling as if she'd never seen such splendor or smelled such clean, crisp air. Or for that matter, heard—as she did now—the untamed intensity of nature's song. Caught up in the beauty that surrounded her, she began to visualize how she would capture it all on canvas and through the lens of her camera.

Taking the final turn toward her destination, she sailed past two of the three properties that claimed access to the private road, knowing that her new employer's estate would be next. And sure enough, minutes later she spotted the entrance to Reddington Manor.

She slowed to a stop alongside the combination keypad and intercom that stood on the outside of the closed wrought-iron gate. There were three buttons on the pad, two that said main house and the third indicating the guest cottage. She pushed the top button and waited.

When a woman's voice floated through the speaker asking Katie to state her business, she said, "I'm Katie Nolan. I have an appointment with Arthur Reddington."

As the gate slowly slid open, the voice said, "Follow the road all the way to the house, Ms. Nolan. I'll meet you there."

Katie did as she was told, steering the car along the dirt and gravel driveway that had been carved out to cut through organized rows of Douglas firs and Oregon pine trees. With sporadic sunlight shining through the treetops, the short drive seemed both surreal and refreshing. When the house came into view, she pulled to a stop at the base of the wrap-around porch and took a minute to gawk at the grandness of the dwelling. It was truly a magnificent representation of old money and excellent taste. And if she believed in such things, she would have sworn that she could feel the watchful eyes of the Reddington ancestors bearing down on her from the rafters.

Arthur Reddington, who was current denizen of the mansion, lived in quiet luxury. This was thanks in part to his grandfather, Angus Reddington, who, in the early nineteen hundreds, sank every last dollar he had into the purchase of a small vineyard located about sixty miles northeast of Abbott county. Over the next thirty years, he acquired two more vineyards and worked extremely hard to keep the businesses afloat—often wearing every hat from laborer to financial analyst. After his death, the properties were passed along to his only son, Liam, who in turn passed the family fortune on to each of his three sons. Arthur, being the eldest son, had received full rights to the vineyard that had started it all.

Over the years, Arthur had proven to be a judicious businessman. By the time he turned forty-five, he had added three high-end restaurants to his portfolio and had secured a reputation of being one of the most revered wine masters of his generation. His two failed marriages had produced no children and now, at the age of sixty-three, he lived a peaceful life at the foothills of the Blue Mountains in the outskirts of Abbott County. Although he still owned the vineyard, winery, and restaurants, he no longer tended to the day-to-day operations—instead, choosing to spend his time running the Reddington Foundation, established in his grandfather's name. Among other honorable causes, the Foundation provided grants to young entrepreneurs who needed start-up money for their business ventures.

Katie knew all this from the research she'd done on the Reddington family when she'd accepted the commission. She had learned early on in her career to gather all the information she could on a client which might help her deal with their eccentricities later on. More than once she'd been caught up in the center of a family feud and wound up as the referee, or even worse, losing out on what could have been a lucrative assignment.

Clutching her shoulder bag, Katie hopped out of the car and headed toward the porch. The door opened as she reached the top step, and she was greeted by a short, thin, middle-aged woman who identified herself as the housekeeper, Nora Blakely.

"Mr. Reddington had wanted to be here when you arrived," she said, motioning Katie inside. "However, he was called away unexpectedly and asked me to pass along his regrets. He said he would contact you tomorrow upon his return. I supervised the arrival of your things yesterday, and I'm sure you'll find everything in order. If you'll wait here, I'll grab the keys to my jeep, and you can follow me to the guest cottage."

The housekeeper turned and drifted toward the back of the house, which gave Katie the opportunity to check out the living room. It was a large, comfortable-looking space, with plump leather furniture and generous geometric windows that invited the beauty of the sunlight to splay across the oriental carpet. Wanting to steal a closer look, Katie took a cautious step deeper into the room. Before she could even form an opinion, the housekeeper's footsteps had her returning to the hallway.

"All set," Mrs. Blakely said as she breezed past Katie on her way to the front door. "We'll take the main driveway to the narrow cut-off road you may have noticed on your way up here."

Katie hurried out the front door behind Mrs. Blakely and down the porch steps to where she'd parked her car. By the time she'd scrambled behind the wheel and turned the key in the ignition, the housekeeper was already making a U-turn in her jeep and heading toward the driveway. Katie quickly put her car in gear and spun around, kicking up dust and pebbles as she raced to keep up. When they got to the edge of the open acreage, the jeep took a hard left and barreled down a narrow trail that ran along the tree line. Katie could see that the path had been used recently, although it didn't appear that it was used often.

Slowing her speed when she saw the jeep's brake lights flash, Katie followed the housekeeper through an opening in the trees where she spotted a small, one-and-a-half story cottage nestled comfortably inside a circle of Douglas firs. The brick structure had a small front porch in addition to a wood terrace in the back, only yards away from the mouth of the dense woods. The trim was red, as was the door, and there were white laced curtains draped behind the sizable front window. Katie loved it.

Mrs. Blakely was already out of her jeep and unlocking the front door when Katie pulled up to the cottage. As she cut the engine and swung out of the sports car, the housekeeper used a wave of her hand to beckon Katie inside.

"Oh, Mrs. Blakely, this is wonderful," Katie exclaimed as she crossed to the center of the living room and slowly turned, taking in the mixture of classic colors in the furniture fabrics and braided rugs. The old country charm of an oversized padded rocking chair, a bulky sleeper sofa, and other strategically placed pieces gave the room a crisp, homey feel.

The open kitchen, which was separated from the living room by an island counter, was both bright and airy. The cabinets and shelves that stretched across the back wall were painted white and had clear glass door panels. Matching white café curtains covered the two narrow windows that looked out over a small floral garden.

The walls in this room were painted a warm periwinkle blue, and another braided rug sat in front of the kitchen sink. It all came together beautifully, Katie thought.

"There are two bedrooms in the rear," Mrs. Blakely said, pointing down a long, narrow hallway, "as well as the bathroom and a laundry room. I had your easels and art supplies put in the south room. Mr. Reddington thought you'd like to use that for your personal studio because it gets the most light during the day, and the transom window should give you an exceptional view of the outdoors. Of course, you'll still have the larger studio at the house for the commissioned work. There's also a small attic area you can access from the back of the cottage, although it's really only good for storage."

"It's perfect," Katie said.

"Here's your key card for the main gate," the housekeeper said as she handed Katie a dark green, plastic card. "If you have visitors," she continued, walking over to a screen that was recessed into the wall near the front door, "you can buzz them in here. It will give you a visual of who's at the gate and you can speak to them as well. Please be responsible when letting anyone onto the estate, Ms. Nolan. Mr. Reddington is a very private man and doesn't like strangers roaming around unsupervised." She gave Katie a final look as she handed over a set of keys. "I'll leave you to get settled in. These are for both the cottage and the house."

Accepting the keys, Katie asked, "Where would be the best place to go for supplies like food and incidentals?"

"If you're looking for the basics, the closest place is about ten miles from here. Go back down Reddington Drive to Brentwood Avenue. Hang a left, and it'll take you directly into the downtown district of Abbott. Of course, there's always the City of Pendleton which will be another fifteen miles or so and it'll have a wider selection."

"You've been very kind, Mrs. Blakely, thank you. And please, call me Katie."

"You can call me Nora. I left my number on the kitchen table if you need anything else."

The housekeeper was already moving toward the front door, and Katie politely followed. "I'm sure I'll be fine, but I'll call if I need anything. Thank you again."

When Nora drove away, Katie went back inside the cottage and took a measured tour of the rest of the space.

Stepping into the first bedroom, she discovered that Nora had been right about using it as her studio. The wall colors were soothing, and the window did indeed invite the natural light to filter into the room. There was plenty of space for her to set up a work table, an easel, and open shelves that she could use to store art supplies.

She moved to the bedroom across the hall which also turned out to be generous in size. A four-poster, queen-sized bed was centered against the wall opposite the door, and a quilt that Katie suspected was a family heirloom draped across the foot of the mattress. The walk-in closet, which stretched the length of the room, would offer plenty of space for her clothes and other belongings.

Alongside the bed was a walnut nightstand with intricate carvings along the top edges and drawers, holding a small Tiffany lamp and a retro princess phone in candy apple red. Positioned near the closet was a waist-high Victorian dresser, crafted from the same dark walnut, with an attached vintage oval mirror. The only other piece of furniture in the room was a padded cedar chest that stood at the foot of the bed. Completing the décor were soft floral curtains covering the corner windows, and two unassuming throw rugs.

Stepping out of the room, she turned down the hallway and found the laundry room containing a washer, dryer, stationary tub, and small folding table. A weathered wooden door stood partially open in the far corner, and upon closer inspection, Katie was both surprised and delighted to discover a moderate-sized room that had probably been used at one time for canned food storage. With some minor modifications, she'd be able to turn it into a dark room for developing her film.

Pleased with the overall layout of the cottage, she returned to her car to unload her suitcases, anxious to begin the next chapter of her life.

The next three hours were spent unpacking, storing clothes, and setting up her studio. It wasn't until Katie found herself stretching cramped muscles that she glanced at the clock and was surprised to see it was past dinner time. Deciding to drive into town to pick up some essentials—and maybe a nice roast beef sandwich—Katie grabbed her oversized purse and dashed out the door.

She climbed into her car and, following Nora's directions, reached her destination in no time at all. It was closing in on eight-thirty but to Katie—who very rarely hit the sheets before midnight—it seemed as if people had already tucked themselves away for the night. Thankfully, the corner convenience store was still open for business.

Parking in the rear and entering through the back door, she picked up a shopping basket and did a quick sweep through produce, frozen foods, and finally health and beauty. She made a mental note to drive into Pendleton toward the end of the week to do a more thorough job, but what she'd thrown in the basket would hold her over until then.

As she handed cash to the older man behind the register, she said, "Is there somewhere you can recommend for a quick sandwich? My heart's set on roast beef."

"Clancy's is down the block. It's a clean, friendly pub that's got great sandwiches. Homemade fries and coleslaw, too. It's your best bet unless you want some greasy, under-cooked fast food, and then

you'll want Billy's Burgers, or as the folks around here call it—
Billy's Belly Burners." His grin was wide as he added an enlightened
wink. "It's on Park Street right past the bank."

"Clancy's it is," Katie said, grinning back.

"It's within walking distance if you want to leave your car in
my lot. Won't be too many more customers coming through here
tonight."

Katie went back to the parking lot and dropped the two bags in the
trunk, locked the vehicle, and walked over to the pub. Once inside,
she was instantly impressed with the clean mahogany tables and
matching chairs, the dark, polished bar that stretched across one side
of the room, and the various sport trophies that were interspersed
among the bottles of premium whiskey and bourbon behind the bar.

Katie was greeted by a woman carrying a tray of food, wearing a
white blouse, black skirt, and green apron. "Welcome to Clancy's,"
she said, slowing long enough to acknowledge Katie. "Hang on and
I'll be right with you."

Giving her a nod, Katie turned her attention to the photographs
on the wall near the entryway. Each pictured a tree—the same oak
tree, Katie was pretty sure—as it transitioned from summer to fall,
to winter, then spring. The photos weren't those of a professional,
but they'd been taken by a fairly good amateur, she thought.

"My boy took those," the waitress said as she sidled up to Katie.
"They're pretty good, don't you think?"

"Yes, they are. How old is your son?"

"He'll be turning eighteen in a couple of months. He wants to
take pictures for a living. Don't think there's much money to be
made in that, but it's what he wants to do, so I encourage him. He'll
be entering college next year," she added with a hint of sadness. "So,
can I get you a table or a booth?"

"I really only stopped in to see if I could get a sandwich to go.
Maybe a soda?"

"Sure. We're not all that busy tonight, so why don't you take that booth in the corner while you wait. There's a menu on the table, and I'll be right over to take your order."

"Thanks," Katie said.

The menu was simple, but each selection looked mouthwatering. She couldn't tell if it was due to the way each item was described, the fabulous smell coming from the kitchen, or the fact that she was famished. The last sandwich listed was—thank you, God—a roast beef on rye.

"My name's Tess, by the way," the woman said when she returned. "You new to Abbott or just passing through?"

"I'm Katie Nolan, and I guess you'd say I'm new but not permanent. Although, if your roast beef is any good, you'll be seeing a lot more of me."

"Oh, you'll be back, guaranteed. That sandwich comes with either chips or fries."

"Fries, and make that a double order."

"Drink?"

"Root beer, please."

"Still want it to go?"

"I do. I've got a lot of work to get done yet tonight."

"What kind of work you in, Katie?"

"I'm a professional artist and photographer."

Tess's mouth dropped and her eyes widened. "You're the one who's going to be working for Arthur Reddington. The folks here have been talking non-stop about it ever since Nora mentioned it to Danny Walsh who then told Owen Franklin . . . have you met Owen? He owns the food mart down the street. Anyway, now that I know who you are, it's truly a pleasure to meet you."

The gossip pipeline was alive and strong, Katie thought. To Tess she said, "And now that I'm no longer a rumor, you can believe me when I say that your son's photographs are very good. He's got potential, and once he gets into college he'll have any number of directions he can go. There are quite a few jobs out there that will pay photographers decent money."

Tess laughed and said, "I'll be the first to admit that money's not everything, but you always want better for your kids. The most important thing is that he's happy. And that he gives me at least three grandchildren to spoil.

"I'll get your order in right away," she continued. "There's a jukebox in the back corner if you want some noise. We don't get live music in here during the week, but you should come back any Saturday night. The place is packed and the music is top notch. Ask anyone." With that, Tess scurried back toward the kitchen.

Katie glanced around and noticed a modestly-sized stage set up against the wall opposite the bar. She also glimpsed the jukebox, although no one seemed to be in the mood for music tonight. For her, the hum of conversations drifting over from the other two occupied tables was noise enough. Even the three men sitting at the bar were being reserved.

Reaching into her shoulder bag, Katie pulled out a paperback book and thumbed it open to where her bookmark was tucked. It was her habit to always have a book on hand, and not only because reading was one of her favorite pastimes. She'd also found herself stuck waiting on too many jobs not to be prepared.

She'd only gotten through three paragraphs when she saw movement out of the corner of her eye. She looked up and spotted one of the men who'd been sitting at the bar approaching the table. Too late to ignore him now.

"Howdy," he said with an exaggerated drawl. "Here alone?"

Oh, please. Next he'll be asking me for my zodiac sign, she thought wryly.

"Waiting for my sandwich," Katie said with little enthusiasm. She glanced down at her book hoping he'd get the hint.

"What a coincidence. I just ordered a sandwich myself. My name's Carl," he said, sliding into the booth across from her. "But everyone calls me C.J."

"Katie," she said, trying to remain polite but not wanting to encourage him.

"Glad to make your acquaintance, Katie. Let me guess. You're traveling across the U S of A and couldn't drive another mile without a hot meal and maybe some sack time." He raised an eyebrow, obviously thinking it made him look irresistible.

"Sorry, not even close," she said.

"Well, whatever your story is, I'm sure glad it brought you into my little corner of the world tonight. Once we finish dinner, we could go find a little action somewhere. Or better yet, go back to my place."

"Don't think so," she said closing her book and returning it to her bag. "It's dinner for one, and it looks like it's ready to go. Nice meeting you Carl."

She slid out of the booth hoping she was close to being right about her food. Unfortunately, C.J. didn't take the hint as he wrapped his fingers around her wrist and held tight. "A pretty girl like you shouldn't have to eat alone. Why don't I follow you back to your place?"

"Why don't you let go of the lady's arm and head back to your buddies, C.J."

Katie glanced up from the man in the booth to the man who had shifted to her side. He was at least a head taller than she was, good looking in a woodsy sort of way, and could easily win any physical contest that C.J. cared to wage. He had a day's growth of beard, which made him look intriguing and dangerous at the same time, and his dark blue eyes flickered in the diffused overhead lights.

"Come on Clay," C.J. whined. "Katie and I are having a pleasant conversation. You got no say in what I do or who I want to talk to."

"My place, C.J. I've always got the final say. Now why don't you go on back to the bar?"

Letting several seconds tick away, he finally looked at Katie and said, "He's the boss, I guess. But my offer stands, anytime, anyplace."

C.J. slipped out of the booth and returned to the bar. One of his buddies slapped him on the back while the other one hooted at his failure. Katie shook her head. "Testosterone fueled by liquor is always precarious."

The pub owner smiled. "So, you're aware of the not so uncommon phenomenon, are you?"

"Afraid I am. I'm Katie Nolan," she said extending her hand. "You have a nice place here."

He still wore that dimpled smile when he took her hand and replied, "Clay Crawford. Sorry about the disturbance. C.J. hasn't quite gotten the hang of bowing out gracefully when a beautiful woman is involved. That doesn't excuse his behavior, but does explain it a bit. He's really not a bad guy."

"I'll take your word for it." Realizing they were still holding hands, Katie cleared her throat and gently slipped her hand from his. "I'm hoping my roast beef sandwich is ready soon," she continued, looking around the room for the waitress. "I've been craving one all day and was ecstatic when I saw it on the menu."

"Well I can guarantee you won't be disappointed, Ms. Nolan. I made it myself."

"Please, call me Katie."

He held her gaze for a moment and then said, "Tess can check you out. It was nice meeting you."

With a nod, he turned and walked past the bar and through the swinging door to the kitchen. Damn, he looked as good from behind as he did when he'd been facing her, she observed pleasantly. Shaking her head in amusement, she walked over to the register to settle her bill.

Back in the car, she opened the cardboard container and inhaled the sinfully calorific aroma of the sandwich and fries. All the necessary condiments were there along with—surprise, surprise— two juicy pickle halves. It appeared that someone had taken a liking to her, she mused. It was either Tess who thought Katie could somehow help her son out, or maybe the owner himself. Either way, she was grateful.

She put the car into gear and happily munched on the fat, lavishly salted, homemade fries as she drove out of the parking lot.

Clay was back behind the bar after shamelessly watching Katie Nolan walk out. Not only was she gorgeous, but she had a very attractive backside that had precisely enough swing in it to stir a man's imagination. What was even sexier though, was that she was totally unaware of the seductive movement. In his line of work, he'd had the pleasure of going up against many a woman who'd used the hip swing to draw wanted attention. But this one? No, he suspected that she was more content to melt into the background and ignore the attention she received from the men who relied only on their one-track minds to round first base.

On the other hand, it wasn't beneath Clay to occasionally be drawn in by a purely physical attraction. Yet, it was more than her adorable derrière that had captured his interest. He'd also been galvanized by that low, soft voice that had floated through deliciously full, appealing lips. And the unreserved handshake, supported by long slender fingers that had wrapped tightly around his. Not to mention the contact that had lingered way beyond the socially acceptable length of time.

His mother, God rest her soul, would have described Katie Nolan as trouble, although she'd had the annoying habit of describing most women under the age of fifty that way. Especially if they were hanging off her son's arm. But what would have escaped her scrutiny this time were Katie's sparkling green eyes. Those sensitive, intelligent, all-knowing eyes that seemed to brighten a room without any effort whatsoever.

But Clay wasn't in the market for a romance right now, and that was certainly something that the fancy California artist would expect from a man. She didn't strike Clay as being the type of woman who would be content with an occasional and uncomplicated liaison between the sheets.

He turned his attention to the two young ladies giggling at the end of the bar. Selecting a nice bottle of white wine, he drifted their way. As he refilled their glasses, he joined in their debate about artificial intelligence—as it related to the current sci-fi flick playing at the Mega Theater in Pendleton. Robots from outer space weren't exactly his specialty, but he was an expert at keeping up with any topic of conversation his customers chose.

When his thoughts drifted back to his encounter with the newcomer to Abbott, he realized that his heart wasn't quite into the chase tonight. The memory of her backside sashaying out of the bar had him smiling, and wondering if she would also intrude his dreams.

Chapter
Six

Katie woke with a jolt, confused at first by the sound of the ringing phone. She rolled onto her stomach and blindly grabbed for the receiver. Her voice was rough and pitched low when she greeted the caller.

"Katie, this is Nora Blakely. Mr. Reddington is back on the estate and would like to meet with you at ten this morning. Does that work for you?"

"Ten will be fine," Katie replied automatically, although she had no idea what the current time was. She had neglected to unpack her alarm clock before crawling into bed but was pretty sure that the thin streak of sunlight filtering in through the half-opened drapes meant that it was still early enough to grab a nice hot shower.

She swung her feet over the edge of the bed and padded off into the kitchen, realizing how much she missed Winston and Tabitha. Seven months after Evan had died, she'd moved out of the condo they'd bought together and into a smaller two-bedroom apartment about a mile from where her mother lived. Winston had been adopted by Bethany and Matt, while Tabitha had gone to an elderly neighbor who had recently lost her own feline companion. Giving her pets away had been a difficult decision at the time, even though she'd known it had been the right one. And from the latest reports, they had both settled into their new homes with little fuss.

When she eventually pulled up to the main house, the efficient housekeeper was waiting at the front door. "I'll show you to the solarium," she said cheerfully, ushering Katie inside. "Mr. Reddington had to take a phone call but will be with you shortly."

Katie was led into a bright, spacious room that looked out onto a splendid country garden that someone obviously kept meticulously well-groomed. She didn't know much about flowers, but recognized a scattering of poppies, daisies, and what appeared to be buttercups. A latticework arbor, covered in climbing roses, was positioned at the outside entrance to the garden. A weathered stone fountain stood in the center, and two benches were strategically placed to offer a peaceful sanctuary. Completing the old country charm was a crushed stone pathway weaving through the assorted plants and herbs.

"The garden is a secret passion of mine. With the Blue Mountains as a backdrop, it's all such a beautiful sight, don't you think?"

Katie turned to see Arthur Reddington standing behind her, his hands clasped behind his back, his deep-set eyes focused on the whimsical garden. He was dressed casually in black pleated pants, a tan polo shirt and soft leather slip-on shoes. His hair curled slightly at the ends and was close to being completely gray, the color matching the highly-groomed mustache she was sure he'd had for more years then he could remember. She noted the amused expression on his face as he scrutinized the garden, making her speculate that he actually spent some quality time on his hands and knees tending to the needs of the flowers.

Shifting her gaze back to the window, she agreed with his assessment. "It is beautiful, although I don't have much luck when it comes to planting flowers, or anything else now that I think about it. My mother is the real expert. Looking at your garden, I can tell that someone must provide a loving hand in maintaining it. It all looks so unplanned and lazy in a way. As if nature has more of a say in it than the caregiver." Turning to face him, she quickly added, "I hope that didn't sound insulting. It's exactly what I would envision a country garden to look like."

"I'm not insulted at all. It's a perfect description."

"You're the gardener," she stated, confirming her earlier thought.

"For the most part, yes. I have someone who comes in to tend the garden as well as provide upkeep on the rest of the property, but I'm out there most days, and I admit that I supervise more than Geno would like."

"What a wonderful talent to have."

"Well, not all talent. A lot of years spent educating myself, as well as picking the brains of some of the best botanists around. Like most things in life, it's hard but rewarding work."

Katie recalled the first time she'd met Arthur Reddington. A small collection of her paintings had been on display at a gallery in Los Angeles, and she'd seen him admiring her work. She had wisely approached him, hoping to make a sale. One thing led to another, and they had agreed to meet the next day to discuss her availability to create three family portraits. The caveat was that she would be using old photographs, as the subjects were all deceased Reddington ancestors. And even though she had cautioned him that she had limited experience with portraits, he had wanted her name scrawled at the bottom of each canvas.

"Regrettably, the photographs are barely recognizable at this point. However, they're all I have left," he'd told her solemnly. "Through the years, I've found other family photos and some old family diaries and newspaper clippings that I hope may be of some help to you."

Katie had listened as Arthur went on to share some of that history, and by the time lunch was over, she had accepted the commission.

Arthur's rich baritone voice cut into her thoughts as he said, "Ah, here's my head of security, Ian Gallagher. I was hoping you two would get a chance to meet today."

Katie turned toward the entrance of the solarium and saw a tall, dark haired man looking to be in his mid-forties entering the room. As he approached, he extended a strong, calloused hand along with a warm smile. "Welcome Ms. Nolan. Have you had the chance to settle in yet?"

"I have, thank you. The cottage is gorgeous and very comfortable."

He nodded, keeping those dark, adventurous eyes softly focused on her.

"I was about to give Katie a tour of the house, and then Nora will serve us lunch on the terrace. Would you care to join us, Ian?"

"Thank you, but I have an appointment in Pendleton. Maybe a rain check?"

"Sounds good."

"Ms. Nolan," Ian said, nodding slightly. "If there's anything you need, don't hesitate to contact me." Turning to Arthur, he added, "I'll need some of your time later today to go over the three resumes I've selected as final candidates for the security team."

"Not a problem. Find me when you're back."

As Ian disappeared out the door, Arthur turned to Katie. "Well, let's take that tour. And I'd like you to call me Arthur. We'll be seeing a great deal of each other during the next several months and, if possible, I want us to become friends." Extending his arm, he motioned her into the main hallway. "We'll go upstairs so I can show you your work area first."

CHAPTER SEVEN

The first two weeks on the Reddington estate flew by so quickly that Katie lost track of the days. The only contact she'd had with the outside world had been a quick trip or two into town for groceries and several late-night phone calls with her mother. The remainder of her time had been spent either at the house working on the first portrait for her employer or at the cottage working on her own paintings.

It was late Tuesday afternoon, and the sunlight that had been filtering into the upstairs room had already begun to dim as Katie stepped back to examine her day's work. She was finding the challenge of recreating Arthur's great-great-grandfather, using only the faded black and white photograph to put the image onto canvas, both a challenging and delicate process. Even with Arthur's help on eye and hair color, her need to capture every nuance—coupled with her obsessive lean toward perfection—was making for a slow and cumbersome progression.

Time to put it away, she decided as she set the paint brush aside and found a rag to swipe at the paint residue on her hands. The kink in her shoulders and the constant throb along her left temple were reason enough to call it a day, yet it was the low, intense growling from her stomach that had her cleaning up.

"It's looking good, Katie."

The deep, penetrating voice had her snapping her head around and taking two steps back. She saw Arthur Reddington standing in the doorway, hands in the pockets of his trousers, watching her.

"I didn't mean to startle you. I apologize."

"How long have you been standing there?" she asked, folding the rag across the bottom of the easel. "I didn't hear you come in."

"A couple of minutes, that's all. I didn't want to disturb you, and I guess I got mesmerized by your intense concentration. But it's more than that, isn't it? It's as if you're one with the painting. And each stroke of the brush pulls you in even deeper. Tell me, do you ever get so totally lost in your work that you have a hard time finding your way back out?"

"I've never thought about it that way, but I guess I am pretty intense when I'm painting," Katie said casually even though she was feeling a bit uneasy with the fact that he'd been watching her. "I didn't think you'd be back until tomorrow."

"I was able to get things sorted out quicker than I thought I would. Have you had dinner?"

"I'm sure I did at least once this week," she laughed. "When I get caught up in a project, I tend to forget about eating."

"Nora is preparing an excellent pot roast, and I would be very pleased if you'd join me."

Katie had planned on a cold turkey sandwich with a side of ridged potato chips for dinner, but when her stomach sent out another hunger alert—one that was loud enough to have Arthur grinning—she didn't think she was on solid enough ground to escape his offer. "If you can give me maybe an hour to clean up, I'd be very pleased to join you," she replied.

Her cell phone vibrated on the workbench, drawing her attention momentarily. Katie preferred working without interruptions. Even the music she occasionally played was set on the lowest volume. But she remembered now that she had left the phone on earlier, after talking to her friend, Christina Freeman.

"Go ahead and take the call," Arthur said. "Dinner at six?"

"That works for me."

Katie picked up the cell phone and answered with a tentative greeting. When no one responded, she tried again to connect with the caller, but no one said a word. Dropping the phone on the table, she muttered words that would have had her mother blushing. But this was the third time this week she'd answered her phone, only to hear dead air on the other end. It was getting frustrating to say the least.

Checking her watch, she reasoned that she had enough time to grab a hot shower and change into more appropriate clothes. As she trotted down the carpeted stairway, she forced herself to let go of the call, choosing instead to focus on the home-cooked meal that lay ahead of her. If the pot roast was even half as good as the lunch Nora had prepared on Katie's first day—creamed spinach casserole served with warm crusty bread and a chocolate nut torte for dessert—Katie definitely didn't want to be late.

Dinner at the Reddington's was the complete opposite of how dinner had been at the Nolan's.

True, when she was growing up, weekend dinners had been served in the dining room, but her family had gathered around the kitchen table for their weekday meals. It had proven to be, for the most part, a fend-for-yourself feast. If you didn't snatch a serving of casserole or potatoes or peas on the first pass, you were pretty much out of luck. Because even if the dish made it back your way, nine times out of ten it would be empty. Her two older brothers, with their bottomless stomachs, would make sure of that. And then there was Biscuit, their spoiled schnauzer, who snapped up the scraps of food dropped by the boys—over the halfhearted objections of her mother, of course. And her father, bless his heart, would try to institute some decorum around the table. Although more times than not, he would end up shaking his head and assuring his wife that her children were merely going through a phase. "They won't always be so unrefined, honey. They'll grow out of it soon enough, trust me."

Sadly, Katie had been the only sibling to survive life's cruelties. Tommy had lost his battle with leukemia at the age of sixteen and Billy—the middle child—had died three years later from congestive heart failure. It had been a difficult period in her life, not to mention the strain it had placed on her parents' marriage.

As Katie now gave the Reddington table a closer look, the comparison to the Nolan dinners was almost comical. There was an elegant lace tablecloth spread beneath genuine silverware, which was lined up perfectly beside plates that matched the saucers that matched the cups. Everything looked way too elaborate for her easy-going lifestyle. The Waterford crystal certainly trumped the colorful plastic glasses her mother had set out in an attempt to keep her hooligans from breaking the good china. Here, pillar candles flickering in the center of the long dining room table completed the extravagant décor. It all reminded her of a classic Grace Kelly film.

"You're going to find that this is the best roast you'll ever taste," Arthur said as Nora served their food, then slipped back into the kitchen. "Nora has been with me for close to ten years now, and one of her best assets is her cooking."

"Is there a Mr. Blakely?" Katie inquired as she lifted her glass and took a sip of wine.

"Nora was married for several years to a communications tycoon in England. When he died, she took on the job of nanny for a widowed gentleman with whom I had occasional business dealings. When his children were all grown, and the last one was getting ready to go off to university, I made her an offer to join me here. Fortunately, she said yes." Reaching for his own wine glass, he gave Katie an amicable smile and said, "So, tell me more about your life in Long Beach."

As dinner was consumed, Katie found it surprisingly easy to talk to Arthur, sharing stories about her work and her family. In turn, Arthur spoke about his wineries and restaurants as well as his love for flying. When the meal was complete, Katie graciously declined coffee and dessert, instead making her excuses.

"It's been a long day, and I'm afraid I'll fall asleep on you if I stay. But thank you for dinner. It was delicious."

"Thank you for accepting the offer. I enjoyed spending time learning more about you, Katie. We'll do it again, soon."

"I look forward to it."

"I'll be leaving again tomorrow, probably gone for several days," Arthur said as he walked Katie to the front door. "If you need anything, Nora will be able to help you."

"Sounds good. Goodnight, Arthur."

"Goodnight," Arthur said, smiling at her as she climbed into her car and drove down the dirt path that led to the cottage.

Arthur stepped into his bedroom a short time later and picked up the remote that operated the assortment of electronics scattered about the room. He programmed an hour's worth of soft music, a ritual that seemed to help relax him most evenings. Next, he stepped into the shower—another nightly ritual—and finally into a clean pair of black silk pajamas.

Walking over to the dresser, he pulled open the top drawer and reached for the wooden box he kept tucked away in the back. Pulling out a small key he kept taped to the bottom, he unlocked the box and removed the photo that was resting on top of the others. For a long time, he stood staring down at the image of himself as a much younger man, his arm wrapped affectionately around a beautiful, smiling woman. He let the memories of that moment in time caress him, remembering how they had both been searching for an escape from the loneliness their lives had shoved upon them. Hers caused by an emotional withdrawal from a husband who for years had sought to find a suitable balance between work and family. His caused by the inability to find a marriage partner who didn't love his wealth and status more than she loved him. So long ago, he thought, yet the memories remained so dangerously close to the surface. He sighed heavily, reluctantly placing the photo back in the box, locking it, and returning it to the dresser drawer.

He crossed the room and crawled into the king-sized bed. Balancing his reading glasses on the bridge of his nose, he opened the book he kept on the nightstand and relaxed back into the pillows, convinced he could manage a few chapters before going down for the night. He wanted at least four solid hours of sleep; six would be even better.

In the end he got the six, and then some.

CHAPTER
EIGHT

Marian Nolan was kneeling in the courtyard of her condominium, bent over the patch of dirt she lovingly called her spring garden. There were eight individual units that led out into the yard, and each had an area that offered the tenant a place to plant flowers, vegetables, or low-growth shrubbery. Today, Marian was making way for a row of petunias that had been given to her by a neighbor whose son owned a nursery across town. Marian loved to spend time in the outdoors.

She recalled how years ago—once her husband had retired—she would join him on the golf course almost every week. Occasionally, when they would organize a foursome with friends, they'd all end up on the outdoor patio of the club, enjoying a glass of wine or beer, along with Cobb salads or BLT sandwiches. Then she'd be right back home changing into her gardening attire and spending another two hours weeding or snipping or digging.

She and Robert had first met at the University of Berkeley, where he was attending the School of Law and she was charting a course that would earn her a degree in mathematics. Robert was the dashing young law student who was not only popular for winning mock trials, volunteering for local non-profit organizations, and setting records as the second baseman on a community baseball team, but also for the energy and dedication he demonstrated in his internship at the Berkeley District Attorney's Office.

It hadn't taken them long to fall in love, and a year after meeting, they married. Following graduation, he accepted an entry-level job in the district attorney's office in Long Beach while she taught at a private high school for girls.

Five years into their marriage, their first child, Thomas, had been born. Marian left her teaching job, choosing to be a stay-at-home mother, as Robert continued to work his way into an assistant district attorney position. There had been a price attached to that assignment, however. The time he spent at the office and in court far exceeded the time he spent at home. On more than one occasion, he'd patiently explained to her that in order to be considered for an appointment to the bench, he needed to put in the time. Which often proved to be an accurate, if not resented, statement on her part.

Their second child, Billy, joined the Nolan clan just over two years later. Four years after that, Katie had been born, and by then it was already being whispered that Robert's appointment was imminent.

The following year, all the hard work and long hours finally paid off. The coveted office in the back of the courthouse prominently displayed his name in gold stenciled letters: Judge Robert T. Nolan.

Robert had spent another fifteen years on the bench during which time they'd suffered a number of hardships, the most difficult being the loss of both their sons. But they'd endured, and when Robert finally made the decision to retire, Marian had been more than ready to enjoy some peace and quiet with him in the ranch-style house where they'd raised their children. But shortly into year three of retirement, Robert had become ill, and within six months, colon cancer had claimed another victim.

Marian had been devastated, but insisted on remaining in the house. She continued to do the occasional entertaining, sometimes offering overnight lodging to an out-of-state relative. But even those familiar connections couldn't fill the emptiness that Robert had left behind. Every morning she would wake up feeling an unalterable void in her life and every night battled with the memories that hovered over her cold, lonely bed.

Eventually, she had said a final good-bye to her old life and taken up residency in Pleasant Horizon Condominiums, which was nestled in a quiet neighborhood not far from Katie's apartment. She'd been forced to downsize of course, but all in all—even though she had less square footage inside, and not as much dirt outside—she had to admit that she was comfortable. Even on the days when she felt the absence of her family it was, for the most part, tolerable.

Marian could feel the heat of the sun now as she patted down the dirt around the last plant. Packing her tools methodically into her garden caddy, she carried them with her as she stepped through the sliding glass door that led to the kitchen. Setting the caddy on a bench near the pantry, she stepped to the refrigerator to retrieve a pitcher of her homemade lemonade.

The sound of the doorbell echoing through the condo had her hesitating. Glancing at the clock, she wondered who could be stopping by this early on a weekday morning.

Delaying the idea of lemonade for the moment, Marian made her way to the front door. As she reached for the knob, she checked the peep hole and froze in place—mind, body, and soul. She stood there for several more seconds until the bell rang again.

Taking a deep breath, she opened the door. Neither Marian nor her visitor offered a greeting. It had been years since they'd seen each other but here they were, face to face, neither able to find the right words.

He'd aged, she thought, but it certainly suited him. The dark eyes looked the same, although they appeared to be wiser now. And the thick gray hair and trimmed mustache gave him an unquestionable air of elegance. He wore charcoal gray slacks, a silver gray dress shirt, and a dark navy suit coat. No tie today, but it didn't change the fact that the man had style when it came to fashion.

"I'm sorry to stop by like this without any warning," he said, breaking the silence. "I was in the area . . . no, that's not true. I came here to see you. I wanted to see you."

"I suppose the proper thing for me to say is that it's good to see you after all these years," Marian said, "but I'm not sure *that's* true. Good manners would also have me asking you to come in, but I'm not sure I want to do that either."

He didn't respond, and she continued to block his way into the condo. But as it had been so many years before, she was the first to concede. Taking a step back, she motioned him inside. When they were both seated in the living room, Marian said, "So tell me, Arthur. To what do I owe this visit?"

Arthur Reddington hadn't been at all certain how Marian Nolan would receive him. It had been ages ago when they'd first met, first fallen in love. And even after she had ended their whirlwind romance, he often felt the heartache and disappointment that the separation had created.

They had both been married at the time—to other people—but that hadn't stopped them from finding comfort in each other's arms. Eventually, and for all the right reasons, they had agreed to end their affair. Occasionally, they would run into each other at a social event or fundraiser, but he had lived up to their agreement to keep their romance locked away.

For Arthur, he had never found a way to completely suppress the love that had continued to smolder deep beneath his heart. The best he'd been able to do was to control his feelings, keeping them hidden from the outside world.

Yet here he was sitting across from the woman he'd never been able to forget. The woman he had shared a secret with for twenty-seven years. A secret that would have easily destroyed two families if it had been uncovered—so they had kept it buried. But now, there remained only one person who could be hurt by the secret that had been created out of their love so long ago. Their daughter—Katie Nolan.

"First, I want to thank you for not stopping Katie from coming to Abbott," he said as he carefully watched Marian. "It must have been a shock when you learned I was the one who had offered her a job, and I understand how difficult it must have been for you."

"I did try to stop her," Marian said tightly. "And yes, it's been extremely difficult. But I don't believe you understand that at all."

"Marian. I've spent twenty-seven years knowing that I have a daughter who thinks another man was her father. A daughter who I never had the chance to be around while she was growing up. And even though I now have the opportunity to spend time with her, she'll still never know who I am. Trust me, I understand."

"You agreed," Marian said with a slow rising panic to her voice. "Katie is not to be told that Robert isn't her biological father. You agreed, Arthur."

"Calm down, Marian." Arthur's voice was both quiet and soothing. "I don't plan on telling her anything. Although I am grateful that we'll have this time together. I didn't come here to upset you, and I certainly don't want to bring any distress to Katie. She believes Robert was her father, and by most accounts he was. I'm only hoping she and I can one day have a relationship we can both feel comfortable with."

Marian pushed out of her chair and walked over to the decorative fireplace. She ran her fingertips across a photo of Katie and Robert sitting on the river's bank, fishing poles in hand, laughing over a joke Robert had told. Marian had been the one who'd taken the picture, and she still felt the closeness that father and daughter had shared. If Katie ever found out Arthur was her biological father, she didn't know how her daughter would react. Would she be able to forgive Marian for being unfaithful to her father?

She didn't object when Arthur approached her and laid his hand on her shoulder. Nor did she try to step away from his touch. There was history between them, and even though it had been brief, it had nonetheless been filled with passion and love.

Yes, she had loved Arthur Reddington even though she'd been wearing another man's ring.

"Will you ever forgive yourself for what we shared, Marian? Will you ever forgive me?"

"We were wrong," she said softly.

"We were both starved for love and attention. We were both lost and alone. And we both found what we needed to fill the void in our souls. I won't apologize for that."

"Robert did the best he could for me and for the children."

"Robert is gone, Marian."

She closed her eyes and placed her hand over the one that was still resting on her shoulder. "You're right. I haven't forgiven myself for what I did. Even though Robert and I loved each other very much, there's always been a little part of you tucked away inside my heart."

Arthur scanned the photos on the mantel as he gave himself a moment to digest what Marian had just told him. A number of the images included a younger Katie sharing precious moments with her brothers, while the rest provided a micro glimpse of Katie's life. There was a photo of Robert Nolan lovingly holding Katie as a baby. Another showed Katie defending her goal in what appeared to be a school league soccer game. The photo on the far end showed Katie in her cap and gown, Marian standing on Katie's right and Robert on her left.

Lifting the graduation photo off the mantel, Arthur understood why he hadn't been allowed to share in these milestones. His presence would have greatly disturbed the balance of the Nolan family. But that was then, he thought, returning the photo to its proper place. What he wanted now, was to be the one to stand with Katie, laughing and enjoying life with the daughter he'd been forced to abandon for way too long.

"You've always had a piece of my heart as well, Marian," he finally said. "You can trust me when I say that I won't tell Katie anything. But I won't deny myself the enjoyment of spending time with her. Not anymore."

He kissed the top of her head and said, "I'm going back to Oregon in the morning. While I'm here, I'm staying at the Concord, suite 502."

Marian remained where she was until she heard the front door open, then close. She slowly moved into the kitchen where she poured herself that glass of lemonade, then sat down at the table and wept.

At roughly the same time Arthur was knocking on Marian's front door, Katie was exiting the cottage. She kept her unsliced bagel and travel mug—which today was filled with a strong, French Roast blend of coffee—balanced in one hand, using her free hand to pull the door open. As she took that first step out, she was surprised by a young woman straddling the porch rail and leaning lazily against the corner post. Katie's hand jerked, sending the bagel flying into the dirt and the freshly brewed coffee sloshing through the sip hole of the cup's lid.

"Sorry to have startled you," the girl said dryly, making Katie believe that she wasn't the least bit sorry.

"Who are you?" Katie asked as she wiped her hand on her jeans. "And why are you sitting here?"

The girl glared at Katie as she slowly lifted her leg over the rail and stood. "I'm Hannah. Hannah Reddington."

"Ah, yes. Hannah. Nora mentioned that you'd be coming for a visit. Your father is Arthur's youngest brother."

"And you're the artistic Katie Nolan that everyone is talking about," Hannah declared smugly.

Great, Katie thought as she watched the girl plant her feet and fold her arms across her chest, attempting to demonstrate that this was her exclusive domain. Dressed in a white T-shirt and tight, stonewashed jeans that were tucked into square-toed western boots, Hannah stood close to five and a half feet tall. Her sassy black hair was styled in a choppy pixie cut which served to highlight the delicate pink rose tattooed below her left ear. She had a round face, expressive eyes, and thin lips that were currently pressed together, emphasizing her territorial challenge.

The last thing Katie wanted was to do battle with one of the Reddington heirs, who had probably been given everything she'd ever wanted by over-indulgent parents. Instead, she took a steadying breath and said, "My contract gives me room and board in this cottage. The house is my workplace. If you have a problem with either, I suggest you talk to your uncle."

She turned to pull the door shut and made a show of engaging the secondary deadbolt lock. She figured Hannah wouldn't have any trouble finding her way inside if she wanted to—and Katie was sure she would—but it was Katie's unspoken gesture of reinforcing her contract with Arthur. Hopefully the girl would get the message.

Fat chance.

"You'll have to excuse me, Hannah, but I have to get to work. Can I offer you a ride back to the house?" Katie had noticed the absence of a vehicle.

"Sure," Hannah said as she stepped off the porch and made her way to the car. "Nice ride," she said once Katie was inside. "So tell me, how did you and Uncle Arthur hook up?"

Katie sighed heavily but kept her temper in check. "How old are you, Hannah? Twenty-one, right?" Katie's research on her boss had extended to the entire Reddington clan. "Don't you live somewhere in the Midwest? Oh, wait I remember. Charlotte, North Carolina. Am I right?"

"So, am I supposed to be impressed that you know about me? Or should I be honored that my uncle deemed you worthy enough to have the information? It doesn't matter. I don't have secrets. Can you say the same Katie?"

Katie glanced over at Hannah as she made the turn that would take them to the main house. "Everyone has secrets, Hannah. Doesn't matter how old you are, or who your parents are, or what you do for a living. So yes, I have secrets." Recognizing the game that Hannah was attempting to play, she added, "I've got to admit that none of those secrets are scandalous enough to force me to leave. Sorry."

Pulling up in front of the house, Katie shut off the engine and climbed out of the car. As Hannah followed her up the porch steps, she said, "We'll have to see about that. It'll be best though, if you learn your place." She pushed past Katie and headed down the hallway toward the kitchen. "You're only an employee here. I'm family."

Katie hesitated halfway up the stairs and leaned over the banister, but Hannah had already disappeared into the back of the house. She continued her climb, wondering how long Hannah Reddington was going to be staying on, and mentally preparing herself for the drama the girl most certainly cloaked herself in everywhere she went.

CHAPTER NINE

Two weeks later, Christina Freeman and her daughter were closing in on Pendleton where they would meet up with Katie for lunch, followed by an afternoon visit with Christina's sister. Melanie was in the back seat, singing along to the radio, which was blasting out a country rock song. Her daughter's pitch was off, by quite a bit in some parts of the song, but her heart and soul were definitely into it. And when she cheerfully slaughtered the words to the second verse, Christina had to catch herself from laughing.

After the photo shoot at the Freeman condo, Christina and her husband had authorized a photograph for *Tailored Elegance* to use, picturing the whole family gathered around the sitting room's fireplace.

Melanie, of course, had been thrilled. The day the article came out, she'd begged her mother to buy her extra copies so she could autograph them for all her friends at school. She'd even had her parents sign a copy that went to Katie.

Christina and Katie had stayed in touch after their initial meeting, and when Evan had suddenly died, she and Andrew flew down to California to attend the funeral. Christina had immediately seen the struggle Katie was going through to accept the cruel reality of the loss of her fiancé. And although they had only known each other for a short time, Christina chose to stay on an extra week to offer her support to a woman she both respected and admired.

Over the next year, the two women built a solid, unbreakable friendship. They would talk every few weeks over the phone to exchange humorous details from their family and work lives, and every couple of months arrange a meeting spot so they could spend face to face time over lunch or dinner. Today, it was a lunch date.

"I can't wait to see Katie," Melanie said when the song finally ended.

Christina reached over to the dashboard to turn the volume down. "I can't wait to see her either."

"And she lives closer now so we should see her more, right?"

"As long as our schedules match up. With both of us working and you in school, it's sometimes hard to find free time to spend together."

"I could always miss school when you and Katie have free time."

Christina caught the humor in Melanie's eyes when she glanced in the rear-view mirror. "I appreciate the extreme sacrifice you're willing to make, kiddo, but it's not going to happen on my watch."

Melanie giggled as she shifted in her seat. "How much longer, Mama?"

"About thirty minutes. Do we need to find a bathroom?"

"I think so. That's a pretty long time to wait."

This time Christina didn't try to restrain her laugh. "Sounds like a quick stop is in order, then. There's a gas station not far from here."

Twenty minutes later they emerged from the ladies' room. When they reached the car, she held the door open while Melanie climbed in.

"Buckle-up, sweetie," Christina said as she slid into the driver's seat and pulled her own seat-belt tight across her chest.

"*Mom*," Melanie said, dragging out the word as she rolled her eyes. "You tell me that every time."

"I tell you that every time because it's important every time."

"But I remember all by myself."

Again, Christina glanced at her daughter through the mirror. When had Melanie gotten so smart? she wondered. Wasn't it just yesterday that she had relied on her mother for everything?

"You're right, Mel. I shouldn't have to tell you every time. So as long as you don't forget, I won't remind you anymore, okay?"

Melanie grinned and gave Christina a victorious thumbs-up.

Christina took another moment to silently watch her daughter. She knew Melanie was growing up and would soon be insisting on spending more time with her friends and less with her mother. But there were still so many things her little girl had yet to learn; other things she would always struggle with. And in addition to all that? For Christina, letting go would be the hardest thing she would ever have to do.

Katie was already seated in the restaurant when Christina and Melanie arrived. She rose as the hostess led them over and bent down to give Melanie a hug.

"Oh, I missed you, squirt," she said as Melanie squeezed her back. "My gosh, will you look at how tall you're getting. And stronger, too."

"I've grown two marks," Melanie said, referring to the pencil marks her father made on the wall inside her bedroom every time he measured her height. "One day I'll be as tall as you, Katie."

"Just keep in mind that I've stopped growing, so you don't have to rush it. There's plenty of time to catch up to me." Pulling Christina in for her hug, Katie said, "How are you doing, champ?"

"Can't complain. How about you?"

"Same old, same old," Katie replied as everyone took their seats around the table.

"I drew a picture for you, Katie. It's in a frame and everything. But Mom said I had to leave it in the car. We don't want to spill anything on it, I guess."

"Thank you, Mel. You know how much I like your pictures. I think it's probably a wise decision to keep it safe until we finish eating. You've seen how sloppy I can get."

"Yeah. Last time you spilled your iced tea."

"Yes, I remember. I still haven't gotten the stain out of that blouse."

"If you need any help ordering ask me okay, sweetie?" Christina said when Melanie sat and opened the menu. "Your eyes are always bigger than your stomach, so keep it on the manageable side."

"*Mom.*"

Katie laughed at the way Melanie had added some real attitude to the word. She glanced at Christina who was trying to control her own laughter.

When the server came to the table, Melanie turned to her mother and said, "Can I get a cheeseburger with bacon? And some French fries. And a chocolate milk?"

"That sounds like a perfectly reasonable lunch, so yes. And I'll have a grilled chicken salad with Russian dressing and coffee."

"I'll take the whitefish," Katie said, closing her menu and handing it to their server. "With a tall iced tea."

"Oh, *no* Katie. Not again," Melanie moaned as she slapped her hands over her eyes.

Thankfully, they all got through the meal with no major incidents, and by the time dessert arrived, the topic of conversation had circled around to Arthur's niece, Hannah.

"As I told you," Katie was saying, "she's living in the main house and has made it abundantly clear that she's not pleased I'm in the cottage. That's where she always stays when she's visiting. I think what bothers her the most is that she can't get away with too much when both Arthur and Nora are so close. The cottage can't be seen from the house so you can pretty much come and go undetected, which I'm sure was a plus for her."

"What does Arthur say about it?" Christina asked.

"I haven't said anything to him, and I couldn't say whether Hannah has or not. It doesn't matter though because I have the contract. And the cottage is mine as long as I'm working there."

"She sounds a little spoiled."

"She's a lot spoiled, although I'm finding it hard not to like her. For example, last week I overheard her talking to one of her friends back home who seemed to be having problems with a neighborhood bully. Hannah sounded truly sympathetic and offered a handful of ideas that could help her friend deal with the situation.

"Sure, she's opinionated, sarcastic, and stubborn, but she's also astute, funny and free-thinking. She has a smart mouth when Arthur is out of earshot, but she can't hide the fact that she both likes and respects him. And Arthur told me the other day how much he adores her. I guess the bottom line is, she's growing on me."

"So you're not afraid she's going to go all psycho on you and slash Arthur's paintings when you're not around?"

"Well thanks for planting that thought in my head," Katie smirked. "Until now it hadn't even occurred to me. But no, she won't. Because we'd all recognize her handiwork. And besides, I think she's kind of in awe of what I'm doing."

"It sounds as if you're happy with the assignment."

"I am. And with the flexibility I have to work on my individual artwork, in another year or two I'll have my own showing, and I can use the profits to open an art gallery."

"Wow. That's a new goal for you, isn't it?"

"I've been thinking about it off and on for a couple of years. Evan and I had discussed it, but I didn't take it seriously until I accepted this job. I've really been motivated out here to produce artwork, and that motivation is going to push me to make it happen."

"That's great, Katie."

"Maybe I can sell some of my drawings in your gallery," Melanie said.

"Well, when the time comes I'll certainly be open to negotiating something with you." At Melanie's perplexed look, Katie added, "When the time comes, we'll work out a deal."

"Deal." Melanie replied while extending her hand for Katie to shake.

No one paid particular attention to the man sitting solo at the end of the bar. He was dressed similar to most of the other men—white dress shirt, suit coat, and tie. He was clean-shaven, average height, and was currently paying more attention to the soccer game on the large flat screen across the room then he was to anything else. But every now and then his eyes shifted to the restaurant and the table by the window.

He knew who the sultry blond was and that the kid sitting to her right was her daughter—thanks to the photograph that had appeared in some design magazine last year. Katie Nolan had taken it, along with the other half dozen photos of the woman's condo that had been featured in the article. Of course, none of that had any bearing on his current plans, but he had always been a believer that the more information you held, the quicker you could react to any unforeseen problems.

That was one of the reasons he was here today. It had only been a short time ago that he'd become aware of Katie's move from Long Beach to Oregon's Abbott County. He'd read that little piece of news in a second-rate magazine that had been sitting on a coffee table in the lobby of the nursing home where he'd recently had to admit his mother.

He thought back on how the decision to turn his mother's care over to complete strangers had been a difficult one. He had been noticing the changes in her behavior, signs that her health—both physical and mental—was deteriorating. Changes that had been validated six months earlier when she'd taken a fall, severely twisting her ankle. A month following that, she'd taken more than the prescribed amount of pain medication and had spent two days in the hospital. He'd had to work hard to convince her doctors that it had been an accidental overdose, and they had finally given her the green light to return to his apartment.

Then, last month, she'd managed to slip out of the apartment while he'd been shopping for groceries, and it had taken him four long hours to track her down. A phone call from their old landlord had eventually led him to the stoop of the basement apartment where they'd lived right after his father's incarceration.

The fear that he could have lost her for good had served as the turning point, and he'd finally acknowledged that he could no longer be her care provider. He'd located an affordable nursing home in western Oregon and had left her there with the promise that he'd come visit her at least twice a week.

The following day, he'd moved out of their Long Beach apartment and headed to Baker County to live in the family cabin that his father had built nearly thirty years earlier. The same cabin that his mother had somehow managed to hang on to after his father's death. He was glad she had, because the place held many fond memories of a time when father and son would go fishing or hunting, bonding the way a father and son should. And now, it was serving as his home base.

Turning his attention back to Katie, he focused on how losing the companionship of his mother had been the final straw. He could no longer ignore the injustice that had been thrust upon his family. It was finally time to set things right. So here he was in Pendleton, observing the target in order to discern if there were a pattern in how she spent her time when she wasn't behind the guarded gates of the Reddington Manor. Anything he could discover about the places she frequented, who she came in contact with, how often she left the estate alone—it would all work in his favor when the time came to take care of business.

Finishing his club soda, he reached into his wallet, left money on the bar, and walked toward the front door. As he swung it open, he stole a final look at the table where she sat, and saw her laughing at something the little girl had said. Christ, that happy-go-lucky attitude made him sick. When he thought about how her family had been the cause of so much pain for his, he had to smother the urge to walk up to her table and bash her brains in. Soon though, he'd wipe that expression off her face and show her what it was like to be afraid and alone. She'd appreciate, once and for all, what he'd had to live through. How he and his mother had ended up with nothing, while the Nolans had ended up with everything.

And when he had her begging for her life, he'd finally be the one laughing. Right before he killed her.

"Next time, I'll meet you guys in Redmond," Katie said when lunch was over and the group was crossing the parking lot. "In the meantime, give some thought to spending a couple of days at the cottage with me."

"I will," Christina said as Melanie ran ahead and pressed a button on the keyless remote her mother had given her to unlock the car doors. "I'm a woman of my word. It would be best if we do it while Melanie is still on summer vacation, though."

"Works for me," Katie said with sincere delight. "There's a traveling dollhouse exhibit on loan at one of the museums in Kennewick that will be there through the end of next month. I'm sure Melanie would enjoy that, and of course we'd have to make time for the mall. We'll make it a day trip. And I'll talk to Arthur and see if he can set up a tour of one of his wineries. No reason you and I can't enjoy some adult time for ourselves."

"And what will my impressionable daughter be doing while we're out enjoying ourselves?"

"Nora is great with kids, and once she meets Melanie, she'll love taking her for a few hours. It's all good."

Saying their good-byes, Christina and Melanie drove off, and Katie made her way to her convertible. Pulling out of the restaurant's parking lot, she turned right and reversed course back to Abbott with the top down, thinking about how life couldn't get much better than it was right now. It never occurred to her that the man in the nondescript, blue Chevy—currently following several car lengths behind her—had been waiting for her to leave the restaurant.

And was now in furtive pursuit.

He kept his distance so as not to appear too interested in the convertible cruising along in front of him.

After he had left the restaurant, his intent had been to call it a day and pick up his surveillance later in the week. Instead, he'd found himself parked in the back of the lot, waiting for Katie and her friends to make an appearance.

He'd watched her get into her car and drive toward the parking lot exit before pulling in behind her and following her into traffic. He couldn't really say why he had changed his plans. Although now that he had, he was hoping that maybe he would get the opportunity to take advantage of the long stretch of highway that lay between the restaurant and the Reddington estate. As they drove toward Abbott, he played several scenarios in his head.

Number one: Her vehicle breaks down. He quickly jumps in to play the good Samaritan, escorting her to his car on the pretense of taking her home. But of course, she'd never make it there.

Number two: She gets a flat tire. Her car pitches off the road and into a ditch. Again, he's right there to save the day. In this scenario, he could even imagine himself using the tire iron to beat her head in before leaving her bloody and half dead along the side of the road.

Although, the best route to take would be to create a scenario that gave him the most control. One where he could catch her off guard, giving her no other choice but to leave with him. Like a well-placed bump to the rear fender of her car that would force her into that ditch. Sure, he could make that work. She'd be angry at first, wondering what kind of lunatic rear-ended someone in the middle of the highway. She'd bitch a little, maybe call him some unflattering names before reaching for her cell phone to call for help. But he would be apologetic—profusely so—and tell her he'd been momentarily distracted and had every intention of paying for the damage he'd caused. Then he'd insist on driving her home, or anywhere she wanted to go. No need to inconvenience someone else to come pick her up when his car was still operational, unlike hers. He would be convincing when he begged her to allow him to make things right.

They would then walk together toward his vehicle, her gratitude now the staple of her emotions. That is, until the fear took over when he physically picked her up off her feet and tossed her into the trunk of his car. He'd slam the lid closed, move to the driver's side door and . . .

The sound of the police siren slashed through his fantasy with a force that nearly had him swerving into the culvert at the side of the highway. He glanced in the mirror and knew instinctively that he was the driver that had been targeted. He reached between the seats and guardedly fingered the fixed blade knife he always carried with him—the one that had once belonged to his father—as he pulled to the side of the road.

Easing the car to a complete stop, he jammed the gear shift into park and watched as Katie moved further and further out of his reach. When he heard the tap on his window, he turned, working hard to control his anger. Rolling the window down, he spoke the clichéd phrase that even a rookie cop must have been tired of hearing: "What seems to be the problem, officer?"

"You have a smashed taillight, sir. I need to see your driver's license and registration, please."

During the next five minutes, he waited. And watched. And fumed, as the officer took his time to run the information. He had no doubt that the ID he was using these days would pass inspection. After all, he'd paid a lot of money for a set of documents that would keep his true identity hidden. Until it was time to reveal it to Katie, that is. To tell her exactly who he was, who his father had been, and why she had to pay for his death.

When the cop approached the window a second time, obviously satisfied with what the computer had told him, he handed everything back, saying, "I'll let you off this time, sir, but you'll need to get that light fixed. The sooner, the better."

"Thank you, officer. I'll take care of it."

With a half salute, the officer returned to his vehicle.

The man behind the wheel of the blue Chevy slowly pulled back onto the road and turned off at the next exit. He once again felt for the knife, soothed by the feel of his hand wrapped tightly around the hilt. "I guess it's score one for Nolan," he mumbled as he headed for home.

Chapter
Ten

Katie had taken the better part of Friday to work on the painting of Thaddeus Reddington, Arthur's great-great-grandfather. When her lower back screamed for her to stop, she thought it best to hang up her paint brushes and retire to her cottage for the evening.

Contemplating whether a grilled cheese sandwich and cream of mushroom soup would satisfy her appetite, she dropped her bag on the floor next to the front door of the cottage and strolled to the kitchen. But instead of reaching for the small fry pan, she merely stood in front of the stove dreading the part where she'd have to go through the motions of grilling the sandwich if she wanted to eat it that way. When Evan was still alive, he had done most of the cooking and selfishly, it was one of the things she missed with his absence.

Great. Now she was feeling hungry, restless, and depressed!

Would it be so bad to have dinner in the city, she thought, hastily making a retreat toward the bathroom to take a quick shower. A little human contact along with that soup and sandwich would be exactly the right combination.

She dressed in an ankle-length, free-flowing olive-colored skirt and a long-sleeved, black tunic top with a soft-draping neckline. Deciding the outfit needed some flair, she clasped on a necklace consisting of three silver cascading strands decorated with varying sized opal, quartz, and glass beads, threaded at varying intervals. She considered slipping on a pair of her three-inch sassy sling-backs but opted instead for her low-heeled black dress boots which were more comfortable. As she checked herself out in the full-length mirror, she smiled at her veiled attempt to make a worthy impression. The fact that she couldn't even remember when she'd last brought out her Friday night wardrobe had her even more determined to have a good time tonight. You only feel as good as you look, she thought. Or was it you look as good as you feel? Either way, she looked pretty darn good if anyone cared to notice.

Driving away from the cottage, she took the dirt road to the front gate, then pulled out onto Reddington Drive. Her plan was to go into Pendleton and check out the nightlife, but for reasons she couldn't quite explain, she followed the highway into Abbott instead. As she drove slowly down Baxter Street, she could hear the laughter floating out of Clancy's when a man held the door open for several other patrons who were coming out. They were all dressed in much the same fashion as she was, and all looking happy and content. Katie took that as a sign that Clay Crawford's place may be a decent enough place to hang for a few hours.

She found a parking space in the side lot and made her way around to the front door. It was still early for the bar crowd to have arrived, so she wasn't all that surprised to see there were a few empty booths. Tess was working, and as soon as she spotted Katie, she hurried over.

"Katie, it's great to see you again. Are you here to eat or just enjoy the band?"

"Truth be told, I'm starving. Any objection if I take that small booth in the corner or do you want to save it for your regulars?"

"Nope, it's first come first serve. And most of the regulars will be in groups tonight so they'll want the bigger tables. Why don't you go on over, and I'll give you a minute to decide what you want." She handed Katie a menu and took off for the kitchen.

Katie settled back in the booth and watched two men enter the pub, both of them carrying instrument cases. One appeared to be holding a keyboard, the other a guitar. The first was wearing a navy polo shirt, loosely-fitted khaki trousers and a dark green baseball cap. The second man was older and taller, dressed in a short-sleeved knit shirt tucked into designer jeans, a brown leather jacket folded neatly over his arm. Both aimed straight for the make-shift stage.

Tess materialized at the table at the same time a third man walked through the door and moved toward the stage. "Do you need me to recite the specials or have you already decided what you want?" Tess asked.

"Oh, I'll take the tuna melt on marble rye with coleslaw, curly fries and a root beer, please. No soup."

"It doesn't come with soup," Tess said, giving Katie a puzzled look.

"Sorry," she laughed. "I was originally going to have soup and a sandwich at home."

"Got it."

"By the way, what time does the music begin?" Katie asked.

"Eight-thirty. Dakota Gold is the name of the band, and it's their first time at Clancy's. I heard that they're pretty good, so if you're not in a hurry you should stay. They'll give you everything from golden oldies to the latest pop rock cover tunes. They may even throw in a few originals."

"Sounds good. I think I'll stick around for awhile."

"Your food should be up in about five."

Tess walked away giving Katie time to casually take in the mixture of individuals who were making themselves comfortable inside the pub. The music wouldn't begin for at least another hour, but the room was beginning to fill up with both young and seasoned patrons. It looked to be a revenue-generating crowd tonight, and Katie smiled as she tried to distinguish the band groupies from the regular customers.

When she shifted her focus back to the stage, designer jeans glanced over and then did a double take. He leaned in to briefly speak to the man behind the keyboard and then both men were looking straight at her. As the first one hopped off the stage and headed her way, she thought about the first time she'd been here being hit on by the testosterone-driven C.J.

As he got closer, Katie thought she saw something familiar in his face but couldn't quite place it. "Excuse me for staring," the man said when he reached the table, "but are you Katie Nolan?"

"I am. And I feel I should know who you are, but I'm not quite—"

And it struck her. Standing before her was Nathan Hunter, the camper who had climbed down to Evan after he'd taken that awful and deadly fall.

"I can tell by the look on your face that you've finally placed me," he said. "And I apologize. I wasn't thinking that maybe seeing me wouldn't put a song in your heart and a twinkle in your eye."

"It was a momentary shock, Nathan, and I've already recovered." Extending her hand, she said, "It is good to see you. Can you sit for a minute?"

"Thank you," he said as he slid into the booth across from her. "How are you doing, Katie?"

"Very well, thanks. And now that my brain is back on track, I have to ask. Are you a musician or a groupie tonight?"

Nathan chuckled. "By day, I'm still a physician with a private practice in Pendleton. By night, I play guitar in the band, Dakota Gold. This will be our first time at Clancy's."

"You'll get a great reception, I'm sure. The folks around here are very friendly."

"Do you live here in Abbott?"

She was about to tell him about her portrait commission when the keyboard player stepped up to the table. "Come on, man, leave the lady alone. The other guys are all here and we need your butt back on stage for a sound check." Turning to Katie he added, "I apologize if the good doctor here has been bothering you, miss. We try to keep an eye on him, but he manages to escape every now and then."

Katie laughed as Nathan gave her an exaggerated eye roll. "Katie, this is Tony Santana. Tony, this is Katie Nolan, and we happen to be acquainted."

"Pleased to meet you, Katie Nolan," Santana said as he tipped his ball cap. "But I must insist that my man here return to his perch, so the rest of us can earn our supper tonight." He gave Katie a pleasant smile and used his deep-set eyes, hidden behind thick black-framed glasses, to search her face. "Hope you enjoy the music tonight," he added, turning back toward the stage.

"I should go," Nathan said. "I'd like to stop back during our first break if you're still here."

"I'd like that."

"Great. See you later."

He slid out of the booth and Katie watched him join the other musicians, confused about what she should be feeling. Here was a man whose only connection to her had resulted from the tragic death of her fiancé. She hadn't even thought about Nathan and his brother for well over a year, and she didn't necessarily want to be dragged back into that connection.

"Here's your tuna melt," Tess said as she set the plate down in front of Katie. "I saw you talking to the guitar player. A friend of yours?"

"Nathan is someone I met back home, but we're not friends so to speak."

"With that smile and exquisitely toned body, it may be worth your while to reacquaint yourselves. Just sayin'," Tess added when Katie gave her a wide-eyed look.

"Thanks for the advice."

"Hey, my pleasure."

As Tess moved off to another table, Katie snagged a fry off her plate. Neither of them had noticed Clay Crawford watching from the corner of the bar. He glanced at the man who had been sitting with Katie and wondered how they knew each other. From what Tess had told him, Katie hailed from California and hadn't been familiar with this part of Oregon. This guy was more local and had been for some years. He turned back to Katie and was surprised to see her studying him. Keeping his expression neutral, he gave her a slight nod, and she smiled before going back to her dinner.

"We need more singles, Clay," one of his bartenders announced as he hurried past him to take an order from an older couple seated at the bar.

"I'm on it." Clay mumbled as he stepped away from the counter. He took off toward his back office where the safe was kept, his thoughts still swirling around the beautiful Katie Nolan.

Clay spent time restocking liquor, helping in the kitchen, and stepping behind the bar to mix drinks before once again slipping away to his office, this time to catch up on paperwork.

It was close to ten o'clock when he signed off the computer. Leaving the office, he made his way to the bar and dining area where he would spend some time visiting with each customer, making sure they were enjoying their time at Clancy's. This was a habit he'd gotten into when he had first opened the pub and one that he continued to indulge in every weekend. Not only was it good for business—an owner who gave customers that personal attention—he truly enjoyed meeting with both the regulars and those who'd be here for the first time.

As soon as he stepped out of the hallway into the main area, he noticed that Katie had abandoned her booth and was now sitting on one of the low back stools at the end of the bar nursing a glass of red wine. He made sure to begin at the opposite end of the room from where she sat, planning on making her his final stop.

Tonight it took him nearly forty minutes to reach the final booth where a couple he'd known since arriving in Abbott was seated. The older man was a science teacher at the local high school and his wife was the school nurse. They talked about the current year's football team, the possibility of Clay sponsoring the little league baseball team next summer, and the impending birth of their second child. By the time he was able to break loose, the band had taken a break and the guitar player was standing next to Katie, talking her up.

Clay walked past them and stepped behind the bar. "Hello Katie. How are you doing?"

"Hi Clay," she said returning his smile. "I'm good, thanks. Quite the crowd tonight."

"That it is." Turning his attention to the musician, Clay reached out to shake hands. "You guys are sounding really good, and I'll admit that's a plus for me. I'm Clay Crawford, the owner of Clancy's."

"Clay, sure. Tony—the guy who talked to you about us playing tonight—told me you'd be here. I'm Nathan Hunter. Thanks for having us at Clancy's. I gotta say that everyone on your staff has been great."

"Glad to hear it. So, how long have the five of you been playing together?" Clay knew the answer because he didn't put anyone on the books unless he checked them out thoroughly. But he needed to make small talk until the guy was ready to go back on stage.

"The band has been together close to two years now, except for Tony. He joined us about a month ago when our former keyboardist moved to Florida and we put out the search for a replacement. Prior to forming Dakota Gold, we each played with different groups off and on. We play mostly in places like Clancy's, although we've scored a couple larger venues in Washington State and Nevada. Reno, to be precise. All of the band members hold day jobs, so we're limited to what we can take. But it's enough to keep us all happy."

"What's your day job, Nathan?"

"I'm a pediatrician. I have a practice in Pendleton."

Of course you do, Clay thought distractedly as he picked up a drink ticket and began filling the order. A doctor with his own practice, who happened to love kids enough to specialize in treating them. Who wouldn't like a guy with all that going for him?

"How long have you owned Clancy's?" Nathan asked, tossing the conversational ball back into Clay's court.

"Going on four years."

"Does the name have any significance?"

"My grandfather owned a pub in Ireland called Clancy's, and I named mine to honor him."

"Ah," was all Nathan could think of to say.

"The food is excellent," Katie piped in, trying to fill the awkward silence. "Roast beef is still my favorite, but the tuna melt is running a very close second."

"I'll be sure to pass your compliments on to the chef." Clay held Katie's eyes for a brief moment, lost in their intensity and beauty.

"Well, I should get back up front." Nathan's voice managed to break the spell. "It was nice meeting you, Clay, and I hope you'll keep us in mind for future gigs."

"I will. The crowd seems to like you, and that's what matters."

The two men shook hands again, and Nathan gave Katie an amiable nod before walking off.

"They really are good, Clay. I've been sitting here watching, and everyone seems to be having a good time. The dance floor has been packed all night. I'll wager that your liquor sales will be rather healthy as well."

"I do pretty good most weekends," he said, taking a bottle

of vodka in one hand and a double-sided jigger in the other. He measured the liquor into a shaker tin already filled with ice, then added equal parts of both fresh and Rose's lime juice. Taking a bar spoon, he stirred it enough to chill the contents, then strained the gimlet mixture into a stemmed cocktail glass.

Katie watched as he continued to mix, shake and pour with the precision of a chemist. She had never been able to hit the right combination when it came to making a mixed drink and had always been relegated to the uncomplicated task of pouring wine whenever she and Evan had been entertaining friends. Something everyone had been grateful for. She smiled at the memory as Clay placed the final drink on a round tray that Tess had left sitting on the corner of the bar.

"So, what brings you to Clancy's tonight?" he asked, using his elbow to lean on the bar in front of her.

"I needed a break from my paint brush. Through the years, I've discovered that if I don't walk away once in a while, I lose focus and my work suffers. I'm pretty finicky when it comes to my art." Katie took a sip from her wine glass before adding, "Although, that wasn't the only reason. I also didn't have the desire to cook for one tonight. It was the kill-two-birds-with-one-stone mentality that brought me here. Refuel both mind and body."

Clay indicated his understanding with a nod. "Been there, done that," he said. "It's good that you came here."

They stared at each other as the band launched into a popular tune from the eighties. It was slow enough so you could hold your partner close, but not necessarily romantic. "Would you honor me with a dance, Katie?"

Her heart foolishly skipped a beat. And then another as he held out his hand. She took it, letting him lead her onto the dance floor.

They were quiet through the first half of the song, blending their steps to the rhythm set by the music. He held her at a respectable distance but she could still feel his warmth. Feel the beat of his pulse as his left hand intertwined her right, his other hand resting comfortably against her lower back. They danced with their heads just inches apart, and the anticipation that at any moment their cheeks might touch stirred something in her that she hadn't felt in a long time.

"I'd like to see you, Katie," Clay said. "Outside the pub, that is. Do you enjoy the opera? There's an afternoon performance of *Carmen* a week from tomorrow in Pendleton. The proceeds will go to the Capplin Center."

She leaned back slightly, looking at him with surprise. Katie was familiar with the organization. It provided opportunities for children with disabilities to attend summer camps designed to handle their special needs. It was one of the charities that Christina and her husband supported.

"How do you know about the Capplin Center?" Katie asked.

"You'll discover that I know a lot of things," he said slyly. "And I may be persuaded to share some of that knowledge if you allow me to escort you to the theater."

Katie laughed and moved back into him, resting her cheek against his, before realizing she'd made contact. Her body tensed and she made a move to correct the impulsive act, but stopped when Clay tightened his hold. "Don't move away, Katie. I won't bite."

"Well, that's good information to have," she said, relaxing against him as they finished the dance in silence. When the music stopped, he led her off the dance floor with his hand still pressing lightly against her lower back. It felt good there.

As she reclaimed the corner stool, Clay asked, "Can I get you another glass of wine?"

"No thanks, I'm good. In fact, I was planning on leaving soon." She thought she saw disappointment in his eyes, but if it was, it quickly disappeared.

"Boss, is it all right if I take off now? I'm sorry to leave you with such a big crowd, but I told my mom I'd be home—"

"It's not a problem, Joel," Clay interrupted, giving the young bartender a manly shoulder squeeze. "You get home. And you take as much time as you need tomorrow. Your family comes first."

"Thanks. I owe you."

Joel took his black apron off and threw it in a basket near the end of the bar that was reserved for dirty laundry. He lifted his knapsack off the floor and hurried toward the door.

"His younger brother is shipping out tomorrow. It's his first tour," Clay said to Katie even though he was still looking at the front entrance. "It's a tight-knit family, and Conrad is the first one to join the armed services. Marines." Snagging a clean apron, he turned to Katie. "As I'm now short a bartender, I'll be working back here until closing. Before I get too busy, though, will you put me out of my misery and say yes to my invitation for next weekend?"

Katie smiled. "I enjoy the opera, and happen to be a supporter of the Capplin Center. So yes, I'd love to go."

"Great. If I can get your number I'll call mid-week and we can work out the details." Again, he graced her with that beguiling smile.

She reached into her handbag and pulled out a business card. "This is my cell phone number, but I'll give you the cottage phone number also." She scribbled the number on the back of the card and handed it to him.

"I'll call you," he said.

She watched him slide easily back into the role of bartender and was impressed with the way he talked up the customers in addition to the speed with which he made their drinks. He was skilled at what he did, and she could tell that he truly enjoyed being at the helm of Clancy's.

Katie sat for another five minutes listening to the music and watching the crowd. Finally deciding it was time to bail, she caught

Clay's eye and gave him a wave. Slipping off the bar stool, she started toward the exit sign. Glancing toward the band, she saw Nathan's gaze following her, and she waved to him as well.

"Calling it a night?" Tess raised her voice to be heard over the music as she and Katie crossed paths.

"I am. But it was fun while it lasted."

Katie made her way through a group of enthusiastic men who were coming into the bar, barely registering their invitation to join their party. Once in the car, she started the engine and backed out of the parking space. Pulling out of the lot, she hit the play button on the car's CD player and listened to the soulful music of Joni Mitchell.

He watched as Katie left the pub. He hadn't realized how intoxicating it would be to see her up close and personal. At one point, when he'd worked his way to the bar for a drink, he'd been so close to her that he had smelled her perfume, a subtle scent that was meant to give a man a reason to linger. But not him. He wasn't interested in her sexually. Not the way other men might be. No, all he wanted was to force her to admit that her father had dismantled his own family, based purely on lies and conjectures. How the unsympathetic swing of his gavel had destroyed their lives. He wanted to make her question the normalcy of her life until every move she made was ringed with uncertainty.

He felt a surge of adrenaline come over him, knowing that when he swooped in for the final kill, his father would finally be vindicated. And Katie Nolan could burn in hell alongside the judge. Oh, what a glorious day that would be.

CHAPTER
ELEVEN

Late Sunday afternoon, after five straight hours of painting, Katie decided to trade in her brushes for a camera. She recognized that there was only an hour or two left of daylight, but the pull to photograph the splendor of an Oregon sunset was too strong to pass up. After making a quick stop to pick up her gear, she trekked through the wooded area directly behind the cottage to find the perfect spot to set up.

Leaning back against a rock that sat alongside her tripod, she waited patiently for precisely the right moment to capture the sun as it set behind a grouping of pine trees. She already had the camera focused between two of the larger trees, anticipating that when the sun dropped far enough, it would spread its fading light through the inner branches of both, creating what she was sure would be a series of spectacular photographs.

She had also brought along her smaller Nikon, intending to digitally snare some of the more ornate portions of the area. She'd already taken several shots of wild mushrooms, a grouping of what she thought was thimbleberry, and now focused in on a hollowed-out log, its chewed bark clothed in brittle leaves that still held their natural color. A minute ago, she'd seen a butterfly resting open-winged on a sliver of that bark, and she was hopeful that it would return.

As she waited, she thought that this would be a great place to capture some winter photographs. A nice frigid morning with mist rising from the floor of the woods. Snow clinging to the branches and blanketing the trunks of the tall, stately trees. There would be more natural light to work with, creating subtle shadows and highlights that would give the photograph a three-dimensional look. She would use black and white film rather than her digital camera, and that way she'd have some flexibility during the developing stage.

She turned away from the trunk to take a quick glance over her shoulder and saw it. The trees—outlined by the sun exploding behind them. She moved fast, checking the focus, the positioning of the lens, the ISO setting, and then clicked off several shots. She re-positioned the tripod once and clicked off several more. Pleased with what she'd been able to capture, she sat back on her heels and quietly watched as another day continued its slide into the history books.

It wasn't until several minutes later when she realized that with the day's light dimming, she'd soon be trapped in the dark of night in woods that weren't familiar to her. She hustled to pack up her equipment, then checked the compass she carried on a thin leather strap around her neck. She knew the cottage was southwest of her current position, so grabbing the camera case, tripod, and backpack, she took off in that direction.

She hadn't gone far before she was forced to stop and pull out her flashlight. It wasn't completely dark yet, but the light was now fading so fast she was afraid that soon she'd be forced to rely on pure survival skills.

She couldn't have strayed too far off a straight line back to the cottage. Weaving through the trees, stepping over aged logs and ducking to avoid a low hanging branch, she continued her jaunt back. It wasn't until she heard a twig snap off to her left that she stopped and focused in on the sounds around her. There was an occasional bird calling out to its mate and a cacophony of insect chatter, but nothing that could be ruled unduly sinister. Moving a bit faster, she continued to check the compass every ten steps or so. Had she actually gone this far into the woods, she wondered? Or was she wrong about what direction she should be heading?

Snap.

That was definitely the sound a twig makes when stepped on by a human's foot, Katie thought. And it was closer. She didn't stop this time, instead picking up her pace as she fumbled with her load of equipment. Several awkward and off-balanced steps later, she found herself on the ground, two of the fingers on her right hand pinched between the legs of the tripod. Quickly freeing the fingers, she released an involuntary grunt as she hurriedly pushed herself back into a standing position. Ignoring the pain, she seized the offending tripod, adjusted the backpack and camera case on her shoulder, and began moving again.

Stepping around a pile of brushwood, she was momentarily frozen in place by a sudden splash of light about fifty yards straight ahead of her. Someone with a flashlight, who was making their way toward her through the darkened woods.

Her heart was racing. Two unknowns now, both within striking distance, and she had no idea where she was anymore. Panic was setting in as she ran through her options. Should she dart behind a tree and hide? Keep going? Change directions?

"Katie? Is that you? It's me, Ian."

"Yes, Ian. It's me," Katie said with a voice dripping with relief.

"What are you doing out here alone?" he asked when he reached her. "And so far off course from the cottage?"

"Guess I got lost," she said looking back down at her compass. Sure enough, she was currently heading almost due north which meant she was traveling further away from the cottage than toward it. "I must have gotten turned around when I fell."

Ian relieved her of the camera case and tripod as he said, "Are you hurt?"

"No, no. A few scrapes probably, but nothing to be concerned about."

"I take it you were out getting some photographs?"

"The sunset, which limits the window of opportunity. I guess I got caught up watching it and started back later than I should have."

"Well, I'll get you back to the cottage."

When he turned away, Katie put her hand on his arm and said, "Are you out here alone?"

"What do you mean?"

"I thought I heard someone else back there," she said, pointing to her left. "But maybe I was already confused by then and it was really you I heard."

Katie's attention was focused away from Ian so she missed the tightening of his jaw and the conflicted look that flickered in his eyes. He was pretty certain that if she truly had heard someone out here, it hadn't been him. But he'd keep that to himself for the time being.

"It probably was me you heard," he said in a calm, reassuring voice. "To be on the safe side though, I'll come back and check everything out once I get you back to the cottage."

With Ian setting a comfortable pace, Katie followed easily. Several minutes into their walk she said, "I'm curious. Why are you out here?"

He glanced over and said, "It's my job to secure the estate. Although we have motion detectors around the perimeter, I still make a visual check every night. I happened to be at this end of the property when I saw your flashlight."

That was partially true, he thought. He always did a routine check of the estate, usually around this same time. But last week when he had suspected that an intruder had somehow bypassed the outlying detectors, he had stepped up those inspections. And now, based on Katie's report, it had happened a second time. He hadn't been able to track the cause of the first disruption, so he'd assumed it had been a computer glitch. But now, he made a mental note to talk to Arthur and recommend getting an expert to come in and find the deficiency in their current system. Better yet, to install a complete security upgrade.

When they reached the cottage, Katie unlocked the front door and reached for the bag and tripod, but Ian squeezed right past her into the living room. "I'll put these in your studio room," he said, not giving her time to object. And while he was back there, he'd do a quick room-by-room search.

Katie was at the sink when Ian stepped into the kitchen. She turned when she heard him clear his throat and said, "Everything clear?"

He saw the humor on her face and cracked a half smile. "Clear."

"Thank you. Would you like to join me for a cup of coffee?"

"I need to finish my rounds, but thanks. Maybe another time."

"Another time, then."

"Lock up, and if you have any problems, call me." He handed her a card with a phone number on it. "That's my cell. Program it into yours."

"I will," she replied. "Thank you again, Ian."

"No problem. Goodnight, Katie."

Once the locks were engaged, Katie activated the alarm. Deciding she no longer wanted the coffee, she went back into the kitchen to turn off the maker, then changed into a loose-fitting pair of sweatpants and a well-worn University of California T-shirt. For the next two hours, she worked in the dark room developing the film from her afternoon shoot. Pleased that she had gotten several high quality photos, she spent another thirty minutes organizing her work before calling it quits for the night.

Moving into the bedroom, she set her clock for an early morning wake-up, then stretched out on the mattress only to find that she was still struggling to fight off a nagging feeling of uncertainty that had dogged her since returning to the cottage. Flinging back the covers, she shuffled back into the living room to double-check the front door. Satisfied that it was locked, she returned to the bedroom, turned out the lights, and moved to the window facing the back of the cottage. For several minutes she stood there, staring into the darkness.

Nothing there, she reassured herself before finally letting the curtain drop back into place. Crawling back into bed, she spent several more minutes trying to shake off the memory of her encounter in the woods. When that didn't work, she pulled the blankets high over her head, much like she'd done as a child who believed there were monsters hiding in the closet, and willed sleep to take her under.

"After I made sure Katie was secure, I did a cursory check around the cottage," Ian was saying into his cell phone. "I didn't find any indications that someone had made their way onto the property, but I'll go back out when it gets light to do a more thorough search."

Arthur listened intently as Ian relayed the details of Katie's encounter in the woods. He routinely phoned his chief of security when he was away on business, and tonight's call had primarily been made to deliver the news that he'd be extending his trip for another two days.

"It could be as elementary as a bunch of kids who ignored the No Trespassing signs and thought they could test the boundaries," Arthur said when Ian had finished.

"My thoughts exactly," Ian agreed. "It wouldn't hurt to have another one of my guys patrolling the grounds. Now that we have a full house on the estate, it would be a logical move."

"Go ahead with that," Arthur said instinctively. "With the cottage being so isolated and Katie sometimes not leaving the main house until well after midnight, well, it makes sense to take some precautionary steps."

After a brief hesitation, Arthur sighed heavily. "You're the only person other than Marian who knows that Katie is my daughter, Ian. I've never had the pleasure of raising any children, and it's hard at this late stage to figure out when to be concerned and when to back off."

"Considering the circumstances, you're doing fine, Arthur." Ian's voice was unruffled yet compassionate. "Katie is lucky to have you in her life. Even if she doesn't know the whole truth."

"I want to change that, but I gave Marian my word."

"Understood."

"I'd be devastated if anything happened to Katie. To anyone on the estate, for that matter."

"I'll offer Glenn some additional hours. His wife is six months along now and I think they would appreciate the extra money before the baby comes. I'll also increase how often we check the property near the cottage."

"I'm being paranoid, aren't I?" Arthur asked with a chuckle.

"You're being fatherly."

The humor in Ian's voice had Arthur grinning. "I should be back in a couple of days. Keep me informed as needed."

"Will do, boss."

Arthur decided on a shower before ordering a wake-up call and breakfast off the room service menu. Climbing into the hotel bed, he leaned against the headboard and mentally went over his conversation with Ian.

It wasn't the first time someone had strayed onto his land, even though he had signs posted. But he couldn't recall anyone having done so completely undetected. In fact, one of the main features of his security system was to expose an intruder crossing onto his property by signaling both the main house and Ian's quarters—one of two bungalows that sat on the northeast corner of the estate. Of course, there were one or two blind spots in the most remote areas that bordered the state-owned land, but it was disconcerting that someone knew where those spots were and had gained access without any of the secondary sensors going off.

He needed to wrap up his business tomorrow and get back to Oregon. He had absolutely no doubt that Ian would keep everyone safe, but he wanted to see for himself where the breach had occurred and have input with any updates.

Closing his eyes, he let his mind drift from the security issues to his recent visit to Marian's condo. It had stirred emotions in him that he'd thought had been dead and buried. No, that wasn't altogether true. He may have buried those feelings, but they had never died. They were a constant reminder of the love he and Marian had once shared.

He remembered one particular fall weekend they'd spent in Washington all those many years ago. It had been rare that they could both get away for that extended amount of time, and it had been magnificent. Their days had been taken up with visiting museums, art galleries, and elegant restaurants. Their nights, wrapped up in intimacy. Regrettably, it had also turned out to be their last time together.

The following week Marian had ended their three-month affair and walked away.

He had been crushed. His heart broken. Then, two months later, she'd called and asked to meet with him, and he had seen his chance to convince her that they were meant to be together. He had already asked his wife for a divorce and she had willingly agreed—for a hefty settlement, of course. And if Marian and Robert agreed to part ways, she would be free to spend the rest of her life with him.

It hadn't worked out the way he had envisioned. Her reason for wanting to see him had been to tell him she was pregnant, and that the child was his. But his excitement over the prospect of being a father had quickly turned to disappointment when she'd pleaded with him to allow her and Robert to raise the child as theirs. At first

Arthur had tried to reason with Marian, but his failure to convince her to leave her husband and marry him, quickly turned into harsh words and hurt feelings. In the end, acknowledging that a fight for custody would do more harm than good, he had agreed to walk away.

As Katie grew, Arthur had made sure to follow her milestones. Made sure he knew about all her birthday parties, her graduations, the boys she'd dated. He had kept a watch on her career, too. What he hadn't been able to do was completely heal from the heartbreak of Marian choosing Robert over him, and the pain that had come from agreeing to let the man raise Arthur's daughter as his own. It had been the right decision at the time though, for everyone else. Or so he'd convinced himself.

But Katie was with him now, and he wasn't going to blow this second chance to create precious memories with his daughter. And if he was being completely honest, rebuild the love he and Marian had once shared.

He reached out and flipped the light switch, pitching the hotel room into darkness. He conjured up a picture of himself spending time with both Marian and Katie. The thought that they could be a happy, well-adjusted family brought a smile to his face.

He'd always been one to believe that dreaming big was the only way to go.

The day following his return to the estate, Arthur heard Katie coming down the stairs. He slipped out of his office and met her in the front hallway.

"Arthur, you're home," she said pausing at the foot of the stairs. "How was your trip?"

"Productive," he said with a smile. "I'm toying with opening another restaurant outside of Sacramento."

"That's a great area, I'm sure it would do well."

"Yes, that's what my accountant thinks, too. I heard that you had a bit of your own excitement this past weekend. In the woods?" he added when she gave him a puzzled look.

"Oh, that. I got a little distracted," she laughed. "Maybe stayed out longer than I should have. I'm embarrassed to say that Ian had to come to my rescue."

"Don't be embarrassed. It's easy to get turned around out there, even for someone who's been around these woods as long as I have. You could always ask Ian or any of the security team to go with you if you think you'll be out past dark. They're all very familiar with the grounds."

"I'll keep that in mind, thanks. But I think when you see this," she said as she shuffled through the large canvas tote bag she used to carry her art supplies back and forth from the cottage, "you'll agree that it was worth a few moments of panic out there." She handed Arthur a framed photograph showing the sun's extended rays encircling the tree tops, as if it were offering a no-strings-attached hug. "I thought maybe you'd like that for your office."

Arthur was speechless. The photo was a flawless replica of the countless sunsets he'd witnessed throughout the years he'd lived here. Moments that he'd never been able to capture on film even though he'd tried.

"It's perfect, Katie," Arthur said with a touch of reverence. "I can't tell you how beautiful this is." He looked up from the photograph and smiled warmly at his daughter. "It's perfect," he repeated. "Thank you."

"Well, I should get back to the cottage," she said picking up her art bag. "Mom is expecting a call from me. Enjoy your evening, Arthur."

Arthur watched her leave, his heart bursting with pride. He walked back to his office to hang the photograph, hoping that one day soon she would appreciate that it was a father's pride he was feeling.

CHAPTER
TWELVE

Katie and Clay left the Pendleton Community Theater, enthusiastically discussing the captivating performance of *Carmen*. The troupe had received three curtain calls, all with standing ovations, and afterward a pre-selected group of patrons were escorted backstage for a meet-and-greet with the performers. Of course, if anyone wanted to make a donation, they were encouraged to do that as well. Clay had graciously responded to the invitation for financial support and Katie was right behind him, check in hand. It had actually been an easy sell once several of the kids who were served by the Capplin Center's programs made an appearance.

"I'm familiar with a place where we can get the best ice cream sundae in the city," Clay said when they reached the bottom of the outside steps. "It's right around the corner. What do you say to a hot fudge delight?"

"A perfect way to top off an already great afternoon. I'm in."

Clay set a leisurely pace as they wove their way through the lingering crowd. "Did you enjoy the performance?"

"Very much. I wish I had that kind of talent. I sang in high school and at a few weddings over the years. But to be able to hit those high notes? Wow." Smiling, Katie asked, "How about you? Any hidden talents?"

"I play bass guitar. Not as often as I'd like to, but I occasionally find the time to plunk away at it."

"Gee, with a little practice we could combine our musical abilities and audition for one of those televised talent shows," she quipped.

"If it's all the same to you, I'll pass. I'm not sure I could handle all the fame and fortune if we won."

As they rounded the bank building on the corner, Katie immediately spotted the ice cream truck parked across the street. She glanced up at Clay and said, "You go all out when you're trying to impress a girl, don't you?"

"I know the best when I taste it. And it's not just me. Read the side of the truck."

Sure enough, in bold red letters the sign read: *Pappy's Ice Cream—The Best of the Best.*

Katie rolled her eyes. "I'll be the judge on whether that's true or false advertising. I happen to be a connoisseur of hot fudge sundaes."

Placing his hand lightly on her back, Clay guided her toward the truck. He ordered two sundaes with the works and then led her to one of several park benches that lined the street.

Katie took several spoonfuls before sharing her assessment. "This is the best hot fudge sundae I've had in a long time."

"Told you so."

"Yes, you did. And you were correct."

She glanced over and saw the little boy inside the man as he licked his spoon, then went in for another scoop of vanilla. It filled her with an overwhelming desire to get to know them both.

"How long have you lived in Abbott?" she asked, digging in for more hot fudge.

"I moved here when I bought the pub. I spent time remodeling the interior and opened for business three months later. That was four years ago."

"Where are you from originally?"

"Kentucky."

Katie poked him when he didn't say more. "Come on, there's more of a story there. Spill it."

Giving his response some thought, he said, "I grew up in Georgetown, did four years in the Navy, came back and went to college, then law school. After passing the bar, I went to work at a large law firm in Louisville. Got married, got divorced, and moved here. Not all that exciting."

"How long were you married?"

"Too long." Clay replied.

Deciding it was best to drop the topic of marriage, Katie said, "So you opened a pub instead of going into private practice. Why?"

"I discovered that I wasn't enjoying the law profession as much as I thought I should. What I really wanted to do was work for myself. Succeed or fail on my own terms, I guess."

"Why Abbott?"

He paused for a minute, swirling his spoon in the river of syrup that congealed in the bottom of the plastic cup. "Once the divorce was finalized, it was difficult running into my ex-wife whenever I needed paperwork processed. She was part of the secretarial pool, and she was very good at her job, so I knew she wasn't going to go anywhere. In fact, most of the attorneys fought for her time." In more ways than one, he thought sadly.

"It was pure luck that I heard about the pub being up for sale. And at the time I didn't even stop to question why Abbott was so appealing. Yet now? There hasn't been a day gone by when I haven't been thankful that I threw caution to the wind. My mother couldn't believe I was being so impetuous. On the other hand, my grandmother told me it was about time I did something honest for a living. Each Thanksgiving she comes out here for a visit and manages to close the bar every night."

"Rock on, grandma! Has your mother ever come out?"

"No, she passed away about six months after I left Kentucky."

He tossed his now empty container in the trash and said, "What about you? Give me the four-minute synopsis of Katie Nolan's life."

Katie began by telling him about her mother and then moved on to her father, brothers and finally Evan. She finished by sharing the story of how she'd met Arthur and ended up in Abbott.

"Without a doubt, I'm enjoying this job, more than I ever thought I would. And the bonus is that I have the time and space to work on my own paintings. I was telling a good friend of mine the other day how I want to eventually open my own gallery."

"Being your own boss has its ups and downs," Clay stated, "but there isn't a job in the world that beats it."

"I hope to find that out one day." Katie stood and disposed of her own empty container. "Ready to go?"

Forty-five minutes later, Clay was driving down Reddington Drive toward the estate. Katie handed him her key card when they arrived, then recited the new passcode she'd been given that morning. Ian insisted that all codes be changed on a random schedule.

"If you're not in a hurry, why don't you come in for a glass of wine," she said when they reached the cottage.

"I'd like that, thanks."

As Katie moved into the kitchen, she asked, "Red or white?"

"Whatever you're having is fine."

Clay listened to Katie's movements in the other room as he stood admiring the two framed photographs hanging on the wall near the front door. The first was a shot of a lighthouse at dusk, the ocean slapping against the rocks at its base, and nothing but dramatic color surrounding its tower. The second was of a sailboat, lounging tranquilly in open waters. This time, the sunrise served as a backdrop.

"I'm guessing these are yours," he said when Katie returned to the living room.

"Yes. I took them back in California."

"They're magnificent, Katie. Add another dimension and I swear I'd be able to hear those waves and smell the ocean air."

"Thank you," she said, touched by his sincere praise. She handed him one of the glasses she was carrying before settling into the couch.

Taking a seat beside her, Clay took his first, slow sip of the rich, garnet-red wine. "This is excellent," he said, giving the glass a swirl, then closing his eyes and slowly inhaling its aroma.

"A Reddington Label Merlot," she replied.

Raising the glass a second time, he savored the taste while nodding his approval. "Arthur's got a real knack for this."

"I'll be sure to pass that on to him," Katie said teasingly.

Clay leaned over to set the glass on the coffee table and said, "I enjoyed spending the day with you. I thought we could maybe try for a second date next week. I'm free most days, but could manage a weeknight. I'm guessing you work days?"

"I try to put in some time every day but it'll vary. Back home there were days that I worked deep into the night if I was in a zone. That's harder to do here of course because I paint up at the house. But Arthur doesn't mind that I keep unusual hours. Do you have anything specific in mind for our date?"

"There's an exhibit and lecture on the life and times of Frank Lloyd Wright this Thursday at the community college. Start time is at one. If it doesn't run too late, we can stop for dinner and I'll have you back here by six, seven at the latest."

"I can make that work," Katie said.

After spending another twenty minutes of casual conversation, Clay realized how comfortable he felt beside Katie. Reaching out to run his fingers against her hair, he said, "We've still got a little bit of daylight left. Are you up for a short walk?"

"That sounds nice. I'll need to change my shoes, though." Kicking off her heels, she disappeared down the hall.

Clay smiled as he carried the empty glasses into the kitchen. Yep, he genuinely liked Katie Nolan. She was charming, intelligent, and possessed a quick and clever sense of humor. It also seemed that they had similar interests, which never hurt. Best of all, Katie's attraction to him seemed to be equal to his attraction to her.

When she reappeared, he followed her toward the small entryway in the front of the cottage. As she opened the door, he immediately saw her body tense and instinctively stepped in front of her, coming face to face with Hannah Reddington.

"Well, if it isn't the handsome man-about-town, Clay Crawford," Hannah said in an exaggerated voice. "What are you doing in our neck of the woods?"

"What are you doing loitering on Katie's porch?" Clay asked with a trace of annoyance.

"I heard Nora say that someone came through the front gates using Katie's security card, and I volunteered to check it out. Make sure our resident artist wasn't in need of rescue."

Katie was sure that there hadn't been any such conversation because she had told Nora that morning that she would be out with Clay. But she let it pass, instead saying, "Aren't you the considerate one." She pushed out onto the porch forcing Hannah to take several steps back to avoid getting stepped on. "But as you can see, I'm alive and well."

Katie turned back to the door and locked it, reaching for Clay's hand as they stepped off the porch stoop. "Have a good evening, Hannah."

Hand in hand, Katie and Clay made their way to the edge of the dirt road that split in two directions—turn left and you'd be on the path leading to the house; turn right and the trail would take you in a wide circle around the cottage.

Katie heard the engine of Hannah's sports car come to life, then watched as the young girl roared past them on her way back to the house. All Clay could do was try to shield Katie from the flying dirt and pebbles.

"I sense that there's a slight problem," he said when the car's taillights were finally out of sight.

"Not really a problem. It's more like she's still testing me. I think it annoys her when I don't take the bait," Katie added as she pointed to the narrow trail that ran parallel to the woods behind the cottage. "Let's go this way."

They were both silent for some time until Clay spoke. "Does she always treat you so badly?" he asked, not yet willing to let go of the incident with Hannah. "You could say something to Arthur, and I'm sure he'd take care of it."

"And I'm sure that's what she wants me to do. It's nothing I can't handle. I've been on photo shoots where the clients have actually thrown temper tantrums. Once I had two family members throwing punches at each other. They were sisters." When Clay gave her an unbelieving look, she nodded. "I've learned how to deal with all sorts of personalities."

"You're right," Clay responded. "I get an assortment of personalities in the pub, too. You need to find a way to deal with each one individually. It's just annoying to see you treated with such disrespect."

"I'm tough," she said as she gave him an elbow jab to the ribs. "In fact, dealing with the poor little rich kid syndrome is my specialty. I once did a photo shoot with a fourteen-year-old daytime actor who was trying to build his portfolio. He was rude, crude, and way too interested in my female body parts. As soon as I caught on to him, I made sure we were never alone. Ever. The last thing I needed was for some pubescent boy to turn it all around and complain that I'd been attempting to entice him sexually. I was still trying to build my reputation as a photographer, and it could have all been ruined by the lies of a spoiled, bored brat."

"But his female co-stars must have seen what he was like. You wouldn't have been the first smokin' hot babe he'd harassed."

She laughed at Clay's choice of words for her and said, "No, I wasn't the first, and I'm sure not the last. The attitude on set was to let someone else call him out on his behavior. And as far as I could tell, the producers, as well as his agent, were of the same mind—boys will be boys. No one was willing to lose their job over this kid."

"Is he still acting?"

"Not in that soap. His character was shipped off to a boarding school in Switzerland. That was about two years ago, and I haven't seen him acting in anything else. But I don't watch much television and rarely get to the movies."

"Maybe we could go together sometime. Catch one of those girly flicks."

"Girly flicks? You mean like *Thelma and Louise*?"

Now Clay laughed. "I see that we have differing definitions of the word girly."

They made it back to the cottage as the daylight started to fade. "I should get back to the pub," Clay said as he pulled his car keys from his jacket. "At the risk of sounding like a broken record, I had a nice time today."

She stood facing him, her back against the driver's side door. "I did, too. Thank you."

He leaned in and touched his lips softly against hers, quickly recognizing that it wouldn't be enough. Stepping in closer, he deepened the kiss as his hands gripped her hips and her arms slid around his neck. Her body was tight against his now, and he totally understood why some fourteen-year-old boy would be interested in her female form. From what he could tell, it was rather awesome.

Pulling back slightly, Clay smiled down at her. "I'm not sure if I can wait until Thursday to see you again. Can you meet me for coffee tomorrow morning?"

"I could do that," Katie said, returning his smile with one of her own. "Say, nine-thirty at Millie's?"

He leaned down for another kiss and was pleased to hear her sigh. This time she pulled back first and when she stepped away from the car, he reluctantly swung the door open and got in. "I'll see you tomorrow then," he said as he brought the engine to life. He made a point to pull away slowly and when he checked the rear-view mirror, she was still wearing the smile, which he had to admit was one giant turn-on.

CHAPTER
THIRTEEN

It had been two weeks since Katie and Clay attended the opera. Clay had gotten his third date, as well as a fourth and fifth—not that he was counting or anything. Today he'd talked her into spending the afternoon browsing through an assortment of trinkets and treasures at a flea market in Umatilla.

Back at Clancy's, Katie transferred her purchases into her car and walked into the pub with Clay. "How about a glass of iced tea," he said as he moved behind the bar and Katie took a seat on one of the stools. "I'd forgotten how exhausting a day of bargain hunting could get."

"Well, let's see," Katie said as she gladly took the tall chilled glass and enjoyed a healthy sip. "Could it be the fact that dragging me through the market once wasn't enough? That you couldn't leave without taking a second look at all the tables?"

"And aren't you glad we did," he said as he guzzled his own tea. "You never would have spotted that porcelain owl cookie jar that will look spectacular on your mother's counter."

"Agreed, but don't forget the tea set with the tiny blue flowers that you're planning to give your grandmother for her birthday."

"I haven't forgotten, and might I point out that the cookie jar—we'll call that Exhibit A—and the tea set—we'll call that Exhibit B—both support my claim that going through a second time was a good idea."

"I guess I'll have to give you this one. It was a good idea, even though my feet might have a differing opinion."

"Hi, guys," Tess said as she swung through the kitchen door. "Have a good day?"

"Long and expensive, but yes, a good day," Katie answered.

"Any problems I need to deal with?" Clay asked.

"Nothing. It's been a slow afternoon, nothing out of the ordinary. Ben's in the back, and Joel should be here shortly."

"Sounds like you have everything under control. Come on, Katie. I want to drag my newly acquired possessions upstairs, and you can help me wrap Gram's gift."

Hand in hand, they walked to the back staircase, stopping to retrieve the packages that Clay had left near the back door.

Once inside the upstairs apartment, he set the packages on the kitchen table and said, "Can you stay for an early dinner?"

"Aren't you needed in the bar?"

"Not for another couple of hours."

"Then yes, I'd love to join you for dinner," Katie said.

"If you'd like, you can take a shower. I know it was hot out there today, and we did a lot of walking." He glanced over at her and the surprised look on her face had him smiling. "I'll be on my way to the food mart while you're cleaning up."

"Right," she smiled back. "A shower sounds pretty good. Thanks."

"Through there," he said, pointing to a closed door to the right of the living room. "I'll be back in a bit." He rounded the kitchen table to stand in front of her, then leaned in for a kiss, tasting the lemon tea when he ran his tongue across her lips. He lingered, enjoying the familiarity. "Umm, that was nice," he said as he reluctantly pulled away. "And I should leave now while I still have all my brain function. You have a way of clouding my better judgment, Katie Nolan." He snatched up his keys and left the apartment.

Katie sighed as she touched her fingers to her lips, feeling the sweet sensation she always felt when he was near her. Touching her. Kissing her.

She turned toward the bedroom and stripped out of her clothes. Noticing the mud encrusted on the bottom of her jeans and the smudges of dirt along the left sleeve of her shirt, she settled on tossing everything into the small washing machine off the kitchen area before taking her shower. Drifting to Clay's closet, she pulled down a long-sleeved denim shirt that would work until her clothes were dry. Laying it across the bed, she made her way to the bathroom.

The warm water felt amazing as it soothed her tired, aching muscles. A corner of her mouth lifted as she remembered how much she had enjoyed the day. First, they had shared an early morning breakfast at a small roadside café about thirty miles into their trip to Umatilla. Then they'd made their way through the marketplace, and on the way back home stopped for coffee and pie at a retro mom and pop restaurant in downtown Hermiston. And now, he was making dinner for her. She grinned when the thought hit her that a good part of their getting-to-know-each-other time had been spent over food.

She used the body wash he kept on a shelf over the shower and rubbed it over her skin, taking care to keep her hair from getting too wet. She hadn't noticed a dryer among his grooming tools and without that, her hair would frizz up and look like a train wreck by the time it completely air-dried. Tossing her head back, she let the spray run down first her front and then her back side.

When she finally stepped out of the shower stall, she felt totally relaxed and . . . happy, she decided. It was somehow strange, this emotion that felt like a second skin, blanketing her so completely. And until now, she hadn't considered that the feeling had eluded her for such a long time. It was nice to have it back.

Wrapping a towel around her body, Katie stepped into the bedroom and stopped dead in her tracks. Standing near the door that led to the hallway was Clay, staring at the bed, a glass of white wine in his hand. He shifted his gaze to her, and in his eyes she could see desire, laced with an undertone of possibility.

Clay found his voice first. "I was going to leave this on the dresser," he said lifting the glass. "I thought you'd be a while yet." His eyes dropped momentarily to her body, and then quickly returned to her face.

"I was hoping you wouldn't mind if I borrowed one of your shirts," Katie said smoothly. "My clothes were coated with mud, so I tossed them into the washer."

Once again, he let his eyes drop below her chin and allowed the devil to weaken his defenses. "Wow, you seriously look hot right now."

Katie said nothing as she took a step forward to stand close enough to stir Clay's imagination, but not enough for him to make a grab for the towel. It was a calculated move and one that had her feeling a bit mischievous, not to mention empowered.

"Is this where I'm supposed to be the gentleman and gracefully back out of the room leaving your honor unscathed?" he asked, setting the wine glass on the bureau.

Katie smiled as she took another step toward him. "What's for dinner?" she asked in a smooth, relaxing voice. "Something that can wait, I hope." She took the final step that placed her within arm's length and let the towel drop to the floor. "Any objections?" she teased, tossing her arms around his neck while pressing her body tight against his.

He lowered his head and kissed her roughly, sliding his hand around to her breast where he skillfully used his fingertips to bring it to life. Katie didn't resist, using her own hands to unbuckle his leather belt.

Lifting her off her feet, Clay carried her to the bed and tossed her on the center of the mattress. He could clearly see the passion reflected on her face, and her smile sent a jolt sparking through his body. He couldn't recall ever having this deep, mind-blowing need for a woman. Not even with his ex-wife, who he'd thought had been the love of his life. Until, that is, she'd jumped into bed—their bed—with his best friend. That betrayal had set him on a course that had kept his heart sealed up tight.

As a result, he had settled into single life again, satisfying his physical needs with the occasional one-night stand. Nothing serious and decidedly nothing intimate. Not once had he invited a woman into his life, his home. He'd kept everyone of the opposite sex at arm's length, convinced that it was the best way to heal his wounds and save himself from that gut wrenching hurt that had nearly destroyed him.

And then Katie walked into his pub. Into his life. Surely into his heart. This woman, who didn't demand anything from him, didn't want to own him or change him. Didn't expect him to be anyone other than who he was.

He quickly dispensed with his clothes, still unable to believe how he'd been given this second chance to enjoy life rather than to merely exist in it. After grabbing a condom from the dresser drawer, he turned toward the bed and found Katie watching him. The sight of her smooth, silky skin catching the fading sunlight angling through the window blinds was intoxicating. It was as if she was begging him to take her—no uncertainties, no regrets.

He climbed onto the bed, straddling her trim, athletic body. With one hand supporting his weight, the other cupping her breast, he bent down and ran slow, evocative kisses down the side of her face, landing once again on her lips. Those soft, feminine lips that were both feisty and ever so inviting were now giving as much as they were taking. Their tongues touched, tasted, and hers sent a jolt of electricity straight down to his toes. He ignored his need to abandon the foreplay and get right down to business. This was a woman who deserved some care and attention. Not a quickie from a man who showed no self-control.

He groaned as Katie leisurely skimmed her fingers down his back, across his hip, and finally around his thigh until she found and took hold of her target. Sucking in a mouthful of air he said, "Not so fast, sweetheart." His voice was deep and strained, and he barely recognized it as his own. "We've got plenty of time."

Her laughter covered him like a cool spring breeze, and the twinkle in her eye only confirmed that she knew exactly what those clever hands were doing to him.

When he finally slid inside her, she pressed her body tightly to his, causing his good intentions to maintain some semblance of control to fly right out the window. He surrendered to the urgent need to give her what she craved while taking what he hungered for. It was fast and it was furious, and when she cried out his name, he followed her over the edge with profound satisfaction.

After both were sated, they remained motionless for several long moments, tethered by the sheer tranquility of mating. Eventually, Clay shifted his weight only enough to give her some breathing room, not quite ready to relinquish this feeling of pure contentment. He released an easygoing sigh, convinced that where he was right now was exactly where he was meant to be.

Until somewhere in the silence of the apartment, a phone rang.

"Crap. That's mine," Clay gasped against her hair. "Just ignore it."

Katie chuckled. "I had no intention of answering your phone."

"Good."

When the ringing stopped, he lifted his head so he could kiss her, contemplating when he'd have the strength to take her again.

Until somewhere in the silence of the apartment, his blasted phone started ringing again.

"Maybe you should get that?" Katie sighed.

"Maybe I deserve a life?"

"I'm not going anywhere."

Clay held her gaze and all seemed right with the world. Her lips curved slightly and her eyes sparkled in the sliver of light that was slowly fading outside the window. "Have I told you how beautiful you are?"

"Is that better than smokin' hot?"

"They complement each other, and on you, both look mighty fine."

He touched his lips to hers and indulged himself in a slow and passionate kiss. And again, somewhere in the silence of the apartment—

"Oh, for the love of . . . Don't move. Stay right there."

Clay jumped out of the bed and jogged into the living room. Katie heard him say, "This had better be good," and she smiled in agreement. A minute later he was back in the bedroom, disappointment clearly painted on his face.

"There's a problem downstairs and if I don't intercede . . ." He already had his pants on and was throwing a sweatshirt over his head.

"I understand, Clay. I'll wait for you up here if that's not a problem."

He stopped, giving her a sympathetic look. "I am so sorry, Katie. I'm such a jerk for getting you into bed and then taking off like this."

"First of all, I think I got you into bed, and it's not like you're disappearing into the night. This is your place. Now go." She swung her legs over the side of the bed and wrapped the sheet around her body. "When you get back we'll have a nice, quiet dinner."

"I was right the first time," he declared as he dashed for the door. "You're one smokin' hot woman."

Her laughter followed him as he took two steps at a time. He cleared the back hallway, running into Tess when he entered the bar area. "Patrick Lynch is drunk again, and he's getting wild. Ben has been trying to control him but it's getting worse. You've got to talk to him, Clay."

Shattering glass greeted Clay as he stepped into the main bar area. He took everything in at once: the shattered mirror, the baseball bat that Ben had pulled out from beneath the bar, the three male customers who had moved away from Patrick—thankfully—and were now gathered around the jukebox. And finally, the two women who were sitting in the corner booth near the window apparently enjoying the floor show.

Clay's eyes fixed on Patrick, a factory worker who was now reaching for an empty beer bottle, intent on doing more damage. With his shirt tail hanging outside his faded blue jeans and his hair standing up in all directions, he'd taken on the appearance of a madman. But what was most disturbing was the look of absolute despair that was painted across his face.

"Tell Ben to stand down," he told Tess, taking another two steps toward Patrick. "Hey, Patrick. Looks like we might have a problem here."

Patrick lowered the bottle and tried to focus in on Clay. "Hey, Clay, how's it going?"

"Good by me. How about you?"

"Hey, I'm on top of the world, my man. Top of the world."

"No problems then?"

"None at all. Everything's great. In fact, I was telling your bartender here that I needed another beer. Just slide another bottle my way, Ben, and everything will be okay." His words were slurred, and Clay could now see the streaks of tears on the man's face as he staggered back, tripped over one of the bar stools and fell hard, landing on his tailbone. Clay figured he didn't feel anything now, but tomorrow when he was sober, he'd be lucky if he could walk straight. Clay went over to Patrick and helped him back to his feet.

"Ben, why don't you bring us some coffee, and Tess, could you kindly rustle up a turkey sandwich? Come on, Patrick, let's take a couple of minutes to catch up."

Clay guided the young man to a quiet corner in the back and got him settled into a booth before taking a seat across from him. He remained silent until Ben had set the cups on the table and gone back to the bar. Patrick lifted his elbows onto the table and dropped his head into the palms of his hands. Clay gave him another five minutes to brood.

When Tess appeared, she set the sandwich down and squeezed Clay's shoulder. "I called Katie and told her what's happening. She said she'll come down and stick around to help where she can."

"Thanks Tess," he said gratefully before turning his attention back to his friend. "Try and eat something, Patrick. It'll absorb some of that liquor you have clogging your common sense."

Patrick Lynch lowered his hands and sat staring at the food. "Sheila's going to leave me. I know I'm going to be laid-off soon and when I am, she won't want to stay. If I can't work, how am I supposed to take care of her?" He looked at Clay, pleading in his eyes. "How?"

"You're not going to find the answer in a bottle of beer. Or at the poker table in the back room of Dooley's. Once you're sober though, I give you my promise that I'll help you figure it out."

"You'll talk to Sheila? Tell her not to leave me?"

"Try to eat something. And then you can use the back room to sleep it off. I'll call Sheila and tell her you'll be spending the night here. No, don't argue with me," Clay said, raising his hand to stop Patrick's objection. "You don't want to go home to her stinking of beer and stale cigarettes. Trust me."

"Yeah, sure Clay. You're right. I am tired, and I probably couldn't make it back home anyway." He rubbed his eyes and ran his fingers through his hair before taking a tentative bite of the sandwich.

An hour later, Patrick was snoring away in the storage room where Clay had an army cot set up in the corner. The women had left, along with two of the men, making C.J. the last remaining customer. As he watched a rerun of an aging legal sitcom that was playing quietly on the set above the liquor counter, Katie sat quietly at the other end of the bar, waiting for Clay.

"Can I get you anything stronger than that hot tea, Katie?" Tess asked as she moved behind the bar.

"This is good. I'll be taking off soon, but thanks."

"Clay is on the phone with Patrick's wife right now, but he shouldn't be much longer."

"Does Clay's friend do this a lot?" Katie asked as she took another sip of the Earl Grey.

"Never used to. He and Sheila have been going through a rough patch and even though Clay tries to stay out of it, he's such a nice guy that he gets dragged in anyway, bending over backward to help. Both Patrick and Sheila are terrific people, so I hope they can work things out."

Katie glanced over as Clay came back into the bar. When he reached her, he ran his hand across her hair. "Hi," he said in a voice dripping with fatigue.

"Hi back."

"Did you get something to eat? It's probably a little late to start the stir fry."

Katie checked her watch and was surprised to see that it was already eleven o'clock. "Tess mentioned that you nibbled on a sandwich while you were talking to your friend and insisted that I have a bowl of her cheese and broccoli cream soup. It was very good, by the way."

"Good to hear. It's not on the menu yet but with your recommendation, I think we'll add it."

"How is Patrick?"

"Sleeping it off. I told Sheila that when he surfaces I'd bring him home. I'm sorry about our evening together."

"I'd be a real schmuck if I was upset about you helping a friend." Katie laid her hand on his arm and added, "It looks like you'll be tied up for the rest of the night so I think I'll head home."

"I had other plans for tonight," Clay said in a low tone, his eyes scorching her with every word. "They included a sleep-over and Olympic-qualifying sex. Can I have a rain check?"

"Any time, any place," she replied.

"Have I told you that you're beautiful?"

"Yes, and I'm still not tired of hearing it. Walk me to my car?"

Clay slipped his arm around Katie's waist and told Ben he'd be back shortly. Out in the parking lot, he backed her against the side of the car and slowly stole her breath away. When he felt her lips part, he slid his tongue through the opening and ravaged her mouth. His hands were wrapped tightly around her waist, and her hands tucked securely in the back pockets of his jeans.

"If you don't stop kneading my ass, we're going to end up in the back seat of your car like a bunch of horny teenagers," he groaned.

Katie laughed. "Sorry. Didn't realize I was stirring your loins."

He pressed his lips to her forehead before slowly backing away from her. "Are you sure you don't want to stay tonight?"

"You've got enough on your plate, and this way you won't be distracted. Take care of your friend and give me a call tomorrow. We'll make plans for another night."

Clay opened the driver's side door, and Katie slid in behind the wheel. He stepped back and watched her pull out of the parking lot and onto Baxter Street. When she was completely out of sight, he slowly walked back into the pub.

CHAPTER
FOURTEEN

Christina and Melanie arrived at the Reddington estate the following Wednesday after having taken Katie up on her offer to spend a few days at the cottage. Katie was waiting on her front stoop when Christina's car made the final turn, slowed, and came to a complete stop.

"Katie," Melanie squealed as she bounced out of the car. "We missed you."

"It's only been a couple of weeks," Katie said as she first hugged Melanie and then planted a welcoming kiss on the young girl's cheek. "I bet I missed you more."

Melanie giggled and returned the kiss.

"This is so charming, Katie," Christina said as she walked around the front of the car and made a slow turn, giving her a panoramic view of the area. "So inspiring. You must be going wild with your photography."

"We can take a walk later, and I'll show you guys everything. But first let's get your stuff inside."

Katie grabbed one of the two suitcases Christina pulled out of the trunk, and the two of them followed Melanie up the porch of the cottage. Once inside, she showed her visitors to the bedroom. "Nora said that if you wanted an extra cot, she's got one in storage and would have someone bring it down."

"The bed is certainly big enough for the two of us, isn't it, Mel?"

"Maybe we can sleep outside tonight. Do you have any sleeping bags, Katie?"

Seeing the horrified look on Christina's face, Katie worked hard to suppress her laughter. "I'm sorry, I don't," she told Melanie. "I left all my camping gear back in Long Beach."

"Well, isn't that a shame," Christina said with faked regret as the trio headed back to the living room. "Where are you sleeping?"

"The couch is a pull-out."

"Let us take the couch," Christina said with much more sincerity. "We shouldn't kick you out of your bedroom."

"Don't give it a second thought. It'll be like I'm on a mini-vacation, too." She poked Melanie in the ribs which got her giggling again. "Arthur has invited us to dinner tonight, and I took the liberty of saying yes. Hope that's not a problem."

"From what you've told me about Nora's cooking, it's no problem at all. Don't have a clue about you guys, but I'm starving."

"Good. I'll call her and confirm the time. You guys relax."

"Katie?"

"Yes, Melanie?"

"I'm glad you wanted us to visit you."

"I'm glad you could make it."

Turning to Christina, Katie asked, "When does Andrew get back from D.C.?"

"He's not sure, but he's going to try and wrap things up by Saturday at the latest. Then he'll join us here. This will be a huge contract if he gets it, so he's taking his time and giving them the royal treatment."

"I know Andrew," Katie said. "He gives all his clients the royal treatment. All the time."

Christina smiled. "Yeah, he does." Looking at Melanie, who had burrowed herself into the rocking chair, she said, "Go wash up, Mel. And then change into a clean pair of slacks and top. We don't want Mr. Reddington to think we're a bunch of slobs."

"Can I wear my new scarf, too?"

"Sure."

When Melanie ran toward the back room, Christina said, "She's getting nervous about going back to school. New kids, new teacher, new classroom. One minute her enthusiasm is off the charts and the next she's ready to break into tears."

"Then we'll help her forget about school for a couple of days. I've got a few things planned, but the two of you can always go off and do some mom and daughter sightseeing if you want. I've adjusted my work schedule for the rest of the week and weekend so I'm at your service."

"Why don't we take it one day at a time," Christina said.

"You go and get cleaned up, too," Katie said. "Take a shower if you want. I'll connect with Nora."

"Thanks, Katie. I'm glad we're here, too."

Christina hugged Katie, then followed the hallway toward the bedroom. When the door shut behind her, Katie wondered if maybe her friend wasn't feeling a few of those going-back-to-school nerves as well.

Clay was behind the bar washing down the mirrors when Katie, Christina, and Melanie walked into Clancy's the following day. It was still too early for the lunch crowd, so Katie knew that this would be the best time for everyone to meet. When Clay spotted them, he put aside his rag and greeted them at the door.

"You must be Christina," he said reaching out his hand. "Katie said you were coming out for a few days." Bending at the waist so he was more at eye-level with Melanie, he added, "And you must be Melanie. Glad to make your acquaintance."

Melanie shook his hand while giving him a reserved smile. "Are you Katie's boyfriend?"

"I am indeed," he said, squaring his shoulders. "Is that going to be a problem?"

"Nope," she replied, scanning the room and pointing to a booth near the jukebox. "Can we sit over there?"

"An excellent choice of seating. Why don't you ladies go on over, and I'll get some menus."

Wrapping his fingers around Katie's wrist, Clay waited until her lunch guests had a head start toward the booth. Leaning in, he gave her a soft, intimate kiss. "Hi."

"Hi back." She touched her fingers to his cheek. "How's life treating you?"

"Can't complain, especially now that you're here."

"Would you like to join us for lunch?"

"Maybe when Tess gets here. She's scheduled to come in at noon."

Katie gave him another kiss then headed toward the booth Melanie had chosen.

After lunch was consumed and Melanie was finishing off a piece of strawberry shortcake, Clay stopped at their table. "Mind if I sit for a minute?"

Katie slid over to make room for him. "As always, lunch was superb."

"What about you, Christina? Was your Clancy burger satisfactory?"

"More than. Andrew is coming in on Saturday, and I already told Katie I'm bringing him back for dinner. She says that you have live music."

"Dakota Gold is playing Friday and Saturday this weekend. You'll like them."

"Mom, I need to use the bathroom."

"It's right down the hall and on your right," Clay said as he pointed to the hallway.

"Maybe I should go with you," Christina said.

Melanie looked at her mother, clearly embarrassed. "I'm a big girl now, and I can go by myself," she spoke in a hushed voice as she pushed at her mother in an effort to escape the booth.

"Fine, fine." Christina stood and let Melanie skirt around her and race to the ladies' room. "She's a big girl, my ass. She'll never be big enough to make me stop worrying about her."

"All mothers worry about their kids," Katie said lightly. "Mine doesn't let me get away with anything, still, to this day. Case in point, she did everything she could to talk me out of moving here."

"I'm glad she didn't succeed." Clay stretched his arm across the back of the bench and pulled Katie close.

"So, tell me Clay, what's it like being a pub owner?" Christina asked.

"It's everything you'd imagine it could be. I've got a great staff working for me and customers who keep us on our toes without being too rowdy. I'm proud to say we've got a good reputation and a good standing in the community."

Tess stepped up to the table and said, "Anybody need anything?"

"I'm good," Christina said, glancing down the hall.

"So am I," Katie said. "Thanks Tess."

When the waitress left, Christina said, "Melanie should have been back by now. I think I'm going to see what's taking her so long."

Katie didn't say anything as Christina slipped out of the booth and made her way to the restrooms. Eventually she would have to give Melanie her independence, but for now her role was that of mom. Melanie was still young, vulnerable, and in need of guidance, especially in a strange surrounding.

"Your friends seem nice," Clay said as he rubbed his hand along Katie's upper arm. "How long are they—"

Clay was on his feet and sprinting toward the bathrooms a split second after hearing Christina cry out. Katie was tight on his heels.

"She's gone. I can't find her," Christina was saying as she made her way toward the alley exit. "Katie, I can't find her."

"She's around here somewhere, Christina. I'm sure she's just exploring."

"I'll check out back," Clay said, reaching the back door first. "Katie, why don't you and Christina check upstairs?"

"Upstairs, of course," Christina said. "We were talking about your apartment, and she probably wanted to see what it looked like."

"Sounds reasonable," Katie said as she exchanged a look with Clay. "Come on, the stairs are this way."

It didn't take long to walk through the apartment, and when they were sure that Melanie wasn't there, Christina was near hysterics. "Why would she do this? I've told her a million times that she's not supposed to go off on her own."

"Christina, honey. Take a breath. This is what kids do. She's found someplace interesting to investigate, and we're at a disadvantage because we're adults. We have no clue which nook or cranny she's exploring."

"She doesn't understand the consequences. I tell her, but she doesn't get it."

"So you tell her again," Katie said gently. "You know all this, Christina. This will become a life lesson for her. When she comes out of hiding, you'll know how to handle it. Come on." Katie led them back downstairs.

The first thing Christina heard when they crossed into the bar area was Melanie's voice. Her relief was evident as she briefly stopped at the end of the bar and clutched the back of one of the chairs. Taking a fortifying breath, she continued toward her daughter.

Clay was on one knee in front of the young girl who sat in the booth, her legs dangling on the outside of the bench. Christina had no trouble picking up on their conversation as she got closer. She also noticed the kitten that Melanie was clutching.

"What did the man say after he gave you the kitten?" Clay was asking.

"He told me that if I didn't like this one, I could pick one of the other ones. He said he had to go to his car and get them and wanted me to go with him, but I told him I couldn't go with strangers. Then I heard you calling me, and the man left." Melanie paused to hug the kitten again. "I didn't really want a different kitten," she said. "I like this one, don't you, Clay?"

"It's a cutie," he replied, stroking the purring animal. "Did you see which way the man went when he left?"

"I don't think so," she said thoughtfully.

"What man is she talking about?" Christina demanded as Clay rose.

Melanie gave her mother a cautious look. "I know I should have come right back. But the man gave me this kitten, Mom. He said there were so many kittens and the mom couldn't take care of all of them. He asked me if I would take care of this one. Don't you think she's cute?"

Christina was struggling to hold her emotions in check as she tried to absorb what her child was telling her. It was only when she heard her name and felt someone touch her arm that she remembered Clay was standing next to her.

"You and Katie stay with Melanie," he was saying. "I'm going to take a walk around the building." He leaned in closer and in a quiet voice said, "It will give you some time to talk to her. She's safe, Christina. First and foremost, she's safe."

Once Clay had disappeared back down the hallway, Christina said, "Katie, could you get us a couple of sodas, please?"

"Sure. I'll be back in five."

"Scoot over, honey." Christina waved her hand in a motion that told Melanie to move deeper into the booth.

"I'm in trouble, aren't I?"

"In a manner of speaking, yes. Do you think it was right to go outside with that man?"

"No," she said dropping her chin to her chest. "You told me never to go with a stranger."

"Not even if that stranger offers you a kitten, Melanie."

"I know. It was a bad thing to do."

Christina was finding it difficult to have this conversation while Melanie lovingly stroked the adorable tan and white kitten she held on her lap. "It wasn't the best choice you've ever made, not by a long shot. Now, we're going over it one more time. Are you listening?"

Melanie looked up at her mother and nodded her head. "I'm sorry, Mom."

"I'm sure you are. But that doesn't change a whole lot right now. Are you ready?"

Melanie nodded again and for the next ten minutes, mother and daughter shared a necessary heart to heart.

When Clay returned from his search, he walked over to Katie who was sitting at the bar, frowning at the cell phone in her hand. He leaned in and kissed the side of her head before taking the seat beside her. "Who was on the phone?"

"Haven't a clue," she replied, setting the phone on the bar counter. "Someone can't get it through their thick skull that they're dialing the wrong number. Anyway, what did you find?"

"Part of what Melanie said is correct. There was a cardboard box near the dumpster with three kittens inside. I didn't find the guy she said gave her the one she's holding."

"What's puzzling to me," Katie said, "is why Melanie would go outside in the first place. It's out of character for her. I think."

"Ben said that he propped the door open when his food delivery came, and that he and the driver spent a couple of minutes in the kitchen talking sports before he left. That's probably when the man coaxed Melanie outside, using the kitten. Ben is going to check with the driver to find out if he saw anyone hanging around. He's sick about what's happened, blaming himself for not keeping a better eye on the back door."

"It's not his fault," Katie expressed with empathy. "He's probably been going through the same routine since the day you opened Clancy's, and this is the first time anything like this has happened."

"It'll be hard to convince him of that."

Katie nodded in agreement. "What about the other cats?"

"They're in my office. I'll take them to the humane society later today or tomorrow. Unless you want them."

"As tempting as that is, I'll have to decline."

"Will Christina be willing to report this?" Clay asked, glancing over to where she was still talking to her daughter.

"I'm not sure. I'll have to ask her."

Clay slid his hand over Katie's and gave it a squeeze. "It's got to be tough for your friend to raise a kid with a disability."

"Mostly they do all right. If you think about it, any kid could have taken the bait. Knowing that doesn't make it any less scary though, does it?"

"No, it doesn't," Clay said. "So, what is Christina going to do with Betty Lou?" When Katie gave him a quizzical look, he added, "Melanie's already named the kitten."

CHAPTER
FIFTEEN

Katie sat on the front porch of the main house with Christina, watching Hannah and Melanie play with Betty Lou. "It looks like Melanie's been able to move past yesterday's interview with Officer Shore," she said.

"It wasn't pleasant, but I think it was necessary," Christina replied. "Not only because there might be someone out there enticing young children, but I think it finally made Mel understand how dangerous it is to be so friendly with anyone who shows her some attention. After taking her statement, Officer Shore gave her the safety talk. He told me that he has three kids of his own, and even though they've started rolling their eyes every time the subject comes up, he continues to give them the stranger talk. He also gave me some ideas to use the next time I discuss the topic with Melanie."

The silence stretched out for several minutes until Katie asked, "Are we still going to Clancy's tonight?"

"I think so. What happened isn't Clay's fault, and Melanie likes it there. I doubt she'll even consider stepping foot out of my sight."

"Can Hannah come with us to Clay's?" Melanie asked as she continued to play with the kitten.

"What did I tell you about eavesdropping, young lady?"

"I wasn't. You were talking too loud, so I heard."

Katie tried, but failed, to suppress her laugh.

"Thanks for the invite," Hannah said to Melanie as she picked up the kitten and stroked its back, "but I've got other plans for tonight." Seeing the disappointment on the girl's face, Hannah added, "Maybe next time."

"Maybe next time, then," Melanie said, adding a long-suffering sigh.

"My daughter will one day win an Oscar, I'm sure of it," Christina declared. "Now what was I saying? Oh yes, with Andrew arriving a day sooner than he'd planned, we'll probably have to make it an early evening. I've booked a room in Pendleton for the three of us tonight, and I'd like to get Melanie down at a reasonable hour. It's going to be a long day tomorrow, and it would make it so much easier if she wasn't crabby because she didn't get enough sleep."

"About that," Katie began but was interrupted by her cell phone. She dug it out of her pocket and glanced at the caller ID. "Unknown Caller," she mumbled, reading the display screen. "Hello?"

When there was no answer, she repeated the greeting. "Hello? Is anyone there?"

Again, silence, and Katie lowered the phone to check the possibility that reception was bad. But she could see no evidence that the signal had been lost, and it appeared as if the caller was still on the line. "Damn," she said as she disconnected the call and jammed the phone back in her pocket.

"We're not supposed to say that word, Katie. Mom said she'd wash my mouth out with soap if she ever caught me using that word."

Christina smiled. "I think Katie is too big for me to hold down while I'm washing her mouth out. But you, I can still handle."

"I can't wait until I get bigger so I can do all the things you and Dad tell me I can't do."

"I would suggest you don't hurry that growing up thing just so you can swear," Katie chimed in while trying to maintain a shred of decorum. "I agree with your mom. Swearing is not a good thing."

Melanie gave Katie a confused look. "Then why—"

"—I should not have said the D word and I apologize for it. By the way, did you feed Betty Lou today?"

"Yes. Hannah and I watched her eat. Do you think I should feed her again?"

"No, I'm sure she's had enough for now. We don't want her to blow up like a balloon and fly away."

"Kittens can't do that," Melanie said grinning. With the swearing episode all but forgotten, she went back to dangling a rubber mouse on a string and watching Betty Lou swat at it.

"Nice redirect," Christina whispered as she gave Katie a shoulder jab. "What was that phone call?"

"Nothing. Or rather, no one."

"Don't tell me. That screwball who hangs up on you is back at it."

"As a matter of fact, the calls never stopped."

"I thought you were going to get a new number."

"Never got around to it."

"Well, get around to it."

"Okay, you win," Katie groaned. "I'll make the time to change my number. Now, what was I saying? Oh, yeah, maybe you guys don't have to leave tonight."

"We don't?"

Katie lowered her voice as she continued. "Remember when Melanie asked if I had any sleeping bags?"

"No, no. I am not going camping with you."

Katie laughed. "I know you better than that. I thought that Melanie and I could camp out and you and Andrew could have the cottage all to yourselves. Ian said he could get his hands on a tent and sleeping bags, and we can set it up right out front here."

"I don't know, Katie. After yesterday, I'm not sure that's a good idea."

"You may not have noticed, but Arthur has an awesome security system here. No one gets through the front gate without a code, there are cameras all over the place, and I'll program the cottage's phone number into my cell so you're only a button push away."

Christina was silent again, and Katie could imagine the internal battle she was having between heart and mind.

"I bet if I ask Ian real nice like, he could find someone to make regular spot checks on us."

"You drive a hard bargain."

Katie smiled. "One of my many skills."

"Let me talk to Andrew."

"Katie?" Nora poked her head out the screen door. "There's an Andrew Freeman out front requesting clearance. Could you please do a visual verification, and I can buzz him up."

Katie jumped up and disappeared through the door. Seconds later she was back on the porch. "Awesome security system," she said in an offhanded tone.

"You told Nora to do that," Christina said, working hard to hide her amusement. She waited patiently for her husband's car to come into sight, and when it did, her heart soared and her smile was bright.

"Daddy," Melanie squealed as she ran toward her father's rental. "Hannah, my daddy's here."

Hannah watched with interest as first Melanie and then Christina hugged and kissed the tall, salt-and-pepper-haired man who didn't seem to mind all the attention. With greetings done, they walked as a trio back toward the house.

"This is Hannah, Daddy. Isn't that a pretty name?"

"Very pretty. Hello Hannah, I'm Andrew Freeman."

"Hello," she said accepting his outstretched hand.

"This must be the devil that caused trouble for my girls." he said, pointing to the kitten that Hannah still held.

"Mom said we couldn't bring Betty Lou home because you're allergic." Melanie reached in and relieved Hannah of the kitten.

"I'm going to miss her," she added as she rubbed her face in the animal's fur.

"It's either her or me, sweetie. And I'd be truly disappointed if you and your mom left me behind."

"I'd never do that, Daddy. And Katie said she'd watch out for Betty Lou, and whenever we visit, I can see her again."

Responding to Hannah's surprised look, Katie said, "Arthur said that as long as she doesn't wreak havoc, he'll look the other way."

"I'm not so worried about Uncle Arthur. What did Nora say?"

"That she'd rip me from limb to limb if I let that scalawag damage anything. I've already cat-proofed the cottage."

"She must be getting mellow in her old age," Hannah quipped. "I wanted to keep a rabbit here one year, and she told me if she found it she'd cook it for dinner."

Melanie pulled on Katie's sleeve. "Will Nora cook Betty Lou if she doesn't behave? Maybe Clay should keep her at his place."

Katie chuckled. "I'll make sure nobody cooks her."

Melanie didn't seem to be totally convinced but let it drop.

"Why don't you get into Dad's car, Melanie, and we can show him where the cottage is," Christina said. Turning to her husband she added, "You'll have time to relax for a bit before we head out to the pub. Our reservation at Clancy's isn't until six-thirty."

Music from the jukebox was playing discreetly when they arrived at the pub. There were still tables available, and all but one of the booths was filled. Tess met them at the door and said, "I saved your booth, Melanie. Why don't you take everyone over there, and I'll be with you in a minute."

"Will do, Tess. I'll grab menus and save you an extra trip."

Tess laughed. "I wish all my customers were as considerate as you. Go ahead."

As they approached the booth where Christina, Katie, and

Melanie had enjoyed their lunch on Thursday, Melanie exclaimed, "Look, Katie. That sign has our name on it."

"Looks like you're a preferred customer."

Melanie gave Katie a puzzled look. "What does that mean?"

"It means that Clay likes you best."

She pulled out a huge smile, evidently pleased with that thought.

A few minutes later, Tess took their orders. When she returned with their drinks, Katie said, "I don't see Clay, is he here?"

"He's in the office. On Fridays he usually doesn't come out until later, unless we need him."

"I'm going to go back and say hello," Katie said.

"Can I go with you, Katie?" Melanie asked as she made a move to exit the booth. "I want to say hi to Clay, too."

"I'm sure Clay will stop by our table later so you don't need to go back there right now," Christina said.

"I promise I'll stay with Katie," Melanie voiced tearfully. "I'm sorry I made you mad."

Christina reached out and took her daughter's hand. "I haven't forgotten what you promised me, sweetie, and I believe you. Right now, I think that Katie wants to see Clay by herself. They want some private time."

Katie knew the instant the light went on in Melanie's head. The clever girl flashed her best smile and said, "You're going to kiss him, aren't you?"

"Never you mind, little Miss Nosy-Rosy," Katie asserted as she turned her back on the laughter of her friends.

The door to the office was partially open. Clay was sitting behind his desk, his fingers flying across the keyboard of his computer. He looked up when Katie stepped into the room and smiled approvingly when she closed the door behind her and engaged the lock.

"Melanie thinks I came back here to kiss you," she said.

"Well then, we shouldn't disappoint the poor girl. Why don't you come over here," he said slapping his hand on his knee, "and we can discuss it right and proper."

Katie complied. She cupped his face between her hands and, starting at the left side of his mouth, slowly slid her tongue along his slightly parted lips. When her hands moved down to his chest, she began to undo his shirt, one agonizing button at a time. She could feel his breathing increase when she spread the shirt open and ran her fingers across his smooth skin. It wasn't until she lowered her head and ran her slow deductive kisses down the side of his neck that he reacted. He squeezed her hips and tried unsuccessfully to suppress his groan.

"We can't do this now," he said on a struggling breath, "although, the only part of my anatomy that's in agreement with that statement is my brain." He lifted her head and kissed her, slowly, meaningfully. "I don't suppose you can stick around until closing and then spend the night with me."

"Sorry, I've got a date later," she said, laughing when he playfully slapped her butt. "I told Christina that I'd give up the cottage to her and Andrew so Melanie and I can camp out in front of the house. I haven't mentioned it to her yet, so don't say anything."

"How about tomorrow night? Can I put you on my dance card for then?"

"Double sorry, this time. I'm driving back to Redmond with the gang tomorrow. Andrew has business in Long Beach on Monday, and I'm flying there with him. My agent wants to see some of my recent work so with any luck, she'll like some of it enough to place it in her gallery for sale. The trip also gives me a few days with my mom."

"When will you be back?"

"Andrew figures he can wrap everything up by Wednesday or Thursday, and he'll fly me back here before he heads home."

"Well, I guess I'll have to spend the next couple of days yearning for you."

"I'm sure you'll find something to keep you occupied."

"Let's hope so." Giving Katie a gentle push off his lap, he added, "Regrettably, you should probably return to the table so I can finish up with this work. I'll be out as soon as I'm done."

"Don't be too long. Melanie's waiting to see you. We had to practically tie her down so I could be alone with you." Leaning in for one last kiss, they separated and Katie left Clay to his computer.

On her way back to the table, Katie spotted Nathan coming through the front door dragging in his guitar case and amplifier. She offered him a wave which he returned with a nod and a smile.

"You're back," Melanie exclaimed as she pushed a French fry into her mouth. "Now your food won't get cold."

"It looks awfully good."

"How's Clay?" Christina asked with a lift of her eyebrows.

"He's fine, thanks for asking," Katie replied with a smile. "He's busy counting his lucre, but when he's done he'll be out."

"What's—"

"Money. Lucre means money."

"How did you know what I was going to ask?" Melanie said with a quick butt bounce.

"Because I get how that brain of yours works," Katie replied, tapping the girl's forehead with her knuckle.

"I'm looking forward to meeting this Clay fellow," Andrew said. "I hear he walks on water."

Katie's laugh was quick and full. "I can tell you straight-out, that's a fallacy. He's a terrific guy but far from being godly."

As Tess was clearing their dishes, Nathan approached the booth. "Hi, Katie. It's good to see you."

"Hi, Nathan. Same here." She made introductions and then said, "I see everyone's here except Tony."

"He called about fifteen minutes ago and said he had an emergency and couldn't make it tonight, leaving us short a keyboard player for the time being. I was able to get hold of a fill-in musician for tonight, but he won't be here for at least an hour, probably more."

"My mom plays the piano, and she's really good. Maybe she could play with you." Melanie piped in. "Chopin is her favorite."

"Well, unfortunately, we won't be doing any Chopin tonight." Turning to Christina, he asked, "Do you do anything other than classical?"

"My wife played in a band in college," Andrew said as he draped his arm around Christina's shoulder and smiled affectionately. "She's able to play most anything. If you're looking for someone to carry you until your replacement gets here, I'm sure she can fit the bill."

"I have Tony's keyboard in my van if you're interested," Nathan said to Christina. "I don't think I'll get any objections from the other guys if you're as good as these two say you are."

"Make that the three of us," Katie said. "I've heard her play, and I think she'll be a good match for Dakota Gold."

"Say yes, Mom. This will be so cool. I can tell all the kids at school that my mom is in a band."

"Why don't you come and meet the guys and I can give you a copy of the song list. We'll be sticking to cover tunes all night, and you can tell us which ones you know."

Christina looked at Andrew, then Katie, and finally at Melanie. "This is going to be so cool," she mimicked her daughter as she leaned across the table and mussed her hair.

Andrew was already on his feet and reaching for Christina's hand. When she was out of the booth, she gave him a quick kiss and said, "Just like the old days."

Clay heard the live music from his office and checked his watch, surprised that it was nearly eight. He shut down the computer leaving the remainder of his paperwork behind locked doors.

He checked with Ben in the kitchen first and was told that everything was going smoothly. Next he stepped behind the bar and made sure that Joel and his other part-time bartender, Rick, were keeping up with the orders. He greeted some of the regulars who were sitting on stools, mixed a few drinks, and then made his way out to the floor to greet the customers seated at tables.

He first noticed Christina Freeman on stage, rocking out to a popular Springsteen song, when he was heading toward one of the corner tables. After taking a minute to listen, totally impressed with what he heard, he continued his rounds, eventually ending up at the booth where Katie sat with Andrew and Melanie. Andrew slid toward the wall to allow Clay to take a seat.

"You must be Clay Crawford," Andrew said extending his hand. "I'm Andrew Freeman, Christina's husband and the father of this little rascal."

Melanie mumbled something unintelligible as she continued to suck on the plastic straw in her chocolate milk. Obviously it wasn't the first time she'd been referred to as rascal.

"You do realize there's someone up on stage that bears a significant resemblance to your wife, don't you?"

"Nathan was short a musician," Katie said as she shifted her gaze to the band. "She's good, isn't she?"

"And she's enjoying herself," Andrew added as he, too, turned toward the stage.

"Nathan has a substitute coming," Katie added, "and until then Christina agreed to play."

With her milk now gone, Melanie was getting bored. Glancing at the people on the dance floor, she looked across the table and said, "Hey, Clay. Do you want to ask me to dance?"

Clay laughed when Andrew said, "Hey, what am I, chopped liver?"

Melanie giggled. "You're my dad. I can dance with you anytime."

"Man, I hate it when she's right."

Clay stood and bent at the waist. "Ms. Freeman, may I have this dance?"

Melanie shot past Katie, who had already moved out of the booth, and grabbed Clay's hand, dragging him onto the dance floor. For the next ten minutes, he did his best to keep up with the little girl's energy. At one point, Katie and Andrew hit the floor and the four mixed and matched dance steps to the beat of an 80's standard song. When the new keyboard player arrived, the band took a break, and Clay gratefully returned Melanie to the booth before slipping into the kitchen. Five minutes later, Christina returned to the table, flushed with excitement.

"Wow, that was fun. I didn't think it would all come back to me so easily, but I felt so comfortable up there and the music seemed to flow out of me."

"You were great, sweetheart," Andrew said through a huge grin.

"I agree, girlfriend," Katie chimed in, sharing a fist bump with her friend. "Nice job."

Andrew glanced at his watch before nudging his wife and nodding at Melanie who was slumped in the corner of the booth with her eyes fluttering. "We should probably get the little one back to Arthur's place. Are you good to go, Katie?"

"Totally," she responded. "Hey, giggles. Do you think you can stay awake until we get back to the cottage? I have a surprise for you."

Melanie sat up in the booth. "What surprise?"

"You'll see once we get there. Do you want to say good-bye to Clay?"

"Yes, please."

"I'll settle the bill, and we'll meet you at the front door," Andrew said as he pulled out one of his credit cards.

An hour later, Katie, Melanie, and Betty Lou were sound asleep in the tent that had been set up on Arthur's front lawn. Andrew and Christina were making the best of their night alone in the cottage, and Arthur was on the computer in his study chatting with his younger brother, who was currently overseas making a circuit of several French wineries. Nora was in her sitting room reading a first edition copy of Jane Austen's *Pride and Prejudice,* and even Hannah was tucked in for the night, phone in hand, listening to her best friend relay all the news from back home. Just another quiet night in the outskirts of Abbott County.

He'd planned on going into Clancy's tonight. But when he'd arrived, he spotted the kid who had been so easily coaxed into taking that stupid kitten from him going through the front door, holding tight to her mother's hand. It hadn't taken a brain surgeon to rationalize the extreme risk of going inside the bar so he could stay close to Katie. Reluctantly, he'd turned his car around and made the ninety-minute drive back home.

As was often the case, memories of his father flooded his heart as soon as the cabin came into sight. When he was a boy growing up in California, he and his father had tried to spend as many weekends and holidays up here as possible, bonding over a fishing pole or tracking small animals in the woods that surrounded their home away from home. He truly believed that the person he was today was a direct result of the rough and tough man he had looked up to as a young boy. The man who had assured him it wasn't wrong to know you were right. That good and evil were simply a state of mind, and that to survive life's cruelties you sometimes had to break the rules. And even though he understood that his father was gone—a reality that hurt like hell most days—he would swear that late at night, when he lay awake on the battered couch, willing sleep to take him under, he could hear his father whistling.

Using the back door to enter the cabin, he allowed himself to think about his own incarceration. Another fallout of Judge Nolan's wrongful decision. If his father hadn't been taken away from him when he was a child, he would have had a better chance in life. Instead, he'd been led down a path where on most days, he'd done whatever it took to survive, and every step forward took him two steps back. Proven by the three years he'd spent in a prison for second degree robbery. Every day had reminded him of the hell his father had gone through, every night spent praying his life wouldn't end with a knife blade through his heart. Oh yes, he had no problem holding Katie responsible for that as well.

On the day he'd been released, he and his mother had moved into a small two-bedroom apartment not far from the Long Beach City College. Rent came out of the money he'd managed to stash away from the burglaries he and his cousin had committed prior to his arrest and conviction. Because they'd stuck to the elite suburban neighborhoods he'd never seen the likes of growing up, it had amounted to a very comfortable sum of money. For all the other household expenses, such as groceries and utility bills, he used the cash he'd get for taking on odd—although not always aboveboard—jobs.

After they'd settled into the new apartment, it had only taken him a few months to realize how sick his mother had become. Dementia was the official diagnosis. Confused about where she was half the time, forgetting the most basic tasks the other half. Always looking for something familiar she could grasp on to.

Resigning himself to the fact that his mother needed more intense care then he could give her, he'd found an affordable nursing home in Medford, Oregon. The first several weeks had been difficult for him, having to witness the agonizing decline in his mother's health. To watch her slowly pulling away from him until one day she hadn't even recognized him. He'd been outraged more than anything else and had carried that fury with him through the next six months as he continued the long drive back and forth from Long Beach to Medford to sit by her side, silently begging the powers that be to give her back her voice. Her mind. Her soul.

When the lease had finally come due on the small apartment, he'd packed all his belongings and moved into the cabin his father had built. Not only was it closer to his mother's nursing home—making visits to her that much easier—it was also closer to Abbott County.

Grabbing the remote off the coffee table, he surfed the channels until he found a popular sports station. He didn't particularly enjoy baseball, but tonight he was hoping the distraction would help alleviate this unbearable loneliness that had been dogging him for the past few days. He had gone through these periods before, but had always had his mother to drag him back out to the lighter side of life. Now, when he would go to her at the nursing home, she would just sit in the rocking chair he'd bought for her, staring out the single window in her room. Which left him to deal with these dark spells all on his own.

Again, his thoughts circled back to his boyhood. When Judge Nolan had lowered that gavel, it had sealed the fate for his family. All the suffering that he and his mother had endured could be traced right back to the day when his father had been hauled away in handcuffs and his mother had left the courtroom in tears.

Well, he was the one swinging the gavel now, wasn't he? Since he'd arrived in Oregon, he'd spent a good share of his time watching Katie's movements, following her as she went about her daily business. The harassing phone calls, the kittens in the cardboard box? Well, those had really been for his benefit—a way to keep himself amused while he perfected his plan to bring her down, hard.

Leaving the sports analyst droning on about whether Chicago had the depth of hitters they'd need to win another World Series, he went to the kitchen for a beer, his thoughts still fixed on revenge. This was only the beginning, and by the time he was done, Katie Nolan would be cowering in the corner, crying for her mama.

He could hardly wait.

Chapter
Sixteen

Marian Nolan knelt in her neighbor's garden picking strawberries. She glanced up when she heard the patio doors at the back of her condominium unit slide open.

"I'm guessing that was your young man calling," Marian said as Katie walked toward her. "It's been a long time since I've seen that bonny smile of yours so wide."

The smile remained as Katie crouched down beside her mother. "Why are we picking these berries instead of letting Mrs. Westbrook do it?"

"Because if I pick them, I get half."

"Makes sense, I guess," Katie replied as she slipped on her gardening gloves. "I'll help you with the rest."

"When your father was alive, I'd spend hours in the garden behind our house. The planting and nurturing of all those vegetables was as enjoyable to me as the harvesting. Some years I would have so many, I'd end up giving a good share of them away."

"I remember," Katie said, sitting back on her heels. "You'd give a healthy share of what you couldn't use to the food pantry and leave small gift baskets at the neighbors' doors. What did we have? Tomatoes, peppers, radishes, broccoli, and my favorites, blueberries and strawberries. Your herb garden was no slouch either if I recall."

"I enjoyed it. The patch behind my place now is smaller, but I'm not as young as I used to be either. A good garden takes a lot of time and movement. The time I've got, but the movement has slowed quite a bit."

Katie leaned over and brushed a kiss to her mother's cheek before giving her a slight shoulder nudge. "I noticed that plant in the corner over there," she said in a hushed voice. "It doesn't quite fit with the rest of Mrs. Westbrook's selection of vegetables."

Glancing over to where Katie was pointing, Marian said, "No, I'd say it's not her typical crop. Millie isn't exactly the *Home and Garden* pinup of a beloved seventy-year-old gardener. She marches to the beat of her own drum, that's for sure. She claims she gets tremendous medicinal benefits from that weed."

Katie laughed, knowing perfectly well the type of plant her mother's neighbor had tucked between her berries. "When it's ready to harvest, do you get half of that, too?" she asked.

"I've never asked, and she's never offered," Marian said, working hard to keep a straight face. "Those blueberries aren't going to pick themselves, young lady. I want to see some action over there."

As Katie once again bent over the berries, she said, "I also remember the flowers you had around the front and side of the house. Arthur keeps an area where he has a nice selection of flowers and herbs. He's got a gardener who watches over it, but I've seen him digging and watering and pruning a number of times." Because Katie's focus was on the blueberries, she missed her mother's reactive smile to the mention of Arthur. "I guess it's relaxing if you like that sort of thing."

"It is," Marian said as she sat back to stretch out her back. "So tell me, how are you and Clay doing these days? When are you planning on bringing him out here to meet your mother?"

"You're always welcome to come visit me in Abbott," Katie replied cheerfully. "I do want you and Clay to meet soon, though. You're going to like him. He's one of the good guys."

"I'll take your word on that for now. He'll still have to pass the mom test."

"Understood," Katie said, dropping the final berry into the basket. "What would you say to us going out to eat tonight? I'm thinking patio seating at Fisherman's Loft."

"I'd say yes and yes." Marian readily agreed.

"Great. Why don't you take those in to Mrs. Westbrook, and I'll go make a reservation."

As Katie scurried into her mother's condo, Marian finished up in the garden. She was glad that her daughter had found a partner who was able to put that sparkle back into her eyes. When Katie had lost Evan, Marian had been concerned that Katie might have closed the door to opening her heart to another relationship. And didn't she know exactly how it felt to lose the love of your life? Or in her case, release it for the good of everyone involved? She'd never deny that she had loved Robert with all her heart, but it had been Arthur who had given her that sparkle. And it was Arthur whom she had once again opened her heart to, giving love a second chance to grow and flourish.

She smiled at the thought that he felt the same way, having proved his feelings when he'd taken her to his hotel room last week and rekindled their love.

Marian lifted the basket of berries and headed to her neighbor's patio door, hoping that Katie had also found that second chance at love.

The air was cool, the night draped in darkness except for the occasional splash of moonlight whenever the clouds separated. He moved carefully through the thickly wooded area on the southeast side of the Reddington property, noting that the only sound being carried over the silence was the inviting call of a cricket or the unintentional rustle of a stray deer.

He'd explored this section of property before—accessible due to its proximity to the state-owned land that bordered it. It had been the day that Katie was taking what she probably thought would be her next award-winning series of photographs. His lips curled now as he remembered the look of panic on her face at the exact moment she'd figured out that the chipping sparrows weren't the only creatures sharing the woods with her.

Tonight's expedition was meant as a dry run of sorts. He hoped to gain insight on how close he could get to the cottage without being detected. Understanding the lay of the land was paramount to any plan he would carry out when the time was right. Preparedness. His father had always stressed how important preparedness was with any job well done.

He stayed close to the fence line, using his binoculars every so often to help him locate the cameras. When he finally spotted the first one, he disabled it with a jamming device that would interrupt any visual activity being sent to all security monitors. If anyone was paying attention, they would think the interruption was a glitch in the system, rather than trouble in the field and would hopefully wait until a second interruption occurred before driving out here to make sure everything was safe and secure.

Staying alert for any signs that the cavalry was on their way, he took a deep soothing breath and carefully moved on to the next segment of land.

Arthur had been asleep less then fifteen minutes when the cell phone he'd dropped on the nightstand sounded an alarm, bringing him instantly out of his slumber. He sat up in bed and grabbed the phone, quickly reading the message on the touch screen. There had been a breach in security somewhere on the property.

Grabbing the remote, he swung his legs over the side of the mattress and activated the monitor that stood on a desk in the corner of his bedroom. It gave him a split view of the cameras that covered his property. Two of the cameras providing a view of the far east corner of the perimeter were dark.

When his cell phone rang, signaling an outside call, Arthur already knew who it was. "Ian, give me an update."

"I'm heading toward the east sector now," Ian said. "Dean is on duty, and he'll swing by the cottage on his way to check out that end of the property. To be safe, keep everyone in the house. I'll call you back."

Arthur had no intention of staying put, but would do as Ian said with regard to anyone else in the house who wasn't yet tucked in for the night. He stepped into a pair of khaki trousers before pulling on a lightweight sweater and slipping on a pair of loafers. Grabbing the S&W revolver he kept in his nightstand drawer, he checked to make sure it was loaded, then hurried out the bedroom door.

By the time Arthur reached the front porch, Ian was reporting in. "I haven't spotted any signs that someone made it onto the estate. If it was someone loitering on the outside who tripped one of the alarms, they probably heard my jeep coming and high-tailed it out of here. It isn't the first time kids have tried to jump the fence. Dean has already started a sweep along the perimeter, and I'll start checking the rest of the grounds."

"What about Katie?" Arthur asked.

"Dean reported that the cottage is locked up tight and there's no sign of her. Nora had mentioned to me yesterday that Katie called saying she'd be away a few more days. I'm guessing she's still in California."

"That fits with the text message she left me." Arthur took a calming breath before adding, "I'll be up for awhile, so call me if you or Dean find anything."

"Will do," Ian replied before disconnecting the call.

Moving back into the house, Arthur secured the front door before making his way to the study. There, he switched on the security monitors that were lined up inside a cabinet set against the wall directly across from his desk. Leaning back in his leather chair, he waited to hear from his chief of security.

Ten minutes later there was a knock on the door.

"Come in," he said, expecting to see Ian on the other side.

Nora entered instead, carrying a tray that held a carafe of coffee, two cups, and a small dish of cookies. "I heard you in the hall and saw Ian walking around out back. I figured that something was up." She set the tray on a table near the couch and poured Arthur a cup.

"There's nothing to worry about, Nora. One of the outside alarms went off. Ian hasn't found any sign that someone's on the estate that shouldn't be. It's more than likely a short in the system."

"I'm confident that you and Ian have everything under control," she said as she handed him the cup. "I also feel very safe inside the house."

"Is Hannah in her room?" he asked.

"Yes. She came home about an hour ago. I checked her room before I came in here and her lights were off, so I think she's down for the night."

"Good," Arthur said, giving Nora a slight nod.

She smiled and started toward the office door. "Ring me if you need anything."

For the next hour, Arthur split his attention between the security monitors and the paperwork he'd pulled out. When Ian phoned with the all clear, he shut down the system and climbed the steps back to his room, slipped under the bed covers, and closed his eyes, hopeful that sleep would follow.

Katie had arrived back on the Reddington estate late Friday evening. She'd been so exhausted, she'd immediately dropped into bed and was asleep within minutes of her head hitting the pillow.

Saturday morning Arthur was in his study when he heard Katie come through the front door of the house. By the time he'd made it to the hallway to greet her, she was halfway up the stairs.

"Hello, Arthur," she said, looking a bit surprised. "I wasn't sure if you'd be here today."

"I'll be around for a few hours yet," he replied. "How was your trip back home?"

"Very relaxing," Katie said, flashing back on how therapeutic the visit with her mother had been. "Mom's as feisty as ever. We spent a lot of time hanging out, eating at restaurants I hadn't been to since I was a teenager, and working in her garden. As well as her neighbor's garden," she added, remembering the budding green plant that had been hidden among Mrs. Westbrook's berries.

"I'm raring to get back to work, though," Katie continued, as she turned toward the staircase.

Arthur grinned. "Before you get too deep into your painting, I'd like to go over some changes in the security system. While you were gone, we put in some new features and enhancements. Can you give me about twenty minutes?"

"Sure. It would be good to do it now before I get started. Will that work for you?"

"It will. Why don't you drop your things upstairs and then meet me in my study."

"Has there been some trouble on the estate?" When Arthur gave her an inquiring look, she added, "I mean, was there a specific reason to enhance the security?"

"One of the alarms went off while you were gone," he began. "We couldn't tell if it was a problem in the system or if some kids were jazzing around on the property. We reevaluate our security twice a year, so I figured now was a good time to initiate an inspection.

There's nothing to worry about. I think once you see how the system works and the safety precautions we've added, you'll feel as safe as if you were living inside Fort Knox."

She gave Arthur a crooked smile. "As long as a net doesn't fall on top of me if I enter an incorrect code, I'm sure I'll be agreeable with any changes you've made. I'll be back down shortly," she said.

Arthur watched her climb the stairs, then disappear down the hallway. He didn't want to worry her unnecessarily, but wanted to be sure she was taking normal precautions for her safety when she was moving around the property alone. Ian was still uncertain what had caused the alarm to go off, and neither he nor Dean had found any signs of an unauthorized entry. Not even the security company had been able to determine for sure what had caused the interruption in the video feed. He'd asked Ian to continue digging into the matter and if there was more to it than a glitch in the system, well, he'd cross that bridge when he got to it. For now, as long as everyone followed the new and improved security measures, the system would do its job.

CHAPTER
SEVENTEEN

Saturday evening Katie was still in the second-floor studio, examining the painting of Thaddeus Reddington. Other than a few touch-ups, she thought she'd done everything she could to capture his true likeness, based on the old family photographs. She was pleased with the final piece and deep inside felt she had captured the real heart and soul of the man.

"It really looks like a Reddington, doesn't it?"

Katie spun around and saw Hannah standing in the doorway. "I wish you wouldn't sneak up on me like that, Hannah. How many times have I asked you to knock?"

"I don't understand what the big deal is. The door's always open."

No, she wouldn't understand, Katie thought. No one did, except maybe Arthur. The first time he'd come to her studio, he'd described her as being one with the painting. He'd seen how she could totally immerse herself into her work, and how the simplest distraction could so easily break the spell.

"Do you need something?" Katie asked politely.

"Nora instructed me to tell you that she's left and won't be back until tomorrow morning. Uncle Arthur is also gone, I think for a couple of days. And I'm taking off, too. Ian and Ted are the only ones left here although I have no idea where they are."

"Thanks for the info," Katie said, encouraged that Hannah had followed through on Nora's request. A week ago, Katie wasn't sure that would have happened. "I'm almost finished here anyway, so I'll be heading back to the cottage."

Hannah hesitated in the doorway for a moment before pitching Katie another fastball. "It's a good painting, you know. You've got some real talent there."

Katie wasn't sure what to say, although it didn't matter because Hannah was already turning to leave. "I'm out of here."

Hopeful that this latest exchange was a sign that she and Hannah had finally turned a corner in their relationship, Katie began the cleanup process, debating her options for the evening. She could go into town and rent a movie or two, then go back to the cottage for a Stooges marathon. Or she could pick up a couple of new books and spend the evening reading.

The best option would be to surprise Clay by showing up at Clancy's. Which is what she really wanted to do. And now that the portrait was done, she could indulge in some downtime that might keep her out the rest of the night, too.

Glancing around the room to make sure everything was put away, Katie hit the light switch and stepped into the hallway as the grandfather clock in the downstairs living room announced the eight o'clock hour. She'd gotten so used to the sounds the antique clock made, she rarely paid attention to it anymore. Tonight, her awareness came from the fact that the house was empty.

As she reached the top of the stairway, her cell phone signaled from inside her tote bag. She stopped, digging to the bottom to retrieve the device.

"Hello?" Katie said as she started down the steps.

Silence was the caller's only response.

"Hello?" Katie repeated after reading the display that identified an unknown number. "Is anyone there?"

"I'm here," the deep, unfamiliar voice replied.

Katie hesitated. "I'm sorry. I don't know who this is."

"Are you sure?" the voice taunted.

"Of course I'm sure. Identify yourself or I'm hanging up."

When there was no response, Katie hit the disconnect button. "Jerk," she hissed as she started back down the stairs, pressing the redial button in hopes of catching the anonymous caller in the act. All she got was a recorded message reporting that her call couldn't be completed. She disconnected once again, muttering a few choice words about what the caller could do with his cell phone.

A faint scraping noise coming from the dimly lit hallway leading to the kitchen brought Katie to an abrupt halt as she reached the front door. She waited, but all she heard now was the rhythmic ticking of the antique clock. She called out, thinking it might be Hannah or Nora, but neither responded.

Katie took three cautious steps down the hall. "Nora? Is that you?" she said firmly. "Hannah?"

A man suddenly stepped out of the kitchen, making Katie jump. He was dressed in a black turtleneck sweater, black jeans, and black boots. Both hands were stuffed in the pockets of his black leather jacket, and because the lights had been dimmed in both the kitchen and the hallway, she couldn't make out his face.

Katie took two steps backward as the man moved toward her. "Katie, it's me. Dean." He'd stopped moving and had taken his hands out of his pockets, holding them loosely at his waist, palms out. "It's Dean Singleton."

Katie swore quietly under her breath, feeling foolish and embarrassed by her overreaction. "Dean, of course. Sorry. I thought I was alone in the house."

"I thought I was, too," he said with a quick laugh. "I came through the back door so I didn't see your car, which I'm assuming is out front."

"It is. I was on my way out."

"Is everything okay?" he asked, moving toward the front door.

"Yes, of course," she replied, even as the phone call she'd received moments before popped into her mind. "I guess I wasn't expecting anyone to be here."

Dean reached out to open the door for her, suspecting that he'd spooked her more than she was letting on. "I can escort you back to the cottage if you want."

"Thanks for the offer, but that's not necessary."

Katie hurried to her car, leaving Dean standing on the porch. She tossed her tote bag in the back seat, slid behind the steering wheel, and started the car. As she made her way down the dirt road, she glanced in the mirror and saw Dean turn to go back into the house.

At the cottage, she quickly changed clothes and was back on the road within thirty minutes. With the windows down and the radio blaring, she made her way into Abbott. By the time she reached Clancy's, her nerves had settled, and she was prepared to enjoy her night out.

Weekends were always busy at the pub, primarily because of the live music. A full parking lot was evidence that tonight supported that trend. It was only by luck that Katie was able to snag a parking spot currently being vacated in the back of the lot. Tonight, whoever the band was, they certainly had done their job of drawing a crowd.

Entering the pub, she saw immediately that there wasn't an empty table in the place. Clay was working behind the bar, systematically filling drink orders that were being dumped on him by Joel, who was apparently waiting tables for new arrivals in-between clearing those that were being abandoned. She cut a path through a group who appeared to be waiting for one of those tables and made her way toward the bar. She passed by the swinging door that led into the kitchen where she saw Ben assembling sandwiches and slapping them into paper-lined plastic serving baskets that were lined up on the prep table. It appeared that Tess had gone AWOL.

"It looks like you're a bit short-handed tonight," she said when she reached the end of the bar, raising her voice above the music so Clay was able to hear her.

He offered her a hasty glance as he continued pouring out margarita mix into the four glasses that sat on top of the rail. "You could say that. Tess's son was in a car accident earlier. And no, I haven't been in my office to check if she's left a message on the machine. We're having a hard time keeping up with everything.

"These are for the ladies in the booth on the other side of the band," he shouted to Joel who appeared to be on overload. Katie was sure that it wouldn't take much to push the poor guy over the edge.

"Mr. Enders said the fries are under-cooked and the chicken is over-cooked," Joel complained to Clay. "He wants new."

"Tell him if he can wait ten minutes, I'll go back and make him a new sandwich and fries."

"Got it," Joel said as he retreated back through the crowd.

"I can help," Katie said to Clay. "I waited tables all through college, I have great customer service skills, and I know your menu like the back of my hand. In short, you need a temporary employee, and I fit the bill." She smiled now as she added, "That was my ten-second interview."

"You had me at two," Clay replied as he tossed a couple of olives into a martini glass. "Grab an apron and relieve Joel so he can relieve me so I can go back and help Ben." He glanced up as Joel dropped another drink order on the bar and then gave Katie a shrewd smile. "Also, sometime in the next thirty minutes you'll have to organize tables in the corner for a party of seven. They called to confirm the reservation right before you came in." The flummoxed look on her face was so readable, he had to chuckle. "Sorry I didn't mention that earlier in our interview."

Katie was laughing now as she dug out an order pad. "I hate to break this to you, Clay, but you don't take reservations. And how do you expect me to displace seven other patrons while I confiscate their tables?"

"You said you went to college, right? You should be able to figure something out."

"You're really enjoying this, aren't you? You owe me, Crawford. And I don't come cheap."

"Didn't expect that you would. Help me salvage some business tonight, and I'm sure I'll be able to satisfy your demands."

As Katie blushed at the implication of his words, Clay pushed a tray of drinks toward her. "Table three. Shake a leg, girl."

For the next three hours, Katie worked the floor while Clay moved between the kitchen and bar. She'd managed to secure two tables near the back of the bar for the unprecedented reservation, even though it was going to cost Clay a double round of drinks for the customers she'd had to uproot.

By midnight the music was winding down, and the customers had thinned to a manageable number. Clay had closed down the kitchen and was back behind the bar, taking over for Joel who was heading out the front door, his shift over for the night.

Katie was wiping down booths along the front wall when she glanced up and saw Clay watching her. He sent her a wink and a smile, and she thought about how it wouldn't be long now before she'd have him all to herself. Then she'd really make him smile.

The spell was broken, however, when Ben called Clay over to the phone. The conversation was short and had Clay coming out from behind the bar and walking toward Katie.

"That was Tess," he began. "They want to send Eli home tonight, but she's afraid that she won't be able to get him inside the house on her own. His ankle and foot are in a cast, and he's still a little unsteady on the crutches they gave him. I'm going to meet them over there and get Eli settled in."

"Of course," Katie said, lightly touching Clay's arm. "Do you want me to wait for you, or should I go home?"

"It shouldn't be more than an hour. I'd like you to stay if you can."

She stepped closer to him and gave him a foolishly romantic kiss. "Go take care of your friends. I'll be here."

As Ben continued to tend bar, Katie finished wiping down the booths before tossing her rag in the laundry basket behind the bar. "There's not much for me to do on the floor until everyone leaves," she said to Ben, "so I'll go check the kitchen and make sure it's clean."

An hour later, Ben rang the bell that signaled last call. Although most of the customers had left when the band had stopped playing for the night, a table of stragglers ordered one more round of drinks and a bowl of pretzels before making their departure. By the time the bar was cleared, ninety minutes had passed since Clay had been called away.

When Katie joined Ben behind the bar, she asked, "Have you heard from Clay?"

"That was him on the phone," Ben replied. "Said he'll make it back in about ten."

"What's the word on Eli?"

"Nothing too serious. He has a slight fracture in his left ankle, along with some cuts and bruises and a slight concussion. It appears as if the driver of the other car ran a red light."

"No doubt Eli's car is totaled, which is going to be a tough break," Katie frowned. "He was relying on having wheels for school next semester. I'll have to give Tess a call in the morning and see if there's anything I can do for them."

"You can always work her shift tomorrow if she can't make it in."

"I'll be sure to make the offer, but somehow I think she's going to need the paycheck."

"Especially if she's going to help the kid pay for a new used car," Ben said sympathetically.

"I'll do the final wipe-down of the tables," Katie said, grabbing a clean rag. "Unless you need help kicking C.J. out."

Ben looked toward the end of the bar where C.J. sat, nursing his beer. "I've got it covered. I told him I'd drive him home." Turning back to Katie, he said, "You were a godsend tonight. I hope you realize that. Thanks for jumping in."

"I kind of enjoyed it. Not what I had expected to be doing on a Saturday night, but I had fun."

When Katie's cell phone buzzed, she was relieved to see it was Clay.

"I was getting worried," she said once they were connected. "We were expecting you to be back by now."

"It took more time then I figured it would to get Eli into the house and comfortable on Tess's couch. I also needed to do some hand-holding. With Tess, that is. Not Eli."

"You're a good friend, and I'm sure Tess appreciates what you're doing for them."

"I just got into my car, and this time I promise to make it back there in ten, fifteen minutes tops. Can you wait?"

"Ben's on his way out with C.J. but I can stay."

"Stay the night?" Clay asked optimistically.

"I can do that, yeah," Katie said quietly.

"Then I can make it in ten."

Grinning as she disconnected the call, she faced Ben and said, "I'm going to stay. Clay's not far out."

"That's cool. Lock up after me," he said as he led C.J. out the front door.

After securing the locks, she walked behind the bar, noting the laundry basket filled with the discarded aprons, rags, and dishtowels. Grabbing the basket, she headed for the back room where Clay kept a small washer and dryer. She started a load, then returned to the bar, noting how quiet it was with the absence of all the talk, laughter, and music that usually filled the area. She let her eyes slowly sweep the room, and for the first time really saw what Clay had built here.

Katie knew that a good share of the décor recreated his grandparents' pub back in Ireland. But here, Clay had successfully blended the old Irish traditions with his more modern American ones, presenting a venue that appealed to a community of people looking for a good, clean place to enjoy a meal, a few drinks and on weekends, some great entertainment.

Running her hand along the now polished bar, Katie tried to imagine the pride Clay must have felt when he'd opened the front door to Clancy's for the very first time. There had to have been pure exhilaration, mixed with a charged sense of accomplishment. Clancy's had been the fulfillment of a dream to honor his heritage, his family. Had he totally understood on that day that he'd succeeded in bringing all that together? she wondered. Did he often think of it still, today?

She heard the back door open before seeing the light in the back hallway go on. "Katie, it's me," Clay called out in that strong, reassuring voice. "You still here?"

When Clay walked through the doorway into the bar, he saw Katie sitting on an end bar stool, her eyes glistening from the lights above, her hands folded neatly in her lap. "I'm here," he heard her say, barely loud enough to carry across the room.

She stood, slowly making her way to him. Cupping his face between her hands, she lightly touched her lips to his. "I'm here," she repeated before kissing him again, this time with a hunger he recognized.

"I need to set the alarm," he managed to say, pulling her toward him so their bodies made contact, making sure she understood his intentions. "Don't move," he instructed. After setting the alarm, he returned, lifted her off her feet and carried her toward the back stairs.

"What about the alarm on the back door?" she asked, trailing those soft, unbearably seductive lips down the side of his neck.

"Set when I came in," he mumbled as he carried her up the stairs, into his apartment, and directly toward the bedroom. Together, they fell onto the bed and immediately began ripping at each other's clothes, tossing aside all the unwanted material.

"This is going to be fast and furious," Clay warned Katie as he dragged her slacks down over her hips.

"I wouldn't have it any other way," she gasped when he moved his lean, naked body over hers. "Give it your best shot, barkeep."

CHAPTER EIGHTEEN

The following morning, Clay had Katie boxed against the side of her car, sharing a passionate kiss.

"Have you recuperated from last night?" he asked, leaning back slightly.

"Depends," she said with humor in her voice. "Are you talking about the party of seven from Pendleton who, by the way, will be calling for another reservation next month? Or maybe the Red Devil softball team that closed the bar? And, by the way, I got three interesting propositions from members of that group. Or, and this is probably the one you're referring to, that award-winning sex I was forced to endure with the pub's owner?"

"Let's start with the sex," he said, smiling down at her.

"The answer is yes. My recuperative powers are amazing."

"Good to know. I was wondering if you'd have time for dinner tonight. We can eat here or maybe go to that Italian restaurant around the corner."

"Sounds tempting, but I've got a list full of things to get done today. Those few days back home put me behind. I'm going into Pendleton later to pick up art supplies, among other things. I also need to restock my kitchen. How about after I hit Franklin's I stop by for a drink?"

"I'd like that. Want to stay the night?"

"You're insatiable." Katie said, shaking her head. "Let me see how the day goes, and we can talk about it later."

Giving her one last kiss, Clay opened the car door for her. "Drive safely."

"Always do," she said, bringing the car's engine to life. "See you later."

Katie drove off, running through a mental list of everything she needed to do. Increasing her speed once she hit the highway, she decided that if she wanted to get Clay on that list, she had to get moving.

Katie drove along Baxter Street in downtown Abbott after spending a long, tiresome day in Pendleton. As she pulled into a parking space in front of Franklin's Food Mart, she debated whether to make a quick stop at the Book-Nook before doing her grocery shopping. As reading was her third greatest obsession behind painting and photography, the debate was a short one.

"Hey there, Katie. How's my favorite customer doing?"

Katie glanced up from the book she'd pulled off the shelf to see the bookstore's owner, Danny Walsh, standing at the end of the aisle holding a cup of hot tea. He was an average-looking man— medium height, medium build, medium skin tone—and was clean shaven. His hair color was a fusion of varying shades of blond, and although it was cut rather conservatively for someone under thirty, there were sections of strands that spiked up uncontrollably, giving it a rebellious look. Small diamond earrings winked from both ear lobes and his thin, frameless glasses were hanging from his neck by a gold-toned braided chain. Katie found him to be an eclectic individual and one who was extremely accommodating when it came to finding her a specific book if he didn't have it in stock. She liked him.

"Hey, Danny," she acknowledged his question with a smile. "Life's not too bad, how about you?"

"Can't complain. Can I help you find something?"

"I'm just browsing right now. You have some new releases here that look pretty good," she added, holding up the book in her hand.

"That one arrived yesterday. We also have some new fiction up front. Some authors I think you'd like. I'm around, so holler if you need anything."

"I will, thanks."

A short time later, Nathan Hunter entered the bookstore to the jingle of a tiny bell that hung over the door. He stopped near the entryway and let his eyes travel along the walls and front shelves, impressed with the way the owner kept his store clean and organized.

A small area next to the checkout counter was reserved for young children, and although it was cluttered, it still seemed controlled and orderly. There was a shoebox filled with crayons sitting on top of the short round table next to a stack of coloring books. A bookrack filled with children's reading materials hung low on the brightly painted wall. Even the two young boys who sat in colorful plastic chairs at opposite sides of the table appeared to be unusually well behaved.

Against the opposite wall was a coffee station offering both decaf and regular—not a mocha latte or raspberry smoothie in sight—and a polished sit-down counter stretched across the front window, six padded stools pushed neatly under it.

He continued through the store, passing by the humor section, skirting around a grouping of half-priced books, and finally winding his way toward the nonfiction aisle. Although he hadn't planned on visiting the Book-Nook today, he'd been inspired to check it out after stopping at Clancy's to work out next month's schedule for Dakota Gold and running into Tess. She'd mentioned a specific writer who'd recently come out with a new book, and he thought it would be a nice gift to give her when he picked her up for their first date. Nathan smiled as he pictured the look of surprise that would cross Tess's face when he handed her the book along with a bouquet of daisies, also her favorite. Swinging a left past the cooking section, he bumped into Katie, practically knocking her off her feet.

"Jeez, Katie. I'm sorry," he said as he reached out to help keep her from losing her balance. "I wasn't paying attention to where I was going, and my mind was on other things. Did I hurt you?"

"It'll take more than a bump in the cooking section to take me down," she said on a half laugh. "What are you doing in this neck of the woods? No sick kids left in Pendleton?"

"Oh, I'd say enough to keep me out of trouble most days," he replied. "I've got the afternoon off so I drove into Abbott. Clay wants us back at Clancy's, so I was at the pub working out specific dates with Tess."

"He'd be a fool not to put you guys on a regular schedule." Katie said.

"That's exactly what Tess said." Pointing to the book in her hand, he asked, "You enjoy cooking?"

"Not even a little," she smirked. "I have a friend in Redmond who lives and breathes cooking, and her birthday is in a few weeks. Her husband gave me a list of books she's been salivating over."

"If you've got time, we can go to the deli down the street for a bite to eat." Nathan said. "I have to grab a book first, but it won't take long."

"I can't," Katie said with regret. "I still have to hit the food mart and then I'm meeting up with Clay. Can we make it another time?"

"Sounds good. Let me know when," Nathan said as he gave Katie a quick wave of the hand and turned toward the back of the bookstore."

Katie's next-to-last stop was Franklin's Food Mart, and she was thankful that she only had a few items to pick up. Although she'd done the bulk of her shopping in Pendleton, Owen always had a nice selection of fruits and vegetables as well as some specialty items she'd found to be both delicious and easy to fix. She would make a quick pass through her favorite aisles, then head over to Clancy's. If she decided to stay the night, she could store the groceries in Clay's refrigerator.

She hit the produce aisle first, deliberating on which fruits and vegetables looked promising. In the end, she randomly tossed some of the more colorful items into her basket and began inching her way around a display of laundry detergent.

She crossed over to the refrigerated section of the store, deciding that she could afford a few frozen dinners now that she had fresh fruit in her basket. As she pulled on the tall glass door, she hesitated when she heard a young angry voice yelling at Owen. She closed the door and slowly edged to the next aisle so she had an unobstructed view of the front counter.

What she saw made her blood go cold. The other man's back was to her, but she could see Owen's frightened, yet restrained face. She could also clearly see the handgun the young man was waving at the owner.

"Stop stalling. Put the money in the bag now or I'll shoot you dead."

Katie couldn't hear any other customers in the store and vaguely recalled that when she'd arrived there had been only one car in the lot. It was very possible that she and Owen were the only two left inside. Well, other than the man who was now pacing in front of the counter as Owen pulled the money out of the cash drawer.

Slowly, Katie set her plastic basket on the floor and reached into her pocket for her cell phone. She backed up several steps so she wouldn't be visible to the intruder and dialed 911.

When the dispatcher answered, she whispered, "I'm at Franklin's Food Mart. Owen is being robbed at gunpoint."

"Ma'am, you have to speak up. Where are you?"

"Franklin's Food. Being robbed. Gunpoint." She tried to punctuate each word without raising her voice, and when the dispatcher didn't respond, she was afraid that he'd hung up.

But then she heard him say, "Franklin's Food Mart on Baxter. We had the silent alarm go off. Are you somewhere safe inside the store?"

"Yes."

"Where is the gunman?"

"Front."

"Is that where Owen is?"

"Yes."

"How many others are in the store?"

"As far as I know, just me. I don't see anyone else."

"Who's back there?" The sharp and nervous sounding voice bellowed from the front of the store.

Katie squatted on the floor behind the shelf that divided aisles six and seven. "He heard me," she desperately relayed to the dispatcher.

"Police are on their way. Can you tell me your name?"

"Where are you, bitch? Come out right now or I'll shoot the old guy. Do you really want that on your head?"

Katie went silent. She could hear the dispatcher relaying information on the other end of the phone, but her attention was now focused on the man's voice coming from the front of the store. She could swear that she'd heard that voice somewhere before tonight.

Suddenly, her fear nearly paralyzed her as recognition bloomed. It was Patrick Lynch, the man who'd created havoc at Clancy's Pub weeks earlier. She remembered the damage he had left in his wake that night, evidence of how out of control he'd been. In addition to the shattered mirror, it had been the only time she'd witnessed Ben bring out the baseball bat normally kept under the bar, keeping it within arm's reach.

Her pulse began to race as Patrick's voice once again rang out, only this time closer to where she crouched. "This is the last time I'm going to ask," he growled. "Who's back there?"

Seconds before he appeared, dragging Owen along by his shirt collar, Katie managed to drop her phone in the shopping basket with the line still open. Patrick pointed the gun at her and said, "Get up. Get up, now!"

She carefully stood with her hands raised. "I'm getting up," her voice quivered. "I'm up."

Patrick pushed Owen in her general direction, and she felt the impact of the man's bulk as he stumbled into her. "Into the men's room. Both of you."

They all began to move toward the front of the store, Katie and Owen several feet in front of Patrick. "I'm going to need you to do what I tell you, you got it? Do what I say and I'll leave, no trouble. Just keep moving and—"

The three of them stopped dead in their tracks as a black and white police cruiser roared toward the store then pulled in tight against the side of the building across the street.

"Damn it!" Patrick spat with some heat.

A sentiment that was echoed silently by both Owen and Katie.

Taking hold of Owen by the back of his shirt, the man said, "You tripped the alarm. You son of a bitch, you tripped the alarm."

"Patrick, listen to me. It's not too late to make things right, son."

"It is too late," Patrick yelled. "I can't make it right this time."

Katie watched in terror as Patrick, desperate to the point of giving up, struck Owen across the face with the barrel of the gun. She heard the sound of metal meeting bone and involuntarily cried out. When Owen fell, she automatically dropped beside him to offer help.

"Leave that son of a bitch alone!" Patrick screamed as he dragged Katie to her feet. Holding tight to her upper arm, he spun around and aimed a vicious kick at Owen's side. Owen cried out in pain, but Patrick didn't care as he took a step back and drilled him with a second kick.

"Patrick, please. Stop." Katie tried to pull him away from Owen, but the young man was too out of control to care that he was making things worse.

She tried again, this time pushing herself into his body. "Patrick. You don't want to hurt Owen. Don't make this worse."

She was standing face to face with him now, looking straight into his eyes. And it frightened her to see that there was no life left in them. No hope.

"This is the Abbott Police," a male voice calmly spoke through a bullhorn. "Lay your weapon down on the front counter and come out of the store with your hands raised. We don't want anyone to get hurt."

Patrick glanced toward the front door and only then realized that he was visible through the glass. He tightened his grip on Katie's arm and pulled her behind the nearest shelf of paper products. "Stick your head around the corner and tell me how many cops are out there. And don't lie to me. If you lie, Owen here is dead."

Katie did as she was instructed and counted three squad cars and five police officers. Stepping back behind the shelf she told him what she'd seen.

"Too many," he said to himself as he pushed her to the floor and paced a few steps down the aisle. Katie moved closer to Owen to check his breathing. She'd noticed that his face was pale, and he hadn't moved since Patrick had administered the second kick. She could tell that his nose was broken, and the blood oozing from it was already soaking the front of his shirt. A long gash trailed down his right cheek, and the area around his eye was swollen and discolored.

She skimmed the shelves around her and spotted the rolls of industrial strength paper towels about two feet away. Patrick was still pacing back and forth, mumbling incoherently, and when he turned his back to pace the other way, she sprang up and grabbed the nearest roll. Returning to Owen's side, she hurriedly tore off the plastic wrapping.

"What are you doing?" Patrick yelled as he swung toward her. "Leave him alone. Get away."

"I need to stop the bleeding, Patrick. I really don't think you want him to drown in his own blood."

Of course, she had no idea what he did or didn't want. She'd already asked herself a dozen times why Patrick had chosen Franklin's to rob, what he might have against Owen. All she knew for sure was that his actions were reckless and unwarranted, making him dangerous. *Tread lightly*, she silently warned herself.

Pointing the gun at her head, he marched back to where she knelt. With the end of the barrel pressed hard against her temple, he bent down and snarled, "Leave. Him. Alone."

She dropped the roll of towels and slowly pushed away from Owen's body.

"He should have given me the money and let me go. If he had just let me go, none of this would have happened."

Clay was behind the bar with Joel talking up some of the regulars who had stopped in to watch the soccer game on the cable sports network. Tess was waiting tables—well, the two tables that were currently occupied—and the jukebox quietly played an old country western ballad. Clay always enjoyed this time of day at the pub. The calm before the storm, so to speak. In another hour or so business would pick up, and even though it wouldn't be as busy as a Friday or Saturday night, he'd still serve enough customers to make a small profit.

When the front door swung open, everyone's attention was drawn to C.J. who sprinted toward the bar. "Owen's store is being robbed," he said, his voice sounding more excited than concerned. "Someone says it's Patrick Lynch and that he has a gun. What the hell is wrong with that guy?"

"What about Owen?" Tess asked.

"I don't think anyone knows. The cops are trying to talk Patrick out right now. They've closed off the street, and Gavin Dorn told me that they've tried to call him on the phone but he won't answer."

Two of the customers who were seated at the bar began wandering out the door as Clay asked, "Any customers in the store?"

"Yeah. They think it's only the one," he said, giving Clay a measured look. "Katie Nolan."

"Clay," Tess said softly, resting a hand on her boss's arm.

"Stay here, Joel," he instructed as he tossed the rag under the counter. "You too, Tess. If anyone comes in, you take the grill."

"Sure," Tess said as she watched him rush out of the pub.

The minute he hit the sidewalk, Clay could see the squad cars parked down the street and heard Lieutenant Bryan Firth, the self-appointed negotiator, trying to make contact with Patrick. What a mess, Clay thought as he tried to remember if there had been any recent problems between Patrick and Owen. The two had known each other since Patrick was a kid, pedaling his bike to the store for a pack of gum and a candy bar. In fact, most everyone in Abbott probably knew Patrick, or at least had heard his name.

It was a not-so-unusual story. Star quarterback who'd played college football until he had blown out his knee his sophomore year. Moved back to Abbott, married his high school sweetheart, and worked for a just-getting-by wage at an industrial factory in Pendleton. Regrettably, he'd squandered most of that money on too many prescription pills, alcohol, and the occasional backroom poker game. In fact, during the past year, Clay had been forced to turn him away from Clancy's on more than a few occasions when he'd become argumentative and abusive with the other customers. He'd also provided a safe place for Patrick's wife to stay when he had turned that abusiveness on her.

Yes, Clay knew both Patrick and Sheila, and he believed that he had a vested interest in making sure this all ended safely. Not only for his two friends, but for Owen, and especially Katie.

He moved up the street and stopped at the barricade where Gavin Dorn was standing. "Sorry, Clay. Can't let you get any closer."

"I think I can help, Gavin. I know Patrick, and I think he'll listen to me. Please, just get word to Bryan that I'm willing to try."

Gavin held Clay's stare for a full five seconds. "Stay behind the barricade," he ordered, turning his back to the crowd. He used his shoulder mic to quietly relay the request to the negotiator. Several minutes later, he motioned to Clay. "Lieutenant Firth says I should take you over to him. Between you and me, I think he's hit a brick wall with this guy."

Waving at one of the other officers keeping an eye on the bystanders that had gathered, he yelled, "Gotta take this guy over to the LT. Watch the line."

The two men moved determinedly toward the squad car that was being used as protective cover for the police who stood facing the food mart. When Lieutenant Firth saw Clay approaching, he was the first to speak.

"You may think you can help, Clay, but this is a delicate negotiation. Tell me what you know about him so I can do my job. What might have set him off?"

"Sheila was talking about divorce," Clay began. "I don't think it was common knowledge, and I didn't think Patrick knew. But if she finally told him . . ."

"Yeah, that would have done it." Firth said. Turning his attention back to the storefront, he scratched his chin, mentally running through a number of strategical moves that might work. He finally turned to Gavin and said, "Let's get Sheila down here."

Gavin nodded and sprinted off.

Neither Firth nor Clay spoke, both deep in thought. Clay trying to figure out the best way to talk Patrick down and Firth, who had recently filed papers for the upcoming mayoral election, speculating about the political ramifications his decisions would have.

It was Clay's own concern that had him breaking the silence first. "I get that I don't have experience in negotiating, and that's why you're reluctant to use me. But Patrick trusts me, and I might be able to get through to him if you let me give it a try."

"It's not how things are done, Clay."

Clay wanted to argue but chose to remain silent, giving the lieutenant the time to figure out on his own that Clay was right.

"Here's what's going to happen," Firth finally said. "I'm going to try the phone one more time. If he still doesn't answer, you can have your shot."

Inside the food mart, Katie sat helplessly watching Owen's irregular breathing. She'd successfully convinced Patrick to let her roll Owen onto his side before packing towels around his face to help slow down the bleeding. But if Owen didn't get medical help soon he would be in serious trouble.

The ringing started up again, momentarily distracting Patrick from his continuous pacing and disjointed chatter. He stopped and turned to stare at the phone hanging on the wall behind the counter.

"I'm guessing that you don't want to cross in front of the windows to answer that, Patrick," Katie said cautiously. "But I can get it. I promise I'll tell you everything the police say. Will you let me answer the phone?"

He looked down at her as if suddenly realizing she was still there. "Sure, why not?"

The casual tone in his voice worried her, but she had to take the chance that he wouldn't shoot her in the back as she crossed the store to the phone. When she reached the front counter, she lifted the receiver off the hook and turned so she was facing him. He stood there, the gun pointed at Owen, his eyes fixed on her.

"Hello? This is Katie Nolan."

"Katie, this is Lieutenant Firth from the Abbott Police Department. How are you holding up?"

"I'm doing good, Lieutenant Firth. But Owen is hurt. He's unconscious."

"Can Patrick hear what I'm saying, Katie?"

"No."

"What did he ask you?" Patrick snapped, raising the gun so it pointed at her now.

"He asked if you could hear him. I told him you couldn't. He wants to talk to you, Patrick."

"Tell him I'm not stupid. Tell him I know that they'll shoot me the minute I come out into the open."

"I heard him Katie. Tell him that I heard him and that I don't want anyone else to get hurt, including him."

Katie relayed the information.

"I'm not stupid," Patrick chanted as he began to pace again. He reached up, rubbing his forehead with the palm of his hand. "Everyone tells me I am, but I'm not. I'm not stupid."

"He's escalating, Lieutenant Firth. He's all but given up that this will end peacefully."

"We can see you through the glass, Katie. Stay where you are. Do not go back behind the shelf. Understand? If you think he's going to start shooting, drop behind the counter, but do not go back to him."

"I hear what you're saying, but Owen needs help," she whispered.

"Stay on the phone, Katie."

She could hear muffled voices as she continued to watch Patrick. For the moment, his attention was diverted to the struggle inside his head and not on either Owen or her, which was good. But she kept herself braced for any change.

The next voice she heard came through the bullhorn.

"Hey, Patrick. This is Clay. I'm guessing that you're having some problems, buddy, and I want to help. But you need to go to the phone so you can talk to me. No one out here wants anyone else to get hurt. We only want to talk this through. Can you go to the phone?"

Katie had seen the change come over Patrick the minute he'd heard Clay's voice. The hand holding the gun dropped to his side, and his whole body seemed to relax. He turned toward the front door, even though he was still blocked from seeing anyone on the other side, and the sound of his friend's voice seemed to soothe.

"He's paying attention," Katie said into the phone. "Tell Clay that Patrick is paying attention to what he's saying."

"I can imagine how rough it's been for you lately," Clay continued, "especially with the trouble at work today." He knew this because Sheila had gotten word to the lieutenant that her husband had been laid off. "But you can get through all that. You know that I'll help you out, but you've got to put the gun down. You've got to come out peacefully and unarmed so we can help you."

Patrick was looking at Katie now, staring at her and shaking his head slowly. "Tell him I appreciate his wanting to help. But it's too late. How does that saying go?" he said scratching the side of his head. "Oh yeah, tell him it's too little, too late."

Katie passed along what he'd said and added, "He's giving up."

"Katie, listen to me," Firth said. "We're about ready to come in through both the back and front doors. When I give you the word, you have to drop to the floor. Flat onto the floor. Do you understand?"

Frozen in place by Patrick's stare, all Katie could manage was a slow nod of the head.

"Katie?" Patrick said. "Be a good girl and hang up the phone now."

The calmness in his voice sent a deadly chill down Katie's back. "But if I put the phone down, Patrick, I won't be able to tell you what Lieutenant Firth says."

"Get ready, Katie," Firth said through the phone's receiver. "We're coming in on three. One—"

"I don't want to talk to the police anymore, so hang up the phone," Patrick repeated quietly.

"Two—"

"Katie. Please," Patrick pleaded. "Will you please hang up the phone."

Katie watched Patrick raise the gun in her direction at the same time she heard Lieutenant Firth give her final instructions. "Now, Katie. Get down."

Katie let the receiver drop out of her hand as she dived for the floor, hearing the sound of glass breaking at the back of the store seconds before the front door crashed opened. Even though the police were shouting out orders, their boots pounding hard as they crossed the tile floor, it was Patrick's quiet voice that reached her. "I'm sorry, Sheila."

The single gunshot had Katie covering her ears and frantically praying that no one had been hurt.

CHAPTER NINETEEN

Daylight had surrendered to night by the time Katie was escorted from the store and taken to the ambulance that was parked in front of the Italian restaurant. Clay sat beside her on the vehicle's back runner, holding her hand loosely in his. She'd already told the paramedic she wasn't injured, but he had insisted she stay put so they could make sure.

Owen Franklin had been rushed to the hospital in another ambulance, and Patrick had been whisked away in one of the squad cars, unharmed. Inside the store, the police continued their investigation, which included digging out the bullet that had wedged itself in the wall directly above the hideous clock that was shaped like a trout. Lieutenant Firth was going with the theory that Patrick Lynch had accidentally discharged his weapon when he saw the cops entering the store, and that he hadn't intended to shoot anyone. Katie was willing to go along with that assessment.

"Are you really all right?" Clay asked her now, concern shadowing his face.

"Yes, I am," she replied, pulling her jacket tight in an attempt to ward off the sudden chill in the air. "I'm sorry about your friend."

"I'm sorry, too. I only wish he'd come to me before . . ."

"Sometimes rock bottom is the only solid ground a person has," she said gently.

"I guess."

"You couldn't have known he'd do this, Clay. And he wasn't willing to let you help. Hopefully that will change now."

"I hope it does."

He stretched his arm around her shoulders and gently pulled her close. "God, Katie. What a mess."

"I know."

His lips brushed across her forehead as he mumbled, "EMT at six o'clock. He'll want you to go to the hospital to be checked out."

"Well, we don't always get what we want, do we?"

He chuckled and dropped his arm as he moved aside to let the EMT examine Katie. When all was said and done, the ambulance drove away, minus a patient.

Clay started toward the one remaining police car where Katie was now standing. Placing his hand lightly on her lower back, he said, "Why don't you come into Clancy's with me. I'll fix you a real Irish coffee to settle your nerves."

"I don't think so. I wouldn't be able to deal with all the questions everyone will have."

"Then let me drive you home. We can deal with your car tomorrow."

"I don't need you fussing over me, Clay. I'm fine." But even as the words came out of her mouth, Katie knew they weren't completely true.

She turned to face the food mart, getting her first clear look at the damage that had been done. How could she be fine after being in the center of all that? How could she simply go home and forget about Owen? He'd looked at her with such pain in his eyes as she'd begged Patrick to stop hurting him. She knew it would be a long time before she could forget that look.

She closed her eyes, unable to stop the vivid memory of how Patrick had held that gun to her head, and how terrified she'd been that with one pull of the trigger, her life would have been over. She had never felt that level of fear before and prayed to God she'd never feel it again.

Clay pulled her into his arms. "You're exhausted, Katie, and the adrenaline that kept you going inside the store is fading. I can see it on your face."

She pulled back slightly to look at Clay. "It's going to take some work to clean everything up, isn't it?" she asked, almost as if she hadn't heard him speak. "I'll have to call Owen tomorrow and tell him I'll help. Someone will board up the broken window, won't they? And make sure the place is locked up?"

"The police will take care of everything," he replied gently. "Come on, sweetie, I'm taking you home."

She hesitated for only a moment before letting Clay steer her toward the alley behind the pub where his vehicle was parked. "I'll have to get Ian or Dean to drive me back tomorrow to pick up my car."

"Don't worry about that now," Clay said. "It'll all work out tomorrow, I promise."

When they reached the car, Clay opened the door for Katie, recognizing that what had happened inside that grocery mart had finally hit her. The look in her eyes had changed, the light that always seemed to be there dimmed. Clay's heart ached for this strong, independent woman who now looked vulnerable.

Tomorrow, when reality set in, she would find a way to deal with it, he thought. For tonight, he would be her strength. He would support her in whatever way she needed. Then, come morning, when he was sure she had her feet planted firmly on the ground, he'd drive her back here to pick up her car.

Because there was no way he was going to leave her alone tonight.

When Ian heard the car's engine, he stepped out of his jeep. He'd been killing time working on his computer tablet while waiting for

Katie to return. Now, as Clay pulled up to the cottage, Ian's full attention turned to her.

"Heard you had quite an ordeal tonight," he began as he held the car door open for Katie.

"You could say that," she replied indifferently. "One I hope I never have to experience again."

Ian had already spotted the cut on her head. Placing one hand on her shoulder, he lifted the other to her chin and gently moved her head to the side to get a better view. "A cold pack should help lessen the bruising."

"I already heard that from the EMT. But thanks."

"Are you okay?" he asked, moving aside so she could make her way to the cottage door.

"I will be," she said. "Owen got the worst of it."

"The good news is that he'll spend the night in the hospital and be reevaluated tomorrow. If everything looks good, he'll be released."

Katie stopped and turned back to Ian. "How *did* you hear?" she asked, her irritability showing. "How did you hear about any of this?"

"Arthur got a call, and he called me. He was concerned about you, and I told him I'd make sure you were okay."

She seemed to consider that for a moment before she used her key to unlock the front door. Once inside, she disengaged the alarm. Tossing her purse on the couch, she started toward the bedroom. "Tell Arthur not to worry, and that I'll see him in the morning. I'm going to bed."

When Clay heard her close the bedroom door, he said, "I guess she's done with us for the night." Moving toward the kitchen he added, "I'm getting something to drink. Do you want anything?"

"No, I'm good, thanks. Are you planning to stay here?"

"I am," Clay said with finality. "I'll sleep in the car if she doesn't want me inside." He pulled a diet soda out of the refrigerator. After popping the pull tab, he took a healthy swig. "She either doesn't want to admit it or isn't fully aware of how this has shaken her. Did you get a good look at her? I've never seen a woman that pale."

"What about you? How are you doing?" Ian asked as he continued to watch Clay. "It must have been hard for you, too. Being stuck on the outside while someone you care about is being threatened at gunpoint."

Clay set the half empty can on the kitchen counter, then ran his fingers through his thick head of hair. "I felt helpless," he confessed. "I consider Patrick Lynch and I to be friends, and I never thought he'd do something like this. Even knowing that he'd been having problems at home, then finding out tonight that he'd been laid-off. I still would never have believed he'd hurt someone he's known all his life just for the few bucks in that man's cash register."

"By all accounts, Owen is going to be back on his feet in no time," Ian said, stepping further into the living room. "Katie will bounce back, too. She's safe now. Here, with you. She might give you a hard time about it, but she's a smart girl. She'll realize soon enough that you're here to provide comfort and support. She needs both right now."

"Whether she wants it or not?"

Ian grinned. "Whether she wants it or not. Need anything before I go?"

Clay gave Ian a long look. "Who called Arthur tonight?"

"Well, I don't think I'm breaking any confidences by saying that it was Sheriff Bradley. He and Arthur go way back, and he's aware that Katie is staying here. He wanted us to have a heads-up."

"Small town, no secrets," Clay mumbled. "It took me a long time to get used to that when I moved here."

Nodding, Ian turned toward the front door. "Katie has my number in her cell phone. Don't hesitate to call if you need me."

After Ian closed the door behind him, Clay moved quietly toward the hallway, not surprised that the bedroom door was still closed.

No problem, he could wait her out. And if she wasn't out in another hour or so, he'd check on her. Like it or not, he did care about Katie Nolan, and she'd have to damn well get used to it.

After Ian left Katie and Clay safely tucked away in the cottage, he drove up to the main house to speak with Arthur.

"It appears as if Katie was in the wrong place at the wrong time," Ian said, concluding his report.

"She could have been killed," Arthur stated in a subdued tone.

"But she wasn't," Ian responded. "After we spoke earlier, I called Bryan Firth, who was the negotiator on scene, and he said Katie did all the right things. He doesn't believe that Patrick Lynch wanted to harm anyone. He just lost control of the situation."

"Where is Patrick now?"

"He'll spend at least tonight in jail. Depending on the charges and bail amount, it may be more."

"And Owen? How is he doing?"

"Better than anyone expected. Facial wounds, lacerations, a battered rib or two that will be more of an annoyance to him than anything else. Knowing Owen, he'll be back at the store tomorrow, if not the next day."

Leaning back in his chair, Arthur sighed. "It's best if I wait until tomorrow to see her, although I want nothing more than to go down there tonight."

"She looked pretty beat when I left her at the door. Said she was going straight to bed. And besides, Clay is there."

"Best if I wait then," Arthur sighed.

Ian rose, prepared to leave, but stopped when Arthur said, "I depend on you for a lot, Ian. I hope you realize how important that is to me. How important you are to me."

"Get some sleep, Arthur," Ian said after a brief hesitation. "You look pretty beat yourself."

"I will. Goodnight."

Arthur stood and moved to the window that faced the back of his land and remained there long after Ian left. His thoughts were scattered, but finally circled around to Marian and Katie.

After he and Marian had gone their separate ways, there had been days when he'd nearly called and begged her to come back to him. Not being able to touch her—to see her smile or hear the sound of her voice—had been hell for him. But he'd made a promise to her to stay away, and he'd kept that promise, until now. Not so surprisingly, it had been Katie's presence in his life that had finally convinced him it was time to reconcile with Marian.

Over the past few weeks, he'd called her on a number of occasions to see how she was doing. He'd also seen her twice on trips to California, the most recent visit turning out to be the most gratifying.

He'd arrived in Long Beach after a day and a half of strenuous meetings regarding his newest restaurant venture. At first, she'd been tentative about accepting his offer to join him for dinner. It wasn't until he'd turned on the Reddington charm, insisting that they could make it an early evening if that was better for her, that she'd finally agreed to see him. He'd sent a car for her, and the driver had delivered her to the elegant restaurant at the hotel where Arthur was staying. They'd dined over candlelight and champagne and talked about everything and nothing. She told him about Katie, sharing stories she thought he would enjoy, and he told her about the success of his wineries and restaurants. She lightly touched his hand when he told her of his mother's passing, and he had repeated the intimacy when she spoke of the struggle she and Robert had endured during his illness. They had been the last couple to leave the restaurant.

"Can you join me for a nightcap, Marian?" he'd asked softly when they reached the hotel lobby. "Please say you'll come up."

Marian had agreed, and for that one night they had rekindled feelings they both had become skilled at suppressing for too many years. For that one night, the feelings that had once been buried memories came back to life. And that one night was all he'd needed to believe there could be more.

"I just got home and saw your light on, Uncle Arthur. What are you doing up so late?"

Arthur was startled from his thoughts by his niece's voice. He gave her the abridged version of what had happened at Franklin's Food Mart earlier.

"Maybe I should go check on Katie," she said. "I admit that she and I haven't always seen eye to eye on things, but this must have shaken her up some."

During the past few weeks, Arthur had seen a change in Hannah that had both surprised and pleased him. It was true that she and Katie had butted heads on more than a few occasions, but he truly believed that Katie was having a positive influence on his niece.

"Ian spoke to her a short time ago, and she said she was going to bed. Clay is going to spend the night there. I'd appreciate you checking on her in the morning, though."

"I will. You should turn in for the night, too. You look tired."

"That seems to be the general consensus. And you're right. I am."

He walked over to his desk and turned off the lamp. "Come on, kiddo. I'll walk you upstairs."

The water had turned cold by the time Katie dragged herself out of the tub and the lavender-scented bath salts had only marginally reduced the stress she'd carried through the front door earlier. Wrapping a towel around her torso, she extinguished the single candle she'd placed on the counter next to the sink, turned out the lights, and headed back into her bedroom.

For the last hour, she'd fought hard to chase away the memories of what had gone down in Owen's store. The pure terror she'd felt every time Patrick had pointed that loaded gun at her. The panic she'd tried to keep in check as she'd frantically tried to help Owen, bruised and bleeding on the floor. She'd seen the total despair shadowed in Patrick's eyes, signaling that he was ready to give up. To relinquish any hope for forgiveness from his wife, from Owen, and from the friend who had tried desperately to talk him into giving himself up. The same friend who was now slumped in the rocking chair he'd pulled in from the living room and set in the corner next to her bed. Clay's legs were stretched out in front of him, his head tilted to one side, held in place by his fisted hand. His barely audible snoring reminded her of the cherished family dog she'd had growing up.

She stood in the doorway for a moment watching him, relieved that he had stayed. Even though the bath hadn't done much to help her forget, it had made her realize that she hadn't wanted to be alone tonight. And what a blessing to have a man in her life who had understood that.

She slipped into her pajamas before going to Clay. Crouching down in front of him, she gently touched his knee. He woke instantly, those deep blue eyes latching onto hers. He leaned forward and touched her cheek, searching her face for signs of how she was coping.

"I wasn't sure if you'd left or not," she said, giving him a reassuring smile. "I'm glad you didn't."

"I'm not going anywhere," he said, returning her smile.

Katie could see the concern in his eyes, reminding her that he had gone through a range of emotions himself tonight. "How are you doing?" she asked.

"I'm good."

"I know it's late," she said quietly.

"I'll stay for as long as you need me," he replied, touching his lips to hers.

Katie rose, taking Clay's hand as she led him to the bed. She climbed in first, sliding her feet beneath the covers while he removed his shoes, belt and jeans. Still wearing his boxers and T-shirt, he moved in beside her. When they were finally laying side by side— her head resting comfortably on his chest, his arm securely wrapped around her shoulders—she released a heavy sigh.

Running his hand across her hair, Clay kissed the crown of her head and said, "Go to sleep now, baby. I've got you."

CHAPTER TWENTY

Several days after the attempted robbery at Owen's store, Katie was sitting on one of the rustic benches in the garden, enjoying the beauty of the rambling roses and wisteria, the fluidity of the poppies and lavender, and the soothing chirp of the lone warbler that perched on the edge of the fountain.

She'd been here for nearly a half hour, ever since experiencing what she referred to as painter's block—the inability to draw a straight line or mix the right colors that would breathe life into her painting. Rather than continue the struggle, she'd taken a leisurely walk around the house, ending up in the center of this cabaret of sight, sound, and smell.

She closed her eyes and raised her head to the sun's warmth when a new scent reached her nostrils. French fries? She turned to find Hannah walking toward her carrying a white paper bag.

"We thought you might be hungry," she said, setting the bag next to Katie on the bench.

"We?" Katie asked as she unfolded the top of the bag to find a cardboard container inside. Lifting it out, she discovered the roast beef sandwich, fries, and four pickle halves.

"I had to go to the Book-Nook and happened to run into Clay. He wanted to make sure you were eating."

Katie glanced up at Hannah, and the expression on her face told Katie the idea hadn't only been Clay's. "This combination," she said, pointing to the container, "could easily become the new comfort food."

"We could start a campaign on Twitter," Hannah said, offering up a grin.

"Why don't you sit down and have half of the sandwich." Katie gestured to the opposite end of the bench, then set the container between them. "Help yourself to some fries, too."

After taking a satisfying bite from the sandwich, Hannah said, "I stopped by the cottage the morning after the robbery, but Clay said you were still asleep."

"Yes, he told me. I've been meaning to thank you, but we always seem to miss each other."

"It must have been terrifying. I can't imagine what Patrick thought he was doing. Owen is such a sweet guy. And you . . . you'd never hurt a fly."

Katie smiled at that. "I think Patrick had a huge lapse of judgment, thinking he was at his rope's end. He didn't mean for it to go as far as it did."

"I guess. I heard he's out on bail."

"He is. Clay phoned this morning with the news."

"Owen's planning to reopen the store tomorrow."

"I heard that, too. In fact, I was helping him with the clean-up yesterday."

"Oh," Hannah said. "If I had known, I'd have pitched in. I like Owen."

"I think he's going to be limited in what he can do for at least a few more days, so you might want to stop by and see if he needs anything. I think he'd appreciate that."

"Yeah, maybe I will."

They were both silent for several minutes until Hannah spoke.

"I'm sorry I've given you such a hard time. I'm usually not that difficult. My only defense is that I became territorial over the cottage and the time I spend here with Uncle Arthur." When Katie didn't respond, Hannah tried to explain. "I've been told that people think I can be selfish. And I admit that there may be some truth to that. But this time, I wasn't aware that Uncle Arthur had hired you until after I arrived, and it surprised me, I guess. Then after being such a bitch to you, I had no clue how to gracefully back down." Looking over, she added, "I really am sorry, Katie."

"I accept your apology," Katie said sincerely. "I never took you for being someone who is selfish to the point that other people don't matter. I think that deep down, you're kind, generous and . . . okay, a little bit selfish. But in a good way," she concluded with a spurt of laughter. "I like you, Hannah. And I think we make better friends then we do adversaries."

"I agree."

Another pause in the conversation before Hannah asked, "Are you having a hard time dealing with what happened at Franklin's? I don't mean to be rude, but from what I heard, it was awful for you and Owen."

Katie took a minute to form her response. "I'd only met Patrick once before, and that had been at Clancy's when he'd had too much to drink and was on the verge of getting physical. So my impression of him wasn't all that positive. However, Clay told me that he was going through a tough time both in his job and at home and told me a little bit about his and Patrick's friendship. When I discovered that it was him holding up that store, I tried to remember the good that Clay had talked about. Although, when he struck Owen, and pointed his gun at my head? It got more and more difficult to hold on to that.

"Then I saw the despair," Katie continued. "I saw Patrick giving up, and I was so scared that he was going to take Owen and me down that dark hole with him. I'm not sure that I've completely forgiven Patrick for the fear he put in me, but I hope that one day I will. I still feel apprehensive once in a while, but it's lessened and only hits me when I'm alone."

"You were able to go back to the food mart. Yesterday, to help Owen."

"Yes. But it was difficult. I refuse to let what Patrick's done rule my life."

"That's a healthy attitude," Hannah said, reaching for another fry.

Wanting to change the subject, Katie said, "You saw Clay today. How is he doing?"

"He's worried about you, I think." Pointing to the food container, she said, "I don't know anyone who gets that many pickles with their meal."

Placing her hand possessively over the pickle halves, Katie said, "They're mine. You're not the only one who can be selfish."

Fair enough," Hannah replied.

When all the food was consumed and Katie was cleaning off the bench, Hannah said, "I'd like to ask you one more thing. Not about what happened. This is personal. Do you think you could give me a few pointers on photography? I've seen what you can do with a camera, and I'd like to see if it would be something I could become good at."

"I can do that," Katie said. "Why don't we spend a few hours together, maybe two or three times a week. Do you have a camera?"

"Yes. Nothing as fancy as yours I'm sure, but it's a good one."

"Let's start tomorrow, then."

They made plans to meet mid-day. When Hannah walked into the house, Katie headed for her car. Amazing how things turned out, she thought as she drove back to the cottage. Could she and Hannah really end up being friends one day? Katie decided that being friendly was a good start.

CHAPTER TWENTY-ONE

The weather in Abbott—not to mention most of the counties located along the Oregon/Washington border—was unseasonably mild for November. Although the mornings were still brisk and the evenings a tad too chilly, the good news was that snow had yet to make an entrance, and the temperatures during the day hours were more tolerable than they'd been in previous years.

Clay was sitting on the Reddington front porch with Katie when Nora came out with hot cocoa and a bowl of tiny marshmallows. "Didn't know if you take your chocolate with or without the fluff, so I put it on the side," she said with an affectionate smile.

"Nora, you didn't need to do this," Katie said as she moved off the porch swing and took possession of the wicker tray. "But, in all honesty, it sure smells delicious."

"I don't mind doing little things for good folks. If there's anything else you need, you'll have to get it yourselves. I'm ready to retire for the evening."

"Will do," Clay said as he reached for one of the mugs. "And thanks for the hot chocolate. It's going to hit the spot tonight."

She offered up another smile as she waved him off. Stepping back inside the house, she said, "Don't sit out there all night you two. The temperature is supposed to drop."

"We won't," Katie replied as she picked up the second cup and went back to the swing. She folded her right leg under her and wrapped both hands around the cup. "This is superior hot chocolate," she exclaimed after taking her first sip. "I wonder what Nora does with her cocoa to get it to taste this good."

"Didn't you say she worked as a nanny once? That would give her a leg up on the rest of us."

"I guess it would. Kids love their hot chocolate, don't they?"

They sat in companionable silence for several minutes, lamp light from the living room spreading a soft, diffused illumination across the porch. It was only when the grandfather clock in the front hallway softly chimed the eleventh hour that Clay finally spoke.

"Remember me telling you that my grandmother visits every Thanksgiving?"

"And that she closes the bar every night she's here? Yes, I remember."

"Well, she'll be here in another week. Flying in on Tuesday. I'm putting together a spread that would make the Pilgrims weep, and I was wondering if you would join us." He was watching her now and saw the surprise cross her face. "I'm hoping you and your mom will be our guests."

Katie was stunned. She didn't know exactly how to respond to the invitation. "Are you sure?" As soon as the words were out she knew how silly they sounded. "What I mean is, don't you and your grandmother want to spend the holiday alone? Together, alone?"

"Trust me, I love my grandmother, but by Thursday we'll have had enough alone time together. Besides, she's used to a crowded Thanksgiving dinner, and she's looking forward to meeting you. Tess and her son will also be coming, I think, and I figured to ask Nora and Hannah and Arthur, too."

"Well, damn, Clay. What's gotten into you?"

He laughed as he reached over and covered her hand with his. "I have a lot to be thankful for this year, and I want to share my joy. Is that so wrong?"

She took a deeper look at the man facing her and saw the truth in his simple explanation. He wanted to share a meal with the people who gave meaning to his life. Period. How could she say no to that?

"I was going to fly home and spend Thanksgiving there, but I'll call my mother and see if she'll come here instead. I told you about my cousin's wedding in Boise that weekend. Having Mom here might even work out better. We can drive there instead of flying, which is something I think she'd enjoy more."

"Great. I'm looking forward to meeting her," Clay said as he pushed to his feet. "Right now, I need to get going. It's my night off, but I want to check on the bar. Walk me to my car?" They climbed down the porch steps and walked around to the side of the house where Clay had parked. "It was nice of Arthur to invite me to dinner tonight."

"We try to have dinner together at least once a week to catch up on things. And he recognizes that you and I have been spending a lot of time together. When are you going to ask him about Thanksgiving?"

"I already have." Again, that surprised look. He was truly getting a kick out of that look. "He said that he'd be honored to share Thanksgiving with me and Grandmother Crawford and even offered to host it here. But I graciously declined that offer. It's become tradition to open up Clancy's for Thanksgiving."

"Open it up?"

"Well, maybe I forgot to mention that we'll be serving a number of Abbott residents who would otherwise be celebrating alone."

"Yes, you forgot to mention that tiny bit of information," Katie said, giving him a not-so-gentle poke. "How many are we talking about?"

"A dozen or so."

As the reality of what he was doing sunk into her brain, her heart swelled. "You do this every year?"

"Every year," he said as if it was no big deal.

"What time do you want my mother and me there to help with set up or cooking or whatever else you need?"

Clay leaned down, touching his lips to hers. "You're my guest."

"Not anymore. What time?"

"I'll get back to you on that. Now, I've got to take off." Stealing one final kiss, he slid into the car and slowly pulled away from the house.

Katie picked up the tray with the now empty cups and went indoors, wondering if anyone was still up. She found Arthur in his study, relaxing in his favorite leather recliner, reading a book. When he looked up, he smiled and gestured for her to come closer.

"Clay told me you're going to Clancy's for Thanksgiving."

"Yes, Hannah and me both. Nora is spending the weekend with her sister in Oklahoma, so she won't be able to join us."

"Don't you spend the holiday with your brothers?" she asked as she set the tray on the edge of the sideboard and took a seat across from Arthur.

"Not this year. One is vacationing in France through Christmas and the other one is spending Thanksgiving in Maine with his wife's family, the likes of which I deplore. So I'm grateful I'll have somewhere else to go."

"Clay's invited my mother and if she says yes, which I think she will, I'll have her stay with me. I think you'll like my mother," she added mildly.

Arthur smiled and put his book aside. "I hope she'll be able to make it."

"Yeah, me too." Picking up the tray, Katie stood and walked toward the door. "Well, all I wanted to do was say goodnight. See you in the morning."

"See you then." After Katie left the room, Arthur rose and extinguished first the desk lamp and then the overhead light. He took his time securing the house, and as he climbed the stairs to his bedroom, he let himself think about the possibility that Marian would say yes and join Katie here for the holiday. And the possibility that maybe when she saw him and Katie together—saw how much he truly loved his daughter—she would agree it was time to share the truth. And what a blessed Thanksgiving that would make for all of them.

CHAPTER
TWENTY-TWO

He stepped through the front door of the nursing home, carrying a dozen tulips—his mother's favorite—tied together with a yellow ribbon. He'd also brought a box of candy for the nurses who'd been taking care of her. Wednesday wasn't his regular day to visit, but he'd been invited to join the staff and residents for a pre-Thanksgiving luncheon. With the hope that sharing a meal with the other women and men at the nursing home might spur his mother to at least try to communicate, he'd accepted the invitation.

He stopped at the front desk to sign in—a mandatory formality that all visitors were required to follow. As he scribbled his name on the form, the young receptionist he remembered from previous visits spoke.

"Our administrator has requested to see you before you go to your mother's room. If you could have a seat in the serenity room," she said, pointing to where she wanted him to wait, "Mrs. Bowen will be with you shortly."

As he walked away from the desk, the slim, quiet-speaking girl lifted the handset attached to the switchboard to contact the administrator. He had no idea what the woman wanted to discuss, although it no doubt had to do with money. When he had first brought his mother to this facility, he'd set up an expense account which was used for her personal needs, and maybe the account was running low on funds. If that were the case, he'd give her a check and their business would be done.

Standing in front of a tall, antique armoire, repurposed into a glass-enclosed aviary, he watched as a handful of bright colored birds leaped from perch to perch, chirping madly. He'd been in this room only once before—the day he'd made his mother a permanent resident. Thinking back, he'd almost changed his mind when, as he was saying good-bye, he saw in her eyes what he thought was a plea for him to take her back home. Of course, that had been him projecting his own feelings onto the woman who had long ago begun her slide into a world where he wasn't permitted to follow. Her Alzheimer's disease had forced her thoughts and memories into a dark corner of her mind where they had been solidly locked away. Not even he, her only son, could bring them out into the light.

When he heard the sound of heels on the tiled floor behind him, he turned to see a middle-aged woman with short, cropped hair making her way toward him. "I'm Mrs. Bowen," she said, extending her hand. "Why don't we move over here."

She directed him to a set of moderately comfortable chairs and waited until they were both seated before continuing. "We tried calling you several times but were unsuccessful in our attempts. I'm sorry to have to inform you that your mother passed away early this morning."

Mrs. Bowen paused for a moment, allowing the information to register. Breaking this type of news to a family member wasn't new to her, yet it was the most difficult part of her job. When she continued, her voice was soft and soothing, filled with sympathy and compassion. "I'm sorry for your loss. Our chaplain is waiting to meet with you if you'd like, or I can show you to the room where your mother has been moved. I've cleared my schedule so I can be available to answer any questions you have and to assist you with her transfer to the funeral home you select."

He slowly turned his head to face this virtual stranger who had just told him that he'd lost the one last person in his life who'd ever meant anything to him. "I'd like to see my mother now."

"Of course," Mrs. Bowen said, a bit taken aback by his stiff, unemotional response. "Right this way."

He followed the administrator down one corridor, and then a second. As they closed in on the small, unadorned room where his mother had been taken, he straightened his shoulders, determined to show strength as he said good-bye. That's what she'd want, he thought. That's what his father would have expected.

The room felt stuffy and smelled of some sort of disinfectant cleaner. It was sparsely furnished and painted in a drab, conservative gray. An ivory-colored phone hung on the wall to the left of the open door, next to a round, large numbered clock. A mirror—which seemed to be absurdly out of place to him—was suspended from a nail by a twisted wire and hung on the opposite wall. There was a steel floor cabinet in one corner, the doors shut tight, displaying a sign that warned only staff were allowed inside. In addition to the rhythmic ticking coming from the clock, he caught the soft sound of classical music that he suspected had consoled previous family members who had crossed the threshold of this room to view their loved ones. For him, it wasn't working so well.

He stepped to the side of the gurney, placing the flowers on top of the stark white sheet that covered his mother's body. "I brought these for you, Mom," he said as he stared at her pale and sagging face. Her eyes were closed, and she looked as if she'd aged ten years since the last time he'd visited her. God, he sincerely hoped this wasn't the memory he'd pull out every time he thought of the woman who had raised him.

He dispensed with the box of candy by tossing it on a stainless-steel tray that stood near the foot of the bed. Turning back to his mother, he lightly touched the side of her face and leaned over to kiss her gently on the cheek. "I'll make them pay, Mother," he whispered close to her ear. "Don't you worry. The Nolans will pay."

Turning to leave, he spotted the administrator standing in the hallway outside the room. "Please select a funeral home you've worked with in the past, Mrs. Bowen. One that will take care of my mother properly. You have my address on file. Please send me the necessary paperwork along with your final bill."

Flustered, the woman said, "You're leaving? But there are decisions to be made. We have to—"

"Do what you need to do. I've entrusted you with my mother's care for over a year now, I can certainly entrust you with this. Just get it done. I have to go."

With that, he fled. Once he was in the car, he started the engine and pulled away from the nursing home, driving through eyes scorched with tears and grief. His intent was to head straight back to the cabin, which was the only place where he truly felt safe and in control. But as he left the streets of Medford behind, rage building inside him, he decided to make a stop before going home.

Leaning down, he checked the ankle holster he always wore, making sure his father's knife was there. He knew this trip would be a risky deviation from his master plan, but he could see no way around it. He needed to do this for his mother so she could finally rest in peace.

A little over two hours into his trip, he crossed the California border and stopped at the first gas station he saw. In addition to the fuel, he purchased two large black coffees, the strongest blend they offered. When he was back in the car, he topped off the first cup with a dollop of brandy from the flask he kept in the glove compartment. He sat at the pump for several minutes more, thinking about what had to be done once he reached Long Beach. Yes, returning to the city where it all began would be cleansing, and then he could devote all his time and effort into eliminating the true source of his misery.

CHAPTER
TWENTY-THREE

Clay had been a bit off on his numbers. By Katie's count it was more like twenty-five—men, women and children—all seated at long tables that had been set up in the main bar area. The round tables that normally took up that space had been moved to the storage room as well as Clay's office, making the seating arrangements more in keeping with the traditional family-style dinner. With all the stools removed, the guests had easy access to the buffet that was spread out on the long, polished bar. The smells of oven-roasted turkey and dressing, green bean casserole, mashed potatoes, and cranberry sauce all mixed with the aroma of homemade dinner rolls, freshly baked bread, and a rich French coffee blend. But what truly made this a Thanksgiving feast were the sights and sounds of the diverse group of neighbors and friends who blissfully took Clay at his word when he encouraged everyone to help themselves to seconds and thirds.

Clay sat at the head of one of the two rows of tables. His grandmother and Katie sat to his right and Marian and Arthur to his left. Hannah had chosen a spot down the line next to Tess, and everyone else was scattered here and there, seated next to a family member or neighbor or complete stranger. But the most unusual pairing in the room was Owen Franklin, who had come alone, and was now seated next to Patrick Lynch and his wife Sheila. Katie could tell that everything that had gone down in the food mart hadn't been forgotten, although it appeared that Owen had opened the door to forgiving Patrick. He'd said as much to her earlier, and she was relieved that he had chosen that path.

"I don't think I've ever enjoyed a holiday meal as much as I've enjoyed this one," Marian told Clay as she rested her hand on his forearm and gave it a gentle squeeze. "I'm so glad you invited me."

"I'm glad that you came," he replied, laying his hand on top of hers. "I know Katie wouldn't have missed spending Thanksgiving with you, and I would have been disappointed if she couldn't have spent it with me. So I guess we're all winners."

"I guess you're right. Now, I insist on helping Katie clear the tables," she added as she rose, offering her daughter a wink of solidarity.

Chuckling, Katie said, "My mother can be subtle when the occasion calls for it." On her way to the kitchen, Katie tapped Hannah on the shoulder and said, "Come on, you're helping." Surprisingly, Hannah didn't argue and was extremely pleasant to the diners as she gathered a tub full of dirty plates and glasses.

"I bet they're going to need an extra set of hands in there," Faye Crawford said as she rose out of the chair.

"Why don't you sit and relax for a minute," Clay responded, guiding his grandmother back down. "You've been cooking since dawn, and you were the point person when it came time to set up. Let the other ladies get the dishes, and when people are ready to leave, you can help wrap up the food."

"Actually my legs could use a bit of a rest, yet. Getting old certainly isn't for the weak, I'll tell you that much."

Smiling, Arthur said, "Now that I'm aware of who's responsible for this delicious meal, I'd like to pass along my compliments to the cook. Thank you, Faye."

"Oh, I had help with everything. My grandson here likes to exaggerate some. But thank you all the same."

"And Clay? Well done. This is quite the gathering."

Clay nodded his thanks and said, "I should go help out with dessert. The crowd seems to be getting restless for those pies."

"No, you stay put with your grandmother," Arthur said as he pushed out of his chair. "I'll see to it, although I'm sure the women have everything organized. Excuse me."

When he stepped through the kitchen doors, he noted that Tess was already slicing up the pies as Marian, Katie, and Hannah were stacking dirty dishes near the sink. "When you girls are through there," Tess was saying, "I'd certainly appreciate your help with these. Marian, I'll continue to cut if you can put the slices on plates. Katie, you and Hannah can use those trays over there to carry the plates out and just give everybody what they want. We've certainly got plenty. There's apple, pumpkin, and lemon meringue—the latter, courtesy of Marian."

"They're the best lemon meringue pies you'll ever have," Katie added with a touch of pride.

"I'll help Marian dish out the slices," Arthur said as he walked over to the prep table. "The natives are going to start banging their forks on the table if we don't get this dessert out there soon."

Marian's hand jerked when she heard Arthur's voice behind her. It had been one thing to carry on a friendly conversation with him during dinner, but now, in the relative quiet of the kitchen, she felt flushed as he took up his position alongside her, close enough so she could smell his shaving cologne and almost feel the heat from his body.

Tess stood across from Marian, observing her reaction to Arthur's offer of help. During dinner, she had entertained herself by watching the two of them as they stole soulful glances when the other hadn't been looking and then pretended to be all nonchalant when they'd conversed. But Tess was a born observer, and she'd known within ten minutes of everyone sitting down that by the end of the evening, sparks would fly. Well, only if the two of them let those sparks take wing, that is.

As Katie and Hannah loaded up the final trays of dessert, Tess said, "Now I want the two of you to sit down out there and enjoy a slice of that lemon meringue."

"I'll come back and help with the dishes, Tess," Katie said as she swung the tray on top of her shoulder.

"Marian and I have got the dishes, now you go on. No arguing."

"Yes ma'am," Katie chuckled. "Jeez, you're as bossy as Mom."

Tess and Marian worked as a team, one rinsing and the other loading the dish racks, as Arthur covered the remainder of the pies and stored them in the refrigerator. "This is a wonderful thing Clay does every year," Marian said as she pushed the first load into the small industrial machine. "He appears to be a very generous and caring man."

"I've been working for him since Clancy's opened, and I can say that I've never seen a scrap of meanness in the man. Sure he gets angry once in a while, and sometimes he needs to assert his authority with customers who step over the line, but he'd rather get through life with a smile and a kind word."

"My daughter seems to have taken a liking to him."

"She has indeed. She's good for him and vice versa."

Marian glanced at Arthur, who was leaning against the counter watching her. "I'm glad she's found someone who makes her happy," she said, thinking of how her relationship with Arthur was much the same as her daughter's.

"He does," Tess said. "I'm going to go out front and make up care packages for folks to take with them. Would you mind finishing with the dishes?"

"Not a problem," Arthur said, still looking at Marian. "We'll take care of what's left here."

Arthur wasted no time once he and Marian were alone. He

walked up behind her and rubbed his lips across her neck while his hands circled her waist. "You smell nice. And feel soft. And you make me crazy with wanting you."

"Arthur, what if someone comes in," she murmured. "How will you explain your hand on my breast?"

Arthur snorted, not realizing he'd moved that far up. "Here's what we'll say. You're having trouble with the dishwasher door, and I'm helping you fix it. How does that sound?"

"No one's going to buy that," she said in a dreamy voice. Turning slightly, she found his lips and kissed him.

"I don't suppose you'd be willing to sneak away from the cottage tonight and join me at the house."

"I don't suppose I would."

"But having you so close, and not being able to hold you, to stroke your hair or make love to you . . . I don't think I can stand it."

Marian was facing him now as he ran his hand through her hair, his eyes fixed tightly on hers. "We need to find some time to talk, Marian."

She closed her eyes and gave in to the moment to wrap herself in the strength and shelter of his arms. "When I get back from the wedding. Give me the next couple of days to think this through." Pulling back slightly, she added, "You want to tell Katie that she's your daughter, and I understand that. I just don't want her to be hurt or to feel deceived. I couldn't stand it if she ended up hating me."

"We'll find a way to tell her so nobody gets hurt. Trust me. I love Katie, and I love you. And it's time the three of us found some happiness as a family."

Marian heard the doors swing open and leaped out of Arthur's embrace. Tess came in carrying an armful of dirty dishes and casually walked over to the sink to set them down. "I'm going to confiscate some more containers, and then I'll be out of your way."

"I'll come out and help you, Tess. What you can't give away

will have to be wrapped and stored, and that's a big job for one person."

"Oh, I've enlisted help. Faye has insisted on jumping in and that daughter of yours has a hard time keeping her butt planted in a chair. Anyway, I should tell you that the kitchen here is going to be getting busy pretty soon, so you might want to rub that lipstick off your cheek, Arthur, and you might want to straighten out that blouse, Marian." Tess had to laugh at the horrified look on Marian's face. "Makes no difference to me what you kids are up to. Just sayin'."

With that, she grabbed the containers and swung back out to the main bar, giving the two love-birds another minute of alone time.

CHAPTER
TWENTY-FOUR

It was late Friday morning when Katie drove into Abbott, her mother riding shotgun. "I'll run into Millie's and pick up our coffee," she said as she pulled into a parking spot on the street.

"No, I'll go in for the coffee, and you go give that man of yours a farewell kiss."

"Why, Mother, if I didn't know better, I would think that you're accusing me of deliberately running out of coffee at home so we'd be forced to stop at the café."

"The café that happens to be across the street from Clancy's," Marian chuckled. "Sweetheart. At your age, I would have done the exact same thing. Now go."

Katie gave her mother a quick hug before jogging across the street. Marian headed in the opposite direction, and once inside Millie's, ordered two bold blend coffees, two blueberry muffins, and the local newspaper. When she emerged from the café, she spotted Katie talking to an attractive, familiar-looking man who had pulled up behind their car.

"My cousin is getting married on Saturday," Marian heard Katie telling the man. "My mother and I are driving out there. And, speak of the devil, here she is now."

Katie grabbed the cardboard tray holding the coffee and muffins. As she leaned into the car to place it on the floorboard, the man said, "Hello Mrs. Nolan. I'm not sure if you remember me. I'm Nathan Hunter. We met—"

"—At the hospital," Marian said, giving Nathan a warm smile. "I remember. You and your brother stayed with Katie when Evan had his accident. Waited with her until Bethany and Matt and I got there. It's good to see you again. I wasn't aware that you lived in Abbott."

"I live in Pendleton, actually, where I run my pediatric practice, but I'm also a musician. My band plays at Clancy's at least once a month. I was on my way to see Tess when I ran into Katie."

"That's right, Katie mentioned your band."

"Are you guys playing this weekend?" Katie asked.

"No, we're not back until next Friday. Down a keyboard player again. Tony quit the band."

"What happened?"

"He told me that he'll be doing frequent traveling for his job during the next couple of months and didn't think it was fair for the band to have to call in a replacement on short notice if he was called out of town. He's right, although he's written a number of the songs we play, and we're going to miss that originality. But having a permanent player works better for us. The only problem for Tony is that I still have his keyboard. We've set up a couple of meets so I can get it back to him, but something always comes up that prevents us from connecting."

"Didn't you say once that he lives in Baker City?"

"Yeah, around there."

"That's not far out of our way." Turning to her mother, Katie added, "We could drop off the keyboard and save Nathan the hassle."

"Of course. I'm always up for a scenic detour. I enjoy getting around to places I've never seen before. Besides that, you stepped in and helped my daughter during a very difficult time in her life when you could have easily walked away. This doesn't come anywhere near repaying that act of kindness, but it's the least we can do."

"You don't need to repay me, either of you."

"Well, for whatever reason, we'll make your delivery, Nathan."

Nathan turned to Katie and she shrugged her consent. "If we run into problems I'll bring it back. How's that?"

Armed with Tony's address, phone number, and vague directions to his place, Katie and her mother pulled away from the curb while Nathan walked over to Clancy's to see Tess—or to be more accurate, talk her into another date.

"I think we've been down this stretch of road twice now," Katie said as her mother tried to reprogram the GPS once again.

"It's three times, but who's counting?" her mother replied. "It might help if you slowed down so that everything I see out the window isn't just a blur."

Katie released a long-suffering sigh, but took her foot off the gas pedal and lightly applied it to the brakes. "Is that better?" she asked in an angelic voice.

"Much. And always remember that your mother knows best. Case in point is directly ahead of us," Marian said as she pointed out the windshield. "There's the bent oak tree that the young man at the gas station a few miles back told us to look for. See the hollowed-out heart in the side of the trunk?"

Katie pulled off the road and coasted up to the tree. Sure enough, the marker they'd been told to look for was right in front of them, the access road leading to Tony's house several feet beyond it.

"Finally," Katie said as she made the right turn. "It would have made everything a lot easier if there had been a mailbox or some sort of signpost."

"I'm sure that's not how things are done this far out, sweetheart. Probably no mail delivery either, and everything is measured in terms of landmarks. It appears that Tony may be a very private person and doesn't like visitors."

"That could be true, but I'm still dropping off his keyboard. If he's not there, we'll leave it inside the door. From your description of how things work out here in this neck of the woods, I'm guessing people don't lock their doors either."

As Katie made the turn onto the access road, Marian said, "I've been meaning to ask why Clay didn't come with you to the wedding."

"I never asked him. It's too soon to expose him to the third degree from all those gossip hungry aunts and cousins that will be there. Not to mention the agony you'd have to endure from the unending amount of questions you'd be forced to answer if I showed up with a boyfriend."

"You mean like, 'So, when is Katie getting married?' or 'Won't it be nice to finally have those grandchildren?'" her mother said, laughing.

"Please tell me you realize that Clay and I aren't even close to having the discussion about marriage," Katie said evenly. "Which means that grandchildren aren't even on the radar at this stage in the game."

"It's not me who's pushing, you understand," Marian said, her voice dripping with innocence. "It's all those pesky relatives we'll be spending the weekend with who are relentless in their quest to see you barefoot and pregnant."

Katie offered her mother an agonizing groan for show. "You've been watching too many chauvinistic movies, and I'm concerned that you're buying into that rhetoric. Does the name Gloria Steinem mean nothing to you?"

"Up ahead," Marian pointed as they drew closer to what appeared to be a solidly-built log cabin. "That must be it."

Katie slowed the car and swung it around so they were parked in front of the porch. "I would have never guessed that Tony lived in such an isolated area."

"Private man," Marian said. "I certainly called that one right."

Both women opened their doors simultaneously and stretched out the kinks. Katie made a sweep of the area surrounding the cabin and, like she always did, visualized the incredible photographs and oil paintings she could create. She walked around to the trunk and dragged the keyboard case out as her mother walked up the porch steps.

"It doesn't look like he's home," Marian said as she knocked on the front door. "I think he would have heard us drive up."

"Let's give him a minute to answer," Katie said as she set the keyboard case down and walked to the end of the porch. She leaned over the rail and tried to see out back, hoping to spot Tony hard at work on the back forty. The only thing she spotted was a wooden shed that looked like it hadn't been used for years. When she heard her mother knock a second time, Katie walked back to the front door and tried the knob. When it eased open, she whispered, "Who's calling it right this time? No locks." Raising her voice, she called out, "Tony? It's Katie Nolan. Are you home?"

When she didn't get a response, Katie stepped into the small foyer and called out a second time. "Hey Tony, it's Katie. From Abbott. I've got your keyboard. Nathan asked me to drop it off."

"It's way too quiet in here, Katie," Marian said from where she stood inside the doorway. "I don't think he's home. Why don't you set it someplace where he'll see it and leave him a note."

Katie nodded. "I'll get my notebook out of my knapsack," she said, setting the keyboard case on top of the couch cushions. "I'll be right back."

As Katie strolled toward the car, Marian stepped out onto the porch and stood near the top step, watching her daughter. A movement off to her left caught her eye, and she turned to see a dark-haired man coming toward them from the back of the cabin. He was about Katie's age and was wearing a short-sleeved T-shirt that accentuated his toned biceps, a pair of comfortable-looking blue jeans, and a dark green ball cap. His focus was on Katie, who had yet to see him approaching.

"Katie?" she raised her voice in order to get her daughter's attention. The man came to an abrupt stop and briefly shifted his attention. She saw what she thought was recognition in his eyes and then watched them go completely blank. Reflex had her taking a quick step backward only to bump up against the railing.

Katie had heard her mother call out and was now moving toward the man. "Tony. Hi. I hope we're not intruding. I brought your keyboard." She stopped about a yard away from him and shoved her hands in her pockets as she continued. "Nathan said that he's been trying to get it to you for several weeks. I offered to drop it off on my way to a relative's wedding. I left a message on your phone about half an hour ago, saying we were coming. I guess you didn't receive it."

Again, Marian observed that the man was intently focused on Katie. Following her motherly instincts, she stepped off the porch and moved close to her daughter. "Hello, I'm Marian Nolan, Katie's mother," she said. "I'm glad you're home. We didn't want to leave something that valuable sitting out." Turning to Katie, she said, "I really don't mean to be pushy, honey, but we need to get moving. Dory is expecting us."

Katie gave her mother a puzzled look, but followed her lead. "Sure, Mom." Turning back to Tony, she said, "We got a little turned around on the way here so we've lost some time. We should be going."

Finding his voice, Tony finally spoke. "I'm being rude. I should be asking you both to come inside. I've been out back chopping wood and could use a nice tall glass of iced water. I think I may even have some cookies. Oatmeal." He focused his attention on Katie, adding, "I'd love for you to join me."

"I don't think so," Marian said as she latched on to Katie's arm and tugged. "Thank you for the offer, but if we don't leave now we'll be late."

"But you can't go yet," Tony said as he made a move to block Katie's path to the car. He saw the quick pull of alarm cross her face mixed with confusion. He was surprised by how electrified he felt by her reaction.

"I'm afraid we do, Tony," Marian spoke up, her voice strong and commanding. "Get in the car, Katie."

Again, Tony gave Marian a dismissive look. "What I mean to say is that you both look like you could use a break," he said, once again directing his statement at Katie. He motioned toward the front door. "I'll go get those cookies."

"That's nice of you, but we should get back on the road," Katie said politely. "As I said before, we're already behind schedule."

Marian made a move toward the car at the same time Tony took another step forward. But Katie's cell phone had them all pulling up short. Grabbing it out of her jacket pocket, Katie smiled when she read the caller ID. "I just need a minute, Mom. I want to take this call. I'll keep it brief. Promise."

As she walked away, Tony heard her say, "Don't tell me you miss me already." When she laughed seductively, Tony realized the caller must be Clay. "We stopped at Tony's to drop off his keyboard," Katie was saying as she walked around the side of the porch and lowered her voice as she continued her conversation.

No longer able to hear what she was saying, he let his gaze drift toward Marian, who was eyeing him suspiciously. "The offer for cookies is still good," he said.

"I'm sure Katie won't be very long. Really, don't trouble yourself." Trying to reign in her discomfort and show some common courtesy, Marian smiled and said, "This is a nice cabin, Tony. How long have you lived here?"

"It's been in the family since before I was born," he said, lifting his foot onto the first step of the front porch and leaning into the railing. "The place holds good memories. My dad and I spent a lot of time here when I was younger." Crossing his arms over his chest, he repeated, "Yeah, some pretty good memories."

"Is your father still alive?" she asked, immediately regretting the question. *If looks could kill* came to mind as she watched Tony's demeanor shift. "I'm sorry, Tony. I shouldn't have gotten so personal."

"No apology necessary," Tony muttered as he fought to hide the sudden flash of anger.

They both turned when Katie rejoined them after finishing her call. "Clay sends his greetings," she said to Tony as she slipped the cell phone back in her pocket.

Tony offered a sociable smile, not wanting to reveal what he was actually feeling. Frustration, rage, repugnance and a strong desire to—

"Well, we should get going, Mom," Katie's voice broke through his forethought. "We'll get our butts kicked if Aunt Marley has to send out a posse for us." Facing Tony, she added, "Take it easy, Tony."

"You, too. Drive safely."

Tony watched as Katie and her mother drove toward the main road. It was only when he could no longer see the car that he moved from his position near the front steps. Crossing the porch, he walked into the house, letting the screen door slam behind him.

Heading straight to the kitchen sink, he began splashing cold water on his face. His hands were shaking, as much from the fact that Katie had slipped out of his reach, as from having her show up on his doorstep in the first place.

At first, he'd thought it had been an apparition, seeing Katie standing there alongside her car. His trip to Long Beach had left him feeling sleep deprived so it had made sense that his imagination was playing tricks on him. But when Katie had smiled at him, it was as if everything had fallen perfectly into place. She had been so close that he could have easily wrapped his fingers around her throat and squeezed while he watched the life slowly drain from her body. His good fortune had crashed and burned when she'd taken that phone call, and he was hit with the realization that at least two people knew she'd come here.

And what about her heartless mother? Asking if his father was still alive. How dare she, when it had been her own bastard husband that had sent his father to prison, all but signing his death warrant. Well, when she got back to her precious condo in Long Beach, she would discover that payback was never pretty.

"And it's just the beginning," he muttered as he grabbed a dish towel off the counter. Wiping it across his face, he conjured up the memory of the time he'd spent taking care of business at Pleasant Horizon Condominiums, followed by a detour through the old neighborhood where he had spent a good share of his childhood.

Thinking about it now, he couldn't come up with any solid reason why he'd felt the need to revisit memories that had kept him up at night, afraid and feeling completely alone. And sadly, he hadn't been surprised to see how totally different that section of the city was from the first. The Nolans had lived in an area filled with prime real estate for the prosperous *haves*. He had lived with his mother in a rat-infested toilet bowl for the forgotten *have-nots*. That's how it had been all those years ago, and nothing much had changed.

Well, that was behind him now, and it was time to finish his business in Abbott. And he knew exactly how he was going to do it.

As Katie and her mother pulled back onto the main road, Katie asked, "What was that all about? You couldn't get out of there fast enough, Mom."

Marian casually waved away Katie's remark. "Maybe I've had too much caffeine," she said. "No, wait. It must be that I'm anxious to get to Boise so I can start fielding all those questions about my favorite daughter's love life."

"I'm your only daughter which automatically makes me your

favorite. Have you ever met Tony before?" Katie asked, still curious about the way her mother had reacted earlier.

"Not that I can recall. He seemed a little strange, though, don't you think? Too intense for such a young man. And the way he looked at you gave me the creeps."

"I hadn't noticed," Katie said honestly. "Maybe he's got the hots for me."

Marian's voice dripped with sarcasm when she replied. "Of course, that's got to be it. If I'd recognized that earlier, we could have invited him along as your plus one."

Katie was amused by the attitude her mother put behind the words. "Okay, okay. I agree that he's a little weird, but I'm sure he's harmless. Now, how about some music? There are CD's in the glove box. You can pick the first one."

"Christmas music?" Marian asked joyfully as she began thumbing through the CD's.

"No. Anything but." Seeing the disappointment on her mother's face, Katie had to laugh. "Okay, give me another day of Ms. Reba, then on the way home you can play all the Christmas music you want."

"Oh, I was right the first time," Marian said. "You are my favorite daughter."

CHAPTER
TWENTY-FIVE

Clay was alone in his office staring at the computer screen. He had opened the inventory spreadsheet over an hour ago and had yet to finalize the bottom line. Of course, it wasn't completely his fault that he couldn't keep his attention on the work. Twice, Joel had called him to handle problems behind the bar, and Ben had popped in to give him some additions to the food order he'd be placing in the morning.

Leaning forward, he positioned his fingers over the computer keyboard and forced himself to concentrate on the rows of numbers on the monitor. He was halfway through the second page when the phone on the desk rang. Reaching over a stack of books, he picked up the receiver, and his attention quickly latched on to the voice that greeted him from the other end of the line.

"Well, it's about time you rang me up. I've been waiting patiently for your call," he said through the grin that spread across his face. "I take it you guys arrived safely, and all is right with the world."

"Well, with the bride's world anyway," Katie said. "When we finally arrived here yesterday, we were bombarded by relatives I haven't seen in years. And during that lost time, the family has multiplied. I haven't seen so many rugrats in the same room since my preschool years." Her voice softened when she added, "I'm sorry I didn't get the chance to call earlier. I hope you didn't worry too much."

"I was frantic, and you'll owe me when you get back."

"You wish," she snorted.

"How was the ceremony? Are the bride and groom legally husband and wife?"

"Indeed. And it was quite the production," Katie said. "Not a single hitch, though. Mom and I are back at the hotel taking a break from everyone. The dinner isn't for another couple of hours."

"Your mom's with you?" Clay asked.

"Yes," Katie said. "You sound disappointed."

"I was planning to ask what you're wearing, but if your mother is there . . ."

Katie made a scoffing noise. "Get your mind out of the gutter and tell me how everything's going at Clancy's."

"It's going. Same old, same old. Getting back to your mother for a minute, how did she enjoy Thanksgiving?"

"We both had a great time. On the way here, she was already talking about what she wants to bring next year. So you better put her on your invitation list."

"Done. In fact, we could invite her for Christmas. Of course, you and I haven't talked about that yet, but I was hoping we could spend it together. At least part of the holiday."

"I'd like that very much," Katie said, touched that he understood how important being together on the holidays was to both her and her mother.

"I should probably get going," she said through a yawn she failed to suppress. "It would be nice to catch an hour's worth of sleep before we have to go to the reception. I miss you, Clay."

"I miss you, too. You and Marian enjoy yourselves tonight. Are you still planning to leave on Monday?"

"Yes. I'll give you a call before we hit the road."

"I'd appreciate that, thanks."

Disconnecting the call, Clay locked his hands behind his head, leaned back in his chair and closed his eyes, not at all surprised how much he missed that woman.

Missed her sultry voice. Her sweet, seductive laugh. The soft, smooth texture of her skin. The whisper of strawberry fragrance in her hair.

This was definitely the woman he had every intention of making his wife. He already had the ring picked out, and he planned on asking her to marry him on Christmas Eve. In fact, when she and her mother returned from their trip, he would ask Marian for her blessing.

He knew there would be a number of logistical issues to discuss about their future. The important thing was that they would be spending the rest of their lives together, happy and in love. There was nothing he could foresee that would prevent that from happening.

It was shortly past nine-thirty when Clay made a run to First National Bank, two blocks down and one block over from the pub. He was always vigilant when he took the short walk to the bank, staggering the times he went and the route he took. Even in a quiet place like Abbott, anyone could become an easy mark if they didn't remain alert after dark.

After dropping the zippered bag into the deposit chute, he started back toward Clancy's. Halfway there, an eerie sense of apprehension struck him with such intensity that he found himself turning to make sure he was still alone. Scanning the area for anything that might seem out of place, he paid particular attention to the shadowed recesses of the dimly lit buildings that bordered Barclay Street—a narrow, rarely used backstreet that intersected with Baxter.

Of course, everything was as it should be. From where he stood, he could see the pub, still a good block away but close enough that he heard the faint voices of a group coming out the front door. He also caught the sound of a car's engine behind him as it motored around the corner of Park Street. Everything was as it should be, he thought again, when he spotted Ben leaning against the far side of the building, smoking a cigarette.

Nonetheless, Clay picked up his pace as he cut through the parking lot of the food mart and into the alley behind Clancy's. As he reached the back door, he stopped again when he felt the hair on his arms stand up. There was a security light on the back of the building which allowed him to see enough of the surrounding area, but again, there was nothing visible to be concerned about. Still, surrendering to the old saying "it was better to be safe than sorry," Clay unlocked the door and stepped into the hallway. He secured the deadbolt, then stepped over to the small window positioned to the right of the door, where he took a moment to reexamine the area.

Confident that there were no evil spirits lurking behind the building, he turned down the hallway, mumbling something crude under his breath as he wondered when he'd become so paranoid. As he passed his office, he paused briefly to make sure the door was still locked, then continued into the bar area.

When his cell phone buzzed, Clay pulled it out of the leather pouch he kept clipped to his belt, sure that it was Katie calling to say goodnight. Glancing at the clock behind the bar, he answered without checking the caller ID.

"This is Clay," he said as he tucked the phone between his shoulder and ear while reaching for a clean mug to draw a beer for C.J.

When no one replied, he repeated his greeting, adding, "Hello? Is anyone there?"

Setting the mug in front of C.J., Clay pulled the phone away from his ear, seeing that the caller had disconnected.

"Hey boss," Joel said as he reached around his boss to grab a handful of napkins. "Reverend Crawley wants to talk to you about sponsoring something going on at his church. He's over there," Joel added, pointing over his shoulder.

Clay took a final look at the phone in his hand and shook his head. Slipping it back into the leather holder he started toward the minister who was now waving to him from the end of the bar.

Tony disconnected his cell phone, throwing it on the front seat of the Chevy. Based on the sounds of music and pub-like banter in the background, he'd just confirmed the whereabouts of the only player left who could have put a fly in the ointment of his plans tonight.

He already knew where Katie and her mother were. Knew that Arthur Reddington was away on a business trip. Had verified that Ian Montgomery was saddled with weekend security detail on the estate. Tony had even taken the time to confirm Nathan's whereabouts, pleased that he was visiting his brother in Nevada, therefore eliminating any chance of them running into each other over the next few hours. Now, as long as everyone stayed right where they were, Tony could make his next move.

Up to this point, he'd been unsuccessful in his attempts to slip onto the estate undetected, but walking through the front door as an invited guest . . . well, that would be like having the key to the castle. Although, to make that happen, he needed Hannah Reddington as his patsy. He'd cultivate a faux relationship with her and in a matter of weeks, if not days, she'd walk him right through the front door and no one would be the wiser. But, first things first, as his mother always said.

He took a minute to mentally replay the conversation he'd overheard earlier in the week between Hannah and a slim, attractive redhead by the name of Denise. He'd been part of a group of people waiting for their drink orders at a popular Starbucks and both girls had been unaware that he was eavesdropping on their conversation. More importantly, they were oblivious to the fact that they had provided him with the time and place where he could find them tonight. He and the Reddington niece had never crossed paths before—a revelation that would only make it easier when he *accidentally* bumped into her at the trendy nightclub in Pendleton.

Tony stole a final look at Clancy's before pulling away from the curb. "Get ready, Crawford," he said into the darkness of the car. "Your girlfriend's world will soon come crashing down and, with any luck, you'll be caught in the crossfire."

CHAPTER
TWENTY-SIX

When Hannah stepped through the doors of Club Alexander in Pendleton, she spotted her girlfriends at one of the premier tables, lost in their animated conversation while the music of the Backwater Blues Band filled the jam-packed room. She made her way through the standing crowd that edged the dance floor and plopped into the vacant stool they'd been saving for her.

"What took you so long?" Denise asked as she signaled the waitress. "We expected you half an hour ago."

"Running behind, that's all," Hannah said, unperturbed. "How's the band sound?"

"Great," Colleen said. "I think I'll bring Kyle back here next weekend and see what he thinks." Hannah nodded, knowing that Colleen had chosen this particular club tonight because she was getting married in six months and was still auditioning bands. "But as far as I'm concerned, they're rating pretty high on my list of probables for the reception."

The waitress stopped at the table, placing a fresh bowl of mixed nuts in the center. "Another round here?" she asked as she began to collect the empty glasses.

"Yes," Hannah said, rubbing her hands together, anxious to get the evening rolling. "I'll have a gin and tonic."

"Then that's two margaritas, a virgin strawberry daiquiri, and a gin and tonic. Be right back," she said, moving on to the next table.

"Hey, the guy standing at the end of the bar keeps looking over here," Denise said as she grabbed a handful of nuts. "I think he's checking Hannah out."

"Why me?" Hannah smirked, although she casually turned to take a look at him. The man was smartly dressed in a white, front-button shirt (the top button undone), striped tie (the Windsor knot loosened), black pleated trousers, and a thin leather belt with a square gold buckle. His short, tastefully cut hair framed a generously handsome face, and the look in those dark, captivating eyes spoke volumes. Hannah approved. "He could be checking out any one of us," she added.

"Yeah, right," Joan said, rubbing her very pregnant belly. "I can pretty much conclude that he's not interested in me. And Colleen certainly isn't going to be giving out her phone number. That only leaves you and Denny here."

"I'm seeing Kevin again," Denise chimed in, "and even though Mr. Club Med over there looks like he's willing and able to give a girl a good time, Kevin's certainly no pushover in that department."

"Anyone care to make a wager who he's got his sights set on?" Colleen joked.

In unison, Denise, Joan, and Colleen chanted, "Hannah, Hannah."

"Stop. Stop, you idiots," Hannah giggled, waving her hands in the air. "You're embarrassing yourselves. Let's show a little decorum."

"Too late," Colleen said. "Prince Charming is on the move and closing in fast."

Sure enough, when Hannah turned a second time, the man who'd been standing alone by the bar was heading straight toward them.

"Are you ladies enjoying yourselves tonight?" he asked as he approached the table, keeping his attention focused on Hannah.

"Very much," she said, tilting her head slightly and giving him an award-winning smile. "I'm Hannah," she added, offering her hand.

Moving closer, he joined his hand with hers and said, "I'm Tony. It's very nice to meet you."

"And these are my friends." As Hannah recited their names, the man shook hands with each of them.

As the last introduction was made, the waitress arrived with their round of drinks, systematically placing glasses on the table. "Let me get this," Tony said pulling out his wallet and dropping several bills on the waitress's tray. "Keep the change," he said, barely giving her a second look.

"That's so nice of you, Tony," Colleen said, reaching for her glass. "Thank you."

Shifting his attention back to Hannah, he placed his hand on the back of her chair and said, "Are you from around here?"

Denise gave Joan an eye roll as Colleen leaned over and said, "I think this is where we become invisible."

"I live in North Carolina," Hannah was saying, "I'm visiting my uncle who lives in Abbott. It's a few miles west of here."

"How long will you be visiting?"

"I'll be here through New Year's, and then I'll be heading back home."

"Maybe we can get together before you have to leave. Take in a few clubs or go out to dinner."

"I'd like that," Hannah said as she pulled a pen out of her purse. She reached for Tony's free hand and proceeded to write her cell phone number on his wrist. "Call me," she added with a wink.

His smile widened as he backed away from the table. "I'll do that. Ladies," he said, tipping an imaginary hat. "Have a great evening."

"How the hell do you do that?" Denise laughed. "You've been here what, ten minutes? And you've already secured a date with one of the hottest guys in the place. I am so jealous."

"If you got it, you got it," Hannah said laughing.

As the music played on, the women enjoyed another two hours

at the club, dancing, singing along with the lyrics they knew, and drinking margaritas, virgin daiquiris, and gin and tonics. When everyone decided to call it a night, Hannah was feeling good—a bit tipsy but not altogether drunk. She parted ways with her friends in the parking lot, hopped into her hybrid, and began the half hour drive back home. Ten minutes into her ride, her cell phone rang. Digging into her purse, she pulled it out—something that her parents and uncle constantly harped at her not to do—and answered seconds before it went to voicemail.

"Hey, Hannah. It's Tony. From Club Alexander."

"Sure, I remember who you are."

"You told me to call, so . . . how about dinner Tuesday night?"

"Wow, you don't waste any time, do you?"

"I don't, no. I go after what I want, when I want it, and I make no apologies for that. And on Tuesday night, I want to have dinner with you."

Hannah couldn't quite figure out whether she should be put off or flattered by his brazen approach. "Tuesday night, huh?" she said as if thoughtfully considering the invitation without sounding too eager to accept. "I have quite the busy social calendar, but I could probably free up some time for you."

"That's mighty hospitable of you, sweetness, and I thank you for that. I can pick you up at eight."

"How about if I meet you at eight. Where did you have in mind?"

"Crosspoints, on Lexington."

Hannah nearly squealed. She had never been to the restricted club because it required a pass-code to get in. If you weren't already a member—or there by invitation of a member—then you weren't getting in.

Trying to play it cool, she said, "I'm impressed, Tony. That place is very exclusive."

"Not so much from the inside looking out. What do you say?"

"Yes. I'd like very much to have dinner with you Tuesday night."

"Great. And if you change your mind about me picking you up, give me a call." He rattled off a phone number that Hannah committed to memory. "Otherwise, I'll be waiting for you in front of the club at eight o'clock."

"Sounds good. See you Tuesday," she said.

Holy crap, she thought giddily as she disconnected the call. Crosspoints! Denise would be so jealous. She'd been trying to find a way into that place for two years.

As Hannah took the final turn onto Reddington Drive, her thoughts were focused on what she would wear for her date with Tony. A shopping trip to Macy's in Kennewick would probably be in order, considering she'd need something fancy and fashionably appropriate. She'd also have to make an appointment at Sterling Salons for a full hair and nail treatment.

Pulling through the front gate, Hannah pumped her fist in the air and let out an enthusiastic hoot. This was undoubtedly going to make her top five visits to Oregon, ever.

CHAPTER TWENTY-SEVEN

Katie was within a mile of the estate, the car radio blasting out an old Bing Crosby Christmas tune. Seated beside her was her mother who was singing right along. There wasn't a Christmas song written that Marian Nolan didn't know the words to and hearing the holiday music so early in December didn't bother her in the least.

As Katie followed the path to the cottage, her mother said, "Are you going to decorate for Christmas?"

"That's weeks away yet," Katie laughed as she parked the car in front of the cottage and got out. Walking to the trunk, she removed two suitcases. "I suppose I could do some holiday decorating inside. Maybe stencil some frosted angels and reindeer on the windows, even though no one will see them."

"You'll see them," Marian said. "And every time you do, it'll make you smile. You should probably get a tree, too. Nothing too elaborate, maybe even a nice artificial one. I can send up some of our family ornaments."

"That would be nice, Mom. I also have a box of stuff that I've collected over the years, and maybe I can get Laura to ship it." Laura Dugan was subletting Katie's apartment for a year while Katie was in Oregon. "Yeah, maybe I'll do that," she added reflectively.

When they reached the front door, Katie saw an envelope taped to it. She took it down as Marian stepped into the cottage. "What's that?" her mother asked with mild curiosity.

"Let's open it up and see."

Katie dropped the suitcases near the front door and pulled out the personalized note card. "It's from Arthur," she said. "He's welcoming us back and wants us to come to dinner tonight if we're not too tired." She handed the note over to her mother and removed her coat. "That's nice of him, don't you think?"

Marian glanced at her daughter and smiled. "But you had other plans for tonight, didn't you?" When Katie stumbled over her denial, Marian said, "Katie, it's fine. I was young and in love once upon a time. And I haven't forgotten what it's like." Probably because she herself was getting a second chance to experience that feeling. "Depending on when I can get a flight back to Long Beach, maybe we can fit in lunch tomorrow."

"I just wanted a few hours with Clay," Katie confessed as she retrieved the suitcases and walked down the hall to the bedroom. "I can probably be back by dinner time. Or maybe we could have dinner with Arthur and then I can go to the pub. That way we won't disappoint him, and I can still have some time with—"

Katie turned and saw her mother standing in the doorway, the strangest expression on her face. She couldn't figure out if it was amusement, tension or . . . intrigue? "Is everything all right, Mom?"

"Of course it is," Marian stated as she entered the room and freed Katie of one of the suitcases. "I'm glad to be out of the car, though." As she started to unpack, she added, "If you don't mind, I'm going to do a load of wash. Do you have anything you want to throw in?"

Katie was still staring at her mother. "Maybe. Look, Mom. If you don't want to have dinner with Arthur, you don't have to. Or if you're uneasy about spending time alone here I can see Clay tomorrow."

"Katherine. I'm perfectly capable of being on my own. You don't have to babysit me." Glancing at her daughter, she said, "Let's do this. We have an early dinner with Arthur, and then you can go to the pub and spend some quality time with Clay." She closed the now empty suitcase and tucked it in the closet. "Don't worry about me. Besides, I think Arthur is a very interesting man. I'm sure we'll find plenty to talk about."

Katie stepped up to the side of the bed and put her arms around her mother for a hug. "I love you, lady."

"I love you, kiddo. Now get your laundry sorted out, I'll do whites first. Then you can call Arthur and find out what time he wants us for dinner. When you've done those two things, you can call Clay."

"Yes, ma'am," Katie said with a mock salute. "And what are you going to be doing while I'm following orders?"

"First, I'm going to load the machine, then I'm taking a nap. Now go."

Later that night, Marian watched Katie drive away from Arthur's house. When the taillights finally faded into the dark, she went back inside.

Nora was cleaning up in the kitchen, and Arthur had retired to the living room. When she joined him, he handed her a glass of wine and motioned her to take a seat on the sofa. He picked up his glass of whiskey and sat beside her.

Taking a sip of the full-bodied Chardonnay, Marian said, "Dinner was very nice. Nora is a wonderful cook."

"She is. She also keeps me organized and honest," he stated. "She's become a good friend over the years."

"And Hannah? Katie tells me she spends several months of the year with you."

"Her parents travel a lot, so she'll usually spend her summers here. They also go on extended holiday this time of the year, and since the age of thirteen, Hannah has spent the holidays with me. It's become a pleasant tradition. I enjoy having her here.

"Are you happy, Arthur?"

"I am, yes. In fact, I haven't felt this content in a long time." He leaned over and lightly pressed his lips to hers. "What about you?"

Smiling, she said, "There's nowhere I'd rather be than here with you."

He took her glass and, setting it on the side table next to his, reached for Marian's hand. "It's a bit cool outside but still a nice night to take a walk in the garden. Interested?"

"I'd like that very much."

For the next half hour, they walked through the flowers and shrubs, holding hands and speaking softly about whatever struck their interest. When they'd finally circled back to the atrium doors, Arthur stopped and pulled Marian into his arms. "Hannah is out tonight, and I'm guessing that Katie will be gone for several hours yet. Will you stay with me for a while, Marian?"

"I'd like that," she said, leaning in to kiss Arthur. First softly, and then with more passion. "I told Katie to feel free to spend the night with Clay. I'd like for us to do the same, Arthur. I want you to make love to me. Will you do that?"

"You never have to ask, darling. Never."

Locking the doors and setting the house alarm, Arthur led Marian to the bedroom, closed the door, and proceeded to show her exactly how much she still meant to him.

CHAPTER
TWENTY-EIGHT

Clay was putting the finishing touches on a round of four cosmopolitan cocktails when Katie walked into the pub. The jolt to his heart came first, quickly followed by the growing need to fold her into his arms and steal as much time as it would take to kiss every inch of her body. Her soft, smooth, beguiling body.

She smiled, blew him a kiss, and then stealthily disappeared into the kitchen where she proceeded to help Ben fill both dine-in and carry-out orders. At around ten, she moved out front to help Tess deliver drinks, clean tables, and talk up the few customers who remained.

By eleven o'clock, the bar crowd had thinned down to a manageable number, so Clay took hold of Katie's hand on his way to the back hallway. "Ben, Tess. You're in charge of the pub," he announced. "Please set the alarm on your way out." Katie laughed as he continued to drag her through the hallway, up the stairs to the apartment, and directly into his bedroom.

He didn't waste any time once they got there. As he backed Katie toward the mattress, he helped her out of her clothes, dispensing with his own before he climbed onto the bed.

"You are the most gorgeous woman I've ever laid eyes on. And your skin is fire under my touch," he said running his fingertips down the center of her torso. Lowering his head, he kissed her gently, controlling the urge to devour her whole. She parted her lips slightly and groaned softly when his tongue drifted between her teeth in a slow and sensuous dance. "I really missed you," he sighed as he pulled back slightly to look into her eyes. The warmth and love he saw displayed there almost did him in.

"You undo me, Katie," he said as he carefully buried himself inside her. "I love you. I love everything about you. And I miss you tremendously when you're gone."

After they'd made love, Clay collapsed on top of her, and both lay perfectly still, exhausted and content.

Several minutes later, when Katie was snuggled in against Clay's side, he asked, "Do you have to leave right away?"

"No. I left my mom in the capable hands of Arthur, who'll see that she gets safely tucked away in the cottage. She told me not to hurry back, and she never says anything she doesn't mean. I'm the one who's feeling guilty that I'm leaving her alone."

"But she's not alone. And if she was feeling uncomfortable about being alone, I have no doubt that Arthur would offer her a room at the house. Don't feel guilty about putting yourself first once in a while, Katie. Your mom wants you to be happy."

"You're right. She's a big girl, and she can take care of herself."

"Then lay back and relax. Besides, I'm pretty sure your mom likes me, so she'd also want me to be happy."

"I'm sure that's true. But before we both fall asleep, I have something to give you." Katie jumped out of bed and walked naked into the living room to retrieve the knapsack she'd managed to grab before Clay had hurled her out of the bar. Returning to the bedroom, she dug inside the bag, pulled out a wrapped box and tossed it on the bed. "Open it," she said timidly as she sat cross-legged at the bottom of the mattress.

Clay smiled as he slipped the ribbon off the box and ripped through the wrapping paper. Lifting the lid, he pulled out a heavy object that had been buried in several layers of green tissue paper.

Katie watched his face as he separated the gift from the paper, feeling both nervous and excited to see his reaction.

Clay was lost for words as he held Katie's gift in both hands. He recognized the door knocker as being an exact replica of the one that had greeted patrons at his grandfather's pub back in Ireland. If he hadn't known better, he would have sworn that the one he held was the original.

When the silence dragged on, Katie began to think that maybe she'd screwed up by presenting him with something so personal. "I noticed the photograph you have hanging over the bar," she began to explain, "and I had Ben slip it to me one day so I could get it enlarged. I wanted to get a better look at the knocker. I sent the design to a shop in Dublin, and they said they could replicate it. I wanted to give it to you on Thanksgiving but . . . God, I'm sorry Clay. I didn't mean to overstep—"

"I love it, Katie. Although, I can't seem to come up with the right words to tell you how much." He ran his fingers over the Claddagh—the Irish symbol for friendship, love, and loyalty—which had been designed to serve as the knocker arm. The Clancy Coat of Arms was engraved in the center of the brass plate. "I think this is the most thoughtful gift I've ever received. I'm not sure you can truly appreciate what this means to me."

"I may have an idea," she said softly, seeing the emotion in his eyes. "I take it you like it?"

"Come here," he murmured, holding out his hand. She crawled up the mattress and nestled into the crook of his arm, her head resting on his shoulder. "The original Clancy's Pub burned to the ground in a fire that the police ruled as arson. Did I ever tell you that?"

When she shook her head, he continued. "Everything was lost except for a few items that granddad kept at home. About three months after the fire, he got sick and never had the chance to rebuild. When he died, the shoebox of memorabilia went to my mother, and then it came to me. There were a few photographs of the bar, and I tried to integrate some of his design into mine, but I never got around to finding a duplicate of the door knocker. In all honesty, I thought I would never be able to find one that would even come close to looking like the original."

He ran his hand down her hair and softly pressed a kiss to her temple. "You hit a home run here. Thank you. Thank you so much."

"You're welcome."

Clay lifted her chin and brushed his lips to hers. "I love you."

"Goes both ways," she said. "Always."

It was close to five when Katie pulled up to the cottage. Knowing the sun would be rising soon, she entertained the idea of taking her camera out and capturing some shots at the east end of the property.

Trying to be quiet, she entered the cottage and removed her dress boots so the heels on the hardwood floor wouldn't wake her mother. As she tiptoed across the living room, she glimpsed Marian standing by the kitchen window deep in thought. "Mom?"

Marian turned and saluted her daughter with a large multicolored coffee cup. "Good morning. I assume you have a good reason for dragging yourself in so late, young lady."

"And how do I know that you didn't just sneak in yourself?" Katie snorted. Because she was hanging her coat on the hook in the entryway and not facing her mother, she didn't see the flicker of satisfaction pass over Marian's face. "Have you been up long, Mom?"

"Oh, I wasn't having any luck sleeping, so I went ahead and made some coffee and toasted a bagel. Can I get you anything?"

"If you could put some of that coffee in my travel mug, I'd appreciate it. I want to go out and take some photos."

"Sure. How about if I go out with you? I don't think I've ever seen you do an outdoor shoot, and sharing a sunrise with my favorite daughter sounds like fun."

Katie threw her mother a curious look as she shuffled down the hallway in her stocking feet. "Sure, if that's what you want. I gotta tell you, though. I don't remember you being this jolly so early in the morning."

Marian laughed. "Things change, baby. Age has a way of mellowing." But Katie was already gone, rummaging around in her bedroom closet for something warm to wear.

"Great sex tends to do the same thing," Marian added quietly through a wide smile.

Chapter
Twenty-Nine

Later that Tuesday, Marian was neatly repacking her suitcase. "It wasn't all that long ago when I was the one sitting in the corner watching you pack," she said.

Katie smirked as her mother tossed another blouse into the case. "When I was getting ready to leave Long Beach and come here. How could I forget? Don't expect me to cry."

"I didn't cry. Well, maybe I shed a tear or two so that you'd feel better, but I knew it would all work out for you in the end. And I was right, wasn't I?"

"You tried to talk me out of coming, Mother. But I forgive you."

"Sadly, you still have that smart mouth."

Katie chuckled and slid off the bed. "It's nice that Arthur offered to fly you back to Long Beach."

"He said that he has business in California, and that it wouldn't be any trouble."

"He's a nice man, Mom. Maybe you should make an effort to get to know him better."

Marian stopped folding the sweater that Katie had handed her. "What does that mean?" she asked.

"It means that you're both single, attractive, intelligent, and easy-going people. I think you'd be compatible." When Marian didn't respond, Katie added, "Daddy's been gone a long time. If you took up an interest in another man, he wouldn't mind and neither would I."

Marian looked up at her daughter and had to swallow hard. She could see so much of Robert in her, but she saw an equal amount of Arthur. And if Katie knew the truth, would she still be so open to the idea of pairing her biological father with her adulterous mother?

"Can you find my shoes, honey? I think they're in the closet." Marian went back to packing and hoped that Katie would take the hint and stay off the subject of romance.

Katie grabbed the shoes along with a square box, wrapped in delicate paper embossed with gold roses and tied with a red ribbon made of velvet. She slipped both inside the suitcase.

"What's that?" Marian asked with curiosity.

"A little something I picked up when Aunt Jenny and I went to the mall on Sunday. Open it when you get home."

"I don't think so. A gift from my daughter deserves immediate attention." Slipping the ribbon aside and gently removing the wrapping, Marian lifted the box lid. Inside was a blown glass unicorn figurine that made Marian grin. "Katie, it's beautiful. And so delicate. It'll fit in nicely with my other figurines. Thank you."

Pulling Katie in for a motherly hug, Marian said, "I had fun these past few days."

"Ditto," Katie replied, swiping her hand under her nose. "Come on, finish packing, and I'll drive you up to the house."

Hours later, the plane's wheels touched down smoothly on the private airstrip. It had been an uneventful flight from Pendleton to Long Beach, and as they taxied to the hangar, Marian turned to Arthur and said, "I've never been in the cockpit of a plane, not to mention riding along in the copilot's seat."

"Did you enjoy it?"

"Very much, yes. The sky is a beautiful canopy from the ground, but from that high up? It's indescribable. When did you get your pilot's license?"

"Around the time we split up." He offered her a reflective smile as he took her hand and brought it to his lips. "I'd always wanted to fly, and the heartache of losing you pushed me to see it through." Releasing his seat restraint, he reached over to help Marian with hers. "Let's go. I need a few minutes to check in and complete my log book, and then we can leave."

Marian wasn't sure how to respond to what he'd said, so she remained silent until they were in the rental car. By the time Arthur finished navigating his way out of the airport, she knew what she wanted to say.

"It was a difficult time back then. For both of us. I hurt you, and I'm sorry that things didn't work out differently, but there was nothing else we could have done."

"I know," Arthur replied. "But knowing didn't stop me from being bitter about the situation. Being angry because I was shut out of Katie's life. But no matter what emotion I was going through on any given day, I always understood."

"She's a wonderful girl. Kind and caring and funny. I'm sure part of that is genetic."

"Thank you, although her upbringing is more likely the reason she's the person she is. You and Robert did an admirable job." He glanced over at her and added quietly, "I kept track of her, Marian. I accepted that I couldn't allow myself to be part of her life back then, but I still wanted to make sure she had everything she needed."

"I saw you at her college graduation," Marian said as she folded her hands in her lap and turned away from him.

Arthur remained silent for a moment, considering his response. "I thought I'd done a better job of keeping to the background," he finally said.

"You're not cut out for background work," she quipped.

"Well, be that as it may, I needed to share in some of her

milestones. And now, for the short time she's been with me, I have no doubts that she's a good person. I've grown to love her, Marian."

"And you think it's time we tell her you're her biological father."

"I do, but you still have reservations, and I'm willing to discuss them. Telling her will be a big step, and the truth may be difficult for her to hear.

"Robert was her father," Arthur continued, "He raised her, provided for her. And I certainly don't want to take that away or shade it by playing the biological card. But I also think that Katie is an intelligent, open-minded woman who'll be able to accept the truth. We've gotten to know each other pretty well, and I believe she holds some affection for me. As a friend and as her boss. I'm ready to take that affection one step further, and maybe she can find a way to love me as, let's say, a surrogate father."

Marian sighed heavily and laid her head back against the car seat. "Let's discuss this over dinner. I'm starving. I'm not sure what I have at home to feed you, though."

"How does this sound. We'll drop off your bags at the condo then swing by the Concord so I can check in. We can have an early dinner at the hotel restaurant."

She smiled without lifting her head. "You can stay with me."

"I appreciate the invitation, but for now, it's probably better if I'm checked in at the hotel. I'll be here for a few days taking care of business, and they have all the office amenities I need."

"Well, how about you spend the days in your office suite and the nights with me. I'll even leave a mint on your pillow if that will make you feel better."

Arthur laughed as he pulled onto the expressway. "An offer I'd be a fool not to accept."

It was nearly four o'clock by the time Arthur pulled up to Pleasant Horizon Condominiums. Shutting the engine down, he climbed out from behind the wheel and rounded the car to open the door for Marian. "I'll pull your suitcase out of the trunk," he said as he pushed the remote button on his key fob.

Marian stepped out of the car, reaching for the smaller bag she had set in the back seat. Closing the door, she turned toward the building at the sound of a male voice calling her name.

"Marian, welcome back," her neighbor said as he stepped out of his own unit. "Wasn't expecting you'd be returning so soon. I was about to go inside your place and do a quick check. Mrs. Doherty caught me out back earlier and said there were some problems over the weekend with kids trying to break into cars. I've been gone myself since Thursday, so I figured it wouldn't hurt to give your place a quick check."

"Oh, thank you, Joe. That was very nice of you to think of me."

"Hey, that's what neighbors do. How was your niece's wedding, by the way?" the neighbor asked as Arthur followed Marian up the sidewalk.

"It was lovely. Everything went perfectly. How about your Thanksgiving? Did all your children make it to your daughter's house?"

"Richie was the only one. The other two girls got stuck working, and then that storm in Maine held up their flight, so they never got there." He moved in front of Marian and stepped up to the door. "Here, I've got the key you gave me for emergencies. Let me get the door for you."

Once both locks were disengaged, Joe pushed down on the door handle and stepped into the open living room. He stopped so abruptly that Marian ran into his backside. "Oh, sorry," she said, moving around him to set her travel bag on the floor near the front closet. "I didn't expect you to stop so quickly." When she turned her attention to the living room, she gasped, raising her hand to her mouth. "Oh, no," she whispered as Arthur stepped up behind her.

One look at the disorder of the room—the broken knickknacks, the smashed lamps, the ripped and toppled furniture—had Arthur quickly rushing Marian back out the door. "Wait outside," he said. "Joe, please stay with Marian."

"Arthur, wait." Marian clutched at the sleeve of Arthur's trench coat. "We should just call the police. What if someone is still inside?"

He handed Marian his cell phone. "Make the call, but from out here." She saw him reach under his coat as he disappeared back into the condo.

Glancing out the studio window, Katie could barely see the outline of mountains through the haze from the overcast skies surrounding them. She checked the clock on the wall and realized that it was nearly six. When her stomach growled, she also remembered that she hadn't eaten since breakfast.

After her mother had left with Arthur, she'd come up to the studio and worked straight through the day. Other than talking to Clay earlier in the afternoon, she hadn't had any human contact, which had allowed her to bury herself in perfecting the facial features on the second commissioned painting. Prior to leaving for the wedding, she'd been having trouble with the shape and color of the eyes, but the break seemed to have given her a fresh perspective, and it now looked as if she'd finally gotten it right. She smiled at the thought that Arthur would be pleased with the end result.

Dropping her brushes into a short jar of paint thinner, she went downstairs and into the kitchen where Nora was cooking. "It must have been the smell of this great southern chili that got my stomach growling." Katie said as she stepped over to the stove.

"It'll be done in about an hour," Nora replied. "Come back down, and you can get a fresh, hot bowl. The homemade bread will be done about the same time so you can take some of that, too. You're skinny as a rail."

"Clay and I are having dinner later, or I'd jump at the offer. Your cooking is so much better than mine." Katie opened the refrigerator door and removed a diet cola.

"There's also some leftover ham. Make a sandwich to hold you over."

"Sold," Katie said, setting the soda aside. She pulled out the large platter and began piling the meat on a slice of bread, adding a splash of Dijon mustard. "The house sounds awfully quiet," she commented around the first bite of the sandwich. "Where's Hannah?"

"She left a few minutes ago. Said she was going over to Colleen's house."

"Oh, that reminds me. I've got to take a quick trip to the art supply store in Pendleton."

"Can't it wait until morning?" Nora asked as she moved to the stove to stir the chili. "You've been working your butt off all day. Take a break and go spend time with Clay."

"Actually, he's coming here tonight. He should be arriving around eight-thirty, so I have plenty of time to get to the city and back." Katie glanced at her watch and added, "Well, enough time anyway." She returned the platter of meat to the refrigerator and grabbed what was left of the sandwich. "I need to go upstairs and clean my brushes first, though."

"You might want to take a minute to change that shirt, too."

Katie looked down and for the first time noticed the paint stains. "Good idea. If I'm not back by the time Clay gets here will you buzz him in?"

"Not a problem," Nora said.

Walking over to where Nora stood, Katie bent to give her a kiss on the cheek. "Anyone tell you lately that you're the best?"

"Go on, get out of here," Nora replied, smiling as Katie strolled out of the room.

CHAPTER
THIRTY

"I'll be available by phone if you need me," Clay said as he walked out from behind the bar.

"Don't worry about a thing," Ben replied as he passed a beer glass to an older man who was a regular at Clancy's. "I expect it to be relatively slow tonight."

Giving his bartender a backward wave, Clay slipped out the front door.

Crossing the parking lot, the cool breeze ruffled his hair, causing strands of it to tickle his ears. Making a mental note to stop at the local barber in the morning, he slowed his pace as he pulled his ringing cell phone from his pocket. "You can't be having any problems already," he groaned. "I'm not even in the car yet."

"As a matter of fact, I do have a problem."

"Katie," he said, reaching out to unlock the car door. "Sorry, I thought you were Ben. What's the problem, babe?"

"First, I want to say that I'm fine," she said, the strain in her voice clearly audible. "I was parked in the municipal parking garage while I was shopping in Pendleton and fell on the way back to my car. Someone called for an ambulance even though I told them it wasn't necessary. And now I'm at the hospital without any way to get home unless I call a cab, which I can do if you're not able to make a stop at St. Michael Hospital."

"Of course I'll come. How bad are you hurt?"

"A few bumps and scrapes. The worst is a twisted knee. I may have hit my shoulder on the step, though. Or maybe it was the wall. Anyway, other than that I'm just hunky-dory."

Clay had slid into his vehicle while Katie described her injuries. By the time he was pulling out of the pub's parking lot, she was explaining how she'd foolishly been spooked in the empty stairwell. "Then I lost my footing, and down I went, and someone called for an ambulance," she concluded.

"They were doing what they thought was best, I'm sure. Has the hospital released you yet?"

"One of the nurses said they wanted a few more tests before they let me go. I'm hoping you can help me convince them that tests aren't what I need. What I need is to go home, Clay."

"Hang in there, honey," Clay said sympathetically. "I'll be there in about twenty minutes."

He disconnected the call and tossed his phone into the auto tray he used for loose change. Fifteen minutes later, he was turning off the highway onto Rosewood Avenue, the main road leading onto hospital grounds.

His cell phone rang again as he was swinging the car into an empty space reserved for emergency room visitors. "This is Clay," he said, retrieving the phone from the tray.

"Clay, it's Ian. Is Katie with you?"

"She will be shortly. She took a fall while she was in Pendleton, and I'm picking her up at the hospital. She's claiming no serious injuries, and I'll get confirmation of that in a few short minutes. Did you need her for something?"

"I got a call from Arthur, and there was some trouble in California. It appears as if someone broke into Marian's condo while she was up here. Arthur is flying her back, and they should be landing in a few hours. Tell me what you know about Katie's accident."

Concern had Clay tensing. "What's going on Ian?"

"I'm working on it. Right now, I need you to tell me what you know. What happened with Katie?"

Clay stepped out of his car and started across the parking lot while relaying what little information he had. "You think there's a connection between Katie's fall and the break-in, don't you?" he asked when he'd finished.

"That's what I'm going to find out. There had been a report at Pleasant Horizon of kids breaking into parked cars, but it doesn't sound as if the damage in Marian's condo was done by kids. Whoever did it knew it was her place. I'll fill in the details later. For now, stick with Katie, and I'll meet you at the hospital."

Clay moved through the automatic doors and into the emergency room with a sense of urgency. As he approached the receptionist, she smiled and said, "How may I help you, sir?"

"I'm here for Katie Nolan. Could you direct me to where she might be?"

After getting her location, Clay headed toward the emergency patient area. He spotted her coming from the opposite direction as he was making his way down the main corridor. She was being pushed in a wheelchair by a chunky, freckle-faced technician in dark blue scrubs. They were both laughing at something the young man had just said.

Spotting Clay, she immediately saw the worry on his face. "Nothing's broken," she said reassuringly. "It's only a sprain. They wrapped the knee and gave me something for the pain. I don't think they plan on keeping me too much longer. At least I hope not."

"What about your shoulder?" he asked as he leaned down to kiss her forehead.

"Didn't break that either. Ramsey here says I'll be back to normal as long as I take it easy for a couple of days."

Clay looked at the young man for confirmation.

"Ms. Katie here speaks the truth," he said. "No broken bones, and only a scattering of bruises. The sprained knee is the worst of it all."

The qualifier had Clay momentarily frowning. "They don't want to keep her overnight? Like, for observation?"

"Not for me to say," Ramsey replied. "That's a decision for the doc to make."

As the tech helped Katie out of the wheelchair and onto the bed, he said, "The emergency room is a little backed up at the moment, Katie. As soon as the doctor has a chance to look at your medical notes, he'll make a decision on your discharge. Kyra is your nurse, and she'll be stopping in shortly."

"Okay," Katie said, unable to hold back a yawn.

"Well, I got other patients to see. Need anything?"

Giving Clay a bemused look, she said, "Do I need anything?"

"I think you're good," he replied, watching Katie yawn a second time.

Aiming the now empty wheelchair toward the door, the tech looked at Clay and smiled. "In case you hadn't noticed, the pain medication they gave her has finally kicked in." Looking back at Katie, he gave her a half salute and said, "Adios, Amiga."

"Until we meet again," she called out.

As the tech moved out into the hallway, Katie motioned Clay toward the bed. When he closed the distance between them, she gripped his hand, pulled him toward her, and surprised him by smacking her lips against his. "Let's blow this Popsicle stand," she said, grinning like a Cheshire cat. "Whataya say?"

"Are you feeling any pain at all?" Clay asked.

"None at all," she said throwing her arms around his neck.

"How much pain medication did they give you?"

"Don't know, don't care," she said happily.

He was laughing by the time he pried her arms away and gently pushed her back onto the bed. "Why don't you rest a minute?"

"Sure," she mumbled. Within thirty seconds, Katie was out like a light.

It was closing in on midnight when Ian took the exit that would lead him to St. Michael Hospital. But instead of going right at the end of the ramp, he guided the jeep in the opposite direction so he could make a short detour before he met up with Katie and Clay.

Fifteen minutes later, he was standing in the parking garage stairwell where Katie had taken her fall, surveying the area in order to comprehend exactly what had happened. According to Clay, she'd been in a hurry to get back to her car, one hand clutching her shopping bags, the other digging in her purse for her keys. She had gotten off the elevator, realizing too late that her car was actually parked two levels down and rather than wait for the elevator to return, Katie had taken the stairs.

It had been right here where she'd heard the footsteps above, Ian imagined. Heard those footsteps stop when she had, then start up again. She might have called out, but he doubted anyone would have answered.

"She said that she got that same uneasy feeling she'd had weeks ago when she was in the woods behind the cottage," Clay had told him. "When she started back down the stairs, she lost her footing and tumbled the last three steps, hitting the cement wall on the landing."

Ian peered over the railing, glancing up to where Katie had first entered the stairwell. He then shifted his attention down to examine the two flights below. As much as he'd wanted to find some evidence of this being more than an accident, he had to admit that there was nothing here that appeared threatening. He didn't even see anything that she could have tripped over or slipped on. Yet, based on his experience, that didn't always mean much.

Stepping out of the stairwell, he started toward Katie's vehicle, mentally running through everything that had happened since she'd arrived at the Reddington estate. The problems with the security alarms, the scare she'd had in the woods, the phone calls. Even the incident at Owen's store, although he was pretty sure that Patrick Lynch had gone solo on that one. Ian still couldn't see any common thread tying all the incidents together, but there had to be one. Especially once you added in Marian's condo.

Reaching Katie's car, Ian peered through the driver's side window, seeing nothing out of place. The vehicle was locked up tight, so he'd wait until he could get the keys to give the inside a more thorough inspection. He moved to the back of the vehicle, where training and sharp instincts had him crouching down to run his hand under the car's framework. Whoever was behind the unsolicited interest in Katie had to have a way of keeping track of her comings and goings.

And there it was.

Palming the tracking device, Ian stood glancing around the structure where only three vehicles remained parked, one of them his own. He circled past the other two cars, surveying the inside of both. Nothing jumped out as being overly suspicious. No visible weapons, no laptop computers, cameras, or telephoto lenses. No camouflaged binoculars or night goggles. Of course, all that would have made it too easy. He walked back to his jeep, climbed in, and began his drive toward the exit.

Pulling onto the main road, he mulled over everything he'd learned so far, coming to the conclusion that someone had the Nolan women in his or her sights.

He increased his speed, more determined than ever that everyone needed to get back to the safety of the estate.

Tony crouched near a broken window on the fourth floor of an abandoned building which stood directly across the road from St. Michael Hospital, asking himself how many times Katie Nolan was going to slip through his grasp.

Thanks to the tracking device he'd placed under the bumper of her vehicle when it had been parked at Clancy's several nights ago, he'd been aware of the exact moment she'd driven off the Reddington property tonight. He'd been driving toward Abbott when the app on his phone signaled that her car was also on the move. Following the signal, he wound up in a Pendleton parking garage thirty minutes later. He pulled into a spot several spaces down from Katie's vehicle and walked to the stairwell where he could keep an eye out for her return. If he could grab her before she made it back to her car, his pursuit for payback would be over.

Unfortunately for him, this improvised plan had been spoiled when, forty minutes into his wait, she'd gone tumbling down the concrete steps, one flight below where he'd been hiding in the shadows. As if that wasn't bad enough, a Good Samaritan who'd been entering the stairwell at preciously the same time, witnessed the fall and had insisted on calling for an ambulance. Luck had him overhearing one of the EMTs radio in to St. Michael Hospital, announcing that they'd be bringing in a patient. Once the ambulance departed, he'd made his way back to his car, ending up once again, waiting in the shadows.

Using the scope mounted on the long-range rifle that once had belonged to his father, Tony brought the entryway of the emergency room into focus. He had learned to shoot from his old man and made it a habit to keep his skills razor sharp. In fact, he considered himself to be a marksman, especially when he used his father's Remington.

Tony had the rifle aimed through a jagged opening that had once been an office window in the now bankrupt food processing plant. Ironically, his father had once been employed here, unceremoniously laid-off with two hundred other unfortunates when management emptied the pension accounts, leaving the workers locked out. That corporate verdict had been the proverbial straw that broke the camel's back, and his family had been forced to move to California where his father had found a new job there. Fortunately, the old man had managed to hang onto the cabin near Baker City.

The building Tony was currently holed up in had been sold a number of times over the years until, finally, it had been left dank and empty. His lips twitched at the thought that where once the father had met failure, the son was determined to embrace success.

It was half-past midnight when Tony spotted Katie's mother rush through the hospital's emergency entrance, Arthur Reddington at her side. He bet that she'd already discovered the damage he'd done to her condo. Maybe he'd gone a little overboard on that one, although, the momentary loss of control on his part had surely gotten the message across that he meant business. Business that was going to end with a bang just as soon as the Nolan women reappeared.

A quick glance at his watch told Tony that it was going on four hours that he'd been sitting in this oppressive shell of a room. He shifted slightly, feeling his hands and legs begin to cramp. He was also painfully aware that the headache slowly inching its way up the back of his neck was causing beads of sweat to take shape across his forehead and upper lip.

"Damn it," he snarled as he eased away from the rifle and shook his head in an attempt to ward off his exhaustion. His eyes felt gritty and dry, and as he rubbed them, he noticed the subtle tremble in his hand.

"What the hell—" Tony shot to his feet and pressed his back against one of the cracked and blistering walls. He was just tired, he told himself as he swiped at his forehead with his shirt sleeve.

Letting his mind drift, he slowly slid his back down the wall and sat with his knees bent to make a cushion for his head. Closing his eyes, he took deep, concentrated breaths until he slowly felt his composure return.

He hadn't realized that he'd let the fatigue take him under until he suddenly awoke, unaware of how much time had passed. The words being spoken in his head were at first confusing until the familiarity of them became a cautionary reminder of a time so long ago.

"Man up," the voice demanded.

It was as if his father was right there in the room, dictating his orders as he'd done when Tony was a young boy.

"You won't get very far in this world if you spend all your time whining about what you should have done instead of getting out there and doing it. You hear me, boy? Or have you forgotten everything I taught you?"

Tony staggered to his feet and squared his shoulders, chastising himself for going soft, especially now when the difference between success and failure could be measured in millimeters.

"I hear you, Dad," he sneered with a renewed sense of energy mixed with rage. "I'll take care of this, you can count on me."

Tony moved back to the window and dropped to one knee, adjusting the rifle as he fixed his eye on the scope. He brought the glass paneling next to the hospital's entrance door back into focus as he realigned his sights and waited for the target to present.

Exactly thirteen minutes and thirty-three seconds later, he took the first shot.

Five hours after her arrival in the emergency room, Katie woke with a dull headache and a dry mouth. Scanning the room, she spotted Clay slouched in a straight back plastic chair, texting on his phone. "Your patience continues to amaze me," she sighed. "You've been here the whole time, haven't you?"

"Here and there. They have lousy coffee in the vending machine but a pretty decent apple pastry."

"I was going to make stuffed pork chops for dinner. And serve an excellent Chardonnay."

"We'll have to put those plans on hold for a few days," Clay said. "I don't think the wine would mix well with that pain medication they've given you."

"Good stuff," she said as she rubbed her hands over her face. "Can we leave now?" she asked pushing herself into a sitting position.

"Soon." Clay stood and walked over to the side of the bed, handing over his half empty bottle of water. "Your mom's here. So is Arthur."

"Why are they here?" Katie asked, still feeling slightly confused from the pain medication.

"Arthur called Ian to let him know they were on their way back, and Ian filled him in. Oh, the nurse brought in a pair of scrub pants for you to wear home," Clay continued, deliberately changing the subject. "You may remember that the EMTs had to cut your jeans to get at your knee. Anyway, she said they'll probably be a little big in the waist but should fit over the bandage."

"Thanks," Katie said, pulling back the top sheet to examine her now bare leg. "Tell me that isn't all swelling," she gasped as she got a look at her knee.

"Most of it is bandage," a voice said from behind Clay. The nurse who had spoken to him earlier about Katie's injury stepped over to the bed. "I gave your fella here some instructions about changing the knee wrap, and by tomorrow you should see improvement." As she helped Katie slip the scrubs up and over her legs, she continued to talk. "You should call your own doctor in the morning and schedule a follow-up. You probably won't need the crutches for long, but use them for at least tonight and tomorrow. Don't overdo it. Even though it's only sprained, it still needs time to heal."

"Got it," Katie said as she eased into the wheelchair the nurse had parked near the bed.

"The doctor gave you a prescription for pain. Take it only if you feel you need it."

"Whatever you gave me seems to have worked extremely well so far," Katie remarked.

"You're all checked out. Someone from our transport staff will be here shortly to take you down to the lobby."

Giving Katie a quizzical look, Clay waited until the nurse left the room. "Transport staff?" he said mockingly. "Sounds like you're getting chauffeur service. I hope that means we all get a ride out of here."

"Very funny," she said.

Katie glanced up when she heard her mother's voice from the doorway. "Katie, you're awake. And it looks like you're ready to leave."

"She's been cleared, and we're just waiting for her chauffeur." Clay laughed when Katie gave him an exasperated look. "What? I thought it was funny."

Turning back to her mother, she asked, "Why are you back here? Was there a problem with the plane?"

"No, no. The flight was magnificent," Marian said. "We came back because—"

Marian's response was cut short by a young girl who breezed through the doorway, making a beeline straight to the wheelchair. Her glossy black hair—which was streaked with sporadic strands of purple—fell to her shoulders. The bangs she wore were cut dramatically short, leaving her sharp, translucent eyes fully exposed. Currently, her jaw was working overtime as she manipulated a wad of gum inside of her mouth, the motion exaggerated by the glittering diamond stud pierced through her lower lip.

"Mia Winters at your service," she chirped, handing Clay a pair of crutches before turning her attention to Katie. "Ready to call it a night?" she asked, releasing the brake levers on the wheelchair so she could roll Katie into the hall.

"We'll talk later," Marian said, as she and Arthur fell into step behind Katie. Clay adjusted his grip on the crutches before grabbing the two shopping bags that had accompanied Katie on her ambulance ride to the hospital, then hurried to catch up with the group.

Ian turned his thoughts to Arthur and Marian as he drove to the hospital.

When Arthur had phoned earlier with the news about Marian's condo, he'd also told Ian he didn't think the break-in had been random, and the details he'd shared were disturbing at best. The intruder had apparently broken in through the patio door, and the unit had been completely trashed—furniture torn, artwork hacked to pieces, vases and glass figurines smashed beyond repair. But Arthur's description of the desecration to the walls was what now worried Ian the most. Words like *Nowhere to hide* and *Someone will pay* were spray-painted in bold black letters throughout the kitchen and living room areas. The bedroom had also been hit with a number of uncomplimentary terms appearing on the wall above the bed.

To Ian's relief, Arthur had enlisted the services of a bodyguard from a firm he often used when traveling. In fact, he'd heard from Arthur a half hour ago and was told that he and Marian had arrived back in Oregon, trouble-free, and were on their way to the hospital. So, for the time being, everyone was safe.

When his cell phone buzzed, he reached into his pocket and pulled it out, immediately recognizing the number that flashed on the screen. "Clay. How's Katie?"

"Good. She's been released, and we're heading for the main doors now."

"I'm pulling into the parking lot now, so wait for me. I don't want you guys leaving—"

The sound of gunfire echoed not only through Ian's phone but directly outside his half-opened window. He dropped the phone in his lap, keeping the line to Clay's cell open, increasing his speed as he weaved his way through the lot, dodging first an ambulance and then a group of hospital personnel who were in the crosswalk, apparently on their way to the employee entrance ready to begin their shift. They had all dropped hard to the ground when the initial shot was fired, but Ian was sure that none of them had been hit. The shooter wasn't interested in innocent bystanders. He was aiming at the entrance to the ER.

Ian pulled up tight alongside a delivery van that appeared to be empty, cursing the fact that he was still too far away from the main doors to see what was going on inside. He grabbed his phone as he exited the jeep and dove behind the van.

CHAPTER
THIRTY-ONE

Before Katie knew what had happened, she was lying on the floor behind the reception counter, Clay shielding her body and yelling, "Stay down, stay down!" Later, she would remember wondering where in the world he thought she'd go considering there was a one hundred ninety-pound body of solid muscle pressed on top of her.

The first gunshot had buzzed past Clay's head and landed with a *whoof* in the back of a leather visitor's chair stationed to the right of the counter. He heard the second shot fire off within seconds of the first and saw it strike the bodyguard who had been herding Arthur and Marian to safer ground. The next shot took out the double-paned glass window to the right of the revolving doors, but Clay wasn't able to identify where the bullet had landed.

But Katie had. From her position behind the desk, she heard Arthur's involuntary grunt as his body jerked against Marian's, followed by her mother's anguished scream. Katie tried to wiggle free from Clay's hold, fear mixing with worry in her voice as she said, "We have to help him. I think Arthur's been hit."

"Stay put, Katie." Clay's mouth was so close to her right ear that she felt the rush of breath as he spoke. "What if the shooter's not done? Do you want to be laying there next to Arthur with a bullet through your heart?"

He turned his head slightly and noticed that Mia was crouched near Katie, her eyes wide with disbelief but otherwise appearing to be unharmed. Continuing his scan of the lobby, he saw a nurse curled up behind a large planter directly across from the counter and then saw Arthur, who indeed had been hit, blood staining his beige pullover shirt at the point of impact.

He couldn't tell how severe the wound was, but when he looked at Arthur's face, he was able to read the man's lips and see the pleading in his eyes when he whispered, "Help Marian."

Clay nodded. Taking a deep breath, he darted from behind the counter, grabbing hold of Marian's arms so he could pull her from under Arthur's body. She fought Clay's efforts to drag her across the floor, crying out Arthur's name, but it didn't slow him down. Even as he heard another round of fire strike the wall inches above his head, he kept moving.

As soon as he got Marian tucked safely into Katie's arms, he moved toward the corner of the desk, intending to go back for Arthur. He was relieved to see that a security guard had used Marian's rescue as a diversion to drag Arthur in the opposite direction where he was now being treated by a physician, out of sight of the shooter.

"Is anyone hurt?" Clay asked as he drew his attention back to the group behind the desk. "Marian?"

"Where's Arthur? He's the one who needs help, Clay. You have to help him."

"He's safe, and he's with a doctor now. We need to stay put right here."

"What's happening? I don't understand what's happening."

"Stay still, Mom. Everything is going to be okay."

But as Katie spoke the words, the look on her face told a different story, and all Clay could do was shake his head, unable to give her any answers.

From the sound of the rifle shots, Ian was pretty sure the shooter was in the rundown building across the street, on the far side of the old county roadway. Although he had watched for a muzzle flash, there had been too many other things he'd needed to concentrate on, so he'd missed seeing any.

Now as he crab-crawled to the front of the van, straining to see through the spider-webbed cracks in the glass doors leading into the ER, he put the phone to his ear and tried to rouse Clay.

"Clay, can you hear me? You there, Clay? What's your status?"

Hearing Ian's voice coming through the phone that had landed beneath the receptionist's chair when the shooting began, Clay scrambled for it and began giving Ian a report. "Arthur's been hit. It looks like they're getting ready to take him into one of the back rooms. The bodyguard who was with him also took a hit. I don't know how bad it is, and we can't get to him because he's too far out in the open. I'm with Marian and Katie behind the reception counter. There are two other hospital personnel in the lobby area, but they're safe for now."

"Are you sure you're all out of the line of fire?"

"I'm sure. Christ, Ian. Whoever is shooting has a laser sight. I'd just helped Katie out of the wheelchair and if I hadn't seen the red dot on her chest she would have taken the first hit."

"I think he's across the parkway in the old Klugmann building," Ian said.

"Do you think he's done?"

"It's been three minutes since the last shot, but stay put. The cops are just pulling in."

Marian remained crouched behind the reception counter watching helplessly as a doctor applied pressure to Arthur's wound while calling out orders to the other hospital personnel who had joined him at the end of the hallway. When the gurney arrived, Arthur was lifted onto it and rushed toward the exam rooms.

It wasn't until the familiar sounds of sirens echoed through the spine-chilling silence in the lobby that Marian found herself being helped to her feet by Clay. She turned as a swarm of cops rushed through the front doors, their shoes crunching on glass that lay in splinters across the lobby floor. Ian was right behind them, and when he reached Marian, he gave her a cursory check to make sure she was uninjured. Satisfied, he escorted her out of the lobby and back into the bowels of the ER.

When they stepped into the exam room where a medical team was working on Arthur, she was only vaguely aware that Katie and Clay had followed and were standing in the corridor behind her. She watched as a man in his mid-forties feverishly tried to stop the bleeding coming from Arthur's chest. She glanced at the doctor's face, thinking that it could only be his years of training that prevented him from displaying the concern he must be feeling.

After twenty-five agonizing minutes of orchestrated chaos, Marian heard the doctor give the order to move the patient to the surgical floor. The nurse who had been working alongside the doctor came over to where Marian stood.

"Is everyone here alright?" she asked.

"Yes, I think so," Marian said as she looked at first Clay and then Katie who was leaning heavily on her crutches. "Except my daughter was here earlier for a sprained knee." Resting a hand on Katie's arm, her mother said, "Do you need someone to look at it?"

"No, it's okay," Katie reassured her mother.

Figuring the daughter knew best, the nurse didn't push it. "Let someone know if the knee becomes bothersome to you." she said.

"I will. I promise."

"Do you have any idea when we'll have some news about Arthur?" Marian asked, even though she knew what the answer would be.

"I'm afraid not," the nurse said in a calm, quiet voice. "I understand that waiting is difficult at a time like this. I can assure you that he's getting the care he needs from an exceptional medical team."

As they'd been talking, the nurse had led the group to an elevator at the end of the corridor where she now stopped to push the call button. "Go to the second floor and turn left. The waiting room will be on your right. Someone will be out to give you an update as soon as they can."

With that, she disappeared through a set of doors restricted to hospital personnel use, and everyone else piled into the elevator.

Over the next hour, everyone was trapped in wait mode. The reality of what had happened in the hospital's lower lobby had finally hit both Marian and Katie, although neither seemed to want to talk about it. Marian's obvious concern for Arthur had also been put on the discussion back-burner.

Ian could tell that Katie was curious. He had seen her watching her mother closely when she thought no one was looking. Katie no doubt suspected that Marian and Arthur had feelings for each other, but Ian knew there was more to their relationship that had yet to be told.

Marian stood when a woman wearing loose-fitting navy scrubs quietly stepped into the room. "I'm Sandra, one of the nurses assisting Dr. Adair. Mr. Reddington is still in surgery. I can only tell you that he's holding his own. He is going to need more blood, and I need to ask if anyone is O-Negative. We only have a short supply in house and—"

"I'm O-Negative," Katie said as she stepped forward. "I'll give you as much as you need."

The nurse offered Katie a gentle smile. "There's only so much we can take in a sitting but even that will help until we can get some more in. Are you a relative?"

"No. I work for Arthur."

"Oh," the nurse said, glancing from Katie to Marian. "Usually with this blood type—well, it doesn't matter," she added as she motioned for Katie to follow her. "Let's get you over to the lab."

"Clay, why don't you go with Katie," Ian said. "I have someone coming in to guard her, but he's about a half hour out yet."

Marian watched the trio leave, and as they rounded the corner at the end of the hallway, she burst into tears. Putting his arm around her shoulders, Ian said, "I know this is difficult, Marian. I wish I could do more for Arthur than just sit here, waiting. And I'm guessing you're feeling the same way."

She turned her head, pressing her face against his chest. "It's not only Arthur's surgery," she said quietly. "I believe that he's in good hands, and there's nothing we can do but trust the surgical team."

When Marian didn't continue, Ian said, "Maybe it's time to tell her."

Marian knew exactly what Ian meant by those words and wasn't at all surprised that Arthur had confided in him. "I've made so many mistakes in my life, and keeping Katie and Arthur apart has been the biggest. I should have told her when Robert died. I don't want it to be too late for them, Ian."

"It won't be too late. Arthur is the most stubborn man I've ever met. He's not going to let a bullet take him out."

Marian desperately wanted that to be true.

During the next three hours, they were joined by Katie and Clay as well as Ted Parker, one of Ian's security team. Everyone took turns walking the halls or getting coffee and snacks from the vending machine until a short, thin woman in scrubs, a stethoscope draped around her neck, stepped into the waiting area.

"Are you Mr. Reddington's family?" she asked in a steady, slightly accented voice.

"Yes, we are," Marian announced as she rose from where she'd been sitting on the couch. Katie silently moved to her mother's side, placing a supportive arm around her waist.

"I'm Dr. Adair, the surgeon who worked on Mr. Reddington. The bullet did some internal damage, creating significant bleeding into his abdomen as well as a rapid drop in blood pressure. We've been able to control both, and his prognosis looks very good. He's being taken to ICU where he'll be closely monitored.

"It may not seem like it," the doctor continued, "but the patient was extremely lucky. My best guess is that the bullet was deflected prior to striking Mr. Reddington, and that's what saved his life. We'll be watching for any post-surgical problems, but based on what I see, there shouldn't be any. He's stable right now, and he'll be under sedation most of the night. It would be best if you all go and get some rest and then come back in the morning."

"Can I see him now?" Marian asked.

"The ICU is on the fourth floor, and you can check at the nurses station for the room number. I have to stress that his body has experienced a huge shock, and the best thing for him right now is sleep. The nurses will tell you two visitors at a time, and they will limit those visits as they see fit. I'll be around for several more hours, and I promise that I'll check in on him. That's really all I can tell you at this point. It's up to Mr. Reddington now."

"Thank you, Doctor," Marian said quietly.

Ian handed the doctor a card. "Here's my number, Dr. Adair, in case you need to get hold of us. I'll also be giving the number to the nurses in ICU."

The doctor slipped the card into the breast pocket of her medical coat and turned to Marian. "Take my advice," she said sternly but with compassion. "Go and get some rest."

After the doctor left, Ian approached Marian. "Why don't you and Katie head over to ICU. I'll check to see if there's a room you can use when you're ready to catch a few hours of sleep. I'll also make sure you don't have any problems getting in to see Arthur."

"You must be anxious to see him yourself," Marian said

distractedly as she glanced toward the hallway where the doctor had stopped to speak with one of the nurses.

"And I will, but later. Ted's going to go with you."

Clay watched as Ted followed Katie and her mother out of the waiting area. When the three of them were out of hearing distance, he turned to Ian, no longer trying to hide his frustration. "What the hell is going on, Ian? While we were waiting for Katie's discharge papers, Arthur told me about Marian's condo. It's hard not to think that the same person who did that is responsible for Arthur's shooting. Although I'm pretty sure that Katie was the intended target."

"I agree with you that the incidents are connected." Ian said, reaching into the pocket of his jacket and showing Clay the tracking device he'd found under the bumper of Katie's car. "And I'm afraid that we need to add Katie's fall in the parking garage to that list. There's no way to tell how long she's been carrying this around, but whoever it was that planted the thing knew exactly where she was tonight."

"She said she heard someone on the level above her and, for some reason, got spooked," Clay said. "That's when she lost her footing and went down."

"I don't doubt that she heard someone, knowing what we do now," Ian stated as he took the device back from Clay. "It's a good thing that woman came along when she did. Otherwise, whoever is doing this could have been the one that came to her aid."

Clay rubbed his hand along the back of his neck, trying to ease the tension that had lodged there. "I certainly hope you have a plan. I'm finding it hard to think straight right now."

"First things first," Ian replied. "Two men from my security team are coming in, so why don't you wait here for them. I have a few things to take care of, but if they get here before I'm back, give me a call." Laying a supportive hand on Clay's shoulder, Ian added, "It's going to work out. I've already got Ethan working a few angles.

Now that we know how far this nut job is willing to go, we can set up the most efficient barriers to his attack. While we're doing that, we'll figure out who it is."

"Whatever you need me to do, just name it," Clay said.

"I will. For now, just sit tight."

CHAPTER THIRTY-TWO

Marian sat quietly by Arthur's bedside watching his shallow breathing, knowing that without the tubes and IV drips, even that simple task would be difficult.

She reached over the side of the bed and took his hand, rubbing her thumb lightly across his wrist. Intellect told her it wasn't her fault that Arthur was lying here in critical condition, but she couldn't stop blaming herself nonetheless. Swiping at the single tear that rolled down her cheek, she whispered, "I'm here, Arthur. I'm right here."

"Mom?" Marian glanced up and saw Katie standing in the doorway. "May I come in?"

"Of course," Marian said, slowly releasing her grip on Arthur's hand. "How's your knee?"

"It's fine," Katie said as she moved to stand near her mother.

"If it gives you any trouble, you need to tell someone."

"I will," Katie said before asking the question that had been weighing heavy on her mind. "Why didn't you tell me? After Dad died, you should have told me."

Marian closed her eyes, ashamed that Katie had been forced to learn of her parentage through a blood test that had probably saved her biological father's life.

"I didn't know how," Marian began, folding her hands tightly in her lap. "I'd kept the secret for so long, I was afraid that things would change between us. I hear how selfish that sounds, but it's the truth."

"Did Dad know?"

After a brief hesitation, Marian said, "Before I met Arthur, your father and I were having problems. We'd spent months being inattentive to each other, arguing over what seemed to be everything, and growing further and further apart. That's no excuse for what I did, simply an explanation. After I told your father I'd had an affair and that I was pregnant, there were a lot of hurtful words exchanged, a lot of sleepless nights. But we slowly found our way back to each other and committed ourselves to fixing what was wrong with our marriage. It took a great deal of time and counseling to rediscover that deep down we loved each other, that we were all a family.

"Even though I'd already cut all ties to Arthur, your father could have easily left us, and I wouldn't have blamed him. But he didn't. He stayed for many reasons, the most important one was his commitment to being a good father. To the boys, and to the daughter who may not have been his biologically, but was his in every other way that mattered. We may have had our problems, your father and I, but you have to believe, Katie, you were never one of them."

"Why didn't Arthur ever contact me?"

"Because I asked him not to. I convinced him that it was in your best interest to let Robert and I raise you. I truly believe that walking away from you had to have been the hardest thing that Arthur ever did."

Shifting in her chair so she was facing her daughter, Marian added, "Robert Nolan was your father. He raised you, took care of you when you were sick, taught you how to ride a bike and kick a soccer ball. He was so proud of you every single day, and he loved you with all his heart. Don't ever doubt that."

After a brief hesitation, Katie asked, "Did you have anything to do with me getting the commission to do Arthur's paintings?"

"No. I was the one who tried to talk you out of accepting the job, remember? It was only after you moved here that Arthur came to see me. Prior to that we hadn't seen or spoken to each other since before you were born. He gave you the commission because you deserved it."

When Katie didn't speak, Marian turned back to Arthur. "Robert is gone, Katie. But Arthur is here. He loves you, and he's proud of you, too."

Again, Katie let the silence settle over the room. Finally, she whispered, "You should have told me, Mom." With that, she turned and left the room.

Marian continued to sit with Arthur until the nurse came into the room and told her she needed to allow the patient to rest. She nodded and rose from her chair. "I'm hoping you can hear me," she said, leaning in close to the man she had never stopped loving. "I have to leave you for a little while. It's not my choice, it's what the doctor has ordered. I won't be far, and I'll be back as soon as I can." Brushing her hand through his hair, Marian said the words she'd left unspoken for too many years. "I love you, Arthur."

When Clay entered the waiting room, he spotted Marian on one of the sofas staring at a magazine that lay open on her lap. Although he'd been out of the room for a good thirty minutes, he was certain that she had yet to turn the page. He crossed the room and handed her a take-out cup, then moved over to where Ian and another man stood near a large window that looked out onto the parking lot.

"Have you talked to Nora?" he asked, lifting the lid on his own cup and inhaling the aroma of a strong Colombian brew.

"All's quiet. Ethan is at the house with her and Hannah." Nodding to the man standing alongside him, Ian added, "I'm not sure if you've ever met Ted Parker. Ted, this is Clay Crawford."

"I've seen you around," Ted said through an easy smile. "Nice to formally meet you."

Clay nodded and extended his hand. "Same here."

"How is Katie doing?" Marian asked as she set the magazine on a side table. Her concern for her daughter was based not only on how she was dealing with everything that had happened in the past twenty-four hours, but also because Katie now knew the truth about her biological father.

After Marian had left Arthur's bedside, she had found Katie sitting in the small meditation room on the third floor and had done her best to explain the circumstances surrounding her affair with Arthur. She had tried to reassure her daughter that Robert had loved his little girl more than life itself. But she wasn't certain how Katie was processing the information.

"She's resting down the hall. The nurse gave her a pain pill, and she finally fell asleep."

"Good," Marian said distractedly as she reached for another magazine. "Arthur's looking better, don't you think, Clay? He's getting some color back in his face."

"I agree," Clay said. "When I glanced into his room on my way back, he looked better than he did even a few hours ago."

"Was he awake? Did he say anything to you?" she asked tentatively.

"I wish I could say differently, but he's still pretty sedated. Sorry."

"It's probably going to be a while yet, Marian," Ian said softly from where he stood at the window staring down at the front entrance of the hospital. "Like the doctor said, this has all been a shock to his system."

Marian opened her mouth to say something, but when she saw the worried look on Ian's face, she rose and walked over to him. "I could use something to eat. I'm going to head down to the cafeteria. I'll bring you something."

"I'm good, but thanks."

"You've been taking care of me for hours. Let me take care of you this once."

Ian glanced at her and smiled. "Not to sound like a broken record, but Ted's going to go with you. Stay close to him, Marian."

"I will. Call if Katie wakes up or if anything changes with Arthur."

After Marian and Ted left the room, Ian said, "Do you feel that? The atmospheric pressure of guilt has dropped by several meters."

"Maybe," Clay responded. "But I don't think that Marian holds a candle to the guilt I bring to the table. I've got so many 'should haves' running around in my brain that there's little room for anything else."

Ian dropped into one of the cushioned chairs and stretched his legs straight out in front of him. "I think we're all suffering a bit too much from what-if-itis," he said. "I realize it's meaningless to second guess myself now, but I should have paid more attention when we were having problems with the security system."

"Well, you're not the only one who suspected there was something off," Clay said, taking a seat across from Ian. Setting his coffee on the end table, he leaned against the sofa's padded back and closed his eyes. "The hang-ups on her cell, the incident at the bar with the kittens. The photo shoot in the woods? She told me about that in passing, made a joke about her poor sense of direction. If I would have just looked at the big picture, I might have been able to piece it all together."

"And the guilt-meter is on the rise once again," Ian said.

Clay frowned. "Yeah, and you're right. Second guessing isn't going to get us the answers we need."

Ian looked hard at Clay, spotting the weariness that seemed to have attacked every inch of his body. "You should get some rest, too," he said. "To quote Miss Jenni Star, you're not going to be any good to anyone if you're half dead on your feet." At Clay's quizzical look, Ian added, "The nurse who was on duty last night. The cute brunette with the sexy smile and big personality?"

"Her name is really Jenni Star?" Clay asked, raising an eyebrow.

"Couldn't say. But if I'd been her mama, that's what I would have named her."

"You're insane," Clay declared jokingly.

"Not really a newsflash."

They sat in silence for several more minutes until Ian spoke. "Someone has a real vendetta against the Nolan clan. I've got some feelers out, and as soon as Marian gets back, I'll be leaving to do some of my own digging. You got any ideas? Anything that maybe Katie mentioned about trouble back home?"

"I've thought about it, but I can't come up with anything," Clay said. "Until you showed me that tracking device from Katie's car, I would never have believed she had a stalker. Not to mention someone who would go to these lengths to seek revenge on her."

"Revenge," Ian said thoughtfully. "An interesting description and an accurate one. Small, irritating things at first, meant to . . . what? Distract her? Maybe punish her? It keeps escalating until one day he finally comes for her and tries to take her down. For what, though?

When he couldn't readily produce an answer, Ian continued. "Dean will be attached to Katie until we have a solid lead on who's behind all of this. If you leave the hospital on your own for any reason, he'll get someone to go with you. Whoever is doing this recognizes that you're important to Katie, which means that you're as much of a target as she is."

"I've got that," Clay said.

A short while later, Ted and Marian returned, and Ian left the hospital with the turkey sandwich she'd brought him. Clay slipped out of the waiting area and headed toward the room the nurses had offered to the family for downtime.

When he stepped through the door, he found Katie sound asleep. He eased onto the bed next to her and closed his eyes, trying to settle his racing mind. Eventually, he too fell asleep, with thoughts of Katie's infectious smile easing back his anxiety.

Katie was sitting against the trunk of a tree with her eyes closed and her breathing slow and steady. The melodious sound of a starling floated from somewhere in the distance, and she could hear the soft rustle of leaves as they were caught by the cool summer breeze. She smiled as that same breeze danced across her cheeks. The sun was warm to both body and soul, and the tranquility of the moment was soothing. This is what heaven must feel like, she thought lightheartedly.

"Katie? Are you with me, baby girl?"

"Daddy?"

"There's my girl. So pretty and all grown-up."

"Oh, Dad, you always say that." But after the words were out of her mouth, she caught her mistake. "I guess I should have said you used to say that. I've missed you."

"I've missed you, too. I see that you and your mother have gotten yourselves into quite the predicament."

"You could say that."

Her father sat across from her in her dream, casually leaning against a Ponderosa pine, the deep cracks of the old tree releasing a mixed scent of vanilla and butterscotch. As he watched her, she found herself thinking that he looked so young and vibrant. She could almost believe he was still alive.

Suddenly, the thought that she could see him caused a jump in her heart rate.

"What's on your mind, baby girl?" he asked.

Katie smiled. "I never could get you to stop calling me that. I used to get so embarrassed when you'd call me your baby girl in front of my friends. Now, it's quite endearing."

Robert Nolan chuckled. "Well, old habits are hard to break, isn't that how the saying goes?"

"Something like that. What are you doing here, Dad? Or better yet, what are we both doing here, together? Am I—"

"No, you're still among the living, although it appears that someone is trying hard to change that."

"I have no idea who hates me so much that they'd want to hurt me. To try to kill me."

"Maybe it's not totally about you, Katie. The best advice I can give you is that you need to sort out fact from fear and look at both past and present."

"Do all dead people talk in riddles," Katie smirked, "or just you? I can't even imagine what that means."

"I raised a smart girl. You'll figure it out. Just make sure you do before you or your mother have to pay the price for someone's misguided truth."

Katie shifted her gaze to her surroundings as she thought about that. The sun's gentle touch flowed through the opening in the trees, and again she felt the gentle breeze as it created a whisper of movement over her hair. She closed her eyes and breathed soulfully, needing to memorize this moment for later when she would try to put it all down on canvas.

After sharing several quiet minutes, Katie opened her eyes and stared at the man who had raised her. His face was still so handsome, and his voice both gentle and strong. His eyes smiled at her, and she knew that if she stayed here with him, just like this, everything bad that was happening to her would disappear. He would hold her and comfort her, all the while keeping the pain away.

"Mom told me about Arthur," she said with sadness in her own eyes.

"And how did that make you feel?"

"Confused. Deceived. Lonely."

"Why lonely?"

"My life turned out to be a lie. Everything I thought was real? All of a sudden it wasn't."

"You're looking at it all wrong, Katie," her father said with empathy. "Your life with your mother and me was as real as it gets. I may not have been the man who gave you your first breath of life, but I was the man who completed it."

"You seem so calm about all this. Didn't it make you angry when Mom told you about her and Arthur?"

"Of course I was. Angry, hurt, confused. You name it, and I probably felt it. But by the time you were born, most of my anger was gone and forgiveness followed. I still remember the moment I first saw you. I cradled you in my arms, held you against my heart, and I knew there wasn't a chance in hell that I'd ever give you up. Arthur could have made things difficult, but he didn't. And I'll forever be grateful for that. I've come to believe that he made the ultimate sacrifice so you could become a Nolan.

"Katie, your mother is one of the most loving, caring women I've ever known. Believe that my time with both of you was blessed. That's all that matters."

Trying desperately to hold back tears, Katie said, "I feel as if I'll be betraying you if I allow Arthur into my life."

"I don't feel that way," her father said gently. "Arthur won't replace me, baby girl. He'll stand alongside me in your heart if you let him."

Katie saw her father's image begin to dim and realized that her time with him was coming to an end. She knew she'd have to let him go soon, and felt an intense ache in that heart he'd spoken so fondly of. "Are you happy, Dad?"

"Very."

"So is everything to your liking up there?" she teased.

"Very much so, smarty-pants," Robert Nolan said with a twinkle in his eyes. "I'd like to ask you to do something for me."

"Anything. Just name it."

"You have a new chapter ahead of you, and it's going to be up *to you which road to take. Choose wisely, sweetie." He stood and walked over to where Katie sat. He crouched in front of her and brushed his hand lightly over her hair. "Don't ever doubt that I'm always with you, and that I'm so very proud of you. Say hello to your mother and tell her I wish her and Arthur all the happiness they can muster." Leaning over, he kissed her cheek. "Go on now. Your mother is worried about you, but you can fix that. I love you."*

He rose, pausing only briefly before turning and walking away. Katie didn't take her eyes off her father until he disappeared into a thicket of weeping willows, and even then she continued to stare. Amazingly, the visit with her father had made her feel both peaceful and content. His words had soothed, and his presence had instilled a renewed energy for life.

She stood and strolled to an opening in the trees, looking first in the direction her father had taken, then turning and walking the other way. She was sure that she would see Robert Nolan again. Just not today.

CHAPTER
THIRTY-THREE

Christina and Andrew arrived at the hospital the day following Arthur's shooting. Clay was coming out of the waiting area when he saw them exit the elevator and detoured down the hall to greet them.

"Thank you for having Nora call," Christina said when they reached Clay. Giving him a hug, she asked, "How is Arthur doing?"

"Still sedated."

"And Katie?"

"She's got a lot on her plate, and I think she can really use a good friend right now."

"I'll do my best. What have you learned from the police about who did this?"

"They aren't saying much at this point. We've all been interviewed, but that's it so far."

"I can make a call," Andrew offered. "I happen to have a client who may be able to give us something."

"We'd all be grateful, Andrew. Thank you."

As Andrew wandered back toward the elevators, Christina looped her arm with Clay's and said, "Where are Katie and Marian?"

"Katie's in with Arthur, and her mom is this way," he motioned, leading her toward the waiting room.

Christina felt the weariness the minute she walked into the room. She saw Marian first, tucked into one end of the sofa, her hands clasped tightly in her lap and her eyes partially closed. It wasn't until Christina moved further into the room that she spotted the man leaning against the wall with his arms folded across his chest. Bodyguard, she thought. Andrew occasionally used security when he traveled out of the country, and she recognized the casual yet intense stance.

As Christina crossed the room, Marian opened her eyes. "Christina." Marian said quietly, her voice heavy with that weariness Christina had felt on her arrival. "Oh, Katie will be so glad you've come."

"I came for you too, Marian," Christina said as she sat next to Katie's mother. "I hope you're taking care of yourself."

"I am. Clay and Katie wouldn't have it any other way. She's in with Arthur now. We take turns because he's not ready to take us all on at once."

Christina leaned over and gave Marian a hug. "There's no one stronger than Arthur. He'll come through this."

Clay watched the women reassuring each other, but he couldn't stop thinking how it had been well over ten hours now since Arthur had been shot. He had yet to wake up. Clay didn't have much experience in the field of medicine, but shouldn't they have seen some improvement in his condition by now? Didn't the prognosis get worse the longer he stayed under?

To be fair though, Dr. Adair had stopped in before she went off duty last night to update them on Arthur's condition, assuring them that Arthur's vitals were good, and that it was up to him when he woke up. And the nursing staff was wearing a path in and out of his room, constantly checking on him.

"My turn to make the coffee run," Clay said, frustrated with nothing to do but wait. "I'm going to the bistro down the street. Call me if anything changes."

"I'll tag along with you," Ted said as he pushed off the wall where he'd been standing. "Ian called and said he's on his way up."

When Clay gave him a look that clearly read, *I don't need a babysitter,* Ted added, "You've been boxed up in here for way too many hours now, and you need some air, I get that. And I need a cigarette. So grab your jacket and let's go."

Arthur woke to the comforting sight of snowflakes delicately swirling past the window, the midday lighting giving them a soft almost illusive appearance. Yet, as soothing as the scene outside appeared, what surrounded him inside momentarily left him confused and somewhat disoriented. It wasn't until he heard the low, steady beep near the head of the bed—combined with the smells and muffled voices in the hallway outside the room—that he remembered hearing someone tell him he was in the hospital, assuring him that he was safe.

An instant later, his mind took a sharp turn, and he remembered the gunfire along with the piercing pain he'd felt when the bullet had struck his chest. Followed by his regret that he hadn't had more time with Marian. As it all replayed brazenly in his head, he tried to control the trembling that had taken over his body.

He needed to find Marian and Katie. Make sure that they were both unharmed. He tried to sit upright, only to discover that the attempt caused a vicious pain that quickly sliced through his back and side. Deciding he'd take a minute before trying again, he cautiously rotated his head to take in the rest of the room. The first thing he saw was a small pressed-wood closet door in a corner near the window. Next, a vinyl high-back chair that held extra sheets and pillows, and a pale green blanket that was carelessly tossed across the chair's arm. The thin clear vase holding half a dozen carnations in varying colors was the last thing to come into view when he spotted the nightstand alongside the bed.

Hearing a familiar voice, he shifted his gaze to the doorway and saw Katie talking to one of his security men. An involuntary reflex had his fingers clutching the edge of the blanket as he tried to speak. His voice came out as a jagged whisper, but it was enough to catch his daughter's attention.

Katie broke away from Dean and quickly moved to the side of the bed. "Get a nurse, Dean," she said, reaching down and gently taking Arthur's hand in hers. "Lie still, Arthur. Just lie still." Smiling, she quietly added, "Everything's okay now."

The elevator doors opened, and Clay followed Ted into the car. As he turned to face the hallway, he saw first one nurse and then a second hurrying in the direction of Arthur's room.

"Wait," he snapped, as his arm flew out to stop the doors from closing. "Something's going on," he added as both men stepped back out into the hallway.

Marian and Christina were walking out of the waiting room just as Clay and Ted reached them. "There's activity in Arthur's room," he said, gently taking Marian's elbow and guiding her down the hallway.

When the foursome reached the room, the nurse that Ian affectionately called Jenni Star was next to Arthur's bed using her stethoscope to listen to his breathing while asking him a series of questions.

"Move aside please," the young resident mumbled as Marian and Clay parted to allow the doctor access into the room. "Everyone needs to leave," he ordered as he pulled his own stethoscope from around his neck.

No one moved.

Arthur's eyes were closed but Marian could hear him answering the questions being tossed at him by the medical staff, and her heart soared. When Katie went to stand next to her mother, Christina and Clay slipped back into the hallway where they found Andrew and Ian waiting.

"Is it good news?" Andrew asked, locking eyes with his wife.

"I think it is," she said moving into his arms.

Ted and Dean were the next to exit the room and quietly moved toward the waiting area with Ian. Not wanting to be too far from Katie, Clay hovered near the door and watched the doctor first check Arthur's incision, then verify that his vitals were within an acceptable range. Finally, he gave the nurse instructions for the patient's immediate care.

Encouraged with what he saw, the tired looking doctor turned to leave. "Everything looks good," he said to Marian. "I've ordered another set of X-rays to make sure his lungs are still clear and some more blood work to make sure his kidney and liver functions are normal. I'll check in with him again later." Noticing the worried look on Marian's face, the doctor added, "Trust me. Everything looks good." Reaching into the pocket of his lab coat to retrieve his vibrating pager, he hurried out the door.

The nurse had been making several notations on the computer notepad she carried with her but now slid it into the pocket of her scrubs. Giving her full attention to Arthur, she said, "We're going to adjust some of your medication, but you let me know if the pain becomes too severe. All you have to do is push the call button if we need to increase the dosage again."

"Thank you," Arthur whispered in a voice he barely recognized as his own.

"He still needs rest," the nurse said as she reached up to make sure the IV was dripping properly. "If he gets sleepy, let him sleep. And don't get him all riled up, or I'll go back to limiting visitors."

"Will Dr. Adair be in tonight?" Marian asked.

"She's expected back in several hours. I think she'll be thrilled to see that Arthur's awake." She glanced at the patient one last time, then left the room.

"Who's Dr. Adair?" Arthur's weakened voice drifted from the bed.

Katie could see that Arthur was struggling to make sense of his surroundings. Concerned she'd be more of a hindrance than a help, she gently laid her hand on her mother's arm. "I'll go wait down the hall, give you and Arthur some time together."

As Katie quietly left the room, Marian stepped closer to the bed and took Arthur's hand, interlocking her fingers with his. "Dr. Adair did your surgery." she said softly. "She's been keeping us all updated and says you're doing great." When a tear trickled down her right cheek, she brushed it aside and leaned down to kiss him. "I'm so glad you're doing great."

When she pulled back, Arthur squeezed her hand and in a soft but determined voice said, "I love you from here to the moon."

CHAPTER THIRTY-FOUR

Two days later, Clay, Ian, and Katie sat on the front porch of the Reddington house drinking coffee and enjoying maybe one of the last warmer days before winter stuck for good. Marian was still spending the majority of her time at the hospital with Arthur, watched over by a rotating security team of highly trained men and women, all handpicked by Ian.

Things had remained quiet on the home front, probably due to the fact that leaving the estate was a rarity for anyone except Clay. Initially, Hannah had weighed in with a substantial protest about the limits put on her social life, but when she walked into Arthur's room and saw what had been done to him, she quickly changed her tune. Of course, Mason—the young, dark-skinned, muscular bodyguard Ian had assigned to her—hadn't exactly hurt. Ian was indeed a wise man.

"Have you had a chance to talk to Arthur yet?" Ian asked idly.

Katie knew exactly what "talk" he was referring to. "Not in great detail. Only to tell him that I know I'm his biological daughter, and that we'd have time to talk about it when he was back home. I didn't want to put more on him then he can handle right now."

"How are you doing?"

"I'm still digesting the news. Although, it doesn't freak me out. Nothing's changed. Arthur and Mom are in love, and I'm happy for them." Her father's words popped into her head: *Arthur won't replace me, baby girl. He'll stand alongside me in your heart.* Sure, they were spoken in a dream, but they were prophetic nonetheless. "It'll work out," she added.

Quiet ensued until Clay finally said, "I've been thinking. What if this whole thing really did begin back in Long Beach?"

Both Ian and Katie understood what Clay was asking. Trying to figure out who was responsible for Katie's stalking—which is what they were officially calling it now—and Arthur's shooting had been the primary topic of conversation for the past seventy-two hours.

"We've been over all that," Katie sighed. "I can't come up with anything else to tell you."

"But maybe we missed something. Maybe we didn't go back far enough."

"How far back do you suggest we go? Maybe a list of anyone who picked a fight with me in kindergarten would be helpful."

"This is tough, Katie, we get that," Ian interjected sympathetically. "But we have to look at every angle."

"Yeah, yeah. Turn every page. Spin every idea. Flip every frickin' rock."

"Maybe we should change the subject for a while," Ian said through a crooked smile.

Clay sat next to Katie on the porch swing, gently rubbing his hand along her thigh for comfort. Ian had his chair leaning on its two back legs, his feet propped on top of the porch rail, and his hat pulled down over his eyes.

"Maybe Clay's right," Katie finally said.

"What? Have you thought of something?" Clay asked, shifting in his seat to face Katie.

"No. Well, maybe. I mean, I don't have anything that will lead us right to the front door of the person responsible for all this."

"But?"

"Look. Mom and I aren't saints by any means, but there isn't anything we've done that would make someone want to hurt us. We don't now, or have we ever held the type of jobs that would draw this kind of attention to us."

"Continue," Ian said, removing his hat as Nora pushed through the screen door and stepped onto the porch.

Katie was thinking about her dream, and how her father's words had made her believe that in order to end this, they had to examine the big picture. *Sort out fact from fear and look at both past and present,* he'd said. *Figure it out before you and your mother pay the price.*

"Maybe this isn't totally about me. Or Mom. Technically, I mean. Like Clay said, this could go back further than we've been looking. Back to my dad."

"That's a good angle," Ian considered, nodding a thank you to Nora as she refilled his cup from the carafe of fresh coffee she'd carried out of the house. "Is there anything in particular you're thinking about?"

"Nothing specific," she replied, shaking her head when Nora offered her a refill. "It's just that if any of us had enemies, it would have been him. He'd gotten a number of threats while he was in public service, especially while he was sitting on the bench. Maybe we should be looking at his cases."

"Which would include a span of how many years?" Clay asked, mentally calculating the number of files they'd need to go through. "And how would we even get our hands on that kind of information?"

"Mom probably remembers some of it. Some of it is public records. And if we want to throw in the cases he handled in private practice, maybe some of the partners from the law firm are still around."

"It's a long shot, honey," Clay said kindly as he accepted a refill from Nora.

"Yeah, but we haven't come up with anything better, and neither have the police."

"When are Christina and Andrew coming back?" Ian asked Katie, buying into the idea more easily than Clay seemed to be.

"Arriving tomorrow and leaving next Tuesday."

"I bet they'll be open to helping us out with this."

"Let's not forget Mom. And Arthur will want to help with whatever he can."

"And I'm no slouch when it comes to problem solving," Nora chimed in as she poured herself a cup of coffee and sat in her favorite wicker chair. "As a former nanny, half my day was spent trying to figure out which child was telling the truth."

"So we have the manpower." Although Clay wasn't totally convinced that Katie's suggestion to go through all her father's old cases was a realistic one, he nonetheless added, "Now all we have to do is get our hands on the files."

"Lucky for you, Ethan is a genius at digging up information," Ian said, "and he knows people who know people who know people. I'd be surprised if he didn't have a contact or two in the court system."

As Ian made the phone call, Clay said, "In the meantime, I think we should put together a timetable of specific incidents and the dates they occurred. In the spirit of staying organized, let's start with Arthur's shooting and work backward."

They spent the next hour piecing together Katie's life, concentrating on the time since she'd moved into the Reddington cottage—dissecting every call, every stranger she'd met, every mile she'd traveled. Clay made a list of people who had moved in and out of the area during the past several months, another list of people who may have shown a particular interest in Katie, and a third list of anyone who had known that Katie and Marian would be out of town the weekend Marian's condo had been broken into.

"All these people need to be cross-checked against the records that Ethan's getting," Clay said as he skimmed the completed lists. "I'd like to think I can vouch for some of them, but they need to be systematically cleared."

"Ethan and I will check out the names," Ian said, "beginning with where everyone was the weekend Marian's condo was trashed." Turning to Katie, he added, "Whoever is doing this has taken an unusual interest in you. With that said, I think it would be a waste of my breath to remind you that you need to watch your back. Better yet, let me or Clay or one of my guys watch it for you."

"I'm sure it won't always be possible for someone to be with me, Ian. I will say though, that if I'll be out there on my own, I'll let you or Clay know where I'm going and check back in when I get there. Because we don't have a clue when or how he or she will strike—or if I'm even the target—I do have one request."

"Name it," Ian said.

"I want you to keep someone on my mother. If we find that this is tied to my father, she'd be a target, too."

"Consider it done."

Although Ian still believed that Katie was the primary target, he had already assigned a rotation of coverage for Marian. Added to that, he had no intention of letting Katie go off the estate unprotected—a discussion best had another time.

They continued to hash out possibilities of who the stalker might be until Ian's phone rang. "It's Arthur, making his daily call demanding I break him out of the hospital." Rising from the chair, he said, "I'm going to do a security check on the property. See you guys later."

Nora also stood and looked at Katie. "I'm sorry you and your mother are going through this. It has to be difficult for both of you. I wish there was more I could do."

"Thank you, Nora," Katie said. "And please, never doubt that you're not doing enough. It's you who's keeping us all on an even keel. I appreciate that. Eventually, we'll find whoever is responsible for this."

Nora went back inside the house, leaving Clay and Katie alone.

Leaning into Clay and resting her hand on his chest, Katie said, "It's going to work out. I meant what I said to Nora. We're going to find whoever is responsible, then fry his sorry ass."

Running his hand down the side of Katie's hair, he totally endorsed her sentiment. "Sounds like a doable plan, sunshine. We'll indeed fry his sorry ass."

It hadn't taken long for the dining room to be transformed into the hub for research gathering. Andrew and Christina had joined Team Reddington shortly after their arrival on Saturday and now sat with Katie, combing through both computer files and hard copy documents.

"How did your visit with Arthur go today?" Christina asked Katie as she sat back in her chair and rubbed her fingers over her strained eyes.

"Good," Katie said with a smile. "He's anxious to come home, which could happen any day now. According to his physical therapist, he's one of the best patients she's ever worked with. Mom is handling it all pretty well," Katie added. "She's been staying with Arthur at the hospital, but he finally talked her into coming back here at night so she can get some real sleep."

Christina had been watching Katie as she spoke and now sat forward, curious about the look on her friend's face. "What is it? Have you found something?"

Katie held up the article that had been paper-clipped to the inside flap of one of the files. "I don't think so," she said as she passed the paper to Christina. "I remember this case, though. Gosh, I must have been ten or eleven. Somewhere around that. It was summer, and Mom took me to the courtroom one day because we were going to have lunch with Dad. We got there early and sat in the back of the room to watch him work. It was the sentencing phase in that case, and I saw the boy in the photo there, sitting in the front row with, according to the article, his mother. It was his dad who was being sentenced."

"That's some memory, girlfriend."

"I guess, although I don't recall anything specific about the case. It's what happened after my dad read the sentence that may be worth mentioning. The woman got hysterical, and they had to usher her into the hallway. But the boy just sat watching as they took his father out of the courtroom through a side door. He wasn't crying or throwing a tantrum—in fact he wasn't showing any reaction at all. Then one of the uniforms went over to where he was sitting and crouched down to talk to him. After a few minutes, he led the boy down the center aisle. When he walked passed me, I remember thinking what an odd expression this kid has on his face. It wasn't sad or unfriendly or even hostile. It was like he was empty of any emotion."

"You got a name?" Andrew asked.

"The kid's name was Adrián Santiago. His father was Anton."

"Do you recognize either name?"

"No, I don't," Katie said, still wondering how many other young boys had been devastated because of a parent who had chosen crime over family."

"It says here that the kid's father was found guilty of second degree murder," Christina read. "The victim was really worked-over, although this Anton guy tried to claim he was acting in self-defense. There were other charges initially, but they were dropped in a plea deal. Armed robbery, aggravated assault, and possession of an illegal substance." Handing the article back to Katie, she said, "Why don't you put this one in the pile that Marian is going to look over."

"Sure," Katie replied, already paging through the next set of documents.

Over the next two hours, cases were divided into three groups—those that were determined to have no impact on the recent events, those that had a slim connection, and finally those that fell into the category of being suspect. The latter group would be reviewed by Marian.

"I take it we're eating in the kitchen tonight," Nora said from the doorway to the dining room. "Although it goes against every hostess gene I possess."

"Having witnessed your absolute culinary skills before," Andrew piped in, "we could be eating that pot roast off the kitchen floor, and you still wouldn't get any complaints out of me."

"And Nora? We've gone way beyond guest status here," Christina said. "In fact, I think its Andrew's turn to do dishes tonight."

Nora smiled as she headed back into the kitchen. "Dinner will be ready in ten. I'll call upstairs to Melanie and tell her to come down."

"Maybe Nora could use a taste tester," Andrew announced as he closed down the document he'd been examining on his laptop. "Ah, the sacrifices a man must make."

"My husband, the connoisseur. While you're in there, offer to set the table."

As Andrew passed behind his wife, he leaned down and kissed the crown of her hair. "I'm on it."

Several minutes later, Hannah poked her head into the dining room. "My date's here."

Katie glanced up from the file she was reading. "I didn't realize you were going out tonight. You'll be missing pot roast. Why don't you ask him to stay?"

"I've been cooped up inside too long. So, thanks, but no thanks."

"Who's your shadow tonight?"

"Dean."

"Don't try to lose him, Hannah."

Hannah heard the concern in Katie's voice that matched the

expression on her face. "It's Dean, Katie. I'm not that good." When Katie tilted her head to the side and gave Hannah a measured look, Hannah chuckled, "I won't try to lose him. Promise."

"Have fun then."

Hannah returned to the atrium where her date, Tony Santana, was waiting for her. When she stepped into the room, he said, "All ready to go, Han?"

Hannah had asked Tony to pick her up at the house tonight, explaining that there were some family issues that required her to have a bodyguard with her at all times. She hadn't given a complete explanation, but he hadn't needed any of the details. He already knew that he was the issue.

When he'd arrived at the house, he'd been hoping that at the very least he'd get a clear picture of how difficult it would be to get Katie off the estate. He'd even entertained the idea that tonight would present an opportunity to grab her outright. From what he'd seen so far, however, the security was tight, although he could probably get around that with timing and a little bit of luck. He'd also have to choose a time when there were fewer people around who wouldn't interfere with his plan. Bottom line—he'd have to wait a little longer, refine the details, and strike when he could control the situation.

"I'm ready," Hannah replied as she slipped her arms through the sleeves of her leather jacket. "Dean should be waiting outside."

"Yeah, he gave me the once over when I got here. I was thankful he didn't insist on a cavity search."

Hannah gave him an elbow jab. "It's not that bad, and he'll stay out of our way. Come on, let's hit the road."

Melanie was standing in the center of the staircase, hugging Betty Lou while running her cheek against the kitten's fur. She watched as Hannah and her boyfriend hurried out the front door, hoping that the man wouldn't turn around and see her. She wanted to run back upstairs but couldn't seem to get her legs to move. All she could think about was the trouble she'd be in if anyone discovered what she knew. She hugged Betty Lou even tighter, which finally had the kitten squirming in her arms.

"What's up, Melanie?"

The little girl jumped at the sound of Katie's voice and waited as she approached the staircase.

"I thought Hannah was going to stay here tonight," the little girl said timidly, fighting the urge to break down into tears. "We were going to play Scrabble."

"Hannah has a date, honey, and I'm sure you'll be in bed by the time she gets home. But I would love to play Scrabble with you later. And maybe we can talk your mom into joining us."

"Nora, too?" she asked, hoping that with both Katie and Nora in the room, her mother might not catch on that Melanie was hiding a secret.

"We can ask her, sure. Now come on, supper awaits us."

Katie held her hand out, and Melanie took it, setting Betty Lou on the floor.

"Nora told me that she made a chocolate cake this afternoon," Katie said as the two headed into the dining room. "If I recall correctly, it's your favorite."

Melanie nodded, thinking that a big piece of chocolate cake, along with a nice cold glass of milk, could be just the thing she needed to help make up her mind whether or not to tell her mother about Hannah's date. She certainly didn't want to get in trouble again, and bringing up what had happened at Clay's place might do that. She stole a final look at the door, half expecting to see the man who had given her Betty Lou to be standing there, holding a box of kittens.

She also found herself hoping that the man didn't get Hannah into trouble, too.

CHAPTER
THIRTY-SIX

The Freeman family flew back home to Redmond on Wednesday morning, leaving Clay and Katie to continue sifting through files from Robert Nolan's days as an attorney, while Ian kept digging into the cases that were flagged. Marian remained on stand-by for any questions the three self-appointed investigators might have.

Late Thursday, Clay and Katie took a break from the files and retired to the guest bedroom where Katie had been staying until her knee completely healed. She had been reluctant at first to move into the house, no matter how temporary the arrangement would be. However, when Ian had pointed out that his security team could work more efficiently if everyone were together in one place, Katie had finally agreed.

Soft music played on the stereo system while the now fading sunlight filtered through the half-closed blinds with soft, comforting buoyancy. Clay could feel its warmth spread across his bare back as he moved over Katie, lost in the love she so generously gave him. And when she smiled—that captivating, lazy smile she reserved just for him—he knew he was the luckiest man alive.

After both lay sated in each other's arms, Katie lightly touched her lips to Clay's shoulder. "Have I told you how much I love you?" she asked.

"You have, but don't let that stop you from saying it over and over again."

She leaned in for a kiss before resting her head on his chest. Within minutes they were both asleep.

When Katie woke an hour later, she gently slipped out from under Clay's arm, whispering for him to go back to sleep when he let out a grunt. She pulled the covers over his body and shuffled to the dresser, grabbing a pair of sweat pants and matching sweatshirt from the bottom drawer. Heading toward the back stairway, she made her way to the kitchen.

"I thought you and Clay were going to take the night off," Nora said, looking up from the apple she was slicing.

"We are," Katie said, spying the oatmeal raisin cookies in the center of the table. "He fell asleep so I thought I'd come down for a snack." Walking over to the refrigerator, she pulled out a carton of milk before going to the cabinet where the glasses were kept. "Will you join me?"

"Not right now, thanks. I can offer you something more substantial than those cookies."

"Yes, but I'd end up eating the cookies anyway, so why not have them first? Then, if I'm still hungry, I can make a sandwich or something."

From her place at the kitchen table, Nora said, "Your logic fascinates me."

Katie reached for a cookie, feeling grateful that she had found such a good friend in Nora. A friend who not only made her feel like part of the family, but one who could out-bake even her own mother. As she took her first bite of the cookie, Hannah swept into the room.

"My, my, doesn't our girl look like the cat's meow tonight."

Hannah laughed at Nora's outdated expression. "If that's another way of saying I'm looking exceptionally hot tonight, then I'll agree. I've got another date." When the buzzer signaled on the security panel, she added, "And there he is now." She skipped over to the control board, identified her date on the monitor then buzzed him onto the property.

"I'm going to put a load of wash in," Nora said as she rose from the chair, knocking the knife she'd been using to the floor.

"Go," Katie said with a brush of her hand. "I'll get it."

"Thanks," Nora said and headed toward the back of the house.

Hannah rushed past Katie, giggling as she scurried to the front door in her remarkably high, yet exceedingly sexy, shoes. A minute later she was back, date in tow.

Katie turned from the sink to get a good look at the man Hannah had taken a liking to, and was dumbfounded when she saw the keyboard player for Dakota Gold.

"Tony?" she said with genuine surprise.

"Katie?" he said, managing to feign his own surprise. "What . . . How did you . . . What are you doing here?"

"I take it you two have met," Hannah said, perplexed.

Katie laughed. "Yes. Tony used to play keyboard for Dakota Gold."

"What the heck," Hannah said, turning back to Tony. "You never told me that."

There was a lot he hadn't told her, he thought, but none of that mattered now. When he'd driven up to the house he'd noted that there was only one vehicle parked outside, reasoning that it belonged to the lone security guard watching the front door. And when Hannah had let him inside, she'd unwittingly told him that he'd have a relatively clear path to grab Katie. "It's been a real zoo around here lately," she'd told him. "But now that Katie's friends have gone back home, things have really quieted down." That's all he'd needed to hear to know that the window of opportunity had been opened. Tonight would be the night that he would begin to even the score.

"I'm on a break from music for the time being," he now said to Hannah. "For the past few months, the company I work for has me

on the road a lot, which doesn't leave a lot of free time to play."
Tony turned to look at Katie when he added, "It shouldn't be too
much longer before my life gets back to normal."

"Will you be able to go back to playing with the band?" Katie
asked.

"I plan on talking to Nathan, although I don't want to disrupt
the chemistry of the band if the new keyboardist is working out."
Wanting desperately to put an end to any more inquiries, he slipped
his arm around Hannah's waist and said, "I didn't know you and
Katie were related."

"Oh, we're not. Katie works for my Uncle Arthur. She's living in
the guest cottage but does a lot of her work here in the main house."

"That's right," Tony said as he casually scanned the kitchen.
"You paint, or take pictures—something like that, right?"

"Something like that," Katie chuckled. Shifting her attention to
Hannah, she asked, "Do you guys have big plans for tonight?"

"We did," Hannah said through a convincing pout. "But Dean
says that the security team is down a guy tonight. Ian's called in a
replacement, but he won't be here for another half hour. We can't
leave until he does, and our dinner reservation at Marcell's is for
eight. So, if he doesn't get here soon, we're going to miss it."

Tony had used Hannah and Katie's momentary distraction to
slide over toward the security screen in the corner of the room to
examine the control panel. It was unlike any he'd seen, although
some of the features looked familiar. All he needed to do was to find
the shut-down function.

"Can't you switch the reservation to later?" Katie was saying,
even though the horrified look on Hannah's face had already revealed
the answer. "I guess that's a no," she added while struggling to hide
her amusement.

"Marcell's is the most exclusive French restaurant in the State of
Oregon. You usually have to wait weeks, sometimes months to get

in. But Tony has connections, don't you?" Hannah said as she dug through her purse for lip gloss.

Tony turned back to face the room. He'd been so intent on trying to figure a way to disarm the security from the kitchen unit that he hadn't been paying attention to the conversation. "Sorry, what did you say?"

"Your friend, Kevin. You said he had to pull a couple of strings to get us into the restaurant tonight."

"Yeah, right. His sister's boyfriend is related to the bouncer who owed him a favor." Another lie delivered flawlessly.

"So it'll be rude if we don't show up on time."

"Don't worry, Han. It's only a ninety-minute drive, and anyone who's important shows up late. We'll make it work." But, of course, Tony had come here tonight, not to wine and dine Hannah Reddington, but rather to take off with Katie Nolan. It didn't matter how many people stood in his way, he was determined to end this tonight.

Hannah took a moment to mull over what Tony had said. "I guess you're right," she eventually said. "Being late is probably in vogue these days."

"It seems awfully quiet around here tonight," Tony commented as he nonchalantly stepped to the open doorway.

"Arthur is still recovering in the hospital," Katie said as she transferred the plates she'd just removed from the dishwasher into an overhead cupboard. "I'm sure Hannah's told you about her uncle."

"Yes, she told me what happened. You all must have been terrified."

"It was unnerving to say the least. But everyone is doing well."

Too bad, Tony thought, but instead said, "Good to hear." He moved back into the kitchen and glanced out the patio doors, not particularly interested in the mountains which were slowly fading away with the sunlight. "This is some great view," he commented, watching Katie who was now sitting at the table folding cloth napkins. *Cloth napkins?* The idea of such a luxury practically made him gag. It was hard to forget how, as a child, he'd been forced to wipe his hands on worn jeans because his mother couldn't even afford paper towels. As he reached behind his back with one hand, he simultaneously pulled the drapes closed with the other.

"Where's Nora?" he asked as he moved to stand beside Hannah.

"In the back," Katie responded slowly. Wondering why he'd closed the drapes, she said, "What's going on, Tony?"

"Who else is in the house?"

Katie began to rise from the chair, but Tony motioned her back into place with a quick jerk of the handgun that had suddenly materialized in his left hand. He'd also taken hold of Hannah's upper arm, a gesture that would no doubt leave impressions from the pressure of his fingers. "No one else is here," she said quietly. "It's just Hannah, me, and Nora."

"And Dean on the door," he said, leading Hannah to the chair directly to Katie's right. "Where's Ian?"

"The last time I talked to him, he said he was heading back to his bungalow."

"You're not lying to me are you, Katie?"

"No."

"Good. That's good." When he placed the barrel of the gun against Hannah's temple, he said, "Now, how many security guys are on the property?"

Katie took a brief moment to do a mental count. "I think there are two besides Ian and Dean."

"And where are they now?"

"I have no idea."

Tony moved behind Hannah and, leaning down so his mouth was close to her ear, said, "Is she telling the truth, Han? Are there only four?"

"Yes," Hannah said in a shaky voice. "Why are you doing this, Tony?"

Tony scoffed. "It doesn't concern you, sweetness. This is between Ms. Nolan and me. Now, Katie. What about that boyfriend of yours? Is he here?"

Katie had anticipated the question and didn't so much as hesitate when she answered. "No. He went back to Clancy's."

Tony stared at Katie for several seconds. Was she telling the truth? He knew that Clay had been spending time here over the past week, but on the other hand, he hadn't seen the boyfriend's car when he'd pulled up to the house. He moved away from Hannah and took a step closer to Katie. "You better not be lying," he said as he pointed the gun at her head. "I want you to call for Nora and get her in here. Now."

"I'm here," Nora said in a strained voice as she moved into the kitchen. "You don't have to hurt anyone."

"Now see?" Tony said as he motioned for Nora to sit. "That's what I call smart. Come and sit down."

Once Nora was seated, Katie took her hand and gave it a squeeze. She continued to hold tight as Tony took the last chair at the table and grabbed a cookie. "These aren't bad," he said, taking a bite. "My mother used to make me oatmeal cookies whenever I did well in school. These aren't as good as hers, but they're pretty darn close. We should take the rest of these with us when we leave, Katie." Tossing Nora a menacing look, he added, "I'm sure you won't mind, will you, sweetie?"

Nora slowly shook her head, not sure if he was really looking for an answer.

"I don't understand," Katie said calmly, trying to draw Tony's attention back to her. "Where are we going?"

"You'll see soon enough." His dark, menacing eyes pinned her in place as he continued. "The important thing is that I'll finally have retribution for the sins of your dearly departed father. Of course, I'd rather have punished him directly, but I've resigned myself to the fact that I have to be satisfied with you."

Nora felt Katie's hand jerk, seconds before hearing the sound of heavy footsteps echoing from the stairwell.

"I smell cookies." The uninhibited voice of Clay echoed down the hallway. "There better be one with my name on it or someone is going to—"

Tony moved so fast he nearly knocked his chair over. He slid in behind Katie, the barrel of his gun now pointed straight at her head. As Clay came to an abrupt halt in the doorway, he immediately absorbed the impact of what was transpiring in the Reddington kitchen. As he slowly raised his hands in a sign of surrender, his mind raced through several options which would give him control of the situation, effectively taking it away from the man holding the gun to Katie's head. Tony Santana.

"Katie said you were at the pub," Tony snarled as he yanked Katie to her feet and re-positioned the gun so it pressed tightly under her jaw. "That wasn't a very smart thing to do, Katie." With his eyes still trained on Clay, he said, "Why don't you join us, tough guy?" When Clay didn't immediately move, Tony tightened his grip on the gun, pushing Katie's chin a quarter of an inch higher. "That wasn't a suggestion, it was an order."

Clay slowly crossed to the table, hands still raised, and sat.

"We've wasted enough time," Tony said, swinging the gun toward Clay and giving Katie a slight shove. "I need you to find some tape to secure these three to their chairs. And if you refuse, or do anything that I believe will contradict my instructions, they'll be digging bone fragments out of your boyfriend's brain in the morning. Get it?"

"Yes," Katie said quickly. "There's duct tape in the utility drawer at the end of the counter." Retrieving the tape, she moved to where Hannah was sitting.

"No," Tony said as he shifted his body so he was directly behind Clay. "Him first."

Clay's mind was working overtime. He had to find a way to disarm Tony or at least get him down long enough so Katie and the others could run.

"Hey Tony, can't we try and work this out, man?" Clay was half out of his chair when he felt the impact from the butt of Tony's gun striking the side of his head. As his vision momentarily flickered, he vaguely heard Katie's strangled cry, then felt her hands as she helped him back into an upright position.

"That was really stupid, Crawford," Tony said as he backed up several steps. "You don't get to play the part of the hero today, asshole. I swear you'll end up like old man Reddington if you mess with me. A bullet straight to the chest." Keeping his eyes glued to Clay, he barked at Katie. "Do what I told you to do. Hands behind his back, ankles taped to the chair legs."

The confirmation that Tony was Arthur's shooter had Katie's stomach rolling. Her mind was on overload as she used the tape to secure Clay's hands and feet, afraid that her failure to do so could have a deadly result for anyone seated around the table.

Once she was finished with Clay, Katie moved over to where Hannah sat, taping her in much the same way. Lastly, she moved over to where Nora was sitting, noting that the housekeeper appeared remarkably composed. When their eyes locked, Katie noticed the quick downward nod Nora gave her, followed by a subtle movement of her left foot.

"When you're done there, I want you to put a strip of tape over their mouths as well," Tony said, steeling a glance down the hallway toward the front door. "Now hurry it up."

Clay was bordering on frantic as he struggled to come up with a way to stop Tony from taking Katie. "Tony, you don't have to do this. Let the others go, and you and I can work it out."

"Well, well. It seems that chivalry is alive and well in Abbott County." Tapping the barrel of his gun against the side of Clay's head, Tony said, "Tape his mouth first or I might be tempted to shut it myself."

As Katie quickly ripped a piece of tape off the roll, she moved over to Clay. "Katie," he whispered, silently pleading for forgiveness.

"Don't worry," she said, touching his cheek lightly before smoothing the tape over his mouth.

Tony jerked the gun toward the front door when Katie was finished. "Time for us to go, Katie."

Giving Clay a final look, she moved down the hall ahead of her captor. Dean was standing at the bottom of the porch steps and came to attention when she and Tony stepped through the front door.

"Katie? What's up? I told Hannah everyone's to stay put until Ethan gets here."

"Well, Dean," Tony said as he raised his handgun and fired. "New game plan."

Katie screamed as she watched Dean's body fold over and drop.

"My car is right over there," Tony said as he gave her a shove toward it.

"Wait, wait a minute," Katie gasped. "We can't just leave him here. We have to help him."

Using the gun, he gave her one quick jab against her backbone. "Shut up and get moving."

When they reached Tony's car, he pushed her through the passenger side door. "Move in behind the wheel, you're driving. And don't try anything because I'll shoot you without a second thought. Then I'll find your mother and shoot her." He smiled when Katie looked at him, the fear written clearly on her face. "Well that got through, didn't it? Stop wasting time and move."

Katie slid under the steering wheel and took the keys from Tony. "Head toward the front gate," he snapped, "and don't do anything to draw attention."

After starting the engine, Katie switched the headlights on and pulled away from the house, praying that she'd find an opportunity to stop this lunatic.

When the gates signaled a visitor, Ian glanced over to the security monitor sitting on the corner of his desk and watched as Tony Santana pulled in and drove up to the main residence. Ian had been aware that the musician was expected tonight. He'd insisted on being given the name of anyone who'd been invited onto the estate, when they were coming, and their purpose for being there. Which Hannah had dutifully done.

He continued to follow the car's progression up the driveway until Dean Singleton—his security man in charge of guarding the house—approached the car and signaled for the driver to pull forward past the porch steps.

Trusting that Dean would buzz him if there was any trouble, Ian went back to his computer where he'd been examining news articles relating to an Adrián Santiago, only son of Anton Santiago, a man who had been sentenced in Judge Nolan's court some twenty years ago. The file had been flagged by Katie and had first drawn Ian's attention when he'd been unable to find a complete background history on the son. His curiosity had continued to grow until he found himself spending well over two hours searching every logical site on the internet looking for information to fill in the gaps. In the end, he hadn't hit on any tangible markers that could point to where Adrián had ended up.

Ian sat back to consider what he had learned so far. The senior Santiago had been brutally stabbed to death three years after being sentenced to life in a maximum security prison. The head of a drug gang operating out of Los Angeles had been suspected of ordering the hit, but as it so often went, nothing could be proven.

The mother, Anna, had been left to raise her son alone. According to Ted's handwritten notes, she had held a number of jobs throughout her husband's incarceration as well as after his death. Throughout the years, she and her son had been forced to move numerous times, although they never ended up far from the run-down neighborhood where the boy had been raised.

Young Adrián had experienced a number of bumps with the law, beginning near the time his father had been stabbed to death. At around age nineteen, he made the decision—which was driven more by opportunity than allegiance—to follow in his father's footsteps. According to court records, he'd approached a guy in a three-piece suit, demanding he turn over his money and expensive jewelry. When the guy resisted, Adrián used his fists to subdue the man long enough to take what he'd been after. The man had survived, successfully identifying Adrián as the attacker, and he'd ended up serving five years, three months, and fifteen days for his crime. After his release, and for reasons Ian couldn't figure out, public records seemed to lose track of both mother and son, leaving him to wonder what the hell had happened to them.

Ian spent another ten minutes searching various websites, finding nothing that would help in his search for the junior Santiago. Scribbling himself a note to make a morning call to a friend in Long Beach who'd been on the police force at the time of Adrián's arrest, he checked the time and decided to put the file aside. He'd take a drive around the land perimeter, and when his rounds were complete, he'd go back to digging into the rest of the judge's files.

He glanced briefly at the security monitor as he rose from the chair, not particularly concerned that he didn't see Dean out front. More than likely he'd gone inside the house.

Grabbing his keys and his handheld radio, Ian stepped out into the cool night air. He loved this time of year, when Mother Nature seemed to be reluctant to let go of fall and commit to the promise of winter. Taking a deep breath, he moved toward the side of the bungalow where he parked his jeep and began to mentally run through a list of what he still needed to get done tonight. When his cell phone rang, he checked the caller ID and saw Christina Freeman's number.

"Hi Christina. How's it going?"

"Ian, thank God. I tried calling both Katie and Clay and neither is answering their cell phones."

"Slow down, honey. Tell me what's got you all wound up."

"Melanie recognized Hannah's date from when we were up there earlier this week. She said he's the one who gave her the kitten. You remember, at Clay's bar? I'm not sure what that means but . . . I didn't know what else to do but call, and now I can't get a hold of anyone."

Ian kicked into high gear, the reality of the situation hitting him like a ton of bricks. The man that Hannah had gone out with on Sunday was the same man who'd been given access to the property less than thirty minutes ago.

"Christina, I've got to go," Ian said, trying to keep his voice calm.

"Is Katie safe? Is she there?"

"She's here, and I'm heading up to the house now. I'll have her call you."

Ian jumped into the jeep and immediately tried to lock down the gates from the unit that was bolted to the dash, but he couldn't activate the command. In fact, he couldn't seem to access any of the main security features. "Damn it," he snapped, as he pulled out of the car port. This wasn't the first time this unit had crashed, but it was certainly the most inconvenient. He hit the computer command for a reboot as he started toward the house.

He reached for his radio when it signaled and quickly engaged the talk button. "This is Ian."

"Ian," a ragged voice came over the unit. "Katie's been taken. Santana."

"Where are you?" Ian asked Dean as he reversed direction and increased his speed toward the front gate.

"House. Shot," Dean replied weakly.

"I'm sending Glenn your way. Hang on."

Ian clicked off and immediately contacted Glenn, one of the other two men he had safeguarding the property tonight. Although he had desperately wanted to ask about the condition of the other occupants in the house, from the sound of Dean's voice, Ian could tell that time was of the essence.

When he heard Glenn's voice over the radio, Ian's instructions were brief and to the point. "There's trouble at the house. Dean's been shot. Go." He then made contact with Mason, the remaining security team member on site. "Meet me at the front gate," he instructed. "Someone's trying to leave with Katie."

As Clay struggled against the tape on his wrists, he heard the gunshot first, followed by Katie's scream. His attempt to free himself intensified as he fought to stay clearheaded, refusing to surrender to the panic which had already increased his heartbeat to an almost unbearable tempo.

He was frantically scanning the room, hoping to discover an easier way to break through the tape, when he caught Nora using head gestures to get his attention. Quickly catching on to what she wanted, he maneuvered his chair across the tile floor until they were sitting back to back. Assuming her plan was to work as a team to rip through their bindings, he was surprised when she began slicing through the tape around his wrists with what he thought was a kitchen knife. Katie, he thought. She had slipped the knife to Nora when Tony hadn't been looking.

While Nora cut, Clay worked hard to keep his patience in check.

When his wrists were finally free, he took the knife and used it on the tape around his ankles before ripping the piece of tape off his mouth. Pushing his chair out of the way, he knelt on one knee and cut through the tape around Nora's wrists.

"Here," he said handing her the knife when her hands pulled free. "I'm going after Katie, so you'll need to track down Ian. Tell him what's happened."

Clay raced down the hallway to the front door. As he approached the porch steps, he saw Dean's body lying motionless off to one side, partially hidden under a large shrub. Ian's voice was still communicating through the compact radio that was clutched in the security team member's hand.

"Dean, are you there? Answer me."

Clay leaped off the porch and snatched the radio, engaging the talk button while he examined Dean for injuries. "Ian. It's Clay. Tony Santana has Katie. He's got maybe a five-minute lead. Dean is down but still breathing."

"I'm on it. I'm approaching the gate now and it's closed. I'm hoping that means Tony is still on the premises."

As much as Clay wanted to storm toward the gate himself, he knew that if Tony and Katie were still on the estate, it would be better if he headed off in a different direction. "Where do you need me to go?" he asked.

"Take Dean's handgun. There should already be a loaded magazine in it and a second one on his belt. Glenn is on his way to you so wait until he gets there, then head for the cottage. That section of property eventually opens up onto public land, and Tony must know that. I'm going to double check the gates first, then meet you there. If I'm right, he'll try to leave with Katie on foot through the woods. Stay alert, Clay."

"Get in touch with Ian and tell him that Katie's been taken," Nora said once she'd cut through Hannah's tape.

"What's happening, Nora? What does Tony want with Katie?"

Nora didn't answer—didn't know what the answer was—as she darted down the hall to Arthur's office. She went straight to the desk and removed a small key from under the desk calendar. Moving to the custom designed gun cabinet, she used the key to unlock the glass double-doors and pulled out one of Arthur's shotguns along with a handful of shells. She dropped one shell into each of the gun's barrels and pocketed the other four.

"Jeez, Nora. What are you doing?"

"I'm not sure what I may encounter out there, so I'm not going unprepared. For all we know, Tony's not alone. Now do what I told you to do. Get a hold of Ian and tell him what's going on." She pushed past Hannah, moving quickly toward the front door. "And for the love of all that's mighty, tell him I'm out there so he doesn't accidentally shoot me."

"Be careful, Nora," Hannah said as she reached for the receiver on the desk phone.

When Nora reached the open front door, she hesitated just long enough to determine what the situation was on the other side. When she saw Clay kneeling next to Dean, she called out to him. "What are you still doing here? He's getting away with Katie."

Clay looked up and was momentarily distracted by the image of Nora clutching a shotgun across her chest. "I'm getting ready to leave," he finally said, shoving the extra gun magazine into his back pocket.

"You need to go now. I'll take care of Dean."

"Do you know how to use that?" Clay asked as Nora hurried toward him.

"Yes. You're wasting time, Clay."

"I'm gone," he said as he raced to the side of the house where he had parked his car, trusting that Nora knew what she was doing. As he pulled away, he glimpsed a set of headlights speeding from the back of the house and he slowed, wanting to make sure it was Glenn. Confirming it was, Clay sped off.

For reasons he couldn't comprehend, Ian still couldn't get the camera views on his jeep's security screen. It had to be more than a software crash, he thought. Someone had to have messed with the system and set up a manual block. Skidding to a stop alongside Mason's vehicle, he reasoned that somehow Tony had gotten to one of the auxiliary units inside the house.

Mason was already examining the gates when Ian swung out of the jeep. "Fresh tire tracks this side of the fence," he began, "nothing indicating a car left this way." Pointing to a patch of torn-up grass at the bottom of the main drive, he added, "That wasn't here this morning, I would have noticed. Someone recently made a U-turn and turned back up the main drive."

"That's because Tony didn't have a key card to open the gates." Ian turned and hurried back to his jeep. "Ethan is on his way in," he said over his shoulder. "Contact him and bring him up to date."

Pulling his cell phone out of his pocket, Ian called Clay.

"It's me," he said when Clay answered. "I've got an update. Katie and Tony are—"

"In the wooded area behind the cottage," Clay interrupted. "I'm tracking them now."

"Copy that. I'm about a minute away yet. Tell me exactly where you are, and I'll follow you in."

As Clay relayed the information, Ian pulled to a stop near the front of the cottage. Putting his phone on speaker, he continued to listen to Clay while grabbing his shotgun off the built-in rack and snagging his ammo vest out of the back seat.

Forced to accept that he had all the pertinent information, he disconnected Clay's call, checked his sidearm, and began sprinting down the gravel road. By the time he was entering the mouth of the woods, he'd convinced himself that he'd done everything he could to secure the estate.

CHAPTER
THIRTY-SEVEN

From somewhere in the distance, Tony heard the muffled ringing of a cell phone. The sound served to fuel him to push ahead even faster, Katie by his side. His fingers were wrapped tightly around her arm as they plowed through the trees and scrambled over fallen logs. He'd initially been concerned that she might draw attention to their position by screaming out, but when he'd pressed the barrel of the gun against her temple, she had no choice but to accept the fact that he was the one holding all the cards.

They continued to sprint deeper into the woods with Tony all but dragging Katie through the mounds of thicket that lined the path he'd chosen. But the pace he had set was too fast for Katie to keep up with, and when she tried to step over an exposed root of one of the tall, overbearing trees, she tripped and tumbled unceremoniously to the ground.

"Damn it," Tony growled as she pulled him down with her. "What the hell are you up to?"

His finger-hold tightened around her bicep, and she couldn't tell which area of her body was producing the most pain—her arm, or her recently sprained knee that had been throbbing since they'd begun their flight through the woods.

She glanced over at Tony, ready to plead with him to let her go, when she realized that his attention had been redirected to the path they had just traveled. His eyes had gone dark again, and his head jerked right, then left, and then right again, all the while tapping the gun against his boot. It was as if he was uncertain what his next move should be.

Well, he may be uncertain what to do, Katie thought decisively, but I know exactly what my next move will be.

Back at the house, she'd found the opportunity to slip Nora's car keys off the kitchen counter and into the pocket of her sweat pants. Attached to the ring was a thin canister of pepper spray, something Nora had told her she'd carried ever since she and her husband had been burglarized in their home in England. Keeping her movements casual but deliberate, Katie slowly slid her right hand toward the side pocket. If she could get the key ring free, she could give him the old one-two punch. Pump him with the pepper spray and then gouge his face with the ignition key.

"Stop wiggling," Tony spat through gritted teeth.

"I don't understand what's going on," she said as he pulled her to her feet and once again began dragging her across the dirt floor in a direction that was taking them further away from the cottage.

"Of course you don't understand. How could you when all you care about is yourself? It's never even occurred to you that your actions affect other people has it? Well, all that changes tonight."

"Tony, please don't do this," she said, struggling to catch her breath. "It's not too late to stop all this."

"But you're wrong, Katie. It is too late."

His glare was deadly as he pushed her to her knees behind a leafy shrub showcasing clusters of inconspicuous berries that continued to flourish despite the cooling temperatures. The pain that shot through her leg nearly had her passing out.

"It wasn't enough that you had the swank house near the beach," he said in an abrasive voice, "or the expensive schools, the lavish vacations, and all those fancy clothes. No, you and your family had to make sure that those of us who weren't born with a silver spoon in our mouths wouldn't dirty up your comfy little world.

"You say you don't understand? Well let me explain it to you." Tony's deep voice vibrated as he fixed his anger-filled eyes on Katie. "Every day at my father's trial, the presiding judge sat up on that bench, listening to the lies that the prosecutor spat out and looking down his nose at my family. He didn't even take the time to glance at the evidence. We didn't have the money or the prestige or the shine, so why bother seeing the truth? Why bother with justice? It was just another case for the all-powerful Judge Robert Nolan. Another day, another dollar, another strike of the gavel.

"But for me it was another day without my father in my life," Tony continued. "Another day my mother had to scrounge for enough money to put food on the table. And because everyone in that courtroom refused to see my father for the great man that he was, he was locked up where he was eventually slaughtered. Your father might have called it a life sentence, but it wasn't. It turned out to be a death sentence."

Katie's mouth had gone dry. The look that a young boy had given her in a courtroom when she'd been ten was the same look on the face of the man kneeling in front of her now. Adrián Santiago had transformed himself into Tony Santana, and both the boy and the man blamed her father for their own father's death.

"You're wondering what you could possibly say to change the outcome, aren't you?" he sneered. "What can you offer me, what sort of deal can you make. Well the answer is nothing. Nothing you can say and nothing you can offer will change what's been taken from me."

He pulled her to her feet, but as soon as she took the first step her knee gave out from under her. As she fell backwards, her head clipped a rock partially buried at the base of a tree. She tried unsuccessfully to swallow her scream.

"Move," he said harshly, gripping the gun in one hand while pulling at her arm with the other. But before either of them could move, the faint sound of a siren tore through the quiet of the night, and he glimpsed the flash of a speeding patrol car's light bar splash across the tree limbs above their heads.

"Well, it looks like you've run out of time, Katie," he said as he dropped her back to the ground. "This won't be as satisfying for me, but maybe ending it here and now is how it's meant to be."

His movements were quick and precise. Laying the gun on the ground near his foot, he reached into his jacket pocket for the roll of duct tape he'd taken from the house. Ripping off a generous piece, he slapped it across her mouth. "It took my father close to an hour to die. He was alone and bleeding out on a filthy shower floor, praying for one of the guards to help him. But no one came," he said as he straddled her, keeping his knees tight against her body, effectively pinning her arms to her side.

"Maybe it'll go quicker for you, Katie," he continued, sliding his father's knife out of his ankle holster. "Either way, when you see that bastard father of yours, give him a message from me. Tell him that payback is everything it's cracked up to be, and more."

Tony raised the knife, clutching the hilt with both hands. Katie screamed, even knowing the sound was being muffled by the tape.

Tony laughed. Lowering the knife slowly until the tip was pressed against the side of her throat, he said, "I'd hoped to have more time with you. But it doesn't look like I'll get my wish. At least not with you."

He didn't even try to hide his exhilaration as he watched tears fill Katie's eyes. "That's right, Katie. With you out of the picture, there's only one person left who needs to repent. It doesn't seem fair to let your mother live when mine is gone, does it? I'm going to take my time with her, too. I only wish you could be there to watch."

Pulling back, he raised the knife for a second time as Katie wrestled to break free. She cried out again, desperate for her voice to be heard. I can't allow my life to end like this, she thought. There's too much I haven't accomplished. Too many people I haven't said good-bye to.

Tony was smiling now, the look of pure evil blazing in his eyes. As Katie watched, the blade began its downward motion, and she screamed one more time.

Then suddenly, Tony's hands stilled. He turned away, frantically searching the darkened shadows that stirred beyond the trees. Katie had no idea what had stopped him but it was enough of a distraction for her to yank her arm from under the weight of his thigh and pull the key ring from her pocket.

When he turned back, she flipped the canister lid and used her thumb to push down on the lever, releasing the blinding pepper spray directly into Tony's face. And even when he lifted his hands to deflect the airborne chemical—even when he howled from the burning in his eyes and nostrils—even then, she continued to spray until the canister was empty.

Tony pushed away from her in a rage, helplessly rubbing at his eyes. "You bitch," he spat as he shot to his feet. Katie kicked out hoping to somehow disable Tony, but her knee felt as if it were on fire, and her foot never connected. Her only hope was to get away.

When she tried sitting up, the fierce throbbing in her head had her releasing another muffled scream. Her brain unsuccessfully signaled her body to ignore the pain as she ripped the tape from her mouth and rolled to her side, hoping she'd be able to use her arms to push off the ground.

She wanted to scream, afraid it was her only hope to alert anyone who may be within hearing distance.

It was the last coherent thought that Katie managed before everything went black.

CHAPTER
THIRTY-EIGHT

Why was she so cold? Katie thought warily. Wasn't that part of the dying process? But she couldn't die, not yet. She had to warn her mother that Tony was coming for her. She had to tell Clay one last time how much she loved him. She tried sitting up, but the pain at the back of her head brought on a serious bout of nausea, and she instantly abandoned the idea.

"Lie still, Katie. Try not to move."

The familiar voice was so calm and reassuring that she fought her initial impulse to break down and cry. Instead, she took a good solid minute to catch her breath.

"Where's Tony?" she eventually managed to ask.

"He's being escorted back to one of the squad cars. A medical team is on their way and should be here any minute. I know it hurts, but we didn't want to take a chance on moving you."

"That son of a bitch was going to stab me," she grumbled indignantly.

"I believe that was his intent," Clay said. "You managed to stop him, although you've got a gash on your head where it connected with a rock."

"I do have a slight headache," she said, looking up, only to see worry on Clay's face. "It's manageable, I swear."

"Well, let's see what the doctor says." At her confused look, he added, "Your next stop is the hospital."

"Clay, I don't need to go to the hospital."

"You could have a concussion."

"I don't have a concussion. Come on, hold up some fingers. Ask me some questions that only a non-concussed person would have the answers to."

"Non-concussed person?" Clay remarked.

"Yes. I have a headache, that's all. Although I am a little confused," she added.

"What is it, Katie? Are you feeling dizzy? Nauseous?" Frantically checking their surroundings, he added, "Where are those EMTs?"

"Clay, relax. What I was going to say is that sometime during my struggle with Tony, I think I heard someone call him a shithead." Watching Clay's expression change from concern to exasperation was comical. "Was that you?"

"Very funny," he said.

"Maybe, but you haven't given me an answer. Was it you?"

"I may have said something like that."

"Yeah? What else did you say?"

"Come on, Katie. How am I supposed to remember every little thing I said?"

"I remember," Mason offered cheerfully as he moved into Katie's line of vision. "He said, and I quote, 'If you move, I'll shoot you dead where you stand. You hear me, you shithead?' It had a real De Niro feel to it if you ask me."

Katie was trying hard not to laugh at Mason's impression of Clay, but she couldn't hide the humor in her eyes. Clay took it as a good sign. It was so much better to see laughter in those beautiful green eyes than pain. Yes, he'd gladly accept the ribbing over the next several days in order to see the laughter.

"Mason's here," Clay said with mock sarcasm. "And so is Ian. The County Sheriff's office is leading the investigation for now, and Sheriff Bradley is on his way."

"My mother," Katie said, suddenly struck by the thought that Marian could still be in danger.

"She's at the hospital with Arthur," Clay said calmly. "They're both safe. Everyone at the house is safe."

"Was Tony doing this on his own? Is there anyone else we need to worry about?"

"Pretty sure he was acting alone, but Ian's on top of all that. Sheriff Bradley said that Tony will be transferred to the county jail tonight where they can begin his interrogation. I heard that the FBI is also getting involved."

"The EMTs are here," Ian said as he crouched next to Katie. "How are you doing?"

"Hanging in there."

"They couldn't get the ambulance all the way back here so they'll have to carry you part of the way back. Clay's going to stay with you and so is Mason. I'll meet up with you at the hospital."

"I already told Clay I'm not going to the hospital. And no one is going to carry me anywhere," she said sternly as Clay helped her to her feet. Although her knee felt as though it were on fire and her vision momentarily dulled, there was no way she was going to consent to being taken out of these woods on a stretcher.

Looking at Clay, she said, "It's not that far back to the cottage. I can make it if you help me. Please. I don't want to be carried out."

"All right," Clay said. "But at the first sign that you're in more pain than you are right now, I'll pick you up myself and throw you on that stretcher."

"I can go along with that."

As they slowly made their way back to where Clay had parked his car, Katie asked, "Has someone told my mother what's happening?"

"Not yet," Mason said as he stepped alongside Katie and offered his shoulder for support. "I'll get word to Ted, and he can bring them up to date. You can tell them the rest after the EMTs have a look at you."

Katie shot him a look of protest.

"At the cottage," Mason said. "A preliminary once over. Come on, Katie. They're the best qualified to assess how badly you're hurt and what you need to do."

"I suppose you're right," Katie mumbled as she, Clay, and Mason continued down the path that was now lit up by the spotlights that had been erected by the Sheriff's department.

After reaching the cottage, exhausted and near tears from the pain shooting up from her knee and down from her head, Katie reluctantly agreed to get checked out at the hospital. But only if Clay drove her. Her days of being Tony's unsuspecting victim were done. She was calling the shots from now on.

Arthur was sitting up in bed when Katie hobbled into his hospital room on crutches. She lowered herself into the visitor's chair before propping the crutches against the wall.

"I heard what happened tonight," Arthur said after releasing a long sigh. "What did the doctors have to say?"

"Other than spraining my knee again, I'm good as new," Katie responded.

"Ian tells me that the person responsible for all of this is in custody. Sheriff Bradley agrees with the lead agent from the FBI that this Santiago kid acted alone. It's over."

"Ian showed me the file a few days ago," Marian said as she walked into the room and stood next to Katie. "As I read through it, I remembered Robert talking about how devastating the case had been. He knew it was going to be hard for such a young boy to grow up without his father, but there was nothing he could have done. The man was guilty of murder." Rubbing Katie's shoulder, she added, "Any case that involved a child was hard on your father."

"Tony made choices." Katie said quietly. "He had a rough life, especially as a teenager when a boy needs more than just his mother's love. But as an adult, he made choices that took him down a murky road. It's not Dad's fault, it's not my fault, and," glancing up at her mother she added, "it's not your fault."

When Marian didn't respond, Katie changed the subject. "Does anyone have news on Dean?"

"He's on the mend, thank God," Arthur replied. "Turned out to be more a flesh wound than anything serious, although he did end up with a couple of bruised ribs. He'll be released in a few hours."

"Then he'll have to wait until he gets back to the estate to see you, Arthur." She smiled at his bewildered look. "The doctor says he's releasing you tonight."

"Hallelujah!" Arthur proclaimed as he pushed back his sheet and blanket. "What are we waiting for?"

"Not so fast," Marian said, moving over to the bed. "There's still some paperwork that needs to be finished. The nurse said she'd bring everything in for your signature as soon as she can get it done."

"I'll give them fifteen minutes. After that, I can't promise that I won't just hightail it out of here."

Marian looked at Katie, who was being unusually quiet. She'd met her daughter in the hospital lobby when she'd gotten word that Clay was bringing her in to be checked out. She'd also stayed with Katie as the medical staff re-bandaged her swollen knee and examined her for any new injuries. At first, Marian had thought that Katie was taking time to process everything but now, she sensed there was something more.

"Hey, Mom," Katie said, turning to face Marian. "Would you mind if I have a minute alone with Arthur?"

"Not at all. I'll go and check on the progress of those discharge papers."

Katie laid her hand on her mother's arm and smiled warmly. "Thanks."

After Marian left the room, Katie had to take a moment to decide how she was going to broach the subject of Arthur being her biological father.

"I bet you're glad to be leaving the hospital," she said, trying to ease into it.

"Beyond ecstatic. It's a good facility with a good medical staff, but it isn't home."

"Agreed." Katie sighed as she took another moment to organize her thoughts. "Is it difficult for you when Mom and I refer to Robert Nolan as my dad?" she finally asked.

"Not really," he said, dropping his gaze to the clasped hands that rested in his lap. "Robert was a good man, Katie. He loved you deeply and by all rights was your father in every sense of the word. I can't replace him. The best I can hope for is that one day you and I will be able to define our relationship as one that is rooted in family."

"I had a dream after Mom told me that you were my biological father. Dad and I were sitting in the forest, and he said that you wouldn't replace him but would stand alongside him in my heart."

"I like the sound of that," Arthur said, nodding in agreement.

"So do I." Leaning forward in the chair, Katie gave Arthur a serious look. "Now, what are your intentions toward my mother?"

Arthur laughed as he reached over and squeezed Katie's hand. "I assure you, they're honorable. But I'll also tell you that I plan to ask her to marry me. Will we have your blessing?"

Katie smiled. "Depends. Can I have a pony?"

CHAPTER THIRTY-NINE

The following week, Arthur and Marian were in the sunroom having Sunday brunch with Clay and Katie when Nora announced that she had buzzed Sheriff Bradley through the main gate.

"Bring another place setting, will you Nora?" Arthur said as he reached for his cell phone. "When the Sheriff gets here you can show him in." Turning his attention to the phone, he said, "Ian. Ed Bradley is on his way up. Could you join us?"

Ten minutes later, everyone was gathered around the table listening to an update on Tony Santana, whose real name was Adrián Santiago. "At this point, he hasn't said much, and he's got himself some superstar lawyer from Portland," Bradley said as he accepted a refill of coffee from Marian.

"You said that you've finished searching his cabin," Arthur said. "Can you share what you found?"

The Sheriff paused long enough to load his coffee with sugar and then said, "The most useful evidence we found was his laptop along with a shoebox filled with photos, newspaper clippings, and magazine articles, all hidden behind one of the walls in the laundry room.

"The clippings were mostly about his father's trial," he continued. "The magazine articles focused mostly on you, Katie, or on your father. Some were about your artwork, others about his high-profile court cases. A good portion of the photos were of the

Santiago family—pictures of Adrián as a baby and then a young boy, snapshots taken during holidays, etc. There were others that looked like they could have been taken on your land, Arthur."

Arthur slid his hand over Marian's. "Ian and I have discussed this, and we think Santiago could have gotten onto my land by crossing through the state forest on the eastern border. It would explain a number of security breaches we've had recently, and why he took Katie that way when he couldn't get out through the main gate. He knew the lay of the land, so to speak."

The Sheriff nodded as he leaned forward. "I'm sorry to say there were also photos of you, Katie. Most of them were taken here in Abbott. He also had photos of the damage at your condo, Marian."

Marian remained silent, unable to respond to the Sheriff's unsettling news.

"It sounds as if you think this all goes back to the father's trial," Clay said, voicing what everyone suspected.

"That would be an accurate assumption, based on everything we've found so far," Bradley said. "Especially when you read some of the entries on his computer. A lot of it didn't make any sense, however, he clearly believed his father was innocent and blamed Judge Nolan for what he termed a miscarriage of justice. If you want my take on the whole thing, he wanted to eliminate the one person he was convinced was responsible for his father's death."

"And because Robert died before Adrián could get to him," Marian interjected, "Katie and I were the only ones left. He was seeking revenge, plain and simple."

"Again, that's my take. Yes."

"But if this was revenge for his father's death, why did he wait until Katie came to Abbott?" Clay asked. "His father's been dead for close to twenty years."

"Regrettably, I don't have the complete answer to that," the Sheriff stated honestly. "What we do know is that Adrián served time in prison himself when he was in his early twenties. During the five years he was there, his mother's health started to deteriorate, and when he was released, he moved in with her, serving as her primary caregiver. Eventually, he was forced to put her in a nursing home." The Sheriff hesitated, taking a good look at the occupants seated around the table, before adding, "Mrs. Santiago died on Thanksgiving Day. My best guess at this point is that her death was the trigger that took him from obsession to aggression.

"As far as the break-in at your condominium," Bradley continued, focusing in on Marian, "the police in Long Beach have concluded their investigation. They're saying that the damage coincides with her death. If you look at all the evidence, there's certainly enough there to file multiple charges. When we interrogate Santiago again later this morning, hopefully we'll learn more."

Katie shuttered, remembering how she and her mother had come so close to Tony/Adrián the day they had gone to the cabin to deliver his keyboard. The day after his mother had died. If Clay hadn't phoned when they were there, and her mother hadn't been so insistent that they leave, he could have easily killed them. She glanced at her mother and realized that she had arrived at the same conclusion.

"This is all too incredible," Arthur muttered as he gently rubbed his thumb on the back of Marian's hand.

"I agree," the Sheriff said. "The FBI has joined the investigation, and they have a whole staff of shrinks who will do their best to get the answers we need."

Bradley's cell phone sounded, and he pulled it out of the leather holder he had strapped to his belt, checking the caller ID. "I'm sorry, I need to take this," he said as he stepped away from the table and walked into the front hallway.

Everyone remained lost in their own thoughts as they waited for the Sheriff's return. Except Ian, whose attention was on Bradley's animated conversation with the caller on the other end of the line. From what he could see, the Sheriff did not look happy.

Disconnecting the call, Bradley took a minute to calm himself. When he returned to the sunroom, he squared his shoulders, mentally preparing himself for the disruption his news was going to create. Be direct, he told himself. Don't offer any frilly lead-ins or ingenuous excuses. Just say it.

"That was my office. Adrián Santiago was found dead in his jail cell about forty minutes ago. He hung himself. One of the Sheriff Deputies performed CPR until medical help arrived, but the prisoner couldn't be revived and was pronounced deceased.

"I'm sorry, Marian. Katie. It would appear that the answers to all your questions died with him."

CHAPTER FORTY

The weather had finally caught up to the calendar. With only two more days until Christmas, the temperature hovered in the mid-twenties, and a fresh coat of snow blanketed the Reddington property.

Katie was standing at the atrium window, mesmerized by the beauty of the mountains that rose tall and unpretentious in the distance. Until now, she hadn't totally appreciated how every day she'd spent in Oregon had been a new and exciting experience. Well, except for the time she'd been hunted by a psycho.

Standing here now, she wondered if her artwork and photographs would ever fully offer viewers the overwhelming feeling of contentment that the majestic landscape rendered. She would come close with her brushes, she thought, but that feeling—that peaceful and inspiring feeling that came with this view—might forever remain elusive.

"Katie?"

Katie turned to see Clay standing in the doorway, his hair matted down by the recent snow burst, his body bundled up tight in a hooded sweatshirt under his heavy leather coat. "I thought we could take a walk."

"It's freezing outside, or hadn't you noticed."

"The cold is just a state of mind. At least the snow stopped. Besides, it's so peaceful out there that it'll be a shame if we pass on it."

Katie wasn't surprised that their thoughts were running a parallel track. She crossed the room and, standing toe to toe with him, said, "I'm game, let's go."

Slipping into her knee-high boots, dark brown, maxi-length coat, and bright red mittens, the two left the house and began walking north toward those far away and unreachable mountains. Clay took her hand as they trudged through the snow, and when they had gotten about a half mile from the house, he turned her to face him.

He didn't speak right away, wanting to take a moment to gather his thoughts. But when she smiled up at him, his heart began to overflow with the love he held inside, and he didn't need time to think. He knew exactly what he wanted to say.

"Katie, I've learned to appreciate the splendor of this place over the past several months," he began. "The grandeur of the mountains, the openness of the land, and the rare beauty of the artist who resides here. I consider myself lucky to have been given the opportunity to experience all three."

He reached into his pocket and pulled out a small velvet box. Dropping to one knee, he said, "For the remainder of my days on this earth, I'll always consider the mountains something I can admire. With respect to the land, I'm hopeful that I will always be welcomed on it. And when it comes to the artist who resides here? I'd very much like her by my side. To have her with me when I admire those mountains and when I'm welcomed on the land. I want to build a life with her, to take her as my wife, and to maybe one day, convince her to be the mother of my children."

Clay took the ring out of the box and slipped the mitten off her left hand. He pressed his lips to her fingers while giving her a winning smile. "Katie Nolan? Will you do me the honor of becoming my wife?"

Katie's eyes glistened with tears as she returned his smile and nodded enthusiastically. She watched as he slipped the ring on her finger then stood, letting out an enormous whoop. "I love you," he said, lifting her off her feet and pressing his lips firmly to hers. "I truly, truly love you."

"I love you, too," she replied, matching his exuberance.

After setting her back on her feet, he kissed her again, but this time added a splash of passion.

"My original plan was to wait until Christmas Day to propose, but I've been carrying the ring around in my pocket for a week, and I couldn't wait anymore." He laughed as he lifted her hand and rubbed his thumb over her ring finger. "I swear this thing was burning a hole in my pocket."

Katie straightened her arm and held her hand at eye level. Admiring the ring, she said, "It does warm my finger some, not to mention my heart. It's remarkable, Clay." She shifted her gaze to him, and her smile widened. "You're remarkable."

He pulled her into his arms and held on. She'd said yes. Man oh man, she'd said yes. He didn't think he could be any happier. When he felt her shiver, he leaned back and said, "Come on, let's head back. I'm no rocket scientist, but I'm pretty sure you're freezing." He squeezed her hand as they jogged back to the house. "Besides, isn't this where you call all your friends and start paging through bride magazines with your mom?"

She laughed along with him as they drew closer to the front porch. "I think I've outgrown the page turning days, and the only friend I have the immediate need to tell is Christina. But she can wait until tomorrow." Scurrying up the steps, she added, "But we should tell Mom and Arthur tonight, don't you think?"

When he pulled her through the front door, she came to an abrupt halt when she saw Arthur standing halfway down the front hallway outside the atrium. His arm was around her mother's shoulders, and his niece and housekeeper were positioned near the staircase. Clay slipped his arm around Katie's waist and leaned close to her ear. "I might have already mentioned my intentions to your mom."

Without warning, her mother released a delicate screech, or so Katie would describe the reaction whenever she recalled this moment. Marian rushed forward and grabbed her daughter's hand. "You said yes. Oh, baby, you said yes."

The women hugged while shedding happy tears and babbled words indecipherable to the men. When Nora and Hannah joined in, Clay stepped away and crossed over to Arthur. "I'd say they approve of me joining the family," he said, nodding to the group.

"I'd say so. Why don't we retire to my study and toast the occasion with a brandy? The women will find us when they're ready."

Once in the study, Arthur poured the top-shelf liquor into two snifters and handed one to Clay. Raising his, he said, "May you and Katie always share the love you're feeling today." He clicked the edge of the glass to Clay's and sipped.

When the women finally strolled into the study, Arthur smiled as Marian crossed the room to him. Standing on the tips of her toes, she stretched to give him a kiss.

"I have a great idea," Hannah chirped as she plopped into one of the leather chairs. "Why don't you guys have like, a double wedding? Uncle Arthur, you and Marian already have your plans in motion for New Year's Day. All you have to do is call everyone and double the order."

"That wouldn't be fair to the two brides, Hannah," Nora chided. "A woman wants her wedding day to be special, and I'm sure both Marian and Katie feel the same way, even though they wouldn't admit to it."

"Besides," Katie said, taking Clay's hand. "I want to enjoy being engaged for a while. We have a lot to think about, a lot to plan out. New Year's is a bit too soon for me, I'm afraid."

"Your mother and I have been talking, Katie, and I'd like to offer you and Clay the guest cottage if you're interested. You can remodel it any way you want, expand it so you'll both have plenty of room.

If you'd rather live somewhere else altogether, though, don't feel guilty about not living here. We'll understand."

"Thank you, Arthur. That's a wonderful offer, and Clay and I will talk about it. For now, I'm guessing we'll keep things as they are." She looked to Clay for confirmation, and he nodded. "Besides, I still have to finish your great-grandfather's portrait. I'm going to need the commission to help pay for the wedding."

For the next several hours, everyone shared the euphoria that weddings tend to elicit. Nora fixed her famous roast beef dinner, and when the clock struck ten, the group disbursed to their separate quarters, and Clay drove Katie back to the cottage.

As they slipped through the front door, he said, "Is this where you want to live after we're married?"

"Not to hurt anyone's feelings, but no. Maybe we can find a house somewhere between Abbott and Pendleton. I'm thinking that I could open that art gallery I've always wanted, and you could keep Clancy's operating, if that's what you want."

Running his finger across her cheek, Clay said, "Sounds doable. Whatever the future holds, we'll work it out. But for right now, all I want to do is to make love to my betrothed."

"I can get on board with that," she said as she pulled Clay into the bedroom and softly closed the door.

EPILOGUE
Six Months Later

A cool breeze filtered through the front door of Clancy's, although the only guests who could take advantage of it were those standing closest to the opening. The music was loud and mixed festively with the sight of good friends and family letting loose on the dance floor. The aroma of barbecue carried easily from the kitchen into the bar area, and every so often, glasses were raised to toast the soon-to-be-married couple.

Clay, Katie, and Ian moved harmoniously behind the bar as Tess and Arthur served guests who were enjoying the festivities from the tables and booths they had been lucky enough to snag earlier in the evening. Christina Freeman was on stage playing keyboard for Dakota Gold while Andrew shared bussing duties with Hannah. In the kitchen, Ben, Joel, and Marian did their best to keep the buffet table out front supplied with food.

"As far as bachelor parties go, this one rates right up there," Ian commented as he passed a round of beer mugs across the bar to the Reddington security team.

"Not bad for a bachelorette party either," Katie added.

"Agreed," Ian nodded. "It was a great idea to combine the two and hold it here."

"It seemed fitting, seeing as how this is where Katie and I first met," Clay said.

Katie glanced over and saw her future husband smiling at her. "You came to my defense when C.J. wouldn't stop hitting on me."

"It didn't take a genius to figure out you weren't seriously interested in his offer."

"Hey," C.J. said from his seat at the end of the bar. "I thought I was spouting some pretty good lines. Wasn't I?"

Katie was laughing as she said, "If I had a dollar for every time someone asked, 'Your place or mine,' I'd be a rich woman, C.J."

"Oh, really?" Clay challenged, trying to sound indignant but recognizing that the attempt fell way short. "And how many times would that be?"

"Stop your bitchin', Crawford," Danny Walsh protested as he signaled for another beer. "You got the girl, didn't you?"

Katie looked up to see the bookstore owner grinning from ear to ear as he swayed to the music. "Hey, Danny. When did you get here?"

"About an hour ago. What a party, you guys. And the band is superb."

"Dakota Gold," Katie said, amused. "I'm surprised you haven't caught them playing here before now."

"I have to confess that I don't get out a lot."

"That's because you spend too much time with your nose in those books you sell," Hannah jibed as she stepped behind the bar to deposit a tray of mugs into the wash sink. "I should take you into Pendleton next week and show you how the other half live."

"Oh, yeah? And what would you do if I actually took you up on that offer?"

"I'd say you can pick me up at eight. You can choose the day." Pleased with herself, Hannah grabbed one of the empty serving trays along with a clean table rag and disappeared back into the throng of well-wishers.

"That girl has some chutzpah," Danny said as he watched Hannah collect more empty glassware while swiping the rag across the tables that sat near the front windows.

Katie hip-checked Clay and grinned. "Looks like another romance blossoms at Clancy's."

"It must be something in the Stout, don't you think?"

"Speaking of which, Owen needs another one."

For the next two hours, everyone ate, drank, laughed, danced, and enjoyed the party. When the crowd began to thin out and all that was left on the food table were scraps of apple pie, Nathan stepped up to the microphone. He gave Tess an affectionate smile when she handed him a flute of champagne, then shifted his attention to Katie and Clay. Arthur, Marian, and Hannah had joined them behind the bar, while Ben and Joel joined Tess where she stood at the edge of the stage. Ian stood near the entrance to the pub with his arm around the shoulders of Lacey Ward, a registered nurse at St. Michael Hospital, who at one time had been affectionately known as Jenni Star.

Tapping the microphone several times, Nathan waited for the room to settle down. "Clay wanted me to thank everyone for joining him and Katie tonight. As you all know by now, the kids are making it legal next Saturday."

"Are you sure I can't talk you into running away with me, Katie?" C.J. shouted over the hoots and hollers.

"Don't think so," she shouted back as she sidled up to Clay. "I'm pretty much busy for at least the next seventy-five years."

When the room had quieted down, Nathan continued. "Clay and Katie. I think I can speak on behalf of all your family and friends when I say that we couldn't be happier that the two of you have found each other and will be continuing your life journey together. I ask that everyone raise their glasses as I toast our dear friends with an old Irish blessing that I learned from my mother when I was but a lad."

As arms were extended toward the couple, Nathan said, "May flowers always line your path, and sunshine light your day. May songbirds serenade you every step along the way. May a rainbow run beside you in a sky that's always blue. And may happiness fill your heart each day your whole life through. *Sláinte*."

"*Sláinte*," the crowd echoed, while watching Clay pull Katie in for a soft kiss.

As Nathan turned to talk to the members of Dakota Gold, Melanie Freeman escorted a group of children into the bar with Faye Crawford and Nora Blakely pulling up the rear. As the youngsters rejoined their parents who were scattered throughout the room, Melanie took Faye's hand and said, "I asked Tess to reserve a booth for us, Grandmother Crawford. It's over there by the jukebox."

Faye allowed Melanie to pull her toward the booth, relieved that she would finally get a few minutes to sit down and relax. Once seated, she said, "Those children were a handful, Melanie. I want to thank you for being such a big help."

"Ah, that's nothing," Melanie said as she sipped from the glass of milk that her father had set in front of her on the table. "I sometimes help the kindergarten kids put away their hats and coats when they get to school. They can be a handful, too."

Andrew sat down next to his daughter and said, "Did you guys have any problems back there?" referring to the babysitting duties that Faye, Melanie, and Nora had volunteered to undertake.

"Nope," Melanie said with pride. "We played games, and I helped Nora bring in the food and juice boxes."

"She helped a lot," Nora chimed in as she slid into the booth next to Faye. "I bet you and Christina are very proud of her."

"You bet," he said as he tousled his daughter's hair.

The group turned toward the stage when Nathan once again tapped the microphone to get everyone's attention.

"We're about to start our final set for the night, but I'd first like to introduce our guest keyboardist, Christina Freeman, who graciously agreed to sit in for tonight's gig."

The bar erupted into cheers and applause as Christina took a dramatic bow.

"Also, you might notice that our bass player has suddenly deserted us. But I have it on good authority that we have someone in-house who can help us out. Clay, come on up."

The cheers and applause got louder even as Clay backed away, shaking his head while looking for the closest exit route. Katie was laughing now and moved behind Clay to push him toward the stage. "Suck it up, Crawford," she said as she gave him one final shove.

"Clay! Clay!" Melanie was standing on the booth's bench now, waving her hands in the air. "Here's your guitar." She gleefully pointed to a spot behind the booth and giggled. "I helped Tess hide it there."

"Well aren't you the sneaky one," he said, giving Melanie's hair a gentle tug as he reached around her to lift the guitar off its stand.

"We'll give you a minute to tune up," Nathan said as he turned away from the microphone. But then, snapping his fingers as if he'd just had a brilliant thought, he stepped back to the mic. "Almost forgot," he said, his eyes skimming the faces in the crowd. "Phil was also one of our lead singers. And I've heard Clay sing, folks, and sorry to say, it's not one of his strengths."

Clay laughed and leaned into his own microphone. "You got that right."

"So, we're going to need some help with our vocals, too."

"Katie sings," Melanie yelled on queue. "You should ask Katie."

Katie's reaction was much the same as Clay's had been. But when Melanie ran over to where she stood, took her hand, and dragged her toward the front of the room, she didn't have a choice.

Stepping into place on the stage—the microphone in front of her, Dakota Gold band members behind her—she smiled at the eager faces waiting for the show to begin. "Remember, this wasn't my idea," she said as the crowd clapped and cheered.

Katie had never envisioned that her future would be this charmed. True, her life back in Long Beach hadn't been unfulfilled, but she hadn't realized how much more of an adventure had been there for the taking until she'd crossed into Abbott County.

She turned to see Clay watching her, and her smile widened when he gave her a reassuring wink. A stand holding the sheet music for her to follow had been placed alongside the microphone, and she fiddled with the pages as the band eased into a popular love ballad. Just let it go, Nolan, she thought with a calming breath. Enjoy the moment, the people, and just let the music surround you.

This was home, she thought as she hit the opening notes. These people were her family. And she didn't know how in the world she could be any happier.

About the Author

Romance and suspense author, **Sara K. James**, has received high praise for her debut novel, *Risking It All*. In this, her newest novel, *Fueled By Obsession* delivers equally strong-minded characters along with an unforgettable story packed with romance and intrigue. Sara, a born and raised Midwesterner, is currently hard at work writing her next book.

www.ingramcontent.com/pod-product-compliance
Lightning Source LLC
Chambersburg PA
CBHW020246200626
46816CB00001BA/159